"DUTY, SIRE? WHAT DUTY?"

Adam kissed her again, taking his time about it. Brielle felt her passion wake and begin to simmer deep in her belly. It angered her to be so easily swayed by this man, and she pulled away. He pulled her back, closer.

" 'Tis the primary duty of every loyal English noble," he answered, and though his eyes still held laughter, his tone was serious, "to breed loyal English sons. You, my love, have made that duty into the greatest of all pleasures."

a love so fierce

joanna mcgauran

A DELL BOOK

Published by
Dell Publishing
a division of
Bantam Doubleday Dell Publishing Group, Inc.
1540 Broadway
New York, New York 10036

ISBN: 0-440-21365-7

Printed in the United States of America

Published simultaneously in Canada

June 1993

10 9 8 7 6 5 4 3 2 1

OPM

My sincere appreciation to Allardyce Hamill, research librarian in the St. Lucie County Library, Fort Pierce, Florida, who pointed the way to more purposeful treks into the past. Each time I asked, she found the answer.

Picardy
October 1349

Adam Dunbarton, second son of the Baron Bruce Dunbarton of Castle on Tyne in Northumbria, had journeyed down to London to cross the English Channel and claim his betrothed bride, and now, some days past the middle of October, he had landed in the English-held port of Calais.

At another time, the city of Calais, with its pretty girls and the gaiety of its entertainments, was well worth a day's visit, even for a man on such a mission. But for the second summer and fall, the terrible plague known as the Black Death had raged through its crowded waterfront and cobbled streets. Sickened by what he saw there, Dunbarton hastened to gather together his cortege of seven knights, all mounted on heavy warhorses, and ride east into the wintry farm country of Picardy.

The eight of them rode with a confidence earned by experience and skill. They were all large and in their prime, armed and wearing mail beneath their warm cloaks. Adam was a giant of a man, well over six feet tall. He was built to match his height, with big bones and a broad, muscular body. Bright yellow Saxon hair blew back from an intelligent Norman forehead, dark blue eyes looked out from a strong, bony face and viewed the world calmly. Adam feared nothing, not death nor plague nor any other danger, but still he wished to rid his nose of the foul odors, his ears from the horrid sounds that gripped Calais, and rest his eyes from the sight of the pitiful, sore-ridden bodies of the dead and dying. The bodies were everywhere, dragged out to lie in filthy, bloodied snow and await the burial carts.

"Here the pestilence is worse than on the Isle of Dogs and the London docks," he said to his cousin Kiernan Comyn, who, once they had left the city and put aside ceremony, rode beside him. "I'd not have believed it possible."

"If it please God," Kiernan said piously, making the sign of the cross on his lean chest, "I pray the disease has not attacked this woman your father intends you to wed. How far is it, now, to Le Fontin Château?"

Adam blew out an exasperated, gusting sigh, his warm breath cloudlike in the cold air. "My father described it as a fast half-day ride from the Calais docks. As for the woman, you are kinder in your thoughts than I. I need a wife, it is true. But I'm not inclined toward the women of France, with their airs and their mincing flirtations. Not that I wish her dead, you understand, but neither would I grieve overmuch if we found it so. I feel my father has done me a disservice in this case."

Kiernan turned aside to hide a grin. Adam was a hooked fish, struggling on a stout line. "Come, now. Sir Bruce said the maiden was quite pretty as a child and had an English mother. And, I recall, her dowry would please an earl. Perhaps she'll suit you better than you think."

"I doubt it," Adam said morosely. "It is said by others that she is tiny and proud. I have never found either trait admirable in a woman. I much prefer a female with meat on her bones and of a quiet and humble nature. They are more comfortable, either in bed or out."

Wisely, this time Kiernan held his peace.

* * *

Close to five hours later, in a paneled upper room of Le
Fontin Château, her family's country home, Brielle Le
Fontin pulled aside the heavy brocade drapery at a
west-facing window and stared out at the falling snow.
Large, light hazel eyes were somber beneath the fans
of dark lashes; her delicate features gleamed in the
pure light like carved ivory. Brielle held her slim,
small body erect, her attitude one of courage and confidence. Her companion, an older woman with graying
blond hair and soft blue eyes, watched her and thought
the Lady Brielle stood like a princess in spite of disas-
ter.

"A dreary day, Honoria," Brielle commented, turning to the tall, wiry woman at the fireplace. "Cold and
lifeless, promising nothing." She spoke in perfect,
unaccented English, as Honoria had taught her, but
the tone of her clear voice was nearly as chilly as the
day. "I grant you," she added wryly, "it suits the occasion, if not the season. I can't remember an October as
miserable as this one."

Honoria Woolford nodded. Brought from England
eighteen years ago by Henri and Catherine Le Fontin
to take on the care of the baby they expected, she had
remained when Catherine died in childbirth. Honoria
had gone from nurse to governess and then to companion, never thinking of returning to England. In
Honoria's lonely heart Brielle had always been her
child, and she was filled now with grief and foreboding. Brielle had lost her beloved father to the plague
two months ago, and word had come last week that
the English nobleman her father had chosen for
Brielle's husband was on his way to claim his bride.
Honoria gave the marriage little chance for success,
yet the contract had been signed and must be honored.

Honoria sighed. Brielle was headstrong, and she'd
learned in these war years to hate the English, think-

ing them uncivilized, murdering beasts, inferior to the
poorest French peasant. How one of the proud English
nobles would react to such scorn from a woman didn't
bear thinking about.

"Perhaps," Honoria ventured, "the weather has
kept Dunbarton in England. The Channel would be in
a rage with this wind."

Brielle shrugged, turning back to the window in a
swirl of billowing black silk skirt and long tunic,
mourning clothes for her father. Bought hastily and
never fitted, the gown was far too big, the black relieved only by the customary stiff white cap and flowing wimple set squarely on her head. Her formal air
was belied by the flood of gleaming chestnut hair that
spilled down her back, and not even the bundle of
chatelaine keys that hung from her belt, nor the gold
crucifix around her neck, gave her the proper matu-
rity. She looked, Honoria thought, like a sad child in
her mother's funeral clothes. But there was nothing
childish about Brielle's mind, nor her next remark.

"We may hope for another day or so of grace," she
said, her voice uneven. "But it will make little difference. The Devil today is still the Devil tomorrow. . . ."
Her voice died away, her face stiffened to attention as
she continued to peer outside. A man on horseback
had appeared on the broad avenue from the public
road to the château and now rode at a brisk trot toward the inner gate, followed by seven knights in full
regalia. Impossible yet to see the insignia on the
shields, which hung now from the saddles, but one
knight held a flying banner showing a gray falcon,
claws outstretched in a hunting stoop, a wild, silvery
threat on a field of blood red. 'Twas the Dunbarton
Castle on Tyne banner her father had described.

For a full minute Brielle was motionless, silent. Behind her, unaware of Brielle's sudden attentiveness or
what she saw on the avenue, Honoria wiped sympa-

thetic tears from her eyes and left the fire, going out of the room rather than add her own misery to the hushed atmosphere of sorrow.

Turning, half glad to be alone now, Brielle dropped the edge of the drapery and left the window to stand before the fire that crackled and smoked on the hearth. She could no longer hope for a change of plans, or an accident, to end this threat to her freedom. He was here. It had been impossible to see the features of the leader or even correctly judge his shape or size in the layers of cloaks and furs and the deeply hooded head-gear he wore against the bitter cold. Still, it was Dunbarton, by the evidence of that banner. From what she had seen she thought him overly large, as so many of the English were, and undoubtedly no more graceful than a lumbering bear. Staring into the fire, large eyes narrowing against a leap of brilliance as a log broke and flamed up, she frowned. Damn the English! Why should they war forever against the French, and yet bargain for wealthy French wives? In her opinion, they were nearly as bad as the plague. Her father had been blinded by his love for his English wife. . . . She whirled, staring, as a slim maid flung open a hall door and stepped in, round-eyed and scarlet with fearful excitement.

"Mam'selle! Old Jacques has sent me to tell you your betrothed is riding toward our gates! There can be no mistake. The banner his knights carry is the one you told us to expect. Must we let him in?"

"Yes, Leone, we must. There is no help for it."

Leone hesitated and then stepped forward bravely. "But, mam'selle! If your papa had seen this man, he would never have consented to the match. He is a giant! Huge and rough looking, like all the English. Horrible! Perhaps I could lie—I could say you are ill. Yes, that will do! He will think it the plague and be gone in the blink of an eye."

Brielle sighed. "I know you are thinking of my happiness, but my father's fortune as well as my honor is at stake. I'll not lie nor allow you to lie for me. Go and see that the gates are opened to my betrothed, unwanted though he is, and say that all must greet him as the sire of this domain."

"As *sire*, mam'selle?"

"As sire," Brielle repeated, swallowing the sour taste of defeat, and turned away as Leone, utterly confused and frightened, scurried to do her bidding.

What she had said first had been true. There was no help for it. Her father's hasty decision had been made two years ago, when King Edward III of England, continuing his deadly campaign against France, had captured the port of Calais after a long and bitter siege, giving England a foothold in France that meant more fighting, more death. Henri Le Fontin had been quite old when Brielle was born; he was fifteen years older in that year of 1347, a widower without other family, and worried sick about his young daughter.

"Before Edward is through," he had told Brielle bitterly, "the noble families of France, already decimated, will lose all the brave young men you might have married. The best I can do for you is to betroth you to an Englishman with a large and honorable family. Then, at the end of this endless war, you will not find yourself alone and uncared for."

Brielle had been horrified, but Henri had persisted. He recounted the long friendship and trust between himself and the Baron Bruce Dunbarton of Northumbria, told her stories of the days when he courted her mother, Catherine of Pembroke, Bruce's cousin, and how Dunbarton himself had aided the two in convincing Catherine's father to allow the marriage.

"If Bruce's sons are as worthy and strong as he," he had ended, "you will be one of the most fortunate of wives. Your children will benefit from both English and French properties, and . . ." Henri had gone on and on, and since a father's word was law, Brielle had been forced to agree. Still, she had hoped that time, and possibly the war, would end the problem.

Instead, her father's sudden death created another, even more disastrous situation. Not only was losing him a terrible blow to her heart, but due to the terms of the betrothal agreement between Baron Bruce Dunbarton and Count Henri Le Fontin, the death impoverished her. When Henri died, the entire Fontin estate passed to Adam Dunbarton and his *wife*, Brielle Fontin Dunbarton! Now, with only enough money in hand to buy food for the château another month, she could not draw a sou from her father's wealth until she married.

The door opened, and Honoria came in, her face white. "Your betrothed is here," she said shakily. "He and his company are dismounting in the courtyard, and John Claude and his nephew are taking the horses around to the stables. You must come to the main hall, Brielle, and greet them. Whatever your feelings, they are your guests."

Brielle straightened. "And one will be my husband," she said in cold distaste. "May God give me strength. I have never managed to learn the humility I need today." Grabbing a long black cloak, she flung it around her slim figure, where it hung in voluminous folds. Then, head high, chin jutting out like the prow of a sailing vessel, she swept from the room, striding rapidly along the gallery to the stairs leading down into the immense stone hall. Honoria followed hastily.

Below, figures moved back and forth in wavering trails of smoke from the open fire in the middle of the hall, for on still days like this one, no draught pulled the smoke upward to the hole in the high ceiling above. There was noise, a great clatter of iron on stone as the men rid themselves of weapons and armor, a swelling rumble of male voices, a roar of sudden

laughter, quickly silenced, and then Brielle caught yet
another sound, weaving into the deeper sounds—the
eager piping of poor Jacques's quivering, high old
voice urging the knights to come in, to draw near the
fire, to rest themselves while he brought them ale—
"good English ale, messieurs!" He capered back and
forth, retreating in front of them, oddly like an insect
in the tight black chausses on his skinny old legs, the
flapping wings of his white tunic waving with his
arms. As soon as she saw him, Brielle knew he was
terrified. She stopped at the top of the stairs and
spoke, letting her clear voice ring out over the other
sounds.

"That will do, Jacques," she said kindly. "Go now to
the cellars and bring the ale, and our best wine. I will
greet our guests."

Her gaze swept the eight strange men peering up at
her through the gloom, taking in the size of them, the
thick, muscular limbs, the untidy hair and great
beards. One of them who stood before the rest was
huge. He had a great mane of golden hair that swept
his broad shoulders, very like a lion, and a golden
beard surrounding a broad mouth that only added to
the illusion. He was the largest, the tallest of them all
and for a moment she simply stared in wonder, forgetting her duty. Behind her, Honoria hissed a reminder.

"Speak to them, my lady! Greet them properly."

She started, snatched from the mesmerizing sight,
and was instantly paralyzed again by the dawning con-
viction that the lion was Adam Dunbarton. Her betrothed. The thought nearly made her faint. Her heart
fluttered like a trapped bird, her horrified eyes refused
to look again, but somehow she grasped the balustrade
firmly and started down. A rumble of whisper reached
her ears in the dead silence, and she looked, seeing the
lion bending to the ear of a dark-haired man at his
side. The whisper was deep but distinct.

"Good God, Kiernan, she's a dwarf! She can't be an ell in height."

A flash of anger bloomed and burst in Brielle's chest. That—that monster of a man dared to criticize her height! An ell! Why, she was a good five feet tall! But no doubt the beast believed he could say anything, no matter how rude, thinking her too ignorant to resent it. Her fear evaporated in the heat of anger that colored her cheeks and strengthened her voice.

"You are all welcome at Château Le Fontin," she said as she reached the flagstone floor of the hall, and this time she spoke coldly. "I am Brielle Le Fontin, and I must stand now and greet you in the place of my father, Count Henri Le Fontin, who died two months past."

The lion stepped forward swiftly, with no sign of the embarrassment she expected to see, took her hand in his, and raised it to his lips in a mechanical courtesy. Lowering it again, he still held her fingers lightly, staring down at her with the bluest and surely the coldest of English eyes.

"I am Adam Dunbarton, Mademoiselle Le Fontin. It was the sad news of your father's death that brought me here. I, too, must stand in Henri Le Fontin's place. Without a father, you must be protected by your promised husband."

Brielle took her hand from his, her lip curling. "I see," she said. "The situation has been forced on us both. Please present me to your knights, sire."

Adam gave her a penetrating look that could be taken as resentment, since she had implied that she was no more pleased than he at this meeting. She stared back at him, her jaw set, her eyes daring him to object. After a moment he shrugged and motioned to Kiernan, beginning the introductions with his cousin. Then followed Charles of Eastham, Philip Tournard, Abel Southers, Henry of Eastham, Charles's brother;

John Worth, and Marsh Nelson. All smiled; all bowed, gazing down at Brielle with the amused indulgence a large man gives a small woman. Brielle frowned, though she spoke with frozen dignity and welcomed each to the château.

By now, Jacques had struggled into the hall with two small kegs of ale, a number of bottles of French wine, earthenware mugs, and a platter of cold pasties to hold back starvation until the cooks managed dinner for eight big men as well as the rest of the château inhabitants. Formalities over, the men crowded around the long table in the center of the hall and left Adam and Brielle standing together. Brielle glanced up at the gallery, seeing Honoria hovering there, anxious and fearful. Brielle gave her a tiny nod and then turned back to Dunbarton, looking up at him with an assessing glance. There was a stern, cold look about him; a feeling of authority, a jaw that hinted at a stubborn nature. But there was no sign of meanness nor cruelty that she could see.

"I, too, have a friend I would like to introduce," she said with as much assurance as she could muster. "And I also ask your permission to have her accompany me to my new home."

His eyes flicked to the gallery and down to her again. So he had noted her glance at Honoria. "Naturally, my lady, you may bring any servants you wish."

"The woman is not a servant. She is my companion."

Thick golden brows climbed the broad forehead. If possible, the eyes grew cooler and more reserved above the high cheekbones, and the broad mouth took on a straighter line. "Few wives," he said flatly, "need a constant companion other than their husband and children."

Brielle took a long breath, meeting his gaze with

eyes colder than his, flecked with frost. "Nevertheless," she said with rigid courtesy, "I do, sire."

Adam's jaw fell and then snapped back, muscles flickering beneath the close-cropped beard. "I think not," he began, but Brielle had turned from him and motioned to Honoria, bidding her to come to her side, and as Honoria hurried down and toward them, Adam looked at her typically English coloring and ladylike appearance and nodded.

"She is of our country, then, and from all signs a gentlewoman."

"That is true, sire." Brielle almost laughed with pleasure. He had given in easily, and she rushed to take advantage. "However, the others I plan to take are French. My maid Leone, her mother Berthe, my cook, and of course, Jacques, the old man who greeted you at the gate." She ignored the amazed irritation on Dunbarton's face and grasped Honoria's arm, bringing her forward. "This is my friend and companion, Mistress Honoria Woolford."

Honoria bent a knee, her skirts billowing, and Adam nodded coolly. "I am pleased to know you, Mistress Woolford. You will be welcome at Castle on Tyne."

"Thank you, sire," Honoria murmured, her eyes on the floor. "You are very gracious." She touched Brielle's arm. "Father Abelard is at the gate. I saw him from an upper window. Did you summon him?"

"No," Brielle said blankly. "I did not. He must need food or money for the poor. Have someone question him—"

"That will not be necessary," Adam broke in. "I summoned the priest myself as we passed through the village. He is here to perform the marriage ceremony. I saw no reason to wait." He looked around. "Kiernan! The priest has come. Bring him in."

Dark-haired and handsome, Kiernan swung around from the table and laughed, setting down his mug of ale. "I have heard of impatient bridegrooms," he began, "but none so impatient as you, Adam. However, I—"

"We need no speeches," Adam snarled. "You well know the reason for speed. Just bring in the priest, damn you!"

Kiernan's amused gaze fell on the face of the bride-to-be, and the beginning of his chuckle died away. The face was suddenly stiff with fright, the brilliant hazel eyes wide and full of hopeless despair. He looked back at Adam and raised his brows.

"Perhaps," he said gently, as the other knights grew quiet and attentive, "it would be well to consult your bride. Women often have their own notions about weddings."

Irritated, Adam glanced down at Brielle. "This time I fear your notions must give to mine, my lady. Perhaps I should have explained to you that this unseemly haste is needed—"

"No matter," Brielle said abruptly. "I, like you, have no sentiment about the occasion. Since it must be done, it is best done quickly." Furious now, two splotches of red burning on her white cheeks, she turned to Kiernan. "Bring in the priest, by all means. Ask your staring, dumbfounded companions to gather around. Let us have done with this accursed ceremony!"

Behind her Honoria gasped in dismay, and Kiernan fled to do her bidding. Adam, staring down at her in surprise, was caught between an unwilling apology and anger.

" '*Accursed?*' "

"Is it not?" Brielle asked savagely. Her eyes were burning gold. "In my opinion, our fathers have burdened us beyond belief! You, poor soul, have been forced to take on the protection and care of a—a dwarf! And I am forced to be wife to a great, lumbering ox of an Englishman who has the manners of a goat!"

Her soft voice had risen until it echoed, full of fury, from every corner of the smoky hall. Adam grasped her shoulders and held her still, glaring down at her. "Be quiet, woman! Perhaps we can yet escape each other. It is not impossible to break this contract! If we agree . . ."

Brielle twisted from his grasp and put her hands on her hips, tossing her hair back and dislodging her cap and wimple, which fell together to the stone floor. She ignored them, and her thick red-brown hair sprang free, falling about a flushed and angry face. Her hot eyes glared, her usually soft voice spat like an enraged cat.

"Oh, yes, you'd like that, wouldn't you? You'd come out very well! You'd have Le Fontin Château, you'd have all the lands and fortune left by my father, and you would *not* have the ugly dwarf!"

"My child! Daughter, please! Control yourself." The village priest strode rapidly into the hall and hurried to clutch Brielle's arm. "Grief has disturbed your mind, my lady." Nervously, he stepped between them, glancing up in near awe at the glowering giant his small friend had been attacking. "She has been severely tried this last month, sire. I am sure she will wish to apologize."

"I will not!"

"It is not necessary," Adam said flatly. "I will make allowances for her nervous condition."

Brielle gritted her teeth and felt the priest's fingers tighten on her arm. He was *warning* her, but he was nodding at Adam and smiling benignly! Priests! They were always on the side of the men.

"Ask her," Adam continued as if Brielle weren't there, "if she still wishes to go through with the ceremony."

"Yes," Brielle said, loudly and recklessly, whirling to face the priest. "I do. I must, since I do not wish to starve while he rolls in wealth from my dowry! But first, you'd better ask him if he's willing to marry a dwarf!"

"My child," the priest said helplessly, "you are distrait. It's the excitement, I presume. Calm yourself."

"Get on with the ceremony," Adam said grimly. "Perhaps when it's over the lady will return to her senses." He turned to Kiernan as the priest hastily began to assemble his cross and prayer book, his holy water, his wine and goblets and documents, taking them from the capacious pockets in his heavy robe and laying them out on the end of the table.

"You have the betrothal pledge and the ring, cousin?" Adam asked, and Kiernan nodded quickly. "Good. There are more than enough witnesses, to be sure." He saw that Brielle had gone white and big-eyed again, and he reached for her arm. She snatched it away, snarling.

"I can stand without your support, sire."

"As you will, my lady."

"But I want Honoria beside me."

Adam motioned to Honoria, and she came in a quick swish of skirts, awkward and frightened, as pale as Brielle. She didn't smile, only stood very close so their arms touched, and Brielle took courage from the familiar odor of the rosewater Honoria always used on her fair English skin. The huge man on the other side smelled of leather and horse, of wine and musk, of man, a scent that curled around her, hot and angrily demanding. She fixed her eyes on the wrinkled face of the priest and listened, shutting off everything else.

The ceremony was short, Father Abelard being as anxious to end it as any. The promises were mumbled, the ring pushed on, the scrawled signatures of the silent, unsmiling witnesses put down. Folding the com-

pleted pledge, Adam handed it to Kiernan, who slipped
it into a small wooden box and put it with their baggage. Returning, Kiernan put a bag of coins into the
priest's hands and stepped back, smiling faintly.

"You will register the marriage, Father," Adam said,
"in the cathedral in Amiens. The rest of the money is
for you."

Abelard, hefting the weight in his hands, beamed
and nodded quickly.

"Mais oui, vraiment! Merci, Seigneur, merci. You are
generous indeed." He hesitated. "You are leaving
here?"

"At dawn. We sail from Calais at noon."

"Ah, Calais," the priest said sadly. "Death rides the
streets there. Not only the Black Death of the plague,
but the deaths from beatings and burnings by the flagellants. Do not stop within the walls, my son."

Moving apart, Honoria clutched Brielle's arm. "You
look as if you may faint, my dear. Will you sit down?"

Brielle shook her head. "No. There is no time to rest.
Let us begin our packing. It will take us all night, I
vow."

"This is your wedding night, Brielle."

"No matter. The giant is no more anxious to bed the
dwarf than the dwarf is to bed the giant. I may well
end my days as a married virgin." Grasping Honoria's
arm, she turned back to her new husband.

"We will start preparing to leave. After dinner
Jacques will show you and your knights to comfortable
rooms."

Adam's blue eyes centered on her sternly. "I will see
to that, my lady. As you have pointed out yourself, I am
now the sire of this ancient pile of rocks. Get to your
duties."

With a soundless gasp Brielle turned, still clutching
Honoria's arm, and dragged her away.

"I am wed to a barbarian," she hissed in Honoria's

ear. "Did you hear that? I am not respected even in my own home—I dread to think what position I will have in his!"

"'Tis your own fault," Honoria said firmly. "You know a wife must honor and obey her husband without argument."

Brielle drew herself to her full height. "I will honor him when he deserves it, and I will obey him when I agree to the order. I have a mind of my own; I can rule my own life."

2

hey left Le Fontin Château the next day, riding toward Calais while the shadows of night still lurked in the forests and the air was still cold enough to waken the drowsy and cool the tempers of the reluctant newlyweds. Behind them, the first faint glow of dawn rose in the eastern sky, silhouetting the dark bulk of the formidable château and the graceful spires above.

Exhausted, for indeed it had taken the whole night to prepare for the move, Brielle had still insisted on leaving the large wagon to Honoria, Jacques, Leone, and Berthe, none of whom were comfortable on the back of a horse. Driving was the grown son of the old man and his wife who were to keep the château clean and orderly until such time as they returned, if ever. Brielle was riding her own small mare, Mimi, who was skittish and wanting to rear and jump from shadows. At first Brielle was fully occupied in controlling her mount, but as they came to the downward slope that led into the valley and farms, she glanced back for a last look at her beloved home.

Dark and empty against the brightening sky, edged and surrounded by snow, the old stone fortress looked lonely. Brielle felt the pain of loss pierce her chest. So much she had loved and valued in life was gone, disappearing within the space of a few weeks. Tears came to her eyes, but she dashed them away impatiently and turned her face to the west again, determined to face the bleak future with courage.

Adam rode beside her, and on her other side rode Kiernan, for Adam had noticed the skittish mare earlier, and with a gesture, he had brought Kiernan in close and moved in himself. With the two large horses bulking high on either side, the mare had behaved herself. Adam's anger was gone; his reason told him his anger and lack of chivalry had added to his new wife's temper. Now, noting how pale she was and seeing the quick flick of her small hand as she wiped away tears, he felt a trifle sorry for the wench, as he might have felt sorry for a homesick child.

"You will like Northumbria," he said gruffly, glancing down at her as he spoke. She looked up at him, the golden eyes clear in spite of tears and fatigue, her expression scornful and as cold as the weather.

"Is that another of your arrogant commands, sire?"

Adam flushed with anger above his unkempt golden beard. His hand itched to strike the insolence from her face, but he had never struck a woman nor would he. He motioned to one of his knights to take his place, and then rode on at a gallop, ranging ahead and disappearing from view. Kiernan, watching the exchange, saw a rueful expression on Brielle's face as she looked after him. She regretted her quick tongue.

"Adam is not an accomplished courtier, madame," Kiernan said easily, "but his remark was meant to engage your interest, not to insist that you approve of his homeland."

"I knew that," Brielle said, embarrassed. "I acted like the child he thinks I am." She looked over and met Kiernan's brilliant green eyes. "I can't stand his superior manner. He acts as if I were some animal he had been sent to rescue. My own manners suffer because of it. This is a difficult time for me, Sir Kiernan."

"And for Adam. But if you give him time enough, you may find a kinder feeling toward him. He's an admirable man in spite of his lack of graceful conversation." Kiernan paused and changed the subject. "There is something both Adam and I would like to

know, my lady. Last evening, before the priest left, he
mentioned with some fear the deaths caused by flagell-
lants in Calais. The remark puzzled us. We have yet to
see the flagellants, but we understood they were reli-
gious men who hurt no one but themselves. We've
been told they go about in the streets half naked, beating themselves with whips and praying that the punishment they give themselves will be penance for all,
so that God will forgive the world's sins."

"They are fools," Brielle said with sudden heat. "Or
they think God is! But what you have just said is what
they have always done before. Now they also claim to
be closer to God than the priests and insist that God
has told them what to do in order to stop the Black
Death."

Kiernan laughed with scorn. "And what is that?"

"Kill the Jews," Brielle said somberly, "and all other
non-Christians. In many cities they have beaten Jews
to death, and in others they have shut them into their
houses and burned them there. They are worse than
criminals. In Calais, they beat a priest to death for
shielding a Jewish family. They are like mad dogs,
turning on all who fail to support them."

"More sins are committed by man in the name of
God than the Devil himself can think of," Kiernan said
grimly. "I will tell Adam what you have told me—and
we will be on guard in Calais."

Brielle nodded. "Good. Tell me, now, of the boat we
will take. I have never been on a boat, and neither has
Jacques. The poor man is terrified. He is sure the boat
will sink and we will all drown."

Kiernan grinned. "And you?"

"I am not afraid. I am merely curious."

Looking at her calm face, he believed her. "There is
naught to fear, my lady. Even the weather has improved. But you may feel a trifle crowded. Our craft is
a carrack, a coastal trading vessel. 'Tis much bigger

than a fishing boat, but t'will be overfilled by our horses and our party."

"How many days must we spend on the boat?"

"Given a bit of favorable tide and not much wind, we will be in Dover this evening and London the day after tomorrow.".

"So soon!"

"And at Castle on Tyne three weeks later." Watching her eyes widen, Kiernan laughed. "That surprises you?"

"I thought the northern border farther."

"'Tis not far around England, no matter what way you take."

She smiled bitterly, lifting her chin. "I am sure your country will resent a Frenchwoman landing on her shores, even in peace."

"Oh, no, my lady." Kiernan spoke warmly. "England will open her arms wide to you, for my country is beautiful and therefore values uncommon beauty such as yours."

Surprised by the lavish compliment, which she put down to Sir Kiernan's chivalry, Brielle smiled and fell silent, looking around at the wintry landscape of snowy valleys and windswept, barren hills. She had always loved the outdoors, spending a great deal of her time in riding and hunting with her father, who was noted for his skill in such pursuits. But for well over a month now she'd been cooped up in the château, due first to her father's last illness, then to the weather and her own somber despair. Now, dressed warmly, if dully, in black cloak and hood, riding Mimi in the crisp air, she felt her spirits rising in spite of her fatigue and her gloomy prospects. Perhaps her life wouldn't be as miserable as she'd feared, she thought now. She'd succeeded in getting her way in the matter of Honoria and her beloved servants—thanks to *le bon Dieu!*—and with them around her, she wouldn't be so lonely. Perhaps there would be other women, too. She turned, her eyes hopeful, to speak to Kiernan again.

"At Castle on Tyne—are there ladies living there, Sir Kiernan?"

"Indeed there are. The Baroness Martha, wife to my lord Bruce and mother to Hugh and Adam; and Lady Candida, who is Hugh's wife. Besides them, there are many other women nearby, though not of the nobility. They are wives of burghers and merchants. Castle on Tyne is very large, possibly the largest castle in northern England. It lies close to an important village called Turnbull, and there are two ancient donjons inside the outer walls, along with many other buildings and a chapel. Then within the inner walls there are three handsome mansions as well as the kitchen house and other outbuildings. You and Adam will have a separate household, but you will often have company, for there is a great deal of visiting back and forth."

"Have they had the Black Death there?"

It was an inevitable question, but Kiernan frowned. "Not yet, my lady. We all pray the plague will never find such an isolated spot. We spoke of it as we set out, fearing that we might bring the disease back with us. But Adam believes the distance from London is far enough, and the onset of the fatal disease so fast, that if one of us is infected he will die before we get to Castle on Tyne's gates."

Brielle nodded. "That could easily be true. But there must be other travelers who come there to trade."

"Not many. Most of our trade is with Ireland, and the plague has not been bad there. In any case, Adam's father, Lord Bruce, has said that if plague comes to Castle on Tyne, we must leave."

"But why? My father told me before he died that every civilized country had been infected. Where would you go?"

"To the hills. There are huts used by hunters scat-

tered in the forests. Each family would live apart from
the others, so the blood of the Dunbartons would have
a chance to survive. Of course the forests belong to the
king, who keeps them as a hunting ground, but King
Edward seldom ventures there for sport these days.''

"True," Brielle said, suddenly bitter. "He takes his
sport by killing Frenchmen instead of deer." Reminded that she was in the hands of her country's enemies, she lapsed into silence again, and Kiernan said
no more.

In midmorning Adam returned from his forays
ahead and took his place, grim and silent, at the head
of the column. Abel Southers, valued by the other
knights for his skill in tracking game, drew up beside
him to ask what he'd seen.

"Nothing you'd find pleasure in tracking," Adam
said shortly. "Only a few starving cows, shut in pens. I
turned them out to forage. They'll find more food beneath the snow than in an empty manger."

"Where are their owners?"

"Gone. I saw only one, and he lay dying in the snow
where he had dropped, the signs of the Black Death on
his face."

Southers crossed himself, and Brielle, her expression worried, spoke stiffly to Adam.

"I know most of the farmers of this valley, sire.
Many of them took fright and fled when their neigh-
bors fell ill, but some stayed to help. Did the man you
found dying have a red beard?"

Adam looked at her curiously, his eyes cool. "He did.
What difference does that make to you?"

Brielle's eyes went dark with pain. "Poor Paul! He
lost his wife and son to the plague a year ago, but still
he was one who stayed. He helped my father and me
with the others, and he came when my father fell ill
and helped with him. I had hoped Paul would be
spared."

A reluctant respect sprang up in Adam's expression. "Your father and you went amongst the dying peasants and eased their way? That was brave, my lady, but foolish. Your father died for his kindness."

"He knew that might happen. But they were our tenants, and our friends. My father lived by certain rules, and nothing could frighten him enough to change them."

"I can easily believe you," Adam said slowly, "for my father described Henri Le Fontin in just that way. I am sorry now that I never met him."

Adam's gaze was in the distance, as if remembering while he talked, and Brielle took the opportunity to coolly study his expression and his rugged face. He was not a smoothly handsome man like Kiernan Comyn, but neither was he ugly, as she had first thought. His skin above the beard was weathered but a good color. His eyes were a strong blue, not the pale, washed-out kind she had seen often on other Englishmen, and very clear, the whites a dazzling white. His nose was straight, arched like a hawk, indented between flaring nostrils. And his mouth, what she could see of it in that great beard, was wide and firm. She had yet to see him either smile or laugh, though the spray of lines at his temples promised good nature.

She shrugged and looked away. So, she thought, he was pleasant looking and from a wealthy and noble family. Many young ladies would think him a desirable husband—if they were English. But this was far worse than she had expected, for he didn't want her any more than she wanted him. And why should he? After all, she was one of the hated French, and to him, as he had made clear, extremely unattractive.

"Calais has moved farther away, I vow," Kiernan said to Adam, only half joking. "Are we on the right road?"

"Indeed," Adam said. "But we travel with a heavy-

laden wagon, not the galloping horses we rode before.
I wager you're hungry, cousin. There's a sunny spot on
that rise ahead. We'll stop there for food and rest for
the ladies."

"We have cold fowl and roast beef," Brielle said,
glancing at Kiernan, "dried apples and bread. Berthe
made up a large basket, along with some wine and ale.
It will be better than anything we could find in Calais."

"We'll not be stopping in Calais," Adam broke in
shortly. "We ride right through to the docks. Even the
air there is foul, like an evil miasma." He turned and
called back through the straggling men and to the
coach. "We stop on the rise ahead!"

There were scattered cheers, and the knights picked
up their pace and headed for the rise, more than ready
to break their journey. Then they were there and all
dismounting, the four in the wagon climbing out with
relief, the women coming together and heading for the
privacy of the woods.

Returning to the open space, Brielle saw that the
knights had not stood on ceremony but opened the
basket of food and drink and helped themselves. She
looked at short, rounded Berthe, properly shaped for a
cook, and grimaced.

"I hope you packed enough, Berthe, or we women
will starve."

Berthe smiled serenely. "They have found only the
first of the baskets, mam'selle. I cooked half the night
and packed enough for a week. In this weather, food
will not spoil."

Later, seated on a fallen tree trunk, finished with the
pork and dried apple pasties, Honoria drank down the
last of her ale and looked at Brielle with foreboding in
her tightly drawn face.

"'Tis pleasant here, and the cold is a wonderful aid
to appetite. Yet I feel that this may be the last easy

moment for us for a long time. I am frightened, dreading the unknown."

Brielle's pretty maid Leone, who had just reached her midtwenties and begun to fear she would never marry—for her betrothed had died in the first wave of pestilence—looked up with great dark eyes.

"'Tis the known I dread, Madame Honoria. The war and the Black Death. Surely the unknown could be no worse."

Brielle put an arm around Leone and hugged her. "Out of the mouth of the babe," she said, "comes strength and knowledge. The Bible itself says that."

Leone smiled shyly, pushing back her tangled brown hair. "I am not the youngest here, my lady. You are but seventeen."

Brielle shook her head. "I feel I have aged a hundred years in the last day, Leone." She looked up and pulled a wry smile. "If that is what marriage does to a woman, no wonder we all fear it."

On the other side of the hastily built fire, Adam looked up at women glancing at him and trying to stifle laughter. He rose, his stern face expressionless, his eyes on Brielle. She was laughing—no doubt at him—and her women laughed with her, unable to hide it well. Brielle's golden eyes were wickedly amused and her soft mouth was open, showing the glint of small white teeth. His jaw tightened. Brielle Le Fontin had spoken to him in ways no man would dare to speak, and he had let it go because of her grief for her father; because of the way they had been forced together. But she was his wife. He would not let her laugh at him long.

"We ride," he said, turning back to the wagon driver and knights. "'Tis well to leave in good time. We may have trouble."

* * *

Clouds had covered the sun as they came through the gates of Calais and saw again the looming, ancient buildings, pressed together and towering over the narrow, cobbled streets, seeming to lean forward in grief at the sight of horrid death below. They came on, aghast at the nauseating odor of rotting bodies, at the sight of thieves and looters going in and out of the homes where the owners had died or run away. Adam and his knights, knowing what they would encounter, had formed a tight wall around the wagon and the small mare ridden by Brielle. As Adam had ordered, they rode swiftly through the streets toward the distant warehouses and the docks that lined the shore.

Berthe had provided squares of linen soaked in vinegar for all, telling them to use the squares over the nose and mouth where the stench was overpowering. It was believed that the plague was carried on the odors of death; therefore the squares were not only helpful but considered necessary to reduce the chance of infection.

The few people hurrying along the gray streets held similar squares to the lower part of their faces, but their eyes glared angrily at the warmly cloaked English knights on their fine horses, and they turned even more vicious when they saw the wagon. The common folk reviled the French nobles who left the country to avoid the plague, saying they were traitors.

Riding near Brielle, Adam watched her closely. She had nursed the dying peasants, he knew she must be used to the horrors of the illness, the blackened swellings called buboes that oozed with blood and pus, the foul odors of breath and blackened excrement, the bloody vomiting. But she was not used to the cruel neglect of victims in the crowded cities. Here, as in other cities, the frightened people brought out their own family members stricken by the disease and threw them in with the rotting bodies to die alone. They feared the disease more than they loved their children, for there were many of the very young, feverish and with the blackened patches of skin, lying amongst the corpses and crying for their mothers.

"Mother of God!" Brielle cried out, and reined in her mare, turning toward the gutter. "I cannot pass that poor child! Look, she raises her arms to me, begging for mercy." She gasped as Adam's wide, strong hand grasped her reins and jerked them away, pulling the mare into step again, his warhorse like a wall beside her. On the other side, John Worth pressed close and held steady. In an instant they were traveling as rapidly as before.

"Damn you!" Brielle flared, struggling to jerk the reins from his hand. "Let me help her! I've helped many before without harm! Surely there is some place I can take her!"

Adam stared over at her, his face like iron, and he gestured toward the ever-more-crowded gutters in the distance. "Look, then, at what awaits you. Which ones will you choose?"

She stared, first angrily, and then as her eyes ranged far ahead, her tears welled up and overflowed. Hands reached up, fell back, reached—too many to count. And this was only one street. She looked away, swallowing. She had been wrong, and she hated to admit it.

"I was foolish," she got out. "I cannot save them, for no one can. I let my pity guide me instead of my mind."

"That is no bad thing in some cases."

Brielle looked up at him in surprise. He stared forward, eyes watchful, jaw set. His expression, she thought, was not angry, but one of tired patience. She lowered her head, shutting out the weak cries of the suffering as well as she could, and kept her eyes on the glistening mane of her little mare. If she could continue to ignore the dying—and she must—they would make the distance to the docks in no more than a half hour now. She had been to the Calais docks many times with her father, to buy the wares of the smallest trading vessels, the little sailing cogs. She fastened her mind on those happy times, hoping to block out the present.

Beside her, John Worth raised his head, alert. "Listen," he said to Adam. "There is a strange sound somewhere in the center of town. It rises and falls, almost like the music of the Scottish pipes."

Brielle grimaced. "No Scot would thank you for that," she said wryly. "What you hear is the groaning of the flagellants and their supporters amongst the watching crowd."

John Worth smiled at her. "My apologies to the Scottish pipers, then. So we will see the foolish men who whip themselves. Are there many, my lady?"

Brielle shrugged. "Often two hundred in the line, at times three hundred or more. It might be better to send the wagon around them. There's little room to pass in these narrow streets."

"A good thought," Adam said shortly, "if we knew the right streets."

"Young Jean Paul knows," Brielle said. "He often drives Berthe to the docks for shopping. If you tell him where the boat is, he will take the least traveled way."

Adam, who had seen the angry glances directed at the English knights, looked at John Worth and jerked his head toward the wagon behind. "Tell the driver that, John. It may be best to separate in any event. Some of these people seem to remember the bitter defeat they suffered at the hands of English knights two years ago. If we have trouble, I'd rather the wagon be out of it."

Worth nodded and was gone, wending back through the riders. Adam looked down at Brielle as they turned into another street. The keening cries and groans seemed closer. "I will lead your mare," Adam said, "if you'd like to join the others in the wagon."

Staring ahead, her eyes again on the bodies, the bloodied snow, Brielle made a suddenly hopeless gesture. "What difference does it make? One can't avoid it. It is all misery, in Calais or anywhere else. All France lies under the curse of this horrible plague."

"'Tis the same in England," Adam said gruffly, "except that France has many more towns, many large cities and many more people. In English cities the dead lie like these. But not at Castle on Tyne."

She started to say that the plague was only playing a game of cat and mouse, that it would come to Castle on Tyne when it willed, for as soon as she had heard the low, continuous groaning begin, she had lost her usually strong will and an insidious despair had taken over her heart. Pain and death seemed certain. But she did not speak, for at that moment they turned another corner and came in sight of the winding line of stumbling flagellants and the crowd of their sympathizers.

Now the sound of groaning rose and rose, until the air seemed saturated with it, a deep, mourning sound torn by shrieks that cracked the air, by the gasping grunts of effort as bloodied arms sent the long, whistling whips up and around, up and around, over and over, while skin split under the constant blows, and blood spurted from the wounds made by iron spikes on the whirling tips.

No more than fifty feet away the men wielding the whips staggered and fell, struggled up and went on, lashing and cutting their own bare backs and splattering blood on the surging, excited crowd that lined the street. Arms linked, faces distorted and bathed with sweat, the watchers moved in waves, bending and shuffling, groaning in deep, wavering howls and shouting to God to forgive the sins of the world.

Adam reached and grabbed Brielle's reins, bringing her mare and his warhorse to a sudden stop. "In the name of God," he said softly, "this is true madness." He turned as the knights crowded up around them and swept the men with a searching gaze.

"What say you? Shall we turn and find another way?"

The men looked at each other in silence, and then Marsh Nelson, a knight noted for his skill in close fighting, laughed and shook his head.

"Push through, Adam, by all means. If they turn on us, we will favor them with even more punishment than they are giving themselves."

"'Twill make little difference to them," Philip Tournard broke in. "Some of those men will die from their own blows if they keep on. Their blood is running out like water."

Charles Eastham fingered his sword, glancing back the way they had come. "I will take the lead, Adam, so you can guard your wife. But let us waste no time—the townspeople gather behind us."

Adam turned. The gathering men behind them were silent, armed with sticks, stones, a knife here and there. He studied the flushed faces, the mesmerized look in their staring eyes. They also swayed; the movement faithfully following the hypnotic rise and fall of the deep groans. "You are right, Charles," he said. "They are also caught up by the madness they see and hear. We'll try for the crowd on the left—it's smaller. Take the lead, but take no lives unless you must." He looked at Brielle's shocked, colorless face sternly, winding her reins more tightly around his hand. "Make sure of your seat, my lady, and keep your head down. The tip of one of those whips can put out an eye." Turning toward Charles, he nodded grimly.

Charles's sword leaped from its scabbard into his

mailed fist, striking shards of light from the pale sun as he brandished it high in the air.

"Make way!" he shouted, rising to his full height in the stirrups. "Make way for Dunbarton of Castle on Tyne! Make way quickly and suffer no harm!"

Beside Brielle, Abel Southers shook out the blood-red banner and thrust it high, the falcon shining silver, flying in the breeze. Then they were off in a surge of powerful horses, small Mimi scrambling to keep up with the others, and heading for the crowd on the left, so to miss the bleeding, staggering flagellants in the middle of the street.

Grasping Mimi's thick mane, Brielle stared in terror as a man screamed, grabbed up a club, and rushed at Charles. Charles swung his broadsword in a swift arc, and the club dropped, the severed hand still clutched around it. The man screamed again, shaking the bloody stump, but the crowd parted to let them through. Swallowing sickness, Brielle clung to the mare and prayed. She fixed her eyes on Adam's big hand, wrapped with her reins and resting calmly on his thigh, and kept her head down.

They were in the thrumming air. The groans, the howls, the knifing shrieks reverberated in her ears. Brielle's eyes were drawn irresistibly to the side, catching glimpses of the naked flagellants through the knights who surrounded her. The acrid odor of sweat and blood came strong to her nostrils, and weaving through it the inescapable sickly taint of the Black Death. Now the pace of the warhorses slowed in the thick crowd, and she felt pounded by noise, horrified by what she saw. The whips rose and whirled and fell, the bleeding men staggered and dropped. One of the crazed flagellants got up to face the knights, his own face a mask of agony, and dropped his whip, raising his arms to God. In his armpits the black buboes of the plague were big as apples, ready to burst. Brielle

turned away quickly, feeling the shock of tragedy as
never before. In that moment it seemed to her that the
whole world was dying.

It was impossible to maintain their speed. The
crowd groaned and shuffled and bent—swaying away
from their path and swaying in again, crowding them.
And then one fell, shrieking, beneath the plunging,
ironclad hooves of Charles Eastham's horse. Only one
man, but then, caught by the mad desire for self-pun-
ishment, another and another ran forward screaming
and howling and cast themselves down before the
horses. In minutes the main part of the crowd surged
out, men and women, braving the hooves of the warhorses. Horrified, Brielle heard Adam roar out a warning.

"Make way, you fools! Make way! We haven't come
here to kill!"

Scrambling, stumbling over the fallen men, rearing
as others threw themselves down, the horses tangled
and slowed, the men cursed, and suddenly the knights
were surrounded. Faces distorted by hate and fear spat
curses at them, hands reached out of the crowd to grab
and pull, to swing a stick or knife. The knights swung
swords, but still the maddened crowd came on, fighting without fear, dying and falling in a frenzy, piling
up under the struggling horses. And Brielle's little
mare was caught by a heavy blow on a slender foreleg,
the club swung by a maddened man. Instantly, Mimi
was down in the moving, groaning pile of the fallen,
whinnying sharply in pain. Brielle slid off, feeling beneath her the cobbled street and seeing over her the
murderous face of the man with the club. He lifted the
club in both hands to bring it down on her head, but
even as she screamed in terror a bright sword sliced
down through his shoulder and half his chest. She was
jerked up and away from the spraying blood and
swung across Adam's empty saddle. He mounted be-

hind her, sheathed his sword, and held her with an iron arm around her waist, urging his big horse on through the thinning crowd. Half fainting, paralyzed with fear, Brielle grasped the edges of his cloak and hid her face between them, hearing his deep voice roar out as he gained the clear end of the street.

"To me, to me, for Dunbarton!"

In a clatter of hooves and blades, the knights broke loose and came galloping to him. Brielle turned her head, looking at them fearfully. Southers's cheek was bleeding, Kiernan's handsome face was bruised badly, his cloak torn; Henry Eastham grinned lazily and bragged that he was untouched; the rest of them shrugged off their cuts and bruises, saying they were nothing. Brielle looked back at the still-seething mass of people and swallowed hard.

"My mare?" she whispered, afraid of the answer.

"A broken leg," John Worth said tersely. "I—gave her an easy death, my lady."

Brielle struggled with tears and lost. She turned her face again into Adam's rough cloak and wept silently. Mimi. Her beloved small mare had been a gift from her father, her last link with his love and the happiness she had known as his daughter. Now all was gone.

3

the townspeople had been drawn to the streets where the flagellants marched, and because of that the streets and alleys on the way to the port were nearly deserted. Adam took them along at a fair speed, for the sun was high and the tide was nearing the favorable ebb. Coming in sight of the docks at last, Adam slowed, the grim look on his face relaxing.

"The others are here," he said, glancing down at Brielle, "and safe."

She had kept her face hidden in his cloak, but now she straightened and looked. The wagon was pulled up and waiting on the shore, empty except for the driver, and beyond it, tied to a dock, was a small carrack, gaily painted in red and blue, swarming with a half-dozen seamen working to unfurl the white sails on its two masts. Standing on the deck were Honoria, Berthe, Leone, and old Jacques, smiling and gesturing to her.

Brielle took a long breath. The sun had come out from the haze and the blue water shone, the boat was new and sparkling clean, and Honoria's smile and out-stretched arms called to her. Suddenly she pushed away Adam's arm and leaped down from his saddle. Picking up her long skirts, she ran out the dock, up the gangplank, and into Honoria's embrace.

Beside Adam, Kiernan chuckled. "It took no persuasion to see your lady aboard, Adam. She seems to have little regret about leaving Calais."

"Nor do I," Adam said shortly. "'Tis full of madmen."

At that moment a group of three English knights rounded the corner behind them, riding with a French monk on horseback, and came hastily forward. The monk called out.

"My Lord Dunbarton! I have a message for you from Aimery of Pavia, now governor of the Castle of Calais!"

Adam looked around at the monk, his heavy golden brows drawing down. "As I recall, Aimery was naught but the captain of the Calais galleys. Has he usurped the position given to Sir John Montgomery?"

"Your pardon, sire. Sir John and his good wife died months ago from the Black Death. Sir John himself appointed Aimery governor till the king finds another. Please, Sir Adam, come with us. 'Twill take less than an hour of your time."

Adam glanced at Kiernan. "I must go. See that you keep the women safe, cousin. If I don't return before the tide changes, set sail. I will follow when I can."

The captain of the carrack had approached and now spoke up. "You've better than an hour before the tide slacks. Unless yon monk lies, you'll be aboard when we leave."

And so it was. In less than an hour, a pleasant hour there on the carrack in the sea breeze, Adam came galloping back alone. Stopping just long enough to wave the wagon on its way—for Jean Paul had waited to see if he returned safely—Adam led the waiting knights aboard the carrack. The knights, each leading a nervous, snorting horse up the swaying gangplank, took them forward to the makeshift stalls set up beneath the fighting platform built over the bow. Another, larger platform in the stern provided a covered space for shelter and sleeping pallets, and this was where the baggage and supplies from the château had been placed.

Honoria had already led Brielle there and to a soft seat on some of the bags of clothes. The rest of her oddly assorted retinue, Leone, Berthe, and Jacques, had followed. They settled down together, wide-eyed and silent, watching the seamen drag the heavy gangplank aboard and stow it beneath the gunwale.

All was done quickly now to catch the tide, the men watching the empty streets with a wariness the women well understood. Then at a shout from the captain the last line was loosed and the sails set for the wind to catch. The idly bobbing craft seemed to wake, to stretch, to turn with decision toward the west and reach out, rapidly gaining speed. Jacques, his thin, wrinkled old face alive with curiosity, got up and went across the slanting deck to the group of knights and seamen standing under the snapping sails. Jacques listened to the talk while he leaned on the gunwale and pretended to watch the heaving water. Knowing Jacques and consumed by curiosity, Brielle hoped he'd overhear what message the English commander of Calais Castle had given Adam Dunbarton.

Coming back in high excitement, Jacques began at once to tell Brielle that the captain of the carrack, who was named John Montford, had said that the pope, Clement VI, had just issued a Papal Bull about the flagellants.

"Now that they claim they have the ear of God," he said, "which is a rank heresy, the pope has decreed that they must be dispersed or arrested. And King Philip has agreed, naturally. He of all people would never dispute the word of Pope Clement. And the king has gone even further, madame, for he's ordered his soldiers to execute anyone seen beating himself in public!"

"Good news," Brielle said, forgetting immediately what she had hoped to hear. "That will save many lives. But it came too late for my little Mimi. She is dead, and so I would be also, had it not been for Dunbarton. He killed the man who would have murdered me."

They gasped, and listened round-eyed while she told all that had happened.

"He is a man of great strength and quickness of mind," Honoria breathed as the story ended. "I thank our Lord and his guardian angels for our sire's presence there when you were so sorely threatened."

"Indeed," Brielle said wryly, "I too am grateful to be alive. But had it not been for Dunbarton I would not have been in that murderous crowd, and Mimi would not be dead. 'Twas the sire who took me away from the safety of my home."

No one answered her. No one spoke at all, nor looked at her. Mostly they stared at the deck on which they sat. She watched wonderingly as Honoria's suddenly downcast face turned pink, and then, alerted by a sound behind her, swung around and looked up into Adam's cold blue gaze. Her own face flamed.

"If you will listen to talk without revealing your presence," she said tartly, "you may often hear something you won't like."

Adam bowed slightly. "Perhaps, though I prefer bitter truth to false compliments. Women are often devious and apt to flatter a man for reasons of their own, but I have heard nothing but the truth from your lips. This pleases me. See to it, my lady, that you continue to say what you mean. I have had enough of flattery and lies from women." He turned, and after seeking through a leather bag brought aboard by Kiernan and taking out a long knife, he left them.

Light winds and the constant easterly set of the Channel current combined to slow the carrack, but the skill of Captain Montford brought them within sight of the Dover cliffs by late afternoon, and in port by time for dinner. Adam took rooms in a nearby inn, ordered a

meal for all, and sent Kiernan off at the head of the
other knights to find a stable for the horses.

They ate in a common dining room, nearly deserted
except for their party. The inn, much frequented by
travelers, had prosperous years behind it but now suffered the same as any business from the growing effects of the plague. The innkeeper lavished attention
on Adam Dunbarton and his knights and treated Lady
Brielle Dunbarton like a queen. After dinner he
showed her to the best room in the inn, a huge square
room on the second floor with a wide double bed, canopied and curtained in heavy red brocade.

"You and Lord Dunbarton will sleep well," the innkeeper said with pride. "'Tis the best room I have, and
better by far than any other in Dover. Your female
companion also will have a room on this floor with a
comfortable bed, and the maid and cook will share a
room downstairs."

Brielle nodded and thanked him, then stood staring
at the bed as he hurried out to settle the others. Naturally, she was innocent, but she knew what to expect in
a marriage bed. Honoria had taken care of that, explaining exactly how a married couple conceives a
child. Brielle had understood immediately, and said
so, because it was the same sort of peculiar activity
that went on between the farm animals when they
were breeding. But Honoria had gone on to say that it
wasn't exactly the same, for a man often had a great
affection for the woman he made his wife, and that
made him so gentle and kind that the woman didn't
mind it at all and, in fact, often liked it.

She stood still now, considering her own case, and
decided the best she could do was to hope Adam Dunbarton was in no hurry to give her a child, for certainly
he had no affection for her—nor, for that matter, any
more reason to like her than she had to like him. No

doubt he thought her not only an ugly dwarf but one with a sharp tongue.

Sighing, Brielle slung off her cloak, going to the baggage to search through her hastily packed clothes for a *chemise de nuit* suitably woolly and warm for a cold night. She had told Leone she wouldn't need her until morning, for she knew the maid was as tired as she was, and besides she was perfectly capable of looking after herself. Laying out the chemise, she poured warm water from a large ewer into a bowl and stripped herself to wash. She had brought her own soap, made at the château with the fat from sheep and the essence of lavender blossoms that grew wild in the valleys. The sweet scent made her homesick as she scrubbed. She worked hurriedly, for the room was chilly in spite of the heat rising from below, and she was tired. Drying herself, she put on the voluminous nightgown and brushed her hair thoroughly. Then, yawning, she put out the lamp, leaving one small candle to light the Englishman to bed, climbed through the red brocade hangings and under the warm covers.

An hour later, Adam lit the lamp again in order to find his way around the strange room. He saw the pool of discarded clothes on the floor, the soapy water in the bowl, the cake of scented soap beside it. He shook his head. A careless woman, and untidy. Used to having everything done for her. Spoiled. Muttering, he flung the water out the window, refilled the bowl, and washed, gasping from the cold. Then, carrying the lamp, he pulled back the red brocade and looked in.

The lamplight fell on a pillow strewn with lustrous chestnut hair. Brielle's face in repose seemed like that of an angel. With the golden, hotly rebellious eyes closed in sleep and the long, dark lashes lying like silken fans on velvety skin, she was the picture of gentle innocence.

Adam stood there for long moments, shivering and

staring. Then, dropping the curtain, he blew out the lamp and set it down. Feeling his way around the huge canopied bed, he drew back the draperies on the other side and eased in, staying well over on his own side of the thick mattress.

There was no doubt in Adam's mind that the girl needed instruction before she would make a good wife, if ever she did. Possibly his mother, he thought, could teach her to watch her tongue, to respect her husband, to obey. To be attentive.

He lay there, thinking and staring up into the darkness, and discovered with some surprise that he had a faint but growing regard for the small, fiery woman he'd married so reluctantly. A sympathy, perhaps. She had been very brave in that melee this morning, and after it her only thought had been of her little mare. At times in his life he'd felt like crying himself over a beloved horse, so he cast no blame for that. She was indeed too proud, too carelessly lazy, and certainly too outspoken, but there was a gallantry about her that he found very touching. He yawned and settled himself to sleep, wondering about it. But why worry? It was better by far to have a kind feeling than to dislike the little creature he'd been forced to take to wife.

Brielle woke to the faintest red glow around her, a feeling of deep, luxurious warmth, a musky scent that gave her random, disturbing thoughts. She shut her eyes again, thinking the feeling was too pleasant to risk losing, like a wonderful dream. But she went on thinking, and the red glow turned into morning light penetrating red brocade; the warmth translated into her woolly chemise—no, not entirely. The warmth began in a heavy weight across her waist, a teasing sensation on a breast, a curl of heat around her back. And it breathed.

She shot upward, pushing his arm and hand away

from her, feeling the hand rise again to grasp her arm.
She squeaked in alarm, but the hand tugged her back
down. She lay still, frozen, staring at the red curtains,
the dim light.

"'Tis . . . morning," she said faintly. "Time to
rise."

"In a little while." Adam rose on his elbow and
loomed over her. He was naked, and to her amazed
eyes he was like some god the pagan Greeks might
have worshipped. In the red glow his shaggy hair and
beard were like the head of a dark gold lion, his bare
shoulders and chest unbelievably wide and massive.
She saw him bending toward her still-exposed breast
and snatched the covers over it. He smiled, teeth glinting inside his beard, and pulled the covers down again.
"I will have you now, wife. We will begin our marriage
properly."

Brielle erupted out of the bed and through the curtains in a whirl of fluttering chemise, shrieking.

"You—you beast! Do you take me for a slut, for some
old worn-out and willing whore who will lie back and
spread her legs for you just because you want to relieve your—your lust? I am your *wife*, curse you! Your
bride! Your *virgin* bride! And—and—you have yet to
court me!"

Adam's head came through the curtains slowly, his
blue eyes astounded. "There was no time to court you,
my lady. We are wed and past that."

She put her hands on her hips and shook back her
hair in a show of defiance. "But there is time now!"

"What?" The eyes above the golden yellow beard
lost their look of amazement and hardened into anger.
He swept the hangings back and crawled out, rising to
his full height before her, naked and aroused. Brielle
shrank away, taking in a long, quivering breath, unable to hide her awe at his size, at his rampant masculinity. He was like a form from mythical times, when

God hadn't yet come to change men into his likeness. He was muscle and bone and hair and passion. A lion in her path, a lion who had the right to satisfy his hungers. She was suddenly warm and dizzy, swaying toward him.

"Put on your clothes," Adam said coldly, and turned away. "I'll not take an unwilling woman."

They left Dover in late morning, Adam having procured a four-wheeled, roofed wagon drawn by four carthorses. The wagon, which also had curtains along the sides that could be lowered in case of bad weather, was the kind used for long journeys by noble ladies or by the ill. It was large enough to hold the food and various household items Berthe and Honoria had chosen to bring, along with all the women. Jacques was a good driver, and though there would be creeks to cross and very few decent roads, the wagon would make the trip considerably easier. Leone, Berthe, and Honoria smiled widely at sight of it, but Brielle looked resigned. She preferred to ride horseback. Adam noted her expression as she waited behind the others to get in, and spoke to her.

"You'd rather ride a horse?"

Since that morning, Brielle had kept her gaze down or her face averted when they spoke, but this question brought her eyes up to his, flaring with hope. Then she shrugged and looked down again.

"I would, indeed. But it would be foolish to buy a horse for me here, my lord. I listened and looked while you bargained for these carthorses. The prices are high, the horses old. I believe the traders are preying on the many travelers who cross the Channel to make the pilgrimage to Canterbury Cathedral."

"True. But how did you know?"

"Every Christian in the civilized world knows of the miracles claimed for the shrine of Saint Thomas. Many

have come here from Calais to give money to the archbishop and pray for healing and have returned saying
they were cured."

"*Saying* they were cured? Were they not?"

She looked up again, her hand now on the edge of
the wagon, and studied his bearded face. He looked,
she thought, stiff and cold—but interested in what she
might say.

"Some of them who paid for intercession may have
been helped," she replied. "That would be hard to
deny, for only they could tell how they felt or how they
were changed. But cripples claimed to have been
made whole, when all could see they were the same
when they came back as when they left. And . . . very
few of those who paid large sums to be delivered from
the plague have survived."

Adam nodded. "I take it you have no wish to stop at
Canterbury Cathedral, then."

Brielle looked at the other women, all listening
closely. Berthe was fingering the crucifix that hung
from her neck, her lips moving, her face filled with
unquenchable faith.

Turning as she stepped back into the wagon bed,
Brielle answered with a shrug. "Stop, by all means, if
you wish. Others may have more faith in miracles than
I."

"If you do stop," Berthe cut in breathlessly, "I will
ask for a long and happy life for you, sire."

Mounting his horse, Adam smiled faintly. "'Tis as
good a place as any to stop for a meal as well as a
prayer."

The road was fine between Dover and Canterbury. At
midday they came to the cathedral. Huge and yearn-
ingly beautiful, its turrets and corona seemed to pierce
the cold blue sky in an ardent search for heaven.
Brielle sat quietly, absorbing the beauty of the carved

stone and graceful arches while the other women and Jacques went inside. Kiernan and Philip Tournard tied their horses to the wagon and went along; the others found shelter from the wind in a sunny spot along the wall. Adam climbed up and sat on the driver's seat of the wagon.

"Sit here," he said brusquely, "and tell me if I have married an unbeliever. Do you deny the existence of God, Brielle?"

She rose, since she had no reason not to, and gathered the full folds of her black silk skirt in her hands. She held it close to her slender hips as she made her way forward, so it wouldn't catch on the bundles and boxes of their belongings. Moving around the end of the high seat, she sat down and looked at him squarely, her amber eyes clear and direct. He caught the faint but sensual odor of warm woman and the lavender soap she used, and he thought bitterly of the pleasure he could have if she chose to honor her vows.

Brielle picked her words carefully as she answered his question.

"I believe in God, sire. But though there are many good and sincere priests, I do not credit the unnatural powers the venial priests claim. I do not believe anyone can buy their way out of sin and into heaven by paying those charlatans to pray for them."

Adam was shocked. Not by what she said, for there were many men in England, and he was one of them, who said the same. But only in private or in the company of trusted friends. Still, he'd never heard a woman express such thoughts. "Do you know that you would be punished severely and perhaps put to death by the churchmen if they heard you deny the divine powers given to them by the pope?"

"Not all of them would, my lord. Father Abelard knows how I feel, and I believe he feels the same. But he is careful and has taught me to be careful also. He says there are cruel and greedy men in every station of life, and there are false priests who love money and power more than they love God. But he has cautioned me not to mention my opinions."

"But you have told me."

Brielle lifted her chin. "You said on the boat that you had heard only truth from my lips, and ordered me to see to it that you always did. Therefore you always will. But had anyone else asked me these questions, I would have avoided saying things that would hurt me —or anyone else."

So she would honor one of her vows, at least. She intended to obey. Oddly gratified, he took her hand in his.

"That would be wise, my lady, even in England, though the English are not as strict as the French and Spanish in their obedience to the pope."

His hand was warm and strong, enclosing hers, as his body had enclosed her body when she woke. Thinking of it, she felt heat rise within her, and she pulled away, clasping her hands sedately and staring down at them.

"Nor were the French, until the pope fled Italy and settled in Avignon. My father said when that happened the French nobility began to think they owned both the Church of Rome and God Himself." She looked up at him, and her eyes were hostile again. "How can they believe that when you English overran our country in spite of all their prayers?"

Adam's face was suddenly flushed with anger. "How little you know! 'Tis our King Edward's right to rule France, by the blood that runs in his veins—royal to the last drop, royal blood from France as well as England. His grandmother was Eleanor of Castile, his mother daughter to the King of France. He is connected by family to Flanders and Burgundy, to Hainault by his queen. Perhaps God has taken note of his just cause instead of the prayers of the cowardly French."

Brielle, furious, was silent. She was sure he was wrong; she was also sure she risked a terrible anger directed at her if she argued. She turned away and watched dourly as Kiernan and Philip brought the women and servants back to the wagon. Adam, still struggling with his temper, rose as they approached and stepped down.

"Have Berthe prepare a meal that can be eaten on the way," he ordered Brielle. "We'll ride on as far as Rochester tonight. There is an inn there that suits me well."

That night they dined all together, seated at two round tables in front of a huge fireplace let into a brick wall, with the host himself serving a good wine and the serving maids in constant attendance, filling plates and bringing bread so hot from the ovens that they had to carry it in baskets.

Later, climbing stairs to a bedroom she was to share with Honoria, Brielle heard Adam's deep voice, soft and coaxing. Glancing down a shadowed hall, she saw him with the prettiest of the serving maids. He had penned the maid to the wall with his thick, muscular arms on either side of her plump body, and he was smiling seductively as he talked. Clearly, he wanted her as a bedmate, and from the way she was giggling, he would get his wish. A wave of mixed emotion sent Brielle running up the steps. Her face was still hot when she crawled into bed.

"Disgusting," she whispered, and wiped at her eyes, wet by anger or jealousy, or possibly both. "How could he?"

4

Riding through South Warke late the following day, Adam Dunbarton and his cortege of armored knights cleared the crowded and odorous streets for the wagon in which the women rode. Children, tradesmen, and beggars all gave way, the beggars running alongside the wagon for a time, whining for copper oboles, then giving way in turn as Jacques threatened them with the whip.

The street they traveled led straight to the Thames and the bridge that would take them across to the walled city of London. The side curtains of the lurching wagon had been rolled up and tied, so that Brielle had an unobstructed view as the bridge loomed up ahead. The span was crowded by houses, small and large, some two and three stories high, leaning precariously out over the water. She stared, then turned her head to look at Honoria.

"People live there, in those houses?"

Honoria nodded. "The bridge is a place for homes, shops, markets, even a chapel dedicated to Saint Thomas à Becket. 'Twas always a busy chapel, that one, needing two priests and a number of clerks. Beside the prayers and offerings to Saint Thomas, there are those who visit the chapel to honor the cleric who built the bridge, Peter of Colechurch, who is buried in the midspan."

"I see." Brielle gazed around thoughtfully and added: "There are few signs of the Black Death here, yet my lord has said that London suffers as much as Calais."

Henry Eastham, riding beside the wagon, spoke up to answer her. "What our sire said is the truth. The condition in London is pitiful. South Warke was full of victims last summer, and the toll in London light. 'Tis the way the plague seems to fall—one year in one place and next its neighbor. Londoners laughed at South Warke last year, but not now."

"Thank you, Sir Henry." Brielle was proper, but not as warmly friendly as she often was with Kiernan Comyn. None of the other knights had made any attempt to befriend her, though they were all respectful. Kiernan was different. He lived up to his lively green eyes, his ready smile. His gaiety raised her spirits—and her spirits needed raising, more all the time. Adam, she thought bitterly, might talk to her of serious things like her belief in God or his belief in Edward III, but he took serving maids to his bed.

Every time she thought of that scene—Adam's taut, eager body bent to that silly, giggling maid, the soft tone of his deep voice as he talked to her . . . begged her for her favors, no doubt!—it made her furious again. Men! Marriage vows meant nothing to them. He had arranged for an excellent room for her and Honoria, with an adjoining one where Leone had slept, and she certainly had no quarrel with that. Still, the way he ignored her now was insulting. He could have been chivalrous enough at least to greet her in the morning and show a concern for her feelings.

But, she thought, it was probable that he didn't care how she felt. She looked ahead, seeing his massive shoulders and flowing cloak between the other big men, and the thick golden mass of his hair waving from beneath the steel and leather helmet. He turned his head, and there was the profile that seemed to be made of the same steel and leather—the clear, hard lines of brow and nose, the close-cropped, gleaming gold beard, and wide, straight mouth. He seemed devoid of any soft emotion, a pitiless, stern man who, though he might be just, might never be merciful.

She looked down, her throat tight, thinking how different her life would be from now on. Then, because her thoughts had sent a shaft of fear into her heart, she stiffened her spine and raised her chin, looking around again. They had come to the bridge and slowed, forming a tighter column to enter. Brielle glanced up and then down again, suppressing a shudder. Above them, ranged about the portico of the gatehouse, there were human heads, blackened by the tar that preserved them, stuck on a row of pikes. A warning, no doubt, a way of showing those inclined to thievery what would happen if they were caught. In her present mood, Brielle considered it less a warning than a sign of barbarity. How, in the name of *le bon Dieu*, had her gentle father ever imagined she could be happy living with an Englishman?

Once inside the walls and narrow streets of London, Leone and Berthe hastily made up new vinegar-soaked cloths for everyone. The streets were befouled with sewage and other filth, though there were only a few bodies lying in wait for the carts. Due to the visits made by King Edward, who strongly objected to the gruesome sights and the chance of infecting more of his subjects, the death carts in London now rolled night and day, and the cry of "Bring out your dead!" resounded in every street.

"'Tis better to ride straight through the city," Adam said, dropping back to speak politely to Brielle. "The farther we go from the ships and docks, the less illness we'll see. We'll be late to bed, but if you are willing to go on—"

"I am willing," Brielle broke in, holding her vinegar cloth over her nose. "I would rather sleep in a field than in this hellish place."

"I doubt that," Adam said dryly. "The fields will

soon be covered with snow. However, we will find shelter outside the city walls in a Benedictine monastery."

"'Twould suit me fine," Brielle answered, and flushed red at the intent look he gave her. She knew as well as he that married couples were never allowed to sleep together in a monastery. He tarried a moment more beside her.

"You seem displeased, my lady. Have you objections to the arrangements I made last night?"

"None whatsoever," she said coldly. "Had I been asked, I would have chosen the same—that is, for myself. Tonight, however, due to the rules of the monastery, there will be no question of where or with whom we sleep."

Adam's face hardened. He said nothing, only bowed stiffly and rode ahead again. Gazing after him, Brielle felt a hand touch her arm.

"Dear Brielle," Honoria said softly, "he is trying his best to please you. Why snap and snarl like a spoiled lapdog?"

"Trying to please me?" Brielle asked scornfully, and shook Honoria's hand from her arm. "He is trying to taunt me instead! In Dover, when we shared a bed, he would have taken me like some bawd from the street, had I not refused! Since then, he's taken a serving maid to bed in Rochester! And he's not asked me once how I am, nor bothered to wish me a good day. The man is grossly lacking in manners."

Honoria's eyes had widened in shock. "You," she said when she got her breath, "are lucky he has not beaten you! Refused him, indeed! It is his right to take his pleasure of you once you are married. I have never known you to be so stupid and argumentive before. Were I he, I too would prefer the serving maid."

Disgusted, Honoria settled back into her seat, noting that they had come to a main street, lined with respect-

able houses. Though an open sewage drain ran down
the middle of the way, it was much cleaner than the
alleys and byways that led up from the docks. She put
aside her vinegar cloth and picked up the yarn and
needles she carried to keep herself busy, her face
regaining its calm dignity as she began to knit. Brielle
gazed at her silently for a time, then leaned back beside her.

"You are right," she said, and sighed. "And I have
no good reason. This is no more Dunbarton's fault
than mine; 'twas no more his wish than mine. Likely
he had a larger and more lusty woman he would have
preferred to wed. He may well think he should have
left me to die with my poor little mare in Calais."

Honoria's critical look softened. She suppressed a
smile at this deep gloom. "Possibly, though the way he
looks at you when you are not looking at him shows a
certain interest."

"What? Oh, that is just you, Honoria. Like a mother
hen with one chick, you always think everyone ad-
mires me."

Her eyes on her knitting, Honoria shook her head.
"That is not what I meant by 'a certain interest.' " She
glanced around, seeing Berthe and Leone at the provi-
sion baskets in the rear of the wagon; old Jacques high
on the driver's seat and watching the oncoming traffic
in the street. She lowered her voice as she looked back
at Brielle. "Sir Adam seems more interested in you
every day, Brielle, and glad to have you to wife. 'Tis a
rare case with the nobility, and a happy chance if you
want a faithful husband. You must act the wanton and
convince him that you want him in your bed."

Brielle gasped. Never had she thought to hear such
words from Honoria! Berthe, yes. Even Leone. But not
virginal Honoria, who never in her recollection had
even looked sidewise at a man! She was too surprised
to even answer coherently. "But . . . but I—"

"Hardly know him," Honoria supplied, and smiled with a tinge of sadness. "That is true. You've missed the excitement of courtship, the first whispered words, the stolen kisses. But that, too, is no more his fault than yours. In the meantime he is attracted to you, and life is short. Try to love him."

Pale, Brielle stared at her for another moment, gave a little nod, and looked away. 'Twas Honoria's own dream she was dreaming, she thought, and wondered at the faithful woman who had given so many years to a motherless child. "I will," she said, to please Honoria. "In time, I will try. But first I must know him better." She curled into her place more comfortably and fastened her mind on other things. From here, as they wended their way through the narrow and crowded streets, she could see what seemed a forest of church spires thrusting into the leaden sky, though they were by no means the only crowded part of the city. When they had crossed over the bridge, she had noted the many vessels trying to keep out of each other's way on the broad River Thames, some driven by sail, some by oarsmen. Then there were the crowded docks on both sides, and the buildings that seemed to press together as if for comfort in these perilous times.

"'Tis hard to believe," she commented to Honoria, "that these men who huddle together here like frightened rabbits are the same people who sweep over France like an army of devils, killing and looting."

"Shh!" Honoria glanced at Henry Eastham, still riding at their side, and saw his glimmer of a grin. "If you must insult the company we ride with, do so in private. You are rude. And do stop feeling that your country is the only one that suffers from invaders. England is a nation of conquerors—but you must remember that the Vikings—and your Norman raiders—came here and made it so, teaching the less warlike natives." She had said all that in Picardy patois and now dropped back into English: "There, look to the north and see St. Paul's Cathedral, the tallest of all the Christian churches in England and also in Europe."

Brielle bent and peered up from under the rolled curtain, drawing in her breath in amazement. Past the streets around them, empty now as the evening came on, over the rooflines of tall buildings extending away like jagged hills, the great cathedral, over five hundred feet high, loomed against the darkening sky. To her wondering eyes, it seemed to spread wide, comforting wings over half of London. She drew her head inside again and straightened her white coif, nearly dislodged as she ducked under the curtain.

"'Tis indeed a great and beautiful building," she admitted, then added contrarily, "but still, to my mind, London seems far less gracious than Paris."

It was near dark as they passed through Newgate and over the River Trent, leaving the city of London. To add to their discomfort, a cold north wind began at nightfall, bringing the smell of snow. Berthe and Leone lowered the side curtains and the women huddled together for warmth, while Jacques, wrapped in two blankets, shivered and shook on the driver's seat. The black bulk of the monastery and its dim lights were a welcome sight when they came into view.

The wagon slowed to turn into the opening gates of the monastery courtyard and creaked to a stop. At once a large hand lifted a corner of the curtain, and Adam's bearded face shone in the light of a lantern he held.

"Women travelers," he said coolly, "have their own common room here, where they eat apart from the men. Your sleeping rooms are curtained alcoves of the same room. Jacques will lead you there and help to serve you from the friars' kitchen."

"Thank you," Brielle said stiffly. "That will be fine."

Adam's gaze, dark blue and expressionless, met hers. "You must rise early. We leave at dawn."

Thinking of Honoria's warnings, Brielle lowered her gaze and spoke softly. "As you command, my lord. We will be ready."

After several moments, during which Brielle could hear the clanking of armor as the other knights dismounted, their muffled complaints, and the stamping of boots to ease their stiff legs, Adam finally replied. "Good," he said, "Sleep well, my lady." He sounded, Brielle thought, surprised. And—perhaps amused?

There was an icy chill in the common room where Jacques led them, though a small fire had been hastily laid and lit. There was a small garderobe leading off from the entry hall, where they could relieve themselves, and a laver in a corner, where they could wash their hands, drying them on the coarse linen cloth that hung beside it. Then they opened their cloaks, holding them wide to capture the heat of the smoky fire. They huddled around the hearth, coughing a little as the smoke stung their throats, but smiling, glad for the rest. Behind them, Jacques and two elderly friars came in with food, laid it on a long, narrow table, and as quickly left. The odor of the food brought all of them to the benches.

They ate for the most part in silence. Then Brielle, the edge of her appetite dulled, looked around the table. "Which of us is the lightest sleeper?"

"Leone," Berthe said, interrupted by Honoria, who claimed the title for herself.

"The slightest noise wakens me," Honoria insisted. "Why do you wish to know, my lady?"

"Our sire demands an early rising," Brielle said, and suddenly laughed, the sound soft but thoroughly amused. "Like a fool, I said we would be ready at dawn. Now I think it extremely doubtful. If the beds behind those curtains I see are comfortable, we may all sleep until noon."

"I'll not," Leone said firmly, and rose to begin clearing the table. "Now that I know we must rise early, I will keep it in mind and the thought will wake me, as sure as a cock's crow." She smiled, her great dark eyes soft as they touched on Brielle. "Your husband will have no reason to complain. We will be ready when they are."

It was after daybreak when Jacques came hurriedly to rap on the door to the women's common room. "Up, Up! We leave in a half hour!"

The door opened under his hand and Berthe came out, fully dressed, including her warm cloak. "A half hour, is it, old man? We were told dawn, and we are ready now. What kept you?"

Jacques, his eyes still fogged with sleep, his clothes thrown on, frowned, opened his mouth, shut it, and motioned to one of the friars in the courtyard.

"Feed these women, brother. Keep this one's mouth busy."

Behind Berthe, a ripple of laughter ran through the waiting women.

"'Tis good," Honoria said, her arm around Brielle's waist. "Laughter will ease this long journey."

Brielle smiled ruefully. "I prefer the journey to its end, I fear. How I do miss our château! Castle on Tyne may be a fine place, but 'twill not be home to me."

"Every bride has misgivings," Honoria said soothingly, and looked around as the two elderly friars who had served them supper came in with steaming bowls of porridge and pitchers of fresh milk. "Come, my lady. Hot food on a cold morning is one of God's richest blessings."

* * *

They had barely finished when the voices of the knights and the creaking of the wagon were heard outside. They hurried out, carrying their bundles, shivering in the cold bright air. As before, Brielle stood back while the others climbed in and packed the baggage into corners to lean against. Adam came to her where she stood, to help her mount the high steps.

"So," he said, standing slightly behind her and cupping her elbows in his palms, "I hear you and your women were up and ready before us. You surprise me."

Her head turned, her clear hazel gaze swept up to his, solemn, her eyes sunstruck with golden flecks. "I cannot take the credit, sire. 'Tis a skill of Leone's, not mine—she can wake when she wishes, tired or not."

He grasped her elbows, swung her to the top step of the wagon, and waited while she climbed in. She was as honest as a child, he thought as he turned away, and wondered how long that would last. It was true that he wanted an honest wife, but he would have relished a little flirtation, a tempting side glance, a meaningful smile. Even as he thought it, he shrugged and let it go. If the imperious Brielle Le Fontin flirted with him, it would doubtless be awkwardly done and certain to be entirely false.

Striding back to his horse, he thought again of his mother. If anyone could change this small, cold woman into a proper and knowledgeable wife, competent in the castle, warm in his bed, and obedient when he spoke, then Lady Martha Dunbarton could do it. Perhaps it would be worth waiting for, and he was willing to wait, though not willing to suffer. Nor would he. So far, there had been only the Rochester serving maid available, but there were many women where they were going now, both lusty and practiced in the arts of love. They would be happy to give him pleasure until his wife grew up.

Swinging into his saddle, Adam adjusted his shield over his left knee, ready to his arm, tested the loose fit of the broadsword in its scabbard, and looked around, finding his knights mounted and attentive; the wagon sides secured against the cold wind; and Jacques, wrapped in his blankets, holding the reins of the carthorses in one hand and his whip in the other.

"Kiernan, did you give the abbot his due?"

"Heaped up and running over, sire."

"Then we ride for Windsor. Aimery of Calais, whether from loyalty or cowardice, gave me an extraordinary message for our king. I am anxious to hear what Edward has to say."

Kiernan's green eyes narrowed, and he laughed. "I've wondered why you never spoke of that summons before. You've given me a puzzle, sire. How could the man's action spring from loyalty or cowardice? Wouldn't one be opposite to the other and therefore be easy to see?"

Adam grinned, knowing Kiernan's curiosity was aroused. "'Twill give you something to think on for the next twenty miles, cousin." He turned and looked back over the group of knights milling around the wagon, raised his shield, and gave a shout. "To Windsor Castle, my friends!"

Heads came up, excitement ran through the column, and scattered cheers rang out. Inside the wagon, having layered the blankets over the bundles and crawled inside the layers, the women huddled together and listened as the warhorses blew through their huge nostrils and, enlivened by the cold, pranced out through the courtyard gates and onto the narrow dirt road. Then they heard Jacques's whip crack in the air and felt the wagon jolt and roll forward, pulled by the patient carthorses.

"Windsor," breathed Honoria as the wagon settled.

She looked at Brielle with wide eyes. "Did you hear that, my lady? We are going to Windsor Castle!"

Brielle yawned and settled deeper in the blankets. "So? Is this Windsor Castle an important place?"

Honoria laughed, breathless. "Windsor is very important, Brielle! King Edward III of England lives there."

Brielle's eyes widened in the faint light. "But—that's very good, Honoria. I'll see my cousin again, Philippa of Hainault. I saw her last when I was but a child." She smiled. "Her son was nine, I recall, and a handsome boy, though bored by a seven-year-old girl—don't you remember, Honoria?"

"Sainted Mary! Of course I remember." Honoria took her hand and squeezed it. "How could I forget? It isn't often that I'm presented to royalty, even as a companion to a young cousin. But you must remember that Philippa is first a queen when she is here in England, not a relative. You must not expect her to take you into her circle, nor to favor you over others." She patted the hand. "Don't be disappointed, my lady, if she fails to remember you."

"She will remember me," Brielle said, her voice sure. "If only for my father's sake. Everyone loved my father."

Honoria looked away. "Yes," she said after a moment, "I know that is true."

5

the way to Windsor was smooth, befitting a road often traveled by a king. The horses went along at a better speed and the wagon no longer jounced and creaked as much as before. Or Brielle thought, perhaps it was only that her spirits had taken an upward leap. The prospect of seeing a member of her family—though she'd been but a child when she knew Philippa of Hainault and therefore had never known her well—made her heart light.

The misty morning gradually brightened and grew warmer, so that the women rolled up and tied the curtains of the wagon, and, pulling the blankets about them, watched the rolling, wintry countryside and the few other horsemen and wagons abroad so early.

On the left the River Thames, though hidden from the road by thickets of trees along its banks, gave away its presence by the lingering silvery fog that hung over the water. On the right great oak trees in the fields were nearly bare, their twisted branches a dark filigree against the pale sky. Here and there a stubborn leaf still clung to a twig, but below, around the gnarled roots, thousands more covered the ground with a gleaming gold patina.

Brielle thought of what Kiernan Comyn had said as they left the château. She had expressed her doubts to him, saying she feared she'd never suit England any more than England would suit her. Sir Kiernan was kind; he'd answered like a true courtier—he'd said she'd suit England better than she thought, for En-

gland prized beauty above all, having great beauty of
its own.

And so it did, she thought now, looking at the pale
blue sky and gently rolling lands, the colors of fading
green, of gold and russet, the streaks of light cream
where chalk broke through the rich dark soil of a
meadow rise. All soft, blended color, and the trees
huge, promising deep shade in summer. It would be a
green and pleasant place then. Though perhaps not in
the north country, where she must live.

"Your homeland is enchanting, Honoria."

"Yes. I'd missed it more than I knew. The sight of it
makes me feel young. I hope we can stay in the south
for a time—'tis more comfortable than the high, barren north in winter. And"—Honoria smiled, though
not with pleasure—"safer. The Scots are inclined to
raid the lands of the English border lords when the
snows come."

"The border lords?"

"Those like your husband, my lady, who guard the
border between Scotland and England. 'Tis a dangerous year, this one. Sir John Worth has told me the
Scots are strong and as many as ever, for the plague of
Black Death never reached them."

"It will, Mistress Honoria," Berthe said piously
from behind them. "God wills it for humanity's sins. I
am sure the Scots are not perfect."

Honoria laughed and picked up her knitting. "None
are, Berthe. Why, even I drop a stitch now and again."

Honoria, Berthe, and Leone went on with the talk,
easy and laughing, glad of the comfort of blankets and
the smooth road.

With them but not taking part, Brielle sat with her
back straight, her face turned toward the land outside,
her expression calm. All her attention had become centered on the big man who rode in the vanguard of the
party. She watched him, but secretly; only her eyes

inside the warm hood moved in his direction. Three times now, since they'd raised the curtains and tied them, she'd seen him glance back. And each time his gaze had sought her face and lingered there, not knowing she watched him from under her thick lashes.

Brielle studied him carefully and decided that unless she misread his expression, what Honoria had said was true. He had some sort of feeling about her, but she could not believe it was admiration. Curiosity, perhaps, in that inquiring gaze. At least he was interested. It came to her that what Honoria had been trying to say was that because she was Adam's wife, she had a weapon that could change her life for the better. A subtle weapon, true, and a weak one. But she was caught in this situation for life, and she must use what she could.

Riding on, she put her mind to work on what she'd learned. In his world Adam Dunbarton was all-powerful, like an earthly god. What he thought was right and what satisfied his needs seemed to be all that mattered to him. It was hard for her to realize that, and even harder to accept it. Her father had been all-powerful in his world, also, but for him his daughter's welfare and happiness had come first. To expect Adam to feel the same way about a cold and critical wife was, as Honoria had said, stupid.

But still—if Adam Dunbarton could be made to feel love for her, or even pride, her lot might be considerably easier to bear. She had been a fool not to recognize that before, instead of expecting this English oaf to treat her with great respect simply because she was a lady.

Thinking it over, she realized that she might have to bend to his wishes with a smile, pretend an admiration she didn't feel, even say flattering things instead of maintaining a cold silence. But she had no other weapons, and if flattering him gave her a chance at the power and respect she wanted, it might be worth the trouble.

Settling back in her seat, she caught his glance again on her face and gave him a bright smile. His brows rose beneath the leathern helmet, and he returned the smile, his teeth shining white within his golden beard before he faced forward again. Simple enough, she thought, but then frowned. Had that smile been altogether pleasant, or had there been a touch of mockery in't? Surely, he could not suspect her thoughts?

By midday, they had crossed on a bridge over to the south bank of the Thames and, turning west, came in sight of the easternmost curtain walls of Windsor Castle. Past them, first a great round tower of stone reared above all else, then a bell tower and a church spire were revealed. Finally, as they came nearer, she made out the castle itself among all the buildings clustered inside, a tremendous castellated building just inside the north wall and east of the round tower. She drew in her breath in amazed admiration. She had not thought the barbarian English could create such noble beauty.

Outside the walls there were many cottages, milling people, sheep and cows wandering everywhere, even in the road, so that the knights and Jacques had to slow, and sometimes to stop and wait. Brielle gripped Honoria's hand, excited in spite of herself.

"How wonderful it is to see children running about, pink-cheeked and strong. The Black Death has forgotten this place."

"Pray that it will continue to do so," Honoria said. "Some must survive. Look! The castle guard has seen Sir Adam's banner. They're opening the gates."

Brielle stared past the waving red banner with its silver falcon, unfurled but minutes ago, past Adam's big figure in the lead, and saw a company of armed men come out through the gates to the north and stand to form a line on either side of the rising road.

Leone leaned forward, her dark eyes full of excitement. "Our sire must stand high indeed in the English court to have the king's men recognize his banner and open for him without awaiting a trumpet call."

"Even an ordinary man might be friend to this king," Brielle agreed coolly. "I have heard he is a man who loves to fight, to hunt, and to play. My father once said Edward III had no patience with the formalities of court life and preferred the company of fighting men everywhere save in bed."

Suddenly conscious of her duties as a companion, Honoria ran a practiced glance over Brielle, taking in the heavy velvet-lined and fur-trimmed cloak, the black silk of her mourning gown, the clean coif of white linen on her dark hair, held to the shape of her head by a filet of gold and half hidden now by the cloak's hood. All satisfactory, given the conditions of arduous travel in these plague-ridden days. No one at Windsor Castle could fault her proper attire.

As for the woman herself, the face that looked back at Honoria was so familiar and so well loved that she had ceased to judge it, but at this crucial moment she scanned it as a stranger would. Dark brows curved gracefully over wide-set hazel eyes, light as clear amber. The short straight nose and forehead seemed carved from ivory, high cheekbones were flushed rose with excitement. A charming half smile curved the full lips. It was a beautiful face, and though Honoria deplored the fact, it was a face that would make Brielle no friends among the high-born ladies who vied for admirers in Edward III's court. But she was satisfied that her child—for that was how she perceived Brielle —was properly dressed and ready for the king's inspection.

"You will do," Honoria said, and settled back to

reach for her knitting and put it away. The knights had picked up their pace when the gates were opened; the carthorses, sensing the end of the day's journey, had broken into a faster trot. Excitement rippled through the column, and smiles broke out. A night or two in royal quarters, with fine food in good supply, would please them all.

Once inside the gates, they turned to the upper ward on their right, the horses' hooves clopping rhythmically on the cobblestones of the courtyard. Led by a pair of liveried men-at-arms, they left behind the huge round tower on its high earthen motte and came finally to a gradual stop before a fortresslike castle. By then, the column of knights and the stout wagon full of women had gathered a staring crowd of peasants, with more running up to join them, curious yet respectful, standing well away from the snorting warhorses and armored knights.

Dismounting, Adam came back to the wagon and lifted Brielle down, giving her a sweeping glance that seemed to judge her appearance critically. "Come," he said. "We go up alone."

Halfway up the flight of wide steps that led to the castle's entrance, they were met by a hurrying man in dark blue silken chausses, a pale blue velvet tunic, and a gold chain holding a chamberlain's insignia about his neck. Anxious and sweating, he bowed deeply to Adam and spoke rapidly.

"My Lord Dunbarton, I bid you welcome. We have only now received word of your arrival. The queen wishes to greet you and your lady in the solar and will give you rooms within her own residence. In the meantime, I will make the rest of your party comfortable in other quarters."

Adam nodded but questioned: "The king?"

"Hunting, my lord, in the forest to the south. His Majesty will return before nightfall."

"Very well, William." Taking Brielle's arm again, Adam went on, ignoring the stiff standing guards at the door, moving inside to a tremendous, high-ceilinged stone hall. Used by lesser guests, knights, and servants, the hall held two long high tables and a half-dozen common tables lined up across from them. There were curtained alcoves in the walls and, beneath the rise of finely polished wooden stairs along the rear wall, several garderobes. Hooded fireplaces held smoldering logs. The stone floor, as in centuries past, was covered with sweet-smelling dried rushes.

Adam took her swiftly up the stairs. Planked with polished wood, screened by a railing of carved panels, the gallery above circled the hall and furnished access to doors let into the stone wall. Burning lamps flickered and smoked in the dim light to mark each door. But at the south end of the gallery, off to the right, double doors were open on a huge solar, and a flood of light and warmth flowed out. With a firm hand on Brielle's arm, Adam swept her along toward the solar. She went willingly, her excitement growing.

Stepping inside the double doors, Brielle was dazzled, first by the blaze of light coming from everywhere, from stained-glass windows, from two roaring fireplaces, from the candles in crystal candlesticks that set rainbows shimmering. She felt the softness of a Saracen carpet beneath her feet and saw the vivid colors of tapestries that covered the walls. Then suddenly, she ignored the tremendous space, the sumptuous furnishings, and treasures of every kind, for she saw the queen coming toward them, and the sight made her breath catch in her throat. She had forgotten how wonderfully large and impressive Philippa of Hainault was.

Tall and strong, with coal-black shining hair and eyes and a bright and ruddy complexion, Queen Philippa came rapidly forward to greet them, her heavy

silk skirts rasping over the thick rug. She wore a loose
tunic of dark red velvet over her cream-colored un-
dergown and a loose gold belt set with varicolored
jewels. The crispinette that topped her luxuriant hair
was embroidered with luminous pearls. Adam had removed his helmet at the door and now he knelt on one
knee, taking her outstretched hand and kissing her fingers. Philippa laughed and murmured to him, and he
stood, smiling.

"I have brought you another subject, my queen." He
turned to the small figure behind him and took her
hand, bringing her forward with a wide, almost gran-
diloquent sweep of his arm. He continued to hold her
hand to give her confidence, for he felt a pang of sympathy for her, so tiny before the large and beautifully
gowned Philippa, and so like a shy child with that
white coif over the long, shining sheaf of dark hair.
"May I present my wife, Brielle Le Fontin of Picardy."

Philippa's dark eyes widened. She stared at Brielle,
who swept her a deep curtsey and a shaky smile. The
queen's strong face crumpled into a tender sympathy,
and tears misted her dark eyes. She opened her arms,
the deep trailing sleeves making them look like welcoming wings.

"*Ma pauvre enfant!* How long it has been since we
met, little cousin! Come, give me the kiss of kinship!"

Startled, Adam let go of Brielle's hand and stepped
aside. Behind the queen three ladies-in-waiting gasped
and spoke softly among themselves. But seeing the
genuine feeling in Philippa's handsome face, Brielle
felt tears spring to her own eyes. She went swiftly forward and embraced the queen warmly, kissing her on
both cheeks. Philippa returned the kisses, holding her
close to her large and comfortable body, stroking her
hair, murmuring words of understanding.

"My poor little one, to lose so dear a father, so wonderful a man. There was no one except my own par-

ents whom I loved more than I loved my gentle uncle
Henri. I wept when I heard of his death, and I grieved
for you, who had no one near to give you comfort. I
thank *le bon Dieu* that Adam has brought you to me."

"Though all unknowing, Your Majesty," Adam said,
and laughed, though the laugh died away as Brielle
turned and met his gaze. There was a subtle, amused
triumph in the golden eyes. He flushed, adding: "My
lady wife neglected to tell me she was related to the
Queen of England."

Philippa's smile was more genuine than Adam's
laugh. "Few husbands know all there is to know of
their wives, Adam, and the Le Fontins have long been
named as a family that keeps its own counsel. Who
knows? Brielle may have many more surprises for
you."

Adam acknowledged that sally with a tight smile. "I
believe you, my queen. I can recall another surprise or
two my lady has given me in the short time we have
been wed. They were not always as pleasant as this
one."

Within an hour Brielle was settling into her own suite
of rooms behind one of the doors she had passed on
the gallery. Honoria and Leone had been summoned
and given a room together in a corner of the gallery,
and they stood ready to help her prepare herself for a
welcoming banquet that evening; Berthe and Jacques
had been sent to join the rest of the household servants
in the quarters behind the big hall.

Adam had ridden out, taking Kiernan along, toward
the forest to the south. He had excused himself to Philippa by telling her the message he carried was of
great importance, and he was anxious to deliver it.

Honoria, amazed and pleased by the queen's welcome for Brielle, sent Leone to the laundry rooms to
carefully clean the best of Brielle's black silk gowns

and to wash and starch the white linen coif. In the meantime, she arranged for a large tub of warm water, placed in front of a roaring fire.

"What an honor," she said, vigorously scrubbing Brielle's thick hair. "The queen is most amiable and great-hearted, taking such notice of a young cousin she hasn't seen in years."

"Not so rough," Brielle said, easing away. "I'll have no hair left on my head. As for the queen's favor, my heart is warmed by her generosity. And I believe part of it is Adam. She seemed glad to see him, before she knew I was his wife."

Honoria raised her brows. "Surely you don't mean there may be something scandalous between them?"

"Heavens, no! I meant only that she felt a tie, as one does in true friendship. When you see her you will know she has not become a courtesan. She tells me she has had eleven children for the king, seven of whom are still alive."

"Seven! How fortunate she has been. Some of them must be quite young."

"Indeed. She has the last two here with her. Mary, who is five years old, and Margaret of Calais, who was born in that city two years ago, when the English took possession."

Honoria looked amused. "I remember you crying bitter tears when Calais was lost. You seem quite calm about it now."

Brielle shrugged bare shoulders. "I was younger then."

"And not married to an Englishman." Honoria saw the spark of argument light up Brielle's eyes and hurriedly changed the subject. "What of the other royal children?"

Brielle composed herself and answered. "The heir, Edward, whom they call the Black Prince, and his sister, Isabella, who is of marriageable age, prefer Lon-

don, even with the plague haunting the streets. The
three younger boys, Lionel of Antwerp, John of Gaunt,
and Edmund of Langley, are all in training at castles
belonging to court favorites, such as one Philippa mentioned, Henry of Lancaster.''

"'Tis a large family,'' Honoria said, pouring water
over Brielle's hair to rinse it. "But I doubt it will grow
any larger.''

"It could. The queen is not yet forty years of age, and
she is big and very strong.''

Honoria laughed, beginning to soap Brielle's back.
"Then why not? The bloodlines are of the best. The
Plantagenet blood showed itself in King Edward's
handsome face and golden hair when he was but a
child, and no one could fault the traits of a daughter of
William the Good, Earl of Hainault.''

"You talk like my father's horse breeder,'' Brielle
said, laughing. "He put all virtue to the blood. But a
man's brain and courage must gain from the training
he receives.''

"No,'' Honoria argued. "You can only teach skills
that come naturally to each man. A brave man will
learn how to fight, but a coward given the same lesson
will learn how to run away faster.''

Squeezing the water from her hair, Brielle laughed
again. She felt wonderful, as if she'd come home. "Perhaps you are right. If you're so good at judging men,
tell me of this king of yours. I seem to remember my
father saying Edward III was crowned when he was
fifteen years old.''

"True, but he did not rule. His mother, Queen Isabella, and her paramour, the wicked John Mortimer,
ruled as regents. They were bitterly resented, for everyone knew they'd conspired to have Edward's father, Edward II, put to death. But the young king had
friends, and there was a palace coup, with Mortimer
captured and Isabella banished from court to live

alone. But then, to give you real understanding of King
Edward, they say he still shows love and respect to his
mother and sees to it that she lacks nothing.''

Standing up in the tub, taking the drying cloth
Honoria handed her, Brielle rubbed her hair and
looked thoughtful. "How do you know these things?"

Honoria sniffed. "I am an English gentlewoman,
and we are told the important news by the men in our
families. The palace coup took place the same year
that your mother asked me to come to France with her.
Since then, Count Henri had often told me news of the
English court, since *you* would never listen to anything
about the 'barbarians.' Now, let me add more to your
wisdom: If you continue to stand there wet and naked,
you will surely catch cold.''

Stepping out of the tub, Brielle wrapped the large
cloth around her and sat on a stool before the fire, still
thinking. "You said the king was handsome when he
was young. Describe him to me, so that I may recognize him when he comes in from hunting.''

"He is many years older than when I saw him last,''
Honoria answered, taking a brush to Brielle's damp
hair. "But unless his face is scarred from fighting, he
would still be handsome, I vow. He was very large,
and his hair and beard marked his Plantagenet blood
with the golden lion color. His features were strong—
why, now that I think on it, he was much like Sir
Adam!" She paused, her brow wrinkling. "*Very* like—I
wonder . . . ah, no. Edward II was more inclined to
dalliance than most men, but Martha Dunbarton
would never have strayed from her own marriage bed.
Not even for a king.''

Brushing away, not noticing Brielle's face, Honoria
went on thinking out loud. "Of course, the king is indeed much older than Sir Adam, some fifteen or so
years, I imagine. But that's the appearance you should
look for.''

"Adam's older half brother?" Brielle's tone was dry and not amused. Honoria paused, holding the brush in midair as Brielle glanced around. Staring down into angry amber eyes, Honoria shook her head firmly.

"Your husband is no bastard, my lady. 'Twould be impossible. Their likeness to each other will have come from generations before, when lusty Plantagenet blood was served in many a lonesome bed. Besides, our present king's father was imprisoned in 1326, a full year before Sir Adam's birth."

The anger faded from Brielle's eyes, replaced by a cool interest. "Yet you believe they have a common bloodline. It will be strange if they turn out to have the same disposition, will it not?"

"Not so strange," Honoria replied. "As I said before, a man's character often comes from the blood he carries."

The Lady Grace of Hainault, aunt of Philippa and one of her ladies-in-waiting, came to fetch Brielle at sundown. She took her back toward the immense solar, saying that the king and the knights with him had been sighted in the distance by guards on the castle wall and would soon be entering the gates.

"No doubt," the Lady Grace added fussily, "we will be forced to listen to their many triumphs in the hunt. Still, in this quiet place, we are lucky to hear of any adventures. I do miss the fêtes and other entertainments in London."

Brielle smiled and nodded, speechless. She was awed by the Lady Grace's ensemble. An elderly woman, she wore a huge ruffled cap of crispinette with a veil, a velvet cloak banded in vair, a printed silk gown that hugged her plump bosom and then swung loose and trailed down to a wide band of royal ermine around the dragging hem. Adding to this odd assortment of styles were several jeweled rings on each wrinkled hand, and a long gold chain that hung about her neck, holding a dangling gold image of a stalking heron, a bird that was known to bring good fortune.

Looking away politely, Brielle thought that if she were to spend much time at court, she would need to change her views on suitable gowns. Of course, being in mourning excused her simple black gown now, but never in the past had she seen anything quite so elaborate as Lady Grace's costume.

Twice on the short trip from the suite to the solar, Lady Grace stopped her and they stood aside, allowing male servants to pass them on the narrow gallery with heavy-laden trays.

Sniffing the tantalizing odors of food that swirled in the wake of those trays, Brielle discovered she was truly hungry for the first time in days. The hollow feeling of loss, the deep anger at being torn from her home and given to a stranger, had dissolved in the warmth of Philippa's welcome.

Entering the solar, she saw open doors on the far wall to the right, and beyond, a formal dining room, its long table covered with gleaming white linen and silver plates, chairs with red velvet pillows brought up, places set for thirty or more. At each place silver goblets were ready for wine, loaves of fresh-baked bread flanked the goblets, and great platters of meat and fowl, fish and oysters, sat along the center.

"Come, have wine with us." Philippa's voice was laughing but kind. She and two of her elderly ladies-in-waiting were standing near the fire in the solar, drinking from jeweled cups.

Brielle's heart lifted with joy. Seeing Philippa there, across the wide room but motioning eagerly for her to come close, was like finding home in a strange land. She left Lady Grace with a murmur of thanks and went to Philippa, pausing to bend neck and knee in a tiny bow as she neared, then looking up and taking the cup of wine Philippa offered. Her throat thick with gratitude, she sipped the wine and thought that there was nothing Philippa could ask of her that she wouldn't give.

"I hear our men below," Philippa said indulgently, as if she spoke of children. "Listen to them. There will be fresh meat in the larder tonight. They've had good hunting when they laugh like that."

Dazzled by the luxury around her, tired from the long journey, Brielle smiled and nodded absently, hearing the sound of booted heels thumping on the gallery planks. Loud talk and male laughter boomed into the solar, and then, as she looked across to the dimly lit doorway, Brielle saw Adam stride into the solar. He was laughing, his head thrown back. Behind him were other men, perhaps a score, accompanied by beautifully dressed women. They all crowded forward, squeezing past each other in the doorway, talking noisily. Brielle kept her eyes on her husband, wondering at his presumption, his easy manner, here in the king's chambers.

"Ha! A pretty sight, Philippa! An extravagance worthy of your guests!"

Brielle stared in shock as he came up to them and caught Philippa in his arms, kissing her mouth heartily. She opened her mouth to protest but no sound emerged, for in that moment she saw the silver hairs in the golden beard and the deep clefts that years had put in the bronzed cheeks.

'Twas King Edward himself, and she on the edge of scolding him! She was cold with the knowledge, thinking how close she had come to earning the king's displeasure. She saw his gaze touch her then with curiosity, and she quickly moved from Philippa's side and dropped into a deep curtsey.

"Your Majesty," she murmured, rising again, "I am sorry indeed to intrude."

Edward smiled and reached out, grasping her arms

in his broad palms and bringing her close. He leaned down, touching his lips to her forehead, then drew back, smiling as he studied her. She stood stock still, gazing up at him in amazement. His blue eyes, as blue as Adam's but surprisingly warm as his gaze roamed over her face, mesmerized her.

"You do not intrude, nor ever will, Brielle of Picardy. Adam has told me of you, and you are welcome here, not only as his wife but as my queen's cousin." He smiled, his thumbs caressing her soft shoulders. "Indeed, I vow your beauty alone would find you a place at my court."

"You are very gracious," Brielle answered faintly. "Very kind. I thank you, sire."

From behind her a hand clasped her waist, and Adam's deep, familiar voice spoke. "Come, my lady— we'll find our places."

As she bowed and moved gracefully away, she thought Adam looked displeased by Edward's attention to her. Still dazed, Brielle saw that Adam was a little taller than the king, broader in the shoulders and much younger in appearance, though the king had such force about him that it belied his age, which could not be forty yet. She glanced back and saw that Philippa was greeting the other knights, but Edward was still watching her as she went with Adam into the dining room. She looked away quickly, her cheeks burning. The warmth in his gaze was almost too openly admiring. But still—'twas an honor, surely, to be admired by a king.

6

"In all my life," Brielle told Honoria later, as the older woman helped her out of her clothes and into a *chemise de nuit*, "I have never seen such drinking and eating. Why, there must have been half a hogshead of red wine consumed within an hour or less, and enough roasted venison to feed an hundred or more men." She spoke more in wonder than in censure, and Honoria, pressing her down on a stool so she could brush out her hair, laughed.

"The Englishmen have huge appetites, my dear child. For everything—for food and drink, for fighting and lovemaking. And revelry! If we stay—and Leone has heard a rumor that we will—you will think of to-night as a paltry feast compared to the delicacies and entertainment of the fetes you will see at Martinmas and later."

Brielle's face was suddenly animated and hopeful. Her head turned to Leone, who sat in a corner of the room mending a torn skirt. "Leone! Tell me of this delightful rumor, and why you believe it."

Leone looked up, her great dark eyes amused, a smile tipping the corners of her lips. "Our Lady Dunbarton is more content with England now, and wishes to stay?" She laughed softly. "And why not? A handsome husband, a comfortable place in the king's own family, and glorious galas to attend. Who could blame her?"

"You are not answering my question, Leone." Brielle's tone chided the maid, though she smiled at the teasing.

Leone stood, shaking down her skirt and picking strands of thread from the rug at her feet. "But I will, my lady. 'Tis only that I am ashamed to say I overheard talk between Lord Dunbarton and two of his knights, Sir Henry Eastham and Sir Abel Southers, who met in the hall below." She paused, looking at Brielle in sudden anxiety. "I must confess to using guile and moving behind a door to hear them better. Does that offend you? I thought you might want to know their plans."

Brielle frowned. "I suppose it was wrong. But I am much too curious myself to place any blame on you. What were they saying?"

"Sir Adam ordered them to ready themselves with a mule, food, and drink and make their way to Castle on Tyne as quickly as they can. They are to explain the absence of the rest of us—by telling Baron Dunbarton that King Edward has ordered Sir Adam, his wife, and the rest of the party to remain with him until a week after Christmas."

Brielle gasped. "After Christmas? Why—why that is near two months away! Are we to stay at Windsor for all that time?"

Leone nodded. "Our sire said 'twas his duty to obey the wishes of the king. 'Tis something to do with the message he brought from Calais. Sir Eastham tried to question him on it, but Sir Adam refused to answer and sent him off."

Brielle sat still, smiling and silent for a few moments, and then rose, yawning. Adam had been much more attentive this evening, as if, she thought, the compliments from the king had made him appreciate his wife the more. She had encouraged him, taking the opportunity to smile and give him compliments, also, and they had talked pleasantly together for the first time. She was sure he would come to her room tonight to begin his courting.

"Perhaps he will tell me, once we are alone. I believe 'tis his intention to join me here, once you and Honoria retire."

"Ah! If that be the case," Honoria said with great satisfaction, "we will leave you now. Come, Leone. Our sleeping room is at the far end of the gallery." Gathering up the clothes Brielle had worn, Honoria started for the door. "'Twould be a good omen," she added, turning to glance back, "to conceive your first child in Windsor Castle. 'Tis the birthplace of King Edward himself."

Startled, Brielle gazed after the two departing women without answering. That Adam might think her smiles and kind words meant she was ready for the full intimacy Honoria implied had not occurred to her. She was *not* ready, and she would tell him so once more, if that became necessary. Surely he wouldn't consider taking her by force? She sat still, going over in her mind what she had heard of men's appetites, and then she rose and went to her wardrobe, where she took out a heavy cloak. Wrapping it about her so that it covered her completely and made her look shapeless, she sat down again in front of the fire to wait.

With Honoria and Leone gone there was silence in the room. Brielle discovered she could hear, even through the thick walls, the occasional tread of someone passing along the gallery; a quick little trill of feminine laughter, the rumbling but pleasant sound of a man's voice. Every lady who sat at dinner, she thought idly, seemed to have many admirers amongst the knights. It was true what she had heard of the present English court. 'Twas all loveplay and flirtation, even amongst the wedded couples—a charming custom, she admitted to herself, if not carried too far. Perhaps it would teach Adam to give her the compliments and attention she wanted.

Time passed. The fire gradually sank lower, the logs turned into coals, the coals became ashes. Brielle shivered in the cooling room. Finally she could ignore the truth no longer, and she rose, took a taper and lit the tall candle by the bed, the one that chased away the spirits of the night when they wished to steal a sleeping soul. Then, dousing the small, guttering candles on the table, she took off her heavy cloak and crawled into the luxurious bed.

So her first efforts to engage Adam Dunbarton's esteem had failed. A wry smile twisted the corners of her mouth as she turned her back on the spirit light and shut her eyes. Certainly she had not been in any danger from raging passion. The wry smile wavered and disappeared as another thought came into her mind. There were other beds, and other women here. There had been many soft glances cast Adam's way at dinner, by women more enticing than a serving maid in Rochester. And far more enticing than a cold wife. Whose bed was he in?

Summoned early the next morning by one of Philippa's tiring maids, Brielle dressed hastily and joined the queen's cortege, consisting of the ladies-in-waiting and various maids and attendants. In sleepy silence the band of women followed Philippa down the stairs and through the great hall, where servants were clattering about, building up the fires and bringing in food. Other women, wives, and daughters of the noblemen who had come for the fall hunting joined them there and followed, giving Brielle sidelong glances, curious about the queen's young cousin. Brielle, wondering which one of them had been the magnet who drew Adam away from her last night, felt the heat of blood rising in her cheeks. She raised her head proudly and walked with a firm step.

The night had been cold, and when they stepped outside, a tracery of frost flowers had etched the windows of the soaring buildings, and a thin crust of rime edged the large paving stones beneath their thin slippers. The air was sharp but pure, as it had been in the country-side of Picardy, and Brielle breathed deep, suddenly glad to be in this place.

Philippa's calm gaze noted Brielle's confident look, her smile. She clasped Brielle's arm, drawing her closer. "We shall attend mass in St. George's Chapel, little one. I wish to offer thanks for your safe arrival and pray for your continued happiness in our coun-try."

"I shall ask blessings for you," Brielle answered, and touched the hand on her arm, smoothing it gently. "I will ask that you shall be always happy wherever you are, for as long as you shall live. You have made me welcome in a strange country, and I will never for-get your kindness."

Around them women nodded approvingly, smiled at them both, and stepped carefully on the slippery stones, clutching one another and uttering small cries when a shoe skidded on the rime. The pale winter sun touched them with light as it slanted above the eastern walls and lit the deep reds and blues and greens of their thick wool cloaks, making glowing spots of color against the snow.

Making their way past the huge round tower and down into the lower ward, they found the chapel nearly filled, for the king and his Knights of the Garter had arrived before dawn and were only now beginning to leave. The queen and her women drew off to one side and waited quietly as the men came out.

Today the men were all dressed in full armor, to be shriven of their sins as warriors. Brielle, who knew this ceremony was usually performed between battles, was taken by a leap of strange foreknowledge. She said nothing, even to Philippa, of what came to her, yet she knew there would be fighting; she knew it had to do with that message Adam had brought. But when? She looked first at Adam and then at the king and was again astounded at their likeness to each other, even in the clear light of day. Glancing up at Philippa, she saw the dark eyes were amused. The queen had seen her interest.

"In private," Philippa bent and whispered in her ear, "Edward calls Adam brother. He swears Adam is his honor and his conscience, brought to life and sent to help him avoid excessive pride in himself and his judgment." Her low laugh was soft. "The king's champion, as in ancient times. Edward swears he's seen the hero light around Adam's head in battle. I never deny it, for Edward truly needs Adam's strength."

Brielle gave Philippa a look of complete trust. She understood nothing of the King's odd fancy—but whatever had been meant, Brielle was sure of Philippa's goodwill. She accepted and would remember the statements; in time, she thought, she might understand the meaning.

Following prayers and mass, celebrated by the dean of the chapel, Bishop John Langley, the women returned to the castle. Walking across the quadrangle of the upper ward, now in full sun, they could see the king and his nobles and knights dressed in hunting regalia, mounting their horses for a trip to the forest. The women slowed to watch, enjoying the spirit of the horses, fresh and prancing in the cold air, and the excitement of the alaunts, the huge hounds used for tracking wolves and wild boars. Held on stout ropes by yeomen, the alaunts gave out their deep, melodious howls and pulled against their collars, trying for the gates and the forest beyond.

"Again." Philippa sighed, and then laughed. "Ah, well. 'Tis one of Edward's best-loved sports, but he'll tire of it soon. He has already sent out challenges for a tournament and feast at Martinmas, scarce two weeks away."

Her eyes on Adam, Brielle smiled absently and nodded, hardly hearing the last words. Adam was different here, easy and full of good spirits, as if a burden had been lifted when he arrived. He seemed younger, happier, even joyous this morning. His taut, muscular thighs clung easily to his saddle as he brought his rearing stallion under control, and Brielle was unable to tear her gaze away from him. He was, she thought suddenly, beautiful to watch. He was like some legendary god of the hunt, so lithe and strong in his tight-knit chausses, the form-fitting tunic of leaf brown leather stretched by the breadth of his chest. The spill of hair from under the cocky leathern cap he wore glinted like gold in the sun. He was laughing, she saw, and as the horse came down and pranced, blowing, he leaned forward and patted the thick neck affectionately.

Brielle smiled without knowing she smiled, liking the way he had gentled his mount. Then, as the horses calmed and cantered toward the gates, she watched until she saw only the men and dogs trailing behind the mounted hunters. She turned back, suddenly aware that Philippa was waiting for her to say something. "I beg your pardon, Your Highness," she said, amazed at herself. "I—was distracted."

Philippa laughed. "I cannot blame you for your interest," she said, taking Brielle's arm and continuing toward the castle. "God knows I've spent my share of time admiring the same kind of man. Handsome, strong, and skillful, possessed of a great joie de vivre. And since one must have faults, a little too fond of other ladies. No, don't frown! These days 'tis not a vice."

Brielle's frown deepened. "Then, ma'am, what is it?"

"The custom," Philippa said, with neither blame or

acceptance in her neutral tone. She looked around, making certain no one of the other women was close enough to them to hear what she said. "A custom taken up by both sexes. I know well what you have been taught of fidelity to marriage vows, for I was taught the same; so I must tell you this. In court and in castle, there is a new law. Courtly love has made dalliance of no more blame than a light flirtation."

Surprised, silent for a moment, Brielle considered it. It was not an entirely new thing to her, for there had been rumors of widespread inconstancy in the French court for years. Still, she hadn't expected to hear these words from Philippa of Hainault.

"'Twill not be my way," she said finally. "I'd rather stay a virgin than sully my vows."

Philippa's dark eyes were soft on Brielle's face. "Adam has told me you are not yet ready to share a marriage bed, and he intends to wait until you are at home in Northumbria. That is why I gave you separate rooms."

"Oh!" Brielle's amazement was apparent. "I—why, I did not know him when we married in such haste, and I—I refused him. 'Twas naught but fright, at that. But since then, though I expected to honor my vows, he has not approached me."

"You refused him?" Philippa struggled with a sudden laugh and lost. "Adam must be amazed! There are few ladies in my court who have not desired Adam—and now all envy you. They would give anything for another chance to lie with Adam."

"They have it now, then," Brielle said, heard the tremor in her own voice, and lifted her head high. "Still, I will not seek to revenge myself in like manner."

They fell silent, for they had reached the palace entrance and the other women were drawing closer. Inside, as the rest of the ladies found seats at the long tables holding steaming oatcakes, buttermilk, and dried fruit pasties, Philippa took Brielle along to the steps and the gallery above.

"You will break your fast with me," she said, "while we discuss the gowns you need. I know you will never forget your beloved father, but I also know Henri Le Fontin would not have you continue wearing that lifeless black now that you are a bride. I have an excellent seamstress here, and a goodly amount of fine cloth."

Brielle's face brightened. "'Tis true, ma'am. My father thought the mourning period overlong and often said so. He would be happy to have me out of these dreary gowns." They were climbing the last few steps, and as she gained the gallery, she turned and looked back at the seated ladies in their colorful clothes, thinking of what she might like to have. One of the women was watching her—studying her, likely, for her expression was intent and unsmiling. A woman, Brielle thought, close to the midtwenties or older, and very pale, with a thick mass of dark auburn hair, worn in coiled braids over her ears. Brielle turned back to Philippa.

"Who is the red-haired woman in forest green tunic and light green underskirt?"

Philippa's strong face tightened. She spoke without looking, making it clear she knew who was meant.

"Alice Montagu, wife of Edward Montagu, Lord of Bungay. Alice is a jealous woman, apt to look down on newcomers here. Pay no attention."

Brielle laughed softly. "Perhaps that is why she frowns. From here, I look down on her."

"That," Philippa said, her tone sardonic, "is what she fears. She holds the attention of—a favored position at court and will not give it up easily."

Curious, Brielle waited; then, as they entered the solar and she realized Philippa was not going to add to what she had said, prudently said nothing more herself.

By late afternoon, the seamstress and her assistants had fashioned the first gown, a cream silk with an overgown of golden brown velvet, the neckline lower than any Brielle had worn before, the bodice tight to her tiny waist. There was a jeweled belt worn low on her hips, and below it the velvet split on the sides to show the graceful flow of silk. She wore a horned headdress, its slanted peaks draped with gauzy amber veils secured by jeweled pins. A necklace of gold with a topaz pendant came from her own jewel box. She could not resist parading about in the small room used for sewing, feeling the soft silk and velvet slide sleekly over her body, looking into a mirror with frank pleasure. In all her life, she had never had a gown so becoming to her. The head seamstress, Bess Miles, smiled as she picked up the scraps and threads.

"Now that we have taken your measure, Lady Brielle, the rest of the gowns the queen ordered for you can be done apace. You will have gowns and habits and cloaks with fur, all new, before Martinmas."

Brielle glanced across the room at Queen Philippa, watching with a smile, and felt her eyes grow damp. "I am grateful, ma'am, much more than I can say."

"And I am well pleased," Philippa said, and rose to leave the room. "The gown does you justice, which could not be said of that bulky black cloth you were bound into. At dinner tonight you will be noticed, and I warrant you, you will be admired even more than before." She paused at the door and added, humorously: "Except, perhaps, by the woman in forest green."

Always, Brielle had looked for reassurance in Honoria's blue English eyes, and she had never failed to find it. That evening, dressing for dinner—delayed again by the tardy king and other hunters—she caught a look of sheer pleasure crossing Honoria's face.

"Beauty has always been yours, my child, but what a difference a good seamstress can make! Tonight, Adam Dunbarton will not resist you. You will be able to lead him where you will."

At first, waiting in the solar, drinking wine with the other ladies-in-waiting, Brielle thought that might be true in spite of what Philippa had told her. Everyone complimented her lavishly, and she knew from her own honest mirror that she did look very well. And when Adam came in with the rest of the noisy crowd of knights, he fell silent at sight of her, his blue eyes widening and warming. She put up her chin, turned her face away a degree or two, and went on watching him carefully from the corners of her eyes, standing as still and graceful as a wary young doe.

Adam came to her, took her free hand, and brought it to his lips. In his tight-fitting leather tunic and knitted chausses, he towered over her like the god she had envisioned, his wind-tangled hair and beard as golden as fall leaves. She drew in her breath soundlessly as his warm mouth touched her hand.

"Good evening, sire. Had you luck in the hunt?"

"We all did well enough, my lady." Now when he came close to her he put her in awe, but pride kept her head up, her gaze on his face. She watched him make a careful inspection that began on the horns of her fancy headdress, skimmed to the neckline that showed the beginning rise of her breasts, then his gaze sharpening and turning cool as he studied the jewels at neck and belt. "'Twould seem you did well yourself, wife. Such a gown and precious stones could only be a gift from your too-generous cousin, Queen Philippa."

There was a hard edge of displeasure in his deep voice. Brielle stiffened, her amber eyes losing their melting softness and growing as chilly as his. "You disapprove?"

Adam frowned. "Not if this gift stands alone. But there will be no more gowns and fripperies unless they are paid for by Dunbarton gold. We need no royal charity. Remember that."

Sudden fury goaded her volatile temper. Not trusting herself to speak, she withdrew her hand from his and turned away, struggling to control her anger. When she turned back, he was gone. When next she saw him, he was talking and laughing with Alice Montagu, whose white hand lay lightly on his arm, her smiling face charmingly flirtatious. While Brielle stared, the king came up and joined them, his arm sliding over Alice's bare shoulders. Between the two leonine heads of striking Plantagenet gold, Alice Montagu's pale face shone with triumph, as if she had gathered to herself all the light in the room. Beyond them, seated amongst her ladies-in-waiting, Queen Philippa looked at them and then looked away, her face shadowed but serene.

"Adam was unfair," Brielle told Honoria later in the privacy of their rooms. "He had never told me not to accept gifts from Queen Philippa, yet he blamed me for doing so, even blaming me for my own topaz pendant, thinking my cousin had given it to me."

Honoria sat before the fire, studying her beloved charge with a sorrowful look. Brielle, her face still set in disappointment, stood leaning against the mantel over the fireplace, watching small flames lick at dying coals.

"From the beginning," Honoria said, "your relationship with the queen was unexpected and, I believe, unwelcome to your husband. Coupled with your pride, it may make him think you intend to do as you please rather than obey him. Still, from what you have told me, he asked only that you accept no more. Had you less temper and pride, you might have quickly agreed that he was right. As it is, your silence is telling him you'll go your own way. If I were you, I'd never chance that with Sir Adam."

The amber eyes flicked to Honoria's worried face. "You wouldn't? Why not? If everything I do makes him angry, what difference will it make? I *will* do as I please! But I won't allow the queen to give me the clothes the seamstress is making. They will be paid for —in Le Fontin gold."

Honoria sighed despairingly. "You are determined to anger him, then. God help us when you do!"

The next morning it seemed to Brielle that God—or perhaps King Edward, since the two seemed much the same in this place—had listened to Honoria and intervened. Coming to St. George's Chapel with the queen and their attendants, Brielle was called aside by Adam as the men came out.

Adam's blue eyes were cold, his jaw set grimly as he spoke to her. "I am sent by the king on an errand to Norfolk, and Edward has asked me to leave you here as a guest of the queen. I trust you will comport yourself with dignity while I am gone."

She would have dearly loved to ask him what dignified custom he was following when he vied with Edward over a whey-faced courtesan like Alice Montagu, but she held her tongue and turned away. His hand caught her arm and turned her back again.

"Do I have your word?"

She shook off his hand, anger flaming her face. "I take pride in the manners and customs I have been taught, sire. To ask me for a promise of good behavior is insulting." Again she turned, and again he whirled her back, so suddenly she lost her balance and fell against him. He held her there, his massive chest as hard as iron against her breasts, his bearded face stern.

"Your manners to me are sadly lacking, my lady. Give me your word!"

Red with anger and embarrassment, she muttered a promise. He let her go, slowly. "I will leave you a purse," he said in a calmer tone. "Buy whatever you need." And then he was gone, taking Kiernan Comyn with him. It was strange, she thought afterward, that with his going she felt no happier.

For Brielle and her attendants, the task of learning the daily life of Windsor Castle—which meant learning the few but sometimes strange rules laid down by a lenient king—took up some of the time they were forced to wait for the first of the fall celebrations, the Feast of Martinmas, which fell in the middle of November.

For three days before the tournament and celebration, which honored both Martinmas and the king's thirty-seventh birthday on November 13, Brielle and Honoria joined the queen and her ladies-in-waiting at the south-facing windows of the gallery. There they sat in comfort on pillowed chairs to watch the colorful trains of the nobles and knights pour past into the snowy quadrangle and pause there to listen to the shouted instructions of the harried chamberlain or his assistants. Then, starting their tired horses again, they headed for the prepared rooms and stables meant for them. All the families who had been invited to attend the Martinmas Tourney had accepted, and the numbers put a strain on even the commodious quarters of Windsor Castle.

"If more arrive," Philippa said in the early afternoon of the third day, "we will have to put them in Colehous, down there in the lower ward."

The queen made few humorous sallies—never one with spite—but this brought a rising, tumbling wave of laughter. Colehous, the oldest and worst of the several prisons at Windsor, came close to being the most mis-

erable in all of England, and most of the ladies knew
from messengers that the last train—sighted by the
lookouts on the towers and reported but minutes ago—
came from Norfolk and sported the flag of Castle Rising. Isabella of France, Edward's mother and the most
scandalous woman in the civilized world, was arriving. The Colehous prison, many of them thought privately, was too good for her.

Even though Honoria had told her that King Edward still gave love and respect to his mother, Brielle
found it hard to believe that the woman once called
Isabella the Fair, the woman who had conspired with
her lover to kill her own husband—Edward's father!—
was truly welcome at Windsor Castle. Shocked, she
listened to the whispered comments of the ladies
around her. They seemed more amused and excited by
Isabella's arrival than surprised or displeased.

"The king's mother comes *here*?" She whispered the
question to the queen as the others tired of the joke
and turned back to the windows.

Philippa's smile was faint but sweet. "Often. Edward is very fond of his mother, now that she is no
longer interested in governing England."

"And you, ma'am?"

"She is a gracious guest and a very intelligent
woman," Philippa said, and winked. "I like her well
enough—more, I suspect, than she likes me. She was
born to royalty, and I am only of noble blood. I believe
she feels she should still be given the respect and adulation due the queen, instead of me."

"What idiocy," Brielle said, and laughed scornfully.
"She is lucky she was allowed to live."

Philippa shook her head in warning. "She has a
good deal of influence with Edward, *mon enfant*. Do
not offend her." Reaching out, she took Brielle's hand
in hers. "Your husband rides guard for her, you know,

he and his Comyn cousin. Edward makes sure of her safety by sending the men he can trust."

"Oh. I—thank you for telling me." Brielle settled back again into her chair, her heart suddenly beating hard enough to flutter the sheer silk she wore. So Adam was once more nearing the gates of Windsor Castle. She felt excitement and, yes, fear, as if a tide suddenly rose from the quiet pool of the last two weeks and swept her with it into an uncertain future. She sat still, collecting her thoughts and pushing the fear away, and then rose from her chair and excused herself to Philippa.

"A simple gown would be best," Philippa said in an undertone. "The primrose silk, perhaps, and the gold velvet tunic." She smiled. "No jewels this time."

Brielle blushed. Philippa had guessed she meant to intercept Adam, though she had only this moment decided. She touched the queen's hand lightly, but with affection. "You are a seer, ma'am."

Philippa smiled. "Isabella will insist on stopping at the round tower first. She is always curious to find out who has been invited and who is here."

Brielle drew in her breath. "Thank you, daughter of Merlin. I will be there to meet them."

7

By custom, the arms and armor of nobles and knights who would enter the Martinmas Tourney were brought into the great hall of the round tower as soon as the parties arrived and were laid out in proud display, even before the visitors presented themselves at court. Prizes won in other tournaments and costly gifts from grateful kings and enamored ladies also were put on show, arranged on tables set up for the purpose.

By now, the tables glittered with polished and lavishly decorated steel, the centerpiece being the priceless jeweled helmet belonging to King Edward, a gift from Philippa's father, William the Good, Earl of Hainault. Swords and daggers captured from the Saracens in the Crusades, damascened with inlaid silver and gold, set with jewels in their handles, lay in nearly every display, and in some the new body armor of articulated plates of steel stood upright, like a headless torso. Newest of all was the armor for the warhorses—thin plate steel fashioned into a chamfron for the horse's head, a crinet to protect the thick neck, and the peytral shield for the chest.

Hurriedly entering the hall from the rear, Brielle slowed her steps and sighed with relief. The hall was empty except for the yeoman guarding the displays; she was in time. She glanced back at Leone, who had accompanied her.

"Are you sure my appearance will do?"

Leone smiled. "You are more beautiful than ever, my lady."

"Good, for I need to be," Brielle said, sighing.

"Adam is used to beauty much greater than mine. Come, then. Let us seem to be wandering through, examining the treasures. Look—see how delicately the gold has been damascened into this dagger."

"How will the dowager queen know just from these displays who is attending the tourney?"

"From the shields that hang over them," Brielle said, pointing. "See? That with the three chevrons sable belongs to Sir Walter Manny, who came to England in Philippa's train and is a great friend, she told me, of the king. And that, with the silver and azure blue, is the Lancaster shield, and that ebony one with the silver lion rampant is that of the Black Prince, Edward's son. Many of them I do not know, but surely Isabella will—" She stopped as Leone whispered hurriedly.

"My lady, they have come in."

Brielle turned. Adam had entered the hall from the long, covered flight of steps that led up from the north courtyard, and Isabella was beside him, her hand clasping his arm. Brielle and Leone were a good thirty feet from that entrance, but Brielle saw Adam's eyes change from boredom to surprise and then a sudden warmth as he saw her there. Her heart leaped. Perhaps he had missed her, too. He looked down at Isabella, who was only an inch or so taller than Brielle, and said something in a low tone, something that made Isabella turn quickly and look at Brielle. Then they came toward her.

Waiting, Brielle lowered her gaze slightly, though not missing a detail in the face or form or fashion of the former queen. In her age, Isabella was no beauty, for she was heavy in belly and hips, her face plump and yet pinched of feature. But her clothes, her jewels, her air of assurance announced her royal blood. Her velvet coat was lined with Russian sable, her gown was heavy China silk. She had pushed back the hood of the coat from her graying but still luxuriant hair, and the chaplet of gold she wore on her head was set with sapphires, diamonds, rubies, and pearls. Grand, Brielle thought, a fortune in jewels and fur, yet 'twas her air of supreme rank that spoke strongest. She glanced again at Adam's bearded face. The warmth was still there, but guarded.

Adam came to a stop, turned, and bowed to Isabella. "I ask permission, Queen Isabella, to present my wife, Brielle Le Fontin of Picardy, daughter of Comte Henri Le Fontin, who died early in this year of the plague."

Brielle swooped down in a deep curtsey, spreading the full skirt of the primrose gown, bowing her head. Isabella stepped forward and extended a hand, bringing Brielle up to stand with her. She was smiling.

"A great pleasure, Lady Brielle," she said. "I must congratulate you both. You have done well. You have found a handsome, virile husband, and you, Adam, a beautiful wife. Also, Adam, I can tell you myself the Le Fontin vineyards will double your fortune. They are among the finest in France."

"Indeed I am fortunate," Adam said smoothly, "though my wife might think herself poorly served."

Brielle took the opportunity at once. She laid a hand on Adam's arm and looked up at him. "Indeed not, sire. Queen Isabella has the right of it. I am happy to welcome you back. I have been lonely without you."

Isabella gave a delighted little crow of laughter. "There, Adam! You've not lost a pennysworth of your charm for the ladies. I doubt you ever will. Stay, talk a bit with your lovely bride, while I look over the shields of the tourney contenders." She looked around at Leone, who had drifted away but kept her eyes on the others. "Come here, maid, and lend me your young arm while I stroll this drafty hall. My legs aren't as strong as once they were."

Leone hurried to obey, and Brielle turned to Adam.

"Will you tilt with the others? I fear for you, now that I've seen the weapons. In France, a tournament is like a game—but here—"

"'Tis still a game, my lady. Rougher here, perhaps, than in France." The warmth left his eyes, displaced by sudden suspicion. "Is this a game of yours, Brielle? Are you playing it with unwarranted compliments and a pretty concern for my safety in the lists?"

Inexplicable tears sprang to her eyes. She turned away, trying to control herself. "No," she said in a low tone, "'tis no game. I want a change for us."

"What kind of a change?"

She glanced around at him and saw by the way he looked that he already knew; he was standing there like a stallion near a mare in heat, neck arched, every muscle taut, waiting for her to surrender. She knew at once that he wanted the mating, but he intended to make her ask for it.

"I—" she began, and swallowed. She felt a searing heat all over her body, as if she were naked and Adam the burning sun. She glanced around, afraid someone would hear, but Leone had taken the dowager queen clear to the other end of the great hall, where they stood admiring a complete suit of armor. Brielle looked back at Adam and forced out words. "I am your wife," she said stiffly, "and I have decided I must be dutiful. I . . . am willing for you to come to my bed."

Adam let out his held breath. "So you no longer scorn the great, lumbering ox of an Englishman with the manners of a goat?"

She stared at him. "Did I call you that?"

"Indeed. Not ten minutes after we met."

Brielle sighed. "I was extremely angry that day, and —and very unwise. I am sorry for my rudeness."

"I am not. Your rudeness was honest. I am not sure you are being honest now. I suspect you are trying to tame me and bring me to heel."

Fury flashed through her, all the hotter because she knew there was indeed something of that intent in her desire to have him. Struggling with this new emotion, she found her pride. She managed to speak softly instead of shouting, but she still said what she wanted to say.

"You are begging the question, sire. If the thought of mating with me repels you, you have only to say so. Certainly I will not insist."

He was silent a moment, staring down at her bent head, and then spoke. "The thought does not repel me. You are a very desirable woman."

Her head came up, the amber eyes suddenly clearing, fixed on him. "Then you *will* come to my bed?"

He raised a hand to her cheek, stroked the satiny skin with the backs of his fingers, then curled the hand around the nape of her neck and held her still, bending to kiss her. She lifted her lips to him willingly, then gasped as the hot mouth within the soft beard opened and covered her lips, forcing them open with a thrust of his tongue. The heat, the musky male taste, the feel of the beard on her skin dizzied her, struck down inside her, roused a feeling she had experienced before only in erotic dreams. She clutched his arms as he drew back, and looked up at him, shaken and mute.

"No," Adam said softly, "I'll not come to your bed. But I will give you permission to come to mine."

"What?" She stared, disbelieving at first, not able to accept what he said, stiffening in fury as it slowly sank in. "To *your* bed? You want me to come begging for you?" She shoved herself away from him, snatching her hands from his arms. Her voice rose into a clear soprano shriek of rage. "Why—why *damn* you for a conceited fool! I'll stay virgin till my dying day before I humble myself like that! Oh!" Gritting her teeth, she aimed a blow at his bearded cheek, her hand caught in midair by steel fingers around her wrist. In futile anger she kicked out at his heavy boots. "Let me go!"

"So you can hit me?" His voice was extraordinarily calm and a little amused. "That would be foolish, would it not?"

She stared up at him, and tears of rage trickled down her red cheeks. "You truly are conceited," she said shakily. "I hate you! But you can let me go without such craven fear. I won't soil my hands by hitting such as you."

He let her go immediately and bowed, his eyes glistening with amusement. Behind her, Isabella spoke.

"Lovers' quarrels," she said, and sighed. "I remember my own." Her plump face broke into a smile as Brielle whirled and looked at her in agonized embarrassment. "Heavens," Isabella added, "don't be ashamed of your anger! 'Tis a good thing in a woman to have a hot temper. It gives a man hope that strong passion hides just behind it."

Later, Honoria listened in shocked silence as Brielle described the meeting in the hall of the round tower. When she had told all, Honoria sat down and wiped her face with a damp cloth, her fingers trembling.

"How did you answer the old queen?"

Brielle shook her head. "I don't know. I can't remember." She looked at Leone. "What did I say?"

"You curtseyed, and then you said 'Please pardon me if you can. My husband has enraged me with his insults.' Then you left. I had to run to get our cloaks and catch up to you. However, Queen Isabella did not look angry. More . . . interested, I would say."

"And Sir Adam, Leone?" Honoria broke in. "Was he terribly angry?"

"That does not matter!" Brielle said hotly. "He is not to be mentioned."

"Our sire," Leone said loftily, "was very calm."

Brielle groaned and sank down into a chair, covering her face with both hands. "He was," she mumbled. "He was calm, and I was a fool." She looked up again. "Didn't I say on that first evening we were married that I might well end my days as a married virgin? I spoke true."

"Perhaps." Honoria looked worried. "Still, if he wishes an heir—"

Brielle's head shot up, her face glowering. "I do not wish to be only a receptacle for his seed!"

Honoria sighed. "Please, do not take Queen Isabella's approval of hot-tempered women as encouragement. Surely you know she's not the best of advisers. Try to conquer your anger."

"I must," Brielle said, her defense suddenly collapsing, "I know I must. I *will*. I can learn to hold my tongue and be civil . . . I think."

Honoria rose and went to find a hairbrush and cool cloths for Brielle's eyes. Leone chose a more elaborate gown than the primrose silk and began hunting out appropriate jewels to wear with it. Both women maintained a discreet silence. The dinner tonight opened the Martinmas fete, and they were aware that Queen Philippa was anxious to have her young Picard cousin looking her best to meet the noble families who would be attending. And, Honoria whispered to Leone, the queen would want her on her best behavior.

"Then 'twould be best," Leone muttered, "to keep our lovers separated as long as possible." She glanced warily across the big room and saw that Brielle was staring into the fire, her jaw set, her thoughts wrinkling her brow. Leone sighed.

"At this moment, they are like flint to steel. 'Twould take but a glance to start a raging fire."

That evening four of the kitchens near to the castle were pressed into service, each preparing food for a

hundred people. Both the private dining room off the
solar and the huge hall of the castle itself were
crowded with royalty and nobles, with squires and
yeomen clustered about the kitchens outside to grab a
portion and take it to a sheltered spot to eat. Tables
were set up among the displays in the tower, and there
was a constant coming and going as early diners gave
way to others. The castle's generous amounts of venison, pork, and fowl, with barrels of oysters and crates
of fresh fish, were dwarfed by the wagonloads of meat
and the first of the season's Gascon wines brought by
their guests.

Always at Martinmas the first of the autumn-killed
beef was eaten, the new wines were drunk in toasts to
Saint Martin, who, it was said, miraculously fermented the wines of Gascony. It was a feast day
brought to England by the Normans some three hundred years ago, and one of the favorite fetes, for its
gaiety warmed the dull month of November. Spirits
were high and growing higher in the royal solar when
Brielle came in and slipped through the noisy crowd to
Philippa's side.

Philippa regarded her approvingly. "Your color is
up," she said, "and charming with that rose velvet.
That is a fine necklace of pearls."

"Thank you, ma'am. 'Tis due to you." Calmer now,
Brielle knew she looked her best. The rose velvet fitted
her closely from shoulder to halfway down her slim,
rounded hips, where a jeweled belt topped the graceful
swirls of skirt below. She glowed, from the rose color
and her own emotions. "The pearls belonged to my
mother," she added, somewhat ruefully. "Honoria insisted I wear them—and told me to touch them as a
talisman when I was tempted to bad temper."

Philippa waved a hand, as if to say the matter was of
little moment. "Isabella has told me of your—shall we

say disagreement?—with Adam. 'Tis a pity you two haven't found your contentment with each other yet."

"I fear we never will," Brielle answered. "'Tis certain I do not suit him well. But 'tis a poor subject for talk on such a festive night, is it not? So much gaiety and laughter."

Glancing around, she smiled and pretended an enjoyment she did not feel. Colorfully dressed players, their lutes hung with fluttering ribbons, strolled the edges of the tight-packed groups and sang to those who requested a song. Always a sad love song, always about a broken heart, Brielle thought, and supposed there must be many more unhappy lovers than she had ever guessed. A player was singing now of tragic and unreturned love to Alice Montagu and her companion, a darkly handsome and brooding man whose face was nearly as pale as Alice's and whose muscular body was set off by the most striking costume Brielle had seen. His short tunic, which barely reached the upper curve of his buttocks, was particolored wool, the right half of it red and the left black. His tight chausses, form-fitting from narrow waist to ankles, reversed the colors. His shoes of black leather were pointed, the narrow points continuing to such a length that they must be arched back and tied just below his knees in decorative bows. Added to that was a velvet shoulder cape in black, dagged around the edge, and arm bands decorated with dagged streamers. Brielle turned to Philippa and smiled.

"Yon dark-visaged knight takes fashion as law. He has counterchanged himself in red and black. I believe him more gaily appareled than the minstrels."

Philippa looked past her and frowned. "A spawn of the Devil, that one. His name is Marc de Rohan, and his ferocity in battle makes him worth his salt to Edward. However, I have heard he cannot be trusted by women. That could be something for you to remember."

"I will remember, yet the man does not look dangerous to me. He is striking, but I am not affected by the kind of charm that is put on with fashionable clothes."

"Shh," Philippa cautioned. "He is coming to us. I will introduce you, for I must, but you needn't stay if he annoys you."

Turning, Brielle caught de Rohan's gaze sweeping over her, studying her with intense interest. Then he was there, taking her hand as Philippa said her name, then kissing her fingers. "Adam Dunbarton is finally captured?" he asked, his dark gaze sliding over her again, dipping into her neckline. His half-mocking smile revealed excellent teeth. "'Tis hard to credit a tale that has Dunbarton wed. I thought him dead set against choosing one of his admiring ladies and losing all the rest. Yet . . . I do see the temptation."

Brielle withdrew her hand from his, managing a smile even though she thought him bitter and crude in his thoughts.

"The queen has told me of your prowess on the battlefield, Sir Marc. Do you plan to enter the tourney?"

"Indeed." His dark eyes held cynical amusement. "May I wear your favor, fair lady? A kerchief, perhaps —a ribbon?"

"Enough of that, de Rohan," Philippa said sharply. "No honorable knight would ask a bride to flout her husband by favoring another man." She turned to Brielle. "Sir Adam has come in, *mon enfant*. Join him."

Brielle looked toward the door and caught sight of Adam, towering over most of the others and staring at her. He too dressed festively tonight. Over gray knit chausses he wore a red velvet tunic banded and embroidered with silver, a jeweled sword belt, and a scabbard of chased silver that held his sword. His golden hair was topped by a cap of red wool, bearing a jeweled pin in the shape of a hunting falcon. He was a man any woman would want to be with, she thought, but she'd planned to wait until he came to her. Still, the order had been given. She bent her head in submission to the queen and left, clutching her skirts about her to keep them from being trodden in the constantly moving mass of guests. She arrived at Adam's side a good bit flushed and disheveled.

"Good evening, my lord."

"Good evening." He looked at her reddened cheeks and twisted skirts in mild disapproval. "I would have made my way to you, my lady, had you been willing to wait."

Willing to wait? Did he think she desired his company so much she had pushed through this troublesome crowd just to be at his side?

"I was very willing to wait," she said coldly, "as long as you wished, or longer. I was ordered to come to you. The queen must have believed you'd be better company than Sir Marc de Rohan. If so, she was wrong."

"De Rohan? He's here?"

"He is." She noted his grim look and prodded again. "He asked to wear my favor in the tournament."

Adam's beard had been trimmed close for the tilting and swordplay tomorrow, and the quick, hard movement of a muscle clenching along his jaw was plain to see.

"You refused, I trust?"

She laughed lightly, knowing the barb had found home. "I hadn't the chance. The queen refused for me, gave de Rohan a lecture, and sent me to you. As punishment, I suppose, though I couldn't say if the punishment was meant for me or for you."

Adam gave her a furious glance. His mouth opened to reply, snapping shut as Kiernan Comyn appeared beside them, wearing an embroidered gray satin tunic with a linked silver hip belt and a velvet cap, gaily cocked to one side on his wavy black hair. He was smiling, his green eyes soft, lingering on Brielle's smiling face.

"My liege lady," he said, accenting his soft Irish brogue, and took her offered hand. "Your beauty grows each time I see you, though 'twould seem impossible to improve on such perfection."

Brielle laughed again, but warmly this time. "You flatterer." She turned between them, taking an arm on either side. She was bound she would show Adam she had forgotten the quarrel that afternoon, as if it were of no importance to her. She wanted him to see the admiration other men gave her, wanted him to know there would be other men eager to come to her bed. Most of all, she wanted him to think she would gladly welcome them if they did, though she had no intention at all of letting them in. She was ready to encourage any and all the knights to flirt with her or admire her—but only as long as it took place within Adam's sight and hearing.

"Come," she said, "we may as well make the most of this celebration. Let us see if we can find places at table and try the beef and the Gascon wine. I may be small, but my hungers—all of them—are as strong as yours."

In the dining room they had to shout to be heard above the loud talk and laughter. King Edward presided, gloriously appareled in his favorite sky blue velvet, the tunic banded and embroidered in gold, worn over a white silk shirt. Around his broad shoulders was thrown a short cloak of snowy ermine, picked out with the tiny black tails. A wide filet of gold, set with diamonds and pearls, held his silver-streaked golden hair. He was flanked by Philippa and Isabella, both gowned in brocaded silk, wearing their best jewels, and seated in chairs as regal as his. Still, when Isabella addressed him, she was careful to sound charmingly deferential. Edward had long since finished the huge joint of beef on a platter before him, and now, face flushed red with wine, lounged back with one hand clasped fondly around his mother's forearm. He hailed Adam with a roar and lifted his full glass to Brielle.

"Come, my friends! Sit near me." His arrogant stare swept the laggard guests on either side, and they scrambled away to make room for the three he welcomed. Seated, Brielle found herself between Adam and Kiernan, who leaned to whisper in her ear.

"A warning, my lady—when Edward is in his cups, stay near your husband. Especially once his mother has retired. Our king grows amorous and insistent when in drink."

"'Tis a common enough fault in older men," Brielle said carelessly. In the din it was possible to talk without worry that anyone else could hear. "Even my father had friends I had to avoid at times."

Kiernan's green eyes gleamed. "No doubt. But none so hard to discourage as our king, I vow. Edward is known to take what he wants. He is used to having his own way, not caring in what manner 'tis managed."

Brielle's chin went up as she remembered the admiration that had been so plain in the king's eyes. Perhaps Kiernan knew of what he spoke. "He may well be, Sir Kiernan. But I am Philippa's cousin. Surely, not even a king would presume . . ." Her voice trailed away as a servant set a slab of roast beef before her, and a goblet of wine. Waiting for the servant to leave, she saw the pale face of Alice Montagu staring at her from across the wide table. The look on Alice's face was displeased and speculative, as if she suspected Brielle of some treachery toward her.

"'Tis nothing," Adam said from her other side, though he had barely glanced at either her or Alice

Montagu. His deep voice was soft but distinct to her ear. "You needn't let the woman bother you. She will forget you at once when she discovers you don't aspire to Edward's favor." He picked up her goblet, handing it to her. "Drink. Eat. Don't sit there with those golden eyes giving every thought away."

So he believed he could read her thoughts in her eyes? He'd come close, at that, but surely 'twas only by chance. She took the goblet and drank deeply, forgetting that new wine was always strong and harsh. For a moment she couldn't speak, and by the time she'd swallowed twice and regained her breath, Adam had turned to listen to something King Edward was saying. Miffed, Brielle took up her knife and began on the slab of beef.

An hour later the minstrels and troubadours gathered in the great hall below, where the center of the huge room had been cleared of tables, and while they wandered gracefully amongst the guests, they played and sang the old folk songs for dancing. The music floated upstairs, buoyed by laughter and shouts as the guests tossed aside what little restraint remained after the strong wine, and leaped to join in.

"Ha!" Edward struggled to his royal feet, no steadier than any other who'd been drinking the new wine, glass after glass, since the dinner began. Seeing him standing there, the guests began rising and leaving the table. Isabella, beautifully gowned but looking weary, rose from her chair and beckoned a maid who stood quietly behind her.

"I'll take my leave now," she said to Edward. "For after the long trip from Norfolk, I need my sleep. Good night, my son."

Edward bowed to her, nearly toppling over, and laughed at himself. "Tomorrow, my mother, we shall talk together. But tonight is for food and drink and dancing and love. Good night, and may your dreams be sweet." He turned again to the others, his red face gleaming.

"Listen, my friends! Can you hear the music? They've started without us, by God! Lead the way, Adam, I'd dance with your wife."

Adam laughed. "And I'd dance with yours. Come with us, my queen."

Philippa, though in high spirits, had drunk little of the potent wine. She stayed her husband with a hand on his wrist. "Hold back," she advised. "We'll make our entrance behind this awkward and stumbling crowd. I'd hate to be caught on those steep stairs with people falling behind us."

Edward wavered, sat down suddenly, and belched. "Very wise, Philippa. Let the others clear out of our way."

Watching, Brielle wondered at the drunken king, and at Philippa's care for him, for that was what it was. The concern in Philippa's dark eyes was apparent; her hand on the king's wrist smoothed the powerful muscles of his forearm, much as a man strokes the neck of an excited alaunt to quiet it.

Glancing around, Brielle realized the others were leaving as rapidly as they could in the crush. Perhaps she and Adam should also leave. She moved her chair back and looked at Adam questioningly.

"Stay," Philippa said quietly, and smiled at her. "We'll manage well together."

Which thought, Brielle discovered, was for the benefit of the king. As if by one mind, Philippa and Adam safely guided Edward down the steep stairs. Adam went first, with Brielle on his arm, and Edward behind him by one step, held steady by Philippa. Twice the king staggered, twice he laughed foolishly and caught himself with a hand on Adam's shoulder, regaining his balance. Then they were all safe at the bottom of the steps and suddenly separated by whirling dancers.

Brielle looked through the flashing bare arms and grinning faces between them and saw Philippa's smile and upraised hand. The noise drowned out her voice, but Brielle could see her lips move.

"Dance," Philippa mouthed. "Enjoy yourself! The evening is yours." Then she turned Edward toward the high table and his pillowed chair. But at sight of the king, the musicians began to play furiously on their wealth of instruments, the English lutes and Welsh crwths, the trumpets and the kettledrums, until the beat of rollicking music filled the enormous hall and echoed from the vaulted ceiling.

Then Edward's handsome head came flinging up, like a warhorse scenting battle, and his laughter rang out. He pulled away from Philippa's firm grasp and whirled, pointing his toes, stepping here, stepping there, his arms spread, dancing gracefully in spite of his size, in spite of his drunkenness.

"Hey, hey," he sang out, "the white swan! By God's soul, I am thy man! Hey, hey . . ." He whirled again, his eyes half closed, alone in the music. His ermine cloak was floating like a cloud, his hair flying, a beatific smile on his red face, his slippered feet never faltering.

Brielle stared at the king in amazement. He swung back to Philippa and grasped her arm, dancing with her now, though more sedately. Then Brielle turned and looked up at Adam. The music, the leaping dancers, the new excitement made her heart beat fast, but she pretended a superior air.

"'Tis very like a dance our château workers liked," she said. "A sword dance, I believe, though they had no swords. They laid their pruning knives in a circle instead and danced wildly around them."

Adam laughed and flung an arm around her shoulders, taking her opposite hand in his, so that they faced the same way, yet were close together. "Put your

right arm at my waist, my lady. Pruning knives or no,
we'll join them.'' He swung her into the line of panting
couples, and they danced, turning first to one side and
then to the other, bowing and kicking and turning
again as the music rose and sang faster and faster . . .
and then he had whirled her out again and she was
free, dancing across an open space and into the arms
of a tall and graceful man, who grabbed her and
laughed aloud at her tiny size.

"You'll not wear me out, I vow. You're light as a
feather.'' He picked her up and whirled her around,
set her on her feet again, and off they went, bowing
and kicking. She tossed back her flying hair and
laughed. Everyone red-faced with mirth; everyone be-
having like children. Wonderful! For nobles to have as
much careless enjoyment as villagers did was unheard
of in her country. To be a noble in France was never to
drop your air of bored superiority.

"My Lady Brielle! How fortunate for me to find you
dancing.''

Swung out and into another man's arms, she looked
up into the dark face of Marc de Rohan. For a moment
her smile wavered, a quick feeling of revulsion came
and went, then she mustered a pleasant look, hoping
Adam had seen the handsome de Rohan choose her as
a partner. There was something about the man she
couldn't like, but perhaps he would do to make Adam
jealous. Turning and bowing, kicking, and turning
again, she laughed up at Marc's sultry gaze and then
found herself pulled from his grip by a long arm in red
velvet.

"Until you know the men who fight for Edward,''
Adam said, leading her away without a word to her
partner, "you'll dance away no more. De Rohan cannot be trusted with a woman. Come, there are others
you should meet.''

Glancing back, Brielle saw that Marc de Rohan

looked not at her but at Adam. Stiff with anger at
Adam's rudeness, he stood fingering the dagger he
wore at his waist. She tightened her fingers on Adam's
arm.

"You've made an enemy, my lord."

Blue eyes looked down at her coldly. "Good. That
one will ever make a better enemy than friend."

Silent, she went with him without protest to the high
table set before a fireplace. Nearly all who sat there
were deep in their cups, two or three of them sprawled
on the table fast asleep. King Edward sat at the head of
the table with Philippa on his right and on his left now
the pale-faced Alice Montagu, who looked, Brielle
thought, much more smugly happy than before. Beside
her, silent and grim, sat her husband, Edward
Montagu of Bungay Castle. A constant flow of men and
well-dressed women passed the table, stopped to greet
the king and queen, and passed on, going back to the
dancing.

Philippa made room for Brielle beside her and motioned a servant to bring wine. Accepting the goblet,
Brielle set it down untouched, watching as Adam
found a seat at the opposite end of the table. Others
rose to dance, among them the king, his blue eyes
glazed, his face as red as fire. He staggered a little,
reaching for the white hand of the Lady Alice, who
rose quickly and joined him. There was a lull in the
noise as they left the table, and in it a half whisper
from a tipsy woman nearby.

"So the white swan tries her bedraggled wings
again."

Immediately loud talk and laughter began again
around them, as if to drown out what was said. Brielle
glanced at Philippa. Calm and serene, Philippa smiled.

"Your husband did not seem pleased by your choice
of partners, dear Brielle."

Brielle grimaced. "My lord shares your opinion of

Marc de Rohan. He too has told me the man cannot be trusted with a woman. But what is that, if the woman herself can be trusted?"

Philippa reached to smooth Brielle's thick and tangled hair with a motherly hand.

"The Lady Rosamunde, de Rohan's wife, could answer that if loyalty—or more likely, fear—had not closed her lips. She is badly crippled, her bones so broken she cannot walk, from what Marc has said was a fall from a horse. No one believes that—my own physician, whom I sent to tend her, says her injuries could have come from nothing less than a terrible beating."

Brielle drew in a long breath. "I see. Neither you nor Adam spoke carelessly, then. Yet you say he is valuable to the king?"

Philippa shrugged. "In battle, yes. As a mad dog might be useful, Edward says, if a mad dog knew enemy from friend. De Rohan delights in killing and is utterly fearless."

"I see." Watching the dancers, Brielle studied de Rohan. He seemed to prefer small women, passing by some real beauties with tall, curved bodies and gloriously blond or red-gold hair, to pick out petite women with long, dark hair. He looked over at the high table once and, catching her gaze on him, gave her a brilliant smile. She turned away as if she hadn't noticed, and saw that Adam had noted the byplay. His face again had the hard, angry look she remembered from the days before they came here to Windsor. Hurriedly, she spoke to Philippa again, before Adam could speak to her.

"Is the Lady Rosamunde here, or is she bedfast?"

"Neither. Rosamunde is wealthy in her own right and now lives alone with her servants in London. They carry her about in a chair, and she can sit comfortably to meals. But the bones of her face were smashed into a grotesque shape, and she will not sit in company."

Chilled, Brielle welcomed the flare of anger that cut through the cold horror she felt. "He should be punished!"

"And would be," Philippa agreed, "if anyone dared put the blame on him. Rosamunde fears him far too much to risk her remaining life by saying a word. She is grateful to be free of his company and able to live in peace."

"Then she is far more forgiving than I," Brielle said, "I would ask the king to see him either dead or in prison." She glanced around and saw that Edward had returned from dancing with the Lady Alice, and just in time. Leaning back in his large, pillowed chair, the king snored, his noble head cocked sidewise and his mouth gaping open in the silver and gold beard. Even as she watched, Alice Montagu gave the snoring king an angry glance and left, urging her husband up to accompany her.

"I believe the king sleeps," Brielle said quietly, and Queen Philippa turned to look.

"Indeed, 'tis time we made our way upstairs." She nodded to Adam, who rose immediately and came to her side, looking at her questioningly. Philippa smiled. "Wake him, then, Sir Adam. Someday he may learn that new wine must be treated with respect."

Adam's broad figure hid Edward from view as he woke him, shielded his dazed face from the others in the hall as they went arm in arm up the stairs, Philippa and Brielle trailing after them. Not that the guests were sober enough to think shame of their king, but Philippa and Adam made sure they had little opportunity to study him.

In the solar everything was again in place, the bed ready for the royal couple, only a few candles lit.

"Off with you, my dears," Philippa said as they entered, and took Edward's arm. "I'll see him to bed.

There will be music for another hour or so, if you care
to dance again."

"Not I, ma'am," Brielle said, and affected a yawn.
"'Tis enough for an evening." Her thoughts had leaped
forward, seeing herself led to the door of her room by
Adam. Honoria must long be in bed, and the last she
had seen of Leone, the girl was dancing with a good-
looking bowman at the back of the hall. Brielle tucked
her hand in Adam's arm and looked up at him. "Do
you agree, sire?"

"I do, my lady. Till the morrow, my queen." He
bowed and left, sweeping Brielle with him, closing the
door.

"I'll see you to your room," Adam said, taking her
along the gallery with a decisive air. "And I'll see that
your maid comes to attend you. Now that you've managed to attract the Baron de Rohan, you cannot sleep
alone, not even in Windsor Castle."

"What? Why, of course I can! There is a stout bolt on
my door." They were almost there, and she thought
fast. "I will show you." Opening the door, she led him
inside and closed it. There was only a guttering candle
here and there, the gleam of dying coals in the fireplace as light in the darkness. But enough that he
could see the evidence she showed him. "See? Once
this bolt is shot, it would take a battle-ax to break in."

The red light of the coals glinted on his arch of nose,
on his cheekbones above the close-clipped beard. It
seemed to her that he smiled, and she moved closer.
"Besides," she said in a softer tone, "I need not sleep
alone, my lord. You are my husband and welcome in
my bed."

He reached for her, and she went into his arms with
a sigh of relief, lifting her face to his. The warmth and
hard strength of his body made her hot with a strange
wanting; when he lowered his face to kiss her and she
felt the leap of passion in his loins, she could have

shouted in joyous triumph. Then, when his mouth closed over hers and she tasted his erotic muskiness, she felt a glorious rush of desire. Her arms tightened around his neck, her tongue played with his. When his hands slipped down and pulled her tight to his body, her hips tilted to him of their own volition.

Adam's breath gushed out as he straightened and stepped away. He would have given anything he owned to take her to bed at this moment, for the heat of her innocent desire promised all a man could ask for. But he had seen the triumph in her eyes, and he could not let her best him. For a moment he was silent while he steadied his voice.

"You are very tempting, my lady. Would you like to follow me to my room?"

Brielle's slim jaw firmed. So he meant to win this duel—but so did she. "We are here, my lord. I see no reason for either of us to go elsewhere."

Adam's teeth gleamed in a sardonic smile. "Then we disagree. I must wish you a good night and take my leave."

Somehow she managed to clench her teeth against her rising fury, to conquer and control it. She would *not* allow him to see she was furious and—well, badly disappointed. Her desire for him had grown until she ached to give in, to feel his arms around her, his body close to hers. Still, her pride made her turn away.

"As you will, sire. But . . . you are—are more than welcome to return."

He heard the quiver in her voice, and he knew she meant it. For a long moment he hesitated, and then he was gone, closing the door softly behind him. Brielle gasped and hurried to the door to open it, to call him back—no! In spite of the still-raucous noise coming from the dancers and the musicians below, she could distinctly hear the sound of his firm tread receding rapidly around the gallery to the north side. She'd be damned if she'd make a spectacle of herself to all those still dancing below. How they would laugh to hear her begging her husband to return to her room! Gritting her teeth, she slammed the bolt home.

8

By the reckoning of the spirit candle beside her bed, Brielle was certain 'twas past midnight when she awoke to the sound of soft knocking. Leone had been in earlier to help her disrobe and had been sent back down to her bowman a half hour ago, so it had to be Adam. He had changed his mind!

Brielle smiled. Quietly, she climbed out of the soft bed and found her robe. She smoothed it down and fastened it at her slim waist with care. It was beautiful, a darkly gleaming Persian blue silk, and she felt beautiful in it. Going to the door, she put her mouth to the narrow crack and whispered.

"Adam?"

A whisper came back. "Yes, my lady."

She laughed softly. "You've come to me at last?"

There was a silence. Then, hoarse and becoming unsteady: "I could not stay away."

Excited, Brielle grasped the heavy bolt and drew it back, flinging the door open. "Oh, Adam, how happy I —" She stopped, staring at Marc de Rohan as he stepped in and shut the door behind him, throwing the bolt. Grinning, his teeth shining in his dark face, he grabbed her arm and jerked her to him. He spoke, and his taunting threat froze her heart.

"Now, pretty bitch, you'll dance with me on yon bed, and no man will want what little I leave."

Brielle screamed, whirling away from him, screamed again at the top of her voice, and was driven to her knees by a heavy blow that shocked her into silence.

"Quiet!" de Rohan growled, grabbing her up. "If you dare cry out again, I'll kill you!" Fastening one of his dark hands in her heavy hair, he grabbed her robe and ripped it open. Brielle gasped and twisted, fastening her teeth in the arm that held her, biting as hard as she could, tasting the salty blood that seeped through the wool. De Rohan staggered, yelped in pain, and knocked her to the floor again with another blow of his fist, then grabbed her, dragging her up with his bleeding arm. She screamed again, terror-stricken, as he grabbed her shift with both hands and tore it apart.

"Fight me, you little whore!" Marc's voice trembled with drunken lust. "Beg me to stop! Beg, or I'll hurt you worse!" He dragged her to the bed, ignoring her screams now, and pushed her naked body down onto the rumpled sheets. Throwing himself atop her, he muffled her noise with his mouth, half choked her with his thrusting tongue, grabbing her small breasts and squeezing them cruelly. He stank of sweat and vomit and strong wine, and even in her fear Brielle realized he was wholly drunk, drunk enough that she might be able to escape him. She gathered her strength and pushed, hope leaping up as feet pounded on the gallery planks outside. She twisted her face away from his and screamed as loud as she could. The heavy door shook as someone slammed into it.

"Let me in!" Adam's voice was easily recognizable at a shout instead of a whisper. Then another tremendous blow, and the sound of splintering wood as the bolt gave way and shattered. Then Adam loomed up over them and Marc was gone, Marc's body slamming against the wall, Adam pinning him there by the pressure of his strong hands around Marc's neck. Marc gurgled and clawed at Adam's wrists impotently, his eyes bulging, his hands falling away as his breath failed him.

Sitting up, Brielle stared at Adam in frozen awe. She

had forgotten how anger seemed to increase his size. Huge, huge like a giant—wearing nothing but his chausses. Huge bare feet, and the naked torso seeming wide as an hundred-year oak, writhing with thick muscles, the massive chest covered with a bloom of golden hair. And oh, *mon Dieu*, his face! His face was a mask of steel and fury, lips drawn back from strong teeth like a wolf, eyes narrowed as he choked the life from Marc de Rohan. . . .

"Adam!" Rushing into the room, Kiernan Comyn threw himself on Adam's arms, pulling hard. "Let him go! Beat him if you will, but for God's sake, don't kill him. Remember where you are! This is Windsor Castle!"

Adam spoke between clenched teeth. "He will die. He has taken my wife."

"No," Brielle said, gasping it out. "He did not." She slid from the bed and pulled her torn robe together. Her voice steadied and became clear. "He hit me and tore my clothes. But he did not take me." She looked up and met the blue flame of Adam's gaze. "It is true. He came to despoil me, but he failed. He is drunk, like most of the men who dined here tonight."

Slowly, Adam released his hold on Marc de Rohan's thick neck. De Rohan slumped to the floor like a dead man, and Kiernan knelt beside him, feeling for a heartbeat. Adam turned away from them and came to stand before Brielle, who now leaned weakly against one of the carved bedposts, one hand holding her clothes together, one cupped over a swelling eye and bruised cheek.

"Do you lie to save him?"

Anger stirred deep in her racing heart. "I never lie!"

"But you tease and flirt. Why did you let him in?"

Color ran up her neck and heated her skin. She thought of how triumphant she had felt, thinking Adam had given in and come to her. How foolish she must have sounded! How foolish she had been. No one must ever know. . . .

"I—he knocked, and then whispered. I thought . . . well, I thought I would be safe. I didn't know who it was."

Adam stared at her. "You opened your door to a stranger who knocked and whispered? Your words either make you a fool, or you believe me one to swallow that tale."

Behind him, Marc stirred and groaned. Kiernan sat back on his heels and looked toward the door. Two of the castle's menservants, alerted by the noise, stood just outside. He motioned them in, and they came, averting their eyes from Brielle.

"Carry the Baron de Rohan to his room," Kiernan told them, "and find his squire. He'll need someone to look after him."

They shuffled off, de Rohan's lax body hanging between them, and Adam turned again to Brielle. He looked at her, she thought, as if he saw a stranger—or an enemy. His eyes were as cold and hard as winter ice.

"You'll finish this night with your companion," he said, and took her arm. "'Twill take tomorrow to mend your door and bolt."

"There are only two beds in that room," Brielle said, trying to disengage her arm, trying not to look at his half-naked body. "I'll not put Leone out of hers."

"Leone has no use for it," Adam said, his tone bitter. "Sensible woman that she is, she's bedded down with her lover."

Morning came, and with it Honoria's fright when she saw Brielle asleep in Leone's bed with a swollen eye and a black and blue bruise covering one cheek. Honoria hovered over her, not wanting to disturb her sleep yet anxious and fearful. The small face was white with fatigue, and the swollen eye and dark bruise seemed unbelievably cruel. Honoria mourned under her breath, wanting to get a cool poultice, afraid to leave. A knock sent her rapidly to the door before it woke Brielle.

"Who is it?"

"Dunbarton. I would speak with my wife."

Honoria, with great presence of mind, opened the door and stepped out, closing it behind her. "My lady still sleeps," she said, looking up at Adam with some fear. As big as he was, to her he appeared both tired and grim, as if he might have been bruised himself, though not outwardly. "She—she doesn't look well. Must I wake her?"

Adam hesitated. "If she sleeps, I'll not wake her," he said after a moment. "But I will see her."

Honoria could do no more, say no more. Strangely, she knew without knowing how that Brielle's injury was not Adam's doing. She opened the door and stood back to let him enter. When he left the door open, she took it as permission to come in, and did so, sidling around to the fireplace and standing there, waiting to see what he would say or do.

Adam stood staring down at Brielle's bruised face silently, his strong profile as still as stone, his hands slowly clenching at his sides. Except for the usual steel and leathern helmet and steel-plated kneeguards, he was dressed for the tourney to take place today. His shirt of light chain mail shone like silver, his leathern chausses clung to him like his own skin. His heavy broadsword hung in a carved leather scabbard, loose and quick to the hand. Honoria thought of the men who might meet him in a real battle and shuddered for them. Then he was moving again, turning from the bed and motioning for her to follow him out onto the gallery. She obeyed quickly, closing the door behind her.

Adam turned to her, looking at her openly, and Honoria was struck by the deep pain in his eyes.

"Do you know what happened, mistress?"

Honoria shook her head numbly. "I only know she is hurt, for that I can see. I have not talked to her."

Adam clenched his jaw. "She was a fool! She opened her bedroom door—mind you, after midnight—to Marc de Rohan, a man who is known to be violent with women. Had she not screamed loud enough to wake the dead, he would have done worse to her than what you have seen."

Honoria gasped. "No! The Lady Brielle would never do that. He must have forced his way in."

"He did not," Adam said grimly. "She told me herself that he knocked softly and whispered to her—and she let him in."

"Then she thought 'twas you," Honoria said at once. He would hear the truth from her, whether Brielle liked it or not. She could not allow Adam to believe Brielle either a fool or an unfaithful wife. "She dreams that some night you will come quietly to her door and ask to come in. That is the reason she sent Leone away and sleeps alone."

Adam's mouth twisted. "Do you think me stupid, mistress? She knows my voice."

"Indeed, sire." Honoria kept her honest eyes on his. "We all do. But a whisper sounds much the same from any man. This de Rohan, whoever he is, will have lied to her."

Adam stood staring at her, wanting to believe. Then he shook his head. "Your loyalty to your lady is great, mistress. But she knew I had no thought of coming to her room. I had made that clear to her only a short while before."

Below them, in the great hall, Charles Eastham came in and looked up at the gallery. "Lots are being chosen," he called, and Adam swung around to listen. "Since you've bargaining to do, you best come now."

Adam nodded and turned back to Honoria. "My wife will likely be too uncomfortable to attend the tourney. But you may tell her I mean to take what vengeance I can on de Rohan. If nothing else, I will make a fool of him."

By the evidence of the broken door and the tales from the menservants, the scandalous news had run fast through the nobles and their wives who had come for the tourney. Philippa heard and hastened to Honoria's room to see Brielle. Brielle was up and dressed, the swollen eye and bruised cheek hidden by a folded veil tucked into coif and gorget. The one beautiful amber eye to be seen was narrowed with determination as she argued with Honoria. As Philippa came in, Brielle turned, gasped, and curtseyed.

"Your Highness is too kind. There was no need for you to come to me. I have just now prepared to come to you and beg your forgiveness for—"

"For Marc de Rohan?" Philippa asked wryly. "'Twas he that caused the trouble, not you, and surely I will not forgive him, nor will your husband. From what I have heard, Adam will make Sir Marc regret his actions in the field today. They meet after the Joust of Peace, in a match of their own."

Brielle flushed. "Once that happens, there won't be a soul at Windsor who hasn't heard of my stupidity."

"There is no one now who hasn't heard the story," Philippa said, and for once her tone was mildly rebuking. "Such talk travels fast. But 'twould be more becoming if your thought was for Adam. Even though the tourney is a'plaisance, de Rohan is a fearless and cruel fighter."

Surprised, Brielle shook her head. "Adam will win, ma'am. I am assured that no one can withstand him."

Philippa laughed, her wide brow clearing. "Then I

am assured you think him a god, as Edward does. In time, the two of you may yet come to a happy union."

Brielle would not gainsay the queen, but her face expressed her doubt clearly. "Perhaps," she said, and left it at that. "I see your manservant carries furs," she added. "You must be on the way to watch the tourney. With these bruises I must stay inside, but I hope you enjoy it."

"I will. And you will, also, for I've given orders to place seats for you and your companion at the gallery windows. You can see it all from there, though you may miss the noise of the crowd and the bows from your knights."

"And I, with my maid, shall sit with them, Philippa," Isabella said from the door. "I have had another two chairs placed there, for I knew you wouldn't mind. The day is raw and windy. Unsuitable, indeed, for a woman my age." She came in, pretending to see nothing unusual, extended a hand to Brielle, and nodded to Honoria. "Come. We will take our seats. Between the events we will talk of France and the golden Mediterranean sands. In this weather, I wish I were strolling there."

Walking around the gallery, behind Isabella by a polite step or two, Brielle watched Philippa go down the stairs and join the noblewomen who waited there for her to lead them on their way to the tournament stands. Much as she appreciated the care and affection Philippa showed in providing a haven for her, Brielle looked after the departing group with longing. She would have loved being outside in the cold air, watching the splendidly caparisoned horses and their gaudy riders and cheering them on. Still, she could imagine the looks when she appeared with half her face veiled because of Marc de Rohan's beating.

"No vain regret," Isabella said, taking one of the center seats and glancing up at her. "Exciting it may be to sit in the stands and cheer, but you'll have a better view from this height."

Brielle gave Queen Isabella a rueful smile. "'Tis my own fault, Your Highness, and it could have been far worse. I will not complain." She sat, and leaning forward to look, she saw that it was true. They would see every move.

"There!" Isabella pointed. "They are parading the prizes. That Arabian filly comes from Edward's finest stock and will make the wife or sweetheart of the winner happy. And see those jeweled daggers on that purple cushion. . . ."

Brielle studied the view as Isabella continued to admire the paraded prizes. From their vantage spot they looked directly down into the centered tournament court, which took up nearly all the quadrangle of the upper ward. Horse-belly high, the colorful stretched cloth that made up the barrier of the Joust of Peace was right below them, and even as they watched the crowds gather and find seats, the younger knights were trying it out. First the challenge, and then the acceptance. Riding proudly into the arena, they took position at each end. Left side to left side, with the barrier of cloth between them, they charged. Locked into their steel armor, peering through the pierced sight-holes of their helms, they could see little more than the head and shoulders of their adversary, but still they thundered toward each other and met with a clash of lance against shield. Each duel continued until one was knocked from his saddle.

Brielle watched the young knights for a few moments; then her gaze wandered to the stands, placed on both sides of the arena, where benches were set up behind a wooden wall draped with swaths of blue cloth and roofed over with red-and-white-striped linen canvas. She could see nothing but the striped top of the stand directly below the windows, but the stand across the way was crowded with laughing, jostling, gaily appareled guests. Servants scurried, bringing extra pillows for the hard benches and hot drinks to warm their bellies. At each end of the arena were the warhorses, held by grooms, and the small tents, each with its identifying banner, where the knights put on their armor. She saw the red banner with its falcon ripple up in a waft of air and was suddenly fearful. She turned to Isabella and spoke hesitantly.

"This Marc de Rohan, Your Highness—do you know aught of him?"

Isabella shrugged plump shoulders. "Only the gossip one hears. A devil, they say, without fear or pity." She smiled at Brielle. "However, I daresay Adam Dunbarton can best him."

Brielle nodded. Faced by the scene below, she was suddenly afraid. "He must. I am told de Rohan shows no mercy."

Unobtrusively, Honoria made the sign of the cross.

A trumpet sounded below.

"Now," Isabella said with a note of anticipation in her mannered voice, "first the presentation, and then the melee begins. Thank *le bon Dieu* they are not as dangerous as they once were. I've seen women faint when their man went down under all those trampling hooves."

"I've never seen it," Brielle admitted, staring down. "But my father said the same." The ill-famed melee, the real beginning of every tournament, was now said to be more like a pageant than a battle, where every man fought for himself. New rules forbade pointed or sharp weapons in the melee; the lances must be blunted, no clubs nor maces were allowed, and every horse must wear a chest guard. Too many men, the king had decreed, and too many fine horses had been lost in the name of pleasure. Still, there were injuries, for excitement ran high and each man vied for the first honors.

Leaning forward, her arms on the wide windowsill, Brielle watched as the knights presented themselves formally and bowed to the king and queen, each man bowing again to the woman whose favor he wore. Every knight was dressed in his finest velvet or wool tunic, girded in shining mail or armor, with tall plumes of white, red, or black feathers tossing on their helmets. For the presentation the warhorses wore silk or velvet body hangings in brilliant colors, banded, tasseled, and embroidered, often with his owner's coat of arms.

Brielle's gaze was drawn irresistibly to the big man with the golden beard who bowed but once and rode on unsmiling, the horse beneath him the same stallion he always rode. There was no scarf nor ribbon tied to his thick arm. She had hoped—but why had she hoped? A man who thought her a faithless flirt would want no ribbon of hers tied about him. She supposed she should be grateful he wore no other woman's favor.

The trumpet blew, and all at once the arena was full of whirling horses, leveled lances, and hoarse shouts. The heavy warhorses needed no more than the blare of trumpet to set them off, rearing and squealing as they pawed the air and came thumping down to rush the nearest horse and rider. Brielle gasped and rose to her feet as the first men went down: four of them, or perhaps more, for the mass of steeds and knights blocked the view. Then another rush by the main body of knights, and Adam caught her eye. He was moving on the edge of the crowd, keeping up as they tried for position, but pulling his horse away when a rush with another knight seemed close.

"My lord will win no prize for this event," she said

dryly, "unless there's a small token for avoiding trouble."

Honoria frowned at the criticism, but Isabella laughed.

"A bloodless melee is child's play for a seasoned knight," she said. "He is showing good manners by taking part, yet giving the young knights a better chance."

"Oh." Subdued, Brielle sat down. She would watch and learn.

Hard tilting followed, and running at the ring, a test of skill with the lance and a suspended target. For the tilting, lances were tipped with a coronel, a blunted metal end that marked the adversary's armor but did not penetrate. In the tilting, which was confined to the barrier of the Joust of Peace, Adam was never unseated by another man's lance, though he was challenged by the others more often than any other. But, Brielle noted, Marc de Rohan also had a perfect score. Smaller but more intense, Marc ran against his adversaries as if he meant to kill. If he was the worse for his night of drunkenness and the choking Adam gave him, he didn't show it.

A manservant came from the great hall below and brought them food and drink. Isabella questioned him.

"Has the king challenged the winners of the tilting?"

"It is said he will choose his challenges tomorrow, Your Highness, if at all."

"I see." As the man left, Isabella turned to Brielle with raised brows. "Edward is feeling his age—or is it his drink? I cannot remember a tourney when he wasn't in it from the opening trumpet call."

"'Twas late when he retired last evening," Brielle said carefully, "and the new wine was harsh and strong enough to sour any belly."

Isabella nodded. "Quite true. Ah well, I needn't worry about my son, for 'tis in the stars that he will

live long and rule until his death. Now look below. The
single matches are beginning."

The single matches began with the young firebrands
at their first tourney. Boys of no less than twelve and
no more than fourteen, mostly dressed in ill-fitting armor and wearing light swords made of dull, silvered
whalebone, rushed each other with blunt lances. Once
one was knocked from his horse and managed to get
up and draw his sword, the other joined him on the
ground, and they whacked away with all their strength
until a judge separated them and declared the winner.

Isabella laughed till she cried at the awkward antics
and crashing falls. "'Tis better than a play with mummers," she said, wiping her eyes. "Yet these boys are
England's champions for the years to come. As your
sons will be, Lady Brielle. Adam Dunbarton will pass
on the excellent traits that make him England's best."

Brielle opened her mouth, and then, seeing Honoria's warning glance, changed her bitter answer to
sweet. "'Tis high praise indeed," she said, using her
best diplomacy, "to be called England's best by Isabella the Fair. My lord will be pleased to hear it."

Settling back in her chair, Brielle waited for the moment to come when Adam took the field against Marc
de Rohan. The fear in her heart grew heavier as the
time passed, and heavier still as she admitted to herself that much of the fault for this grudge fight was
hers. She had been warned of de Rohan by the queen
herself. She shouldn't have smiled at him, nor made
him think himself welcome on the dance floor. But
even worse, her vanity had caused her to let him into
her room. She should have known Adam Dunbarton
would never give in and come begging to her door.

She stared below, noting that the day was growing
long as the young knights and then the more seasoned
men matched their strength and skill in single combat.
Shadows laid across the open courtyard, and the chill

of evening was settling over the crowd. The spectators were restless, leaving their seats to stroll back and forth and talk with others. Bottles of wine were passed, and a keg of ale broached, and laughter rose. Women began to make their way toward the buildings around them, shivering in the cold wind. Then, as a trumpet blew for the final match and two men rode into the arena, the laughter slowly died away.

Riding in from the west, Adam wore only the light chain mail tunic over a wool cotte, and a leathern helmet instead of a casque over his head. His long legs, clad in heavy wool chausses, were unprotected save for leather boots. For weapons, he carried his lance, his shield, and his broadsword.

Marc de Rohan, galloping into the center from the east, pulled up and waited there for Adam's arrival. He carried the same weapons—approved weapons for the tourney—but in contrast to Adam's light armor, Marc wore a steel headpiece that spread like a collar on his shoulders, protecting both head and neck, a suit of heavy mail, and articulated plates of beaten steel that served as kneeguards.

"Ah," Isabella said, her eyes lighting with interest. "A brave entry there by de Rohan, come to try his skill against a knight like Adam. However, some will decry his courage—and possibly his common sense—when they note the excessive amount of his armor. He is dressed for battle, not tourney."

Brielle scarcely heard her. Her throat tight, she gazed down at the scene and watched Adam ride at an easy trot to the center of the field, his pennon fluttering from the top of his upright lance. Facing the box where Edward and Philippa sat, he bowed and lifted the lance high. Beside him, Marc de Rohan also bowed to royalty, then turned and faced Adam.

"He is saying something," Isabella murmured, fascinated by the scene. "How I would love to know if it is an insult or an apology. Oh! Oh!'' She leaned back and laughed. ''From the look on your Adam's face, 'twas no apology. More likely a threat—what a foolish man!''

Brielle groaned, her eyes terror-stricken. ''A wicked man—a spawn of the Devil, Queen Philippa says. May God protect my husband!'' Behind her, she could hear the rapid mumble of earnest prayer from Honoria, who could not bring herself to look.

Below, the two men wheeled their horses and rode to the opposite sides of the arena, turning to face each other again. Couching their lances, fitting their shields on their arms, they awaited the trumpet blast.

To Brielle, the scene was magnified, crystal clear, burning bright. She absorbed every detail. She saw that Adam had loosed his reins, giving his horse freedom to move, but de Rohan held his reins tight, the stallion's neck bowed from the pull on his jaws, his big body moving restlessly, jerking back and forth.

Glancing back at Adam again, she swallowed the bitter taste of fear. He seemed uninterested; he acted as if this were only another Joust of Peace. His face was calm, and his couched lance rested on his thigh, pointing at a distant spot of ground. She twisted her hands together anxiously.

''Our sire is careless of his safety! Not only does he come to this match without the proper armor, he ignores the order to make himself ready, and—''

The rest of her complaint was lost in the blast from the herald's trumpet, and below the two men drove hard toward each other. Mouth open, Brielle saw Adam's horse leap into a thundering gallop with the first trumpet note, saw the lance begin to straighten and point at Marc de Rohan's chest, saw Adam's body thrust forward, his calm face turn to steel. She gasped, turning to look at Marc, who had to force his whirling horse to settle and head toward the center of the field. His lance wavered as he came, his heavily armored

body swaying, his shield coming up as he neared
Adam. Then, just before they met, de Rohan tilted his
lance down and thrust hard against the peytral chest
armor on Adam's horse, a dishonorable ploy meant to
force the horse to rear up and throw his rider.

Lifted from his saddle by the force of Adam's lance
and falling heavily to the ground, Marc de Rohan still
succeeded in his treachery. Glancing off the smooth
steel surface of the peytral, his lance had gone between
the stallion's front legs, tripping him. The horse somer-
saulted, throwing Adam over his head. Struggling up,
the horse limped over to Adam, nosing him as he lay
on his back in the dirt. Dazed, Adam grasped the bridle and pulled himself up, staggering, shaking his head
to clear it. His helmet was gone, flung off in his fall,
and his hair sprang free and wild, more like a lion's
mane than ever before.

Clambering to his feet, impeded by his heavy armor,
de Rohan started toward his fallen adversary, reaching
down and pulling a long dagger out of his boot, a dagger that glinted hard and sharp in the slanting rays of
setting sun. Eager to kill, he forgot to hide his weapon
from the onlookers.

A great roar rose in the chilling air. Watchers in the
gallery had leaped to their feet, pointing at the dagger:
"No! No! For shame! For shame!"

Brielle screamed as de Rohan raised the dagger, her
eyes wild with fear. "He means to kill Adam!"

Honoria took one look and slid to her knees again,
clasping her rosary. Isabella, white-faced, wrung her
hands.

"De Rohan will be put to death if he succeeds in
wounding Adam," she said. "No deadly weapon can
be used in the a'plaisance tourneys—oh, but look!
Adam has seen the danger, and his sword is drawn!"

"And he is fighting! Oh, thank the saints and our
good Lord Jesus—he is fighting and he is winning!"

Leaning far out on the windowsill, Brielle watched eagerly, her fears and guilt forgotten.

Below, Adam stood with his feet apart and wielded his heavy broadsword with ease, swinging it like a toy, clanging away on the armored de Rohan with the flat side of the blade, knocking him down again and again. Finally de Rohan gave up his deadly weapon, flinging it away with a shouted obscenity, and drew his own broadsword, raising it high and rushing at Adam with a roar of rage. Adam flipped it out of his hands with the next stroke. Then, as de Rohan bent to pick it up, Adam sent the fully armored man sprawling with a whack across his buttocks.

There was another roar—this time laughter, and jeering catcalls. De Rohan grabbed up his sword in haste and swung it hard at Adam's unprotected face, missing by inches as Adam leaned out of its arc. Then the sword was gone again, sent flying by Adam's swing, and de Rohan's buttocks caught the next blow. And the next. The stands rocked with laughter. Battered and helpless, the dark knight finally raised both hands, empty, to admit defeat.

Adam stepped back, lowering his sword, and de Rohan stood up. Facing Adam, de Rohan slowly removed his casque and held it under one arm. He was seen to say something to Adam and then turn away, mounting his horse and riding out of the arena.

Brielle let go of the deep windowsill and sat down, letting out her held breath and smiling at Honoria. "'Tis over, my dear friend, and Adam whole and healthy."

Still pale from her fright, Honoria nodded somberly. "That is true, my lady. But he has gained a dishonorable and crafty enemy. That terrible man will never forget that your husband made a laughingstock of him."

9

Brielle's shame over her foolishness was searing; she wanted no curious stares to remind her of it. She took her meals in her room until the swelling and bruises de Rohan had given her faded away. But in the privacy of afternoons, her injuries veiled and her smile in place, she joined Philippa and Isabella, who stayed on for a time as an honored guest, in the solar. They spent their time talking and embroidering in company with the ladies-in-waiting.

Brielle thought constantly of Adam but seldom saw him, and then only at a distance, when he was riding out with Edward and other men to the hunt, or when the men came from chapel and passed the women waiting their turn outside. Then she kept her hood up, covering her hair and shadowing her face, and her eyes down, though she couldn't resist an occasional quick glance at him. Adam, his face grim, seemed never to look her way. She told herself it was better if he didn't, considering how she looked and how her bruises must remind him of that night. Still, it scalded her heart that Adam could believe her faithless and dishonorable.

The talk now was all of London and the festivities that would mark the approaching Christmas season. Philippa took it for granted that Adam and Brielle would stay with the royal family when they removed to London for the holidays.

"I would stay at the white tower," Philippa told her one day when by chance they sat alone, "for 'tis far more cozy and comfortable than Westminster Palace.

But at Christmas our subjects expect us to entertain in Westminster Hall." She smiled at Brielle. "Please don't look so stricken. There is room for us all and more in the palace there, and privacy when we need or want it. Besides, Edward would not miss the great festivals of the season."

Brielle had left off her veiling today, for there was but a small shadow over the eye and no swelling. She felt reprieved, exonerated at last from her own stupidity. She was also resolved never to be so foolish again.

"I could have hazarded the king's delight in festivals," she said, "for I've seen that he loves gaiety. If I looked stricken, 'twas because my time with you grows short. When the Christmas holiday is over, we will be leaving for Northumbria."

Philippa's face fell. Looking at the cloth in her hand, she plied her needle thoughtfully. "Yes, and I hate to think of it. Having you with me has been a bit of home, and I will miss you. But"—she bit off her thread with her strong teeth and took up a skein of blue silk to thread the needle again—"you have a home with me if ever you need it. You and Adam Dunbarton are two of a kind, willful and stubborn and strong in your passions. I believe that either you two will make a union that will last an eternity, or you will fly apart in rage." She smiled, noticing Brielle's guilty look. "I hope," she added, "'twill be the first—for to see such a pair bound in love would be a sight worth remembering. But if not, you must come to me."

Brielle saw genuine love in Queen Philippa's dark eyes. "Thank you, ma'am," she answered, full of gratitude. "I will remember. However"—she paused, surprised by words that rose in her throat and must be said—"I mean to stay with Adam. I made my vows, and I do not break a promise easily."

"Nor I," Philippa said, "as you may have seen. My mother was the same: Though my father strayed occa-

sionally, she never thought of separating from him."
She smiled wryly. "The Le Fontin women are faithful,
n'est-ce pas?"

Later, Brielle kept to herself what Philippa had said,
though she knew Honoria could be trusted not to repeat it. Of course the queen knew about pale Alice
Montagu, the king's "white swan"! No one could miss
the byplay between the two; nor did Alice try to hide
her triumph. What Edward Montagu thought of it was
yet to be seen. He was a good twenty years older than
his wife, and perhaps he didn't care, though the tight
set of his jaw most of the time seemed to promise even-
tual trouble.

Brielle sighed and went back to her sewing. 'Twas
no different for her. She suspected—nay, she knew, for
no man here was celibate—that Adam must have a
woman. Likely more than one, for in the hall below
during the evening hours, the most brazen of the ladies
were forever hanging on the arms of the knights,
pressing against them, laughing and teasing, encouraging any who showed interest in taking them to bed.

Perhaps, Brielle thought with sour amusement,
there should be a tourney for women, so a wife could
challenge her rival and teach her to leave husbands
alone.

Sitting on a stool before the fire, while Honoria
brushed her long, thick hair, Brielle humorously
broached the subject of a Wives' Tournament as the
next entertainment.

At first scandalized, Honoria finally laughed and
continued the tale. "The Wives' Tournament, dear
Brielle, has been going on for centuries. 'Tis played at
every gathering. The weapons of beauty and charm
vary widely, but the battle is never resolved except by
the prize."

"The prize?"

"The man himself. He chooses the one he wants."

"Oh." Wheeling around, Brielle looked up, frowning. "Are you saying the women in the lower hall are more charming and better-looking than I?"

"You well know there is not one who could come near to your beauty. But as to charm—their bright smiles and eager welcome surely are more attractive to a man than your chilly frowns and haughty looks."

Instant fury swept Brielle. "How do you dare to blame *me*? 'Tis Adam who thinks me a wanton and a liar and refuses to come near me. Refuses, in fact, to come to my bed! Aha! I see that surprises you, my friend. 'Tis true, damn him! He has insulted me!"

Honoria stared, shocked and disbelieving. "Refused? Do you mean you *asked* him?"

"Yes!" Brielle was close to shouting. "I asked him! And do you know what he said? He said he would not! And then—and *then*, he said I could come to *his* bed! Can you even think it? I, trailing along the gallery in my nightwear, humbly knocking on his door and asking to be serviced?"

Dragging in a long breath, Honoria shook her head. "I cannot think it. I would not believe it if I saw it. Yet —I wish I could imagine such a thing, and bring it to pass. 'Twould undoubtedly solve all the hurts and misunderstandings between you."

"Sainted Mary," Brielle said, suddenly deflated. "Even you are against me." She whirled away from Honoria's reaching hands and began working with her own hair, creating a thick and crooked braid bound to trouble her when she tossed about in her sleep. "Go! Go to bed, Honoria. And never mention Adam to me again."

That night she lay staring into the flame of the spirit candle and thought deeply. For the first time, she tried to imagine how she would feel if she bowed to Adam's demands. If she humbled herself. Could she stand it? She thought of him laughing when he opened his door and saw her there, and her jaws came together with an audible click. *Damn* him! But what if 'twas the only way?

After mid-December the king's household began the move to London. Carts were loaded with sacks of beef and venison, with bags of hares and pigeons, with barrels of salt fish and live oysters, with pipes of Gascon wines. They groaned away from the storehouses and, with a company of bowmen as guards, began the haul to the city.

"The more we carry to London, the less we burden the city merchants," Philippa said in answer to Brielle's inquiring look. They had been watching from the gallery windows as a train pulled out. "'Tis a time of feasting, and supplies run short in the city." Brielle nodded, and having thought of feasting, thought of Berthe. It had been weeks since she had talked to Berthe and Jacques, though she had seen them often enough in the beginning to know they were satisfied with their positions.

"I must see to my servants," she told Philippa, and left, going down the steep stairs to the great hall and through it to the kitchens in a separate building outside. Berthe saw her coming and came out of the busy kitchen to meet her, motioning to Jacques, who stood in a corner talking to another old man.

"Which would you like," Brielle asked, once they all stood together, "to see London or remain here at Windsor until I return?"

"I've seen all I ever wish to see of London, my lady," Jacques replied, and Berthe agreed.

"But Leone will wish to go," Berthe added. "Her lover Harald marches with the wagons and stays in London until the king returns."

"Then she shall go." Brielle turned to leave and then turned back, looking from Berthe to Jacques's old face and thinking of the hardships and bitter weather to come on the next trip, as they made their way to northern England in January.

"I wonder," she said slowly, "if 'twould be well to leave both of you here in Windsor Castle until spring. The trip north will be arduous, the ice and snow worse than ever we've seen in Picardy. What think you, Jacques?"

Jacques straightened and thrust out his bony chest. "'Tis my duty and pleasure to look after you, my lady, when you leave the king's protection. Of course I shall accompany you." He looked at Berthe sternly. "You agree, do you not, cook?"

Berthe sniffed. "Of a certitude! How else would our lady taste again the flavors of Picardy? Allow me to remind you once more, old man, that I do not need your instructions in my duties! I am well aware that . . ." Her voice continued, indignantly.

Brielle smiled and left them to their interminable arguments. Neither of them would be happy without the other, that much she knew. It had always been so, as long as she could remember. Their quarreling bound them together.

Some few days later, after most of the noble guests had left—some willingly and others, such as Alice Montagu, not so willingly—the royal remove began. Again there were wagons, a good half dozen, filled with personal possessions and clothing. They left at dawn, with a quiet, clear day promised, and only an inch or so of snow on the ground.

Everyone but the wagon drivers rode astride a horse, even Honoria and Leone, who were riding two huge but calm dray horses. Brielle rode a beautiful snow white mare from the king's Arabian stable, graceful, obedient, and light of foot, so there was no jarring nor awkwardness in her gait. Brielle noticed that Edward often looked back at her and smiled when he caught her eye. Finally, after an hour or so of riding, he wheeled his black Barb and came to ride beside her. Staring down at her with a warmly speculative blue gaze, he nodded approvingly.

"The mare is yours," he said grandly. "She suits you too well to take her away at journey's end. I will tell Adam to find room for her in London when he stables his own mount."

Brielle studied his expression. No matter what Adam said, the king was no saint, and his usual paramour had gone home.

"Your Majesty is much too generous," she said. "I would find myself too deep in your debt if I dared accept the gift. The mare is worth a fortune."

Edward moved closer, his broad mouth widening in a suggestive smile. "A small tribute to your beauty, my lady. Your pleasure in riding her would be my reward."

Her amber eyes, brilliant as topaz in the sunlight and suddenly just as hard, met his gaze squarely.

"'Twould be your *only* reward, Your Majesty," she said. "She'd not buy you a new mount for your stable. Think it over before you sell the mare so cheap."

Edward's mouth fell open as he stared at her, and then he threw back his head and laughed, his roar of genuine merriment resounding through the broad and snowy valley in which they rode. Heads turned; relieved smiles welcomed the king's good humor. Edward was not always cheerful.

"By God," Edward gasped out, "there's wit in that small body, and spirit enough for a warrior! No need for me to think over my gift, Lady Brielle. The mare is yours, with neither gold nor favor asked."

Later, when the walls of London were in sight, Adam dropped back from the forefront of the column and edged in beside Brielle, riding in silence. She had

seen him, and also Kiernan, the only Dunbarton
knight in the cortege, in close conversation with the
king, for Edward grew restless in the slow pace and
changed positions often, talking to this favorite or that
during the dull hours. Still, Adam said nothing to her,
only rode there bulking high and looking stern. But
when she caught him studying her, she thought his
gaze friendlier than it had been lately.

The magnificence of Westminster Hall took Brielle's
breath away. They approached it with the light of the
westering sun just touching the great towers and striking shards of gold from the arched windows. The sun
shone also on banners and lances, on tossing plumes
and prancing horses, for they were expected, and the
Westminster Palace Guard had turned out in force to
greet their king and queen.

The grandeur overwhelmed Brielle. She had found it
easy at Windsor to feel the family connection between
herself and Philippa, but the formal trappings of royalty, the huge castle, the uniformed guard awed her,
made her feel the real distance between her estate and
this tremendous power. Even Philippa, dropping back
to ride beside her as Edward took the lead alone,
looked grave, more serious and burdened than she had
ever seemed at Windsor.

In truth, Brielle thought, the arrival seemed to affect
most of the train. Faces changed, growing serious;
smiles disappeared, as if each man felt the burden of
duty fall on his shoulders. But—not Edward! Staring
at the king as he led the column of knights that gathered and fell in behind him, Brielle noted the change
in him with fascination. She leaned to whisper to
Philippa.

"King Edward approaches his palace as a Greek god
hails Olympus," she said softly. "Just see how straight
he sits his warhorse, how proud he looks! Like Zeus
himself."

Philippa smiled, her dark eyes resting on Edward as he led them into the palace yard. "'Tis true, little cousin. He is exalted by his power and rank, and has ever been." She laughed a little. "Fortunately for England, he was born into the role. Otherwise, he might have swept others from his path and made himself king by violence, as many have done before him." She turned toward Brielle and studied her rapt face. "But 'tis unfortunate that he believes a king entitled to everything—and everyone—he wants."

"I know." So close Brielle and Philippa had become in the weeks they had been together that there could be no misunderstanding between them, and there was none now. "He may be powerful and wise in his governing," Brielle said quietly, "yet he can be a child who envies his brother's new toy. Is that not so?"

"You put it very well," Philippa said, and took a deep, relieved breath. "I am glad you understand. He is not perfect. To carry it further, he is sometimes careless with other men's belongings, so that they are ruined and cast aside. I—would not see that happen to someone I love."

"You will not." Brielle's eyes met Philippa's squarely. "I promise you that for many reasons, both of love and pride."

They had not been noticing what was going on around them, and they found their horses nudged and crowded by others as the column swung out and away from the palace yard and proceeded down the towering side of the long hall. As their horses broke into an eager trot, Philippa pointed.

"There," she said, "at the end of the hall, we turn toward the Thames again and come to the courtyard of Westminster Palace. Soon you will see where we spend our Christmas holidays."

* * *

Now Brielle saw the sense in sending half of the servants and most of the supplies ahead of the main party. The odors of baking bread and roasting meats swirled in the small courtyard enclosed by the wall, and the palace—first seen as they went up the back stairs as great, luxurious suites with lofty ceilings and wonderful rugs and tapestries—was swept and freshened, ready for them all.

Directed by the chatelaine, Adrienne Parsons, a round ball of a Frenchwoman with a cherubic smile and silver-streaked dark hair, Brielle and Honoria examined the suite they were given. A large sitting room was furnished comfortably, with a row of small glassed windows that looked out over the Thames. Leading off from the large room, three smaller ones were furnished with enormous featherbeds. With smiles, Honoria and Leone set about disposing of the luggage. Adrienne opened the wardrobes, wafting a scent of lavender through the rooms, and left them, hurrying to settle others. She was back in less than a half hour, pink-faced and apologizing.

"I am very sorry, Lady Brielle, for my mistake. This room is for your maid and your companion. Follow me, and I will show you yours. 'Tis in another passage."

Brielle signed for Leone to come along and learn the way. They followed Adrienne along the echoing hall, turned a corner, and proceeded along an inside hall lighted with tapers. The chatelaine showed them into a room at the end with windows on all three sides, overlooking a courtyard, the river, and a long view of the main part of London in the distance. The furnishings in the room were luxurious to an extreme; even the royal blue velvet hangings of the tremendous bed were weighted with bands of gold filigree and rough stones of lapis and ruby. Beneath their feet, the rug felt thick as clover in summer. Brielle took a long, suspicious glance around and set her jaw hard.

"Please tell my cousin Queen Philippa that I much prefer the first suite with my maid and companion near, and I'm sure I shall be the happier in it. But do thank her for her kind thoughtfulness."

Adrienne gasped and stared at her. "But, my lady, 'twas the king himself who ordered the change."

Aha. 'Twas as she suspected. Her chin jutted. "Then tell my wishes to the king, by all means. Come, Leone."

White-faced, Leone followed Brielle's rapid stride, hurrying, peering at her in utter confusion. "How do you dare to disobey the king's orders?" she whispered in the hall.

Brielle cast her a rebuking glance. "What you cannot understand," she said sharply, "you need not question. 'Tis better for us all that I stay with Honoria and you. Therefore, that is what I shall do. The king will not gainsay me."

Leone was silent but not for long. As they reached the door of the first suite, she dared to lay a hand on it and hold it closed until she could speak her mind. Her great dark eyes searched Brielle's face.

"I would sleep elsewhere, my lady, if you allow it."

Brielle's set jaw softened with warm amusement. "I would not build walls between two lovers, dear Leone. All you must do is pretend you sleep here, with Honoria and me. Slip out and meet Harald whenever you wish."

Leone let out a long, shaky breath. "Thank you, my lady. I will never forget your kindness. Now, we will finish our settling in."

That night they dined in the palace hall at a table glittering with silver and crystal, with golden goblets and a multitude of candles in sconces on the walls. The room was crowded, for no less than forty diners were there, most of them strangers to Brielle, though she did recognize the charming nobleman with whom she had danced that fateful night before Marc de Rohan became her partner. The noble guests wore lavish silks and satins, velvets and fur-trimmed wools. The soft candlelight gleamed back from jewels of every color, in necklaces, in rings, in rows sewed on the men's satin or velvet tunics, in pins that held the floating veils fluttering from the women's headdresses.

Entranced, Brielle gazed about, seeing something new at every turn. The soft, sparkling light, the warmth, and the wonderful colors made the old men handsome, the women beautiful and very charming. She glanced down at herself, at the soft amber silk and the golden-brown velvet of her favorite gown, fingered her topaz necklace, and was satisfied. Then from a corner of the room the first lute player softly strummed a romantic song of love, and Brielle's spirits rose like bubbles in wine.

"You are looking well, my lady," Adam said as he stepped from behind her. "The trip didn't tire you, then?"

She turned quickly, hearing a new softness in his voice. In this sparkling light Adam's eyes were like sapphires, deep glowing blue above his weathered cheeks and close-clipped golden beard. His mane of golden hair was brushed smooth and topped with a dashing black velvet cap that tilted over one eye and sported a rough-cut ruby and diamond pin.

Brielle looked him over admiringly. The present style of skin-tight chausses and extremely short tunics, unkind to many men who lacked the means of filling out the tights, was kind indeed to Adam, showing off his long, muscular legs and potent masculinity.

"The trip was easy for me," she said, and looked away, conscious of her quickening heartbeat. "The mare I rode was like a feather in the wind."

"And now she is yours, I understand."

She glanced up at him quickly, but there was no censure in his voice. "I—did not say I'd keep her, sire."

"You may if you wish," Adam said, surprising her. "Edward has told me neither payment nor favor will be asked in return. I believe he truly wants you to have the mare as a gift."

Brielle stared into the distance, frowning. Had it not been for the offer of the luxurious, out-of-the-way boudoir, she would have already felt the mare was hers. But it seemed possible to her that Kiernan had been right when he warned her about the king. Perhaps Edward's seduction had only started. She turned back, shaking her head.

"I will take no such expensive gifts from the king," she said. "I think it wrong."

"'Tis for you to decide," Adam said. His voice was calm, but beneath the calm she sensed something else he seemed to want to say but didn't. Then, after a moment, he took her arm and turned toward the table. "Come, I've been asked to present you to England's chiefest warrior, the invincible Henry, Earl of Lancaster."

Brielle smiled up at the tall and graceful man she remembered from the dancing at Windsor. "If the Earl of Lancaster fights as well as he dances, he is worthy of the name you gave him," she said, and offered her hand.

Taking the hand, Henry raised it to his lips. "Many conquests I have made, but none so glorious as Adam's. Now I understand what tempted England's chiefest bachelor lover, the sorrow of many languishing ladies, to choose at last to marry."

Adam's laughter rang out. "What a wonderful fool you are," he said, clapping an affectionate arm over Henry's shoulders. "So full of fancy phrases that mean nothing. Come sit with us and dampen that blathering tongue of yours with wine."

Henry raised his elegant brows. "I accept with pleasure, if I am to sit by your wife. I need practice in compliments for the season, and though she is bound to you, she provides excellent inspiration." He took Brielle's arm, tucked her neatly into the small space between Adam and himself, and drew them both toward the table.

Brielle was laughing. "You hold a treasury of flattering wiles, Sir Henry. You need no more."

Henry's light, clear eyes danced. "Ah, but the need is tremendous, my lady. With this new style of courtly love, the ladies have become exceedingly demanding. Why, less than nine or ten years ago, I had but to say their eyes were like stars, and they allowed me to kiss them. Now I must write poems to earn a smile."

Adam laughed. "Poor Henry! Had you thought further than blaming the ladies, you might have recalled that nine or ten years ago there was neither silver in your hair nor wrinkles in your face. Be thankful you have your poems to enthrall them."

Henry looked sad. "I thought you my friend, Adam. 'Twas an unkind cut, indeed, to remind me of my advancing years. For that, I shall flirt dangerously with your wife."

Slipping into a gilded chair, waiting for them to settle beside her, a maneuver which took a great deal of clattering of scabbards and shuffling of large feet, Brielle was smiling. This lightness of spirit, this beauty around them, this comfort and security was what she had hungered for ever since the war had come to Picardy and taken those blessings away from Le Fontin Château. Strange it was that now she received them from the conquerors of Picardy. But though she had once scorned King Edward's right to rule France, she had begun to see that the war was not between countries but was a struggle for power within the ranks of English and French royalty, all of whom were related by blood. 'Twas truly a family fight, always more bitter than any other.

10

The next morning the French chatelaine, Adrienne, came to Brielle's door.

"Lady Dunbarton, I am commanded by the queen to escort you to her breakfast room," she said with a little bow. "Her Highness said there would be no need to dress formally."

Brielle put on a simple gown and a warm tunic, for the long halls were chilly. Honoria brushed her long dark hair, allowing it to flow down her back in waves, and fastened a narrow gold filet around her head to keep it in place.

"You look as you did years ago," she murmured as she fastened the filet, "young and eager. You feel safe with Philippa, don't you? As you did with your father."

"Yes," Brielle said, and smiled, surprised at Honoria's perception. She rose and joined Adrienne in the hall and followed her to a small room on the east end of the palace. Flooded with early sunshine, the room was warm and cheerful, and a table was set with plates of hot bread, a crock of butter, and jellied preserves of summer fruit. A pitcher of mead, its warm honey odor rising from it, waited.

"Her Highness will—" Adrienne began uncertainly, and then stopped, making a deep curtsey as Philippa came in from another door. Philippa, smiling at sight of Brielle, was in deshabille, her heavy dark hair on her shoulders and her strong body dressed in only a shift and a royal blue silk robe, with soft slippers on her feet.

"Thank *le bon Dieu* that last night is over," she said

to Brielle, and motioned for Adrienne to rise. "The first dinner after an absence is hard—everyone wants to be invited, and if they are not, they stay angry until the next holidays." She turned to Adrienne. "Please send my son Edward and my daughter Isabella to me as soon as they arise." She sat down at the breakfast table as Adrienne left and indicated a chair on her right. "Sit, child. No need for ceremony within the family."

Brielle sat, pouring a cup of mead for Philippa and one for herself, reaching hungrily for the new baked bread. "I am pleased to be meeting the Black Prince and Princess Isabella, but I thought they were living in Pountney's Inn."

Philippa laughed. "Indeed they were, and they wished to stay there, too, but their father sent orders ahead for them to join us here after dinner last night."

"Orders?"

"Indeed. Otherwise, we'd not see them. Oh, they came, but not willingly. It does not suit them to be ordered home when they've become used to their freedom. They've been looking forward to the winter festivals, hoping to play their way from Devon to York and from London to Wales."

Buttering bread, reaching for the honey pot, Brielle was thoughtful. "Perhaps they value the freedom they have now because they know they will lose it later. One will be a king, the other may be a queen in another country. They will have little time for play then."

"I know. But Edward insisted on having his son here this time, and I cannot let Isabella stay on her own." Sipping the warm mead, Philippa shook her head. "A charming but wayward daughter, I fear. Edward gives in to Isabella's every whim."

"My father did the same, I admit. I am only now beginning to realize I cannot expect Adam—or any other man—to accord me the same treatment."

The queen smiled. "A lesson all women must learn.

So far, Isabella is not willing to change her lenient father for a domineering husband. She has been betrothed three times—to Pedro of Castile, to the son of the Duke of Brabant, and to Louis of Flanders—and married none of them."

Behind them, the door to the hall opened and a clear young voice spoke.

"But I *would* have married dear Louie, *Maman*, had he not run away and married someone else!"

Brielle quickly rose to be presented to royalty, dipping a knee and giving a small bow as Philippa introduced her. The Princess Isabella was well named, for she resembled her grandmother, Queen Isabella, both in looks and in her air of confident royalty. Short but regal, her hair a light brown and her features small but regular, the princess was pretty enough and broad in the hips, an advantage in the marriage mart. But the Black Prince, Edward, who came in behind her quietly, was muscular and tall. The heir apparent had shining black hair and jet black eyes, a smooth olive skin and calm manner, all Philippa's legacy to her first son. He was also, Brielle thought, exceedingly handsome. But he seemed to have none of the flamboyant spirit, the wild and joyous nature of his father the king. Instead, the Black Prince seemed cool and quiet, almost somber in his effect, though his expression when he saw Brielle was pleasantly admiring.

"I remember you, my lady," he said as they took their places at table. "You have become a lovely woman, yet you still look much the same as the charming little girl I met in Picardy ten years past."

"Your Highness is too gracious," Brielle answered politely. "A seven-year-old girl must have been indeed boring to a boy of nine."

"Indeed not. As I recall, you took me out in the courtyard where your father's hawks were mewed, and the falconer took us hawking. 'Twas the most enjoyable day of the whole visit." He turned to Isabella. "At seven, the Lady Brielle flew a hawk better than you do now."

Isabella laughed. "I am glad you told me. I shan't challenge her to a match." Spreading fragrant preserved peaches on a slice of hot bread, she smiled mischievously.

"Come to think of it, Lady Dunbarton, you trapped England's most prized silver falcon when you married. Tell me, have you managed to tame him?"

Caught unaware, Brielle could think of nothing to say for a moment. Then, blood mounting up her slender neck and spreading over her cheeks, she lowered her gaze to her plate and shook her head.

"No, Your Highness. I cannot lay claim to such skill."

Isabella leaned back, laughing. "Had you said yes, I would have known you lied. Adam will never be tamed. But still, you are fortunate in your choice. He must make a delightful bed partner."

Philippa broke in, her usually warm voice chilly. "Do be quiet, Isabella. Your tongue runs away with you, giving you the manners of a common courtesan. Ignore her, Brielle. She pretends great knowledge of men, yet she knows very little."

Isabella was silent, splotches of red on her fair-skinned face, but after a few minutes she stretched an arm across the table and touched Brielle's fingers. "I am sorry indeed if I embarrassed you, Cousin Brielle. I meant no harm."

Brielle looked up. Isabella's light blue eyes were regretful, her smile friendly and full of hope. Brielle smiled back, her embarrassment easing. "If no harm was meant, no harm was done, Your Highness."

"Good!" Isabella sat back, adding brightly: "We shall be friends, I know it. Edward and I will take our

midday meal at his residence in Pountney's Inn, and if
Adam agrees, I want the two of you to join us."

Brielle's gaze flew to Philippa questioningly. Philippa nodded. "Adam will likely approve the visit. The
threat of the plague is over for the year, and
Pountney's is a pleasure you will enjoy."

Prince Edward set aside his mug and plate and
stood up. "I will find Adam and tell him our plans."
His dark gaze flickered over his mother's face. "From
what I heard last night, he also has a plan to put before
me."

Philippa gave an almost imperceptible shake of her
head, warning her son. "Perhaps. But go, by all
means. We ladies have the task of making ourselves
look wonderfully grand for the pageants of Christmas,
and the dressmakers are coming within the hour."

Brielle dressed with care for the trip to Pountney's
Inn. Her heavy silk samite riding gown of forest green,
powdered with a design of silver falcons, had a light
green overgown with open sides, the color soft as
spring leaves. Her shaped cloak of dark gold wool was
fully lined with vair, so that the warm fur framed her
face inside the hood. Aware that she looked her best,
she joined Princess Isabella and accompanied her
down the back stairs. They stepped out into light snow,
seeing across the courtyard the Black Prince and
Adam riding toward them, accompanied by a guard of
mounted knights and a stable man leading two mares,
one a bay and one the white Arabian Brielle had ridden before.

Adam, resplendent in dark blue chausses and a red
tunic with a silver hip belt, a dark blue wool cloak and
dagged hood, swung down from his horse to help
Brielle mount her mare. She needed little help. Agile
and strong in spite of her small size, she seemed to
barely touch her small foot to his cupped hands before

she was in the saddle, taking up the reins with a practiced hand. Still feeling confident, she smiled down at him but was suddenly chilled. His eyes were granite hard inside the dark blue hood. Puzzled and hurt, for he'd been most companionable last evening, Brielle looked away.

"Thank you, sire."

Adam didn't bother to acknowledge her thanks. "We must set a fast pace once we leave the courtyard," he said coolly. "'Tis only a short ride into the city before we come to Chepeside and Pountney's, but when the Black Prince rides, we take the least dangerous way."

"Least dangerous? What danger awaits us in the streets with a company of knights around us?"

"Royalty always has enemies," Adam said, "and the season when they gather together in London brings assassins to our shores. 'Tis wise to avoid trouble." Mounting his stallion again, he turned away, choosing to ride in the van with Prince Edward rather than with his wife. It made no difference, for immediately the company of armored knights ranged themselves around the four and, as they left the courtyard, drew their swords and held them at the ready.

Watching the guards as the company rode slowly past the great hall, seeing that they never looked toward the prince or princess but instead swept the snowy fields and the gates ahead with a constantly searching gaze, Brielle questioned Isabella in a whisper.

"Does it seem to you that the guards expect trouble? They look so grim!"

Isabella shrugged. "They always look grim. 'Tis their uncertain life, I believe. Why, if Edward receives so much as a cut, they will be put to death."

Brielle gasped. "That is barbaric!"

"I think so myself," Isabella agreed. "Yet as my father says, the custom sharpens their eyes wonderfully well.''

The pace picked up as they left the gates of Westminster and turned first north along the curve of the Thames and then east, toward London's gates and its close-packed houses and soaring church spires. There was a haze of smoke from the sea-coal fires hanging over the city, and a soft fall of snow on the ground that muffled the sound of the horses' hooves as they broke into an easy canter.

Brielle laughed aloud in the sheer pleasure of being outside and on a horse. The air was icy on her cheeks; frost starred her long lashes and spiked the fur that circled her pinkening face. She saw Adam turn to look at her and sent him a nod and a careless smile, holding his gaze as if she would share her enjoyment. Without warning, strong emotion blazed up in his narrowing eyes. His wide mouth tightened and went flat within his close-cropped beard. She stared, sensing that he fought himself hotly, denied himself some hidden desire. Then as he slowly turned away, his face tightening, it struck her like a lick of flame: He desired *her*.

Breathless, she lowered her gaze to her gloved hands, dragging in a deep breath, staring unseeingly at her clenched fingers. She gave the little Arabian her head, trusting her to follow the lead of the other horses. She was dazed; the world around her disappeared as long-held sensation broke loose and raced through her blood, hot and revealing. She saw in her mind a vision of Adam in her dark room at Windsor, fireglow glinting on his face, his strong arms pulling her against his aroused body, his mouth fastening on hers. She tasted again the musky sweetness of his tongue, felt again the spread of his hands against her buttocks, and was forced to bite down hard on her lower lip, fighting a wild passion. Damn him! He had wanted her then, by the evidence of his own body. Had

he given in and stayed that night, they'd be truly wedded now—and none of the trouble and doubt that had
begun that night would have happened. By God's
bones, the man was far too stubborn!

The cortege slowed, for they entered now the wide,
cobbled street of Chepeside, London's chief market-
place and the site of Pountney's Inn; built there, Isabella had told Brielle that morning, by John Pulteney,
four times Lord Mayor of London. He had meant it for
the comfort of nobles and their ladies. The rich, Isabella had said, often came to London to buy jewels and
tapestries, Saracen rugs, the silks of China, and the
cloth woven by the excellent weavers of Flanders, who
started coming here to ply their trade when Philippa of
Hainault began her reign as queen.

"However," Isabella had added, "since my brother
has taken the inn over as his London residence, 'tis no
longer open to trade."

Now, as they slowed to a walk and turned toward
the inn, Isabella laughed and moved close to Brielle to
speak. "As you will see, the inn is still home to the
same nobles that used to frequent it. Only now they are
guests."

The inn, with its walled courtyard, took up a full
corner on Chepeside and one of the narrow streets of
market stalls that ran toward the Thames. Brielle studied it and then looked at Isabella curiously. "Prince
Edward is too generous to his friends. That practice
could impoverish him."

Isabella gave her usual tiny shrug. "They bring lavish gifts. The gifts are always worth more than the
price of the stay. My brother is no fool, nor ever will
be."

They were in the courtyard, and the heavy iron gates
closed behind them, an inn guard strolling the walls.
The cortege of knights climbed down from their horses
in high spirits. Grooms rushed to their duties from the

stables behind the inn, and an old man, wearing the long tunic and badge of a domestic chamberlain, came from the entrance to the inn, leaving the doors wide in welcome and hurrying to assist Princess Isabella from her horse.

Going in through a magnificently paneled hall, following the prince and princess with Adam beside her, Brielle saw in Edward and Isabella some of the quality seen in their father when he paraded before his subjects. They stood straighter, they walked with dignity, they wore benevolent smiles, they nodded graciously to the bowing and scraping of the inn workers. But, she thought, they did it all by rote. His children had none of Edward III's vibrancy in them, nor the glorious, flamboyant happiness that shone from the king and warmed his subjects like a fire in the heart. They were his children, but neither son nor daughter had inherited the flame.

A score or more of guests were seated in the main dining room, which was huge and paneled like the hall. The round oak tables held as many as a dozen noble diners, and the chairs were padded and covered with red wool. The guests came to their feet as Edward appeared, as if the Black Prince were in his own court. Going on through to a private room, Edward waved them down again into their chairs. They sat obediently, but they looked pained, as if they had thought he'd join them. Brielle, guilty of being one of the more favored today, was sure she felt their eyes boring into her back as she passed.

The private room was lavish but cozy. A small fire leaped and spluttered merrily in a chimney corner; another huge round table sat in the center of the room, with chairs as soft as goosedown. They were barely seated when a maid came in with bottles of wine and a tray of goblets, followed by a footman to pour and pass the wine around.

"A meal, Felix," Edward ordered, "a good one. The cold day whets hunger." He sat down, smiling at Brielle. "No grouse, I fear. Surely none so fat as the birds we ate that day in the Château Le Fontin."

"You loved the hunt," Brielle said, remembering, and forgot to say Your Highness. "As for the grouse, they are always sweeter when the game is yours."

He laughed. "That day they were yours." He turned to Adam, still warming himself at the fire, keeping a little apart. "I hope I'm with you when you take your bride hawking this spring. She will surprise you."

Adam's icy blue gaze swept Brielle with a definite chill. "I have learned to expect that," he said, and smiled without humor. "I've had a continual round of surprises, from the very beginning of our marriage." He turned away, as if he tired of the subject, and spoke to Isabella. "And you, Izzy? Are you as well as you look?"

"How can you ask?" Isabella sighed theatrically, winking at Brielle. "I've been deep in despair since I learned you had wed. Where am I to find another handsome bachelor to squire me about?"

"Marry," Edward said, draining his glass. "Make our mother happy at last. As she often tells you, marriage is a woman's natural state."

"Poo," Isabella said. "Poo, poo, poo! I'll marry when I find a man I want. Had it not been for our father's poor taste in killing Louie's father, I'd be happily wed now, and the Countess of Flanders. Louie never forgave that deed."

"True," her brother said lazily, "but be careful you don't hang on the vine till you shrivel." He poured more wine and sent the footman around with the bottle. "Drink," he ordered them. "Enjoy yourselves. Adam and I need bright faces around us, ladies."

Isabella laughed. "We will brighten like polished sil-

ver if you promise to accompany us to the Street of the
Jewelers after we dine.''

Brielle was silent, wanting to say what she was
thinking—that she needed no jewels. But the Black
Prince had already agreed, saying he needed Isabella's
advice in choosing a gem for ''a charming female who
shall not be named.''

"And I," Adam said, breaking a long silence, "will
buy a bride's gift for my wife. 'Tis long overdue.''
Lounging back in his chair, his booted feet propped on
the underpinnings of the table, he seemed to be studying the wine in his cup, which he held in both hands.
"This makes the duty easier. The gift is bound to please
if the lady chooses it herself.''

Brielle's heart had leaped up with his first words;
the last let it fall again. She would have been happy to
accept a gift Adam had chosen, but if she had to
choose it, she would pay for it herself. She would ask
him for nothing. "I need no jewels," she said stiffly. "I
have more than enough.''

"Dear, foolish Brielle," Isabella breathed, amazed.
"Every year the London jewelers surpass themselves
with rich designs. How could you know you don't
want a thing when you haven't seen it yet?''

Edward waved a hand. "First, we dine. Let no argument spoil the meal. Later we can decide the question,
on full and comfortable bellies.''

In the end, they visited the Street of the Weavers and
that of the Jewelers, causing a great commotion in the
narrow ways. They walked, and the knights who
guarded the heir apparent marched around them, creating a solid wave of armored bodies and flashing
swords that drove other customers to take refuge
wherever they could, there to stand and stare at the
famed Black Prince as he strolled by.

"Our bodies are safe enough here in these crowded
ways," Isabella told Brielle. "'Tis our money that is in

danger. When these robbers see royalty, they show
their respect by doubling their prices. Oh! Do look at
this, Brielle!" She held out a necklace of gold filigree,
set with diamonds. "Isn't it lovely and fine? 'Twould
suit you perfectly."

Brielle smiled but shook her head. "It is beautiful,
indeed, but it is nothing I need or want, Your Highness. I truly do have quite a few jewels—Honoria tells
me my mother was fond of them, and my father fond
of giving her gifts."

"Well, then," Isabella said, "I'll turn my talents to
helping Edward find a gift for his nameless lady." Still
holding the filigree necklace, she turned to her
brother. "Would this be suitable, do you think? It is
quite different from the usual thing—" Her voice
stopped as a large hand gently lifted the necklace from
her fingers.

"You have an excellent eye, princess," Adam said,
holding the delicate filigree high, turning it back and
forth so that the diamonds flashed and swung. "Find
something else for Edward's paramour. I know the
lady well. She will prefer a large and gaudy bauble."
He dropped the necklace into a pocket in his cloak and
got out a bulging leather bag, glancing at the suddenly
glistening eyes of the shopkeeper. "The price?"

The shopkeeper bowed. "Twenty *francs d'or*, Lord
Dunbarton, thirty if silver, fifty if a signed paper."

Adam laughed, truly amused. "I offer you ten *francs
d'or*, Lord of the Thieves."

The man's broad face shone with avarice. "Fifteen,
then. I will make no profit, but 'twill put me in your
good graces."

Adam took the necklace from his pocket and eyed it
dubiously. "Five."

"I'll take the ten *francs d'or*," the shopkeeper said
hurriedly, "as a tribute to your exalted company."

Accepting the gold coins, the shopkeeper bowed to

Edward. "I wish Your Highness good health and prosperity, and may you come again with your wealthy friends."

In the next open booth they warmed themselves at a charcoal fire while Edward haggled for a gem-encrusted brooch and a matching ring from a one-eyed trader who looked more like an outlaw than a jeweler. While they dickered, a light fall of snow commenced, and the guardsmen rapidly grew restless, for snow provided a convenient veil for assassins. Edward's calm gaze took in their worried looks and shifted to Adam's face as they left the booth.

"Back to the inn, Adam?" he asked, and Adam nodded, taking Brielle's arm.

"A wise move, Your Highness. The weather worsens."

Isabella grumbled at the pace of the long-legged men but kept up, laughing breathlessly as they dodged 'round the gates into the sheltered courtyard of the inn.

"Good! We've time to warm ourselves by the fires inside."

"Not so, little sister. We ride at once." Edward motioned to one of the knights to bring out the horses from the stables. "The snow is setting in," he added to Isabella, "and I promised our mother we'd not stay here the night. Don't look so gloomy. 'Tis but a short ride."

"I know." Isabella glanced at Brielle and grimaced. "I'd hoped we'd find an excuse to stay over so you could see the gaiety of the inn and the saucy entertainments provided."

"Perhaps another time," Brielle said, and shivered, drawing her cloak around her. "I would not worry Philippa."

"You call our mother by her Christian name?" Isabella's tone was only curious, not accusing, but Brielle blushed.

"We have become friends," she said, "yet I should watch my tongue. Thank you for reminding me, Your Highness."

"Quickly, now," Adam said, coming up to them with their two mares. "Mount and be ready to ride. Here, I'll help you."

They left in a crowding rush through the narrow gates, the armored guardsmen thick around the prince and the two women. Outside, the knights urged the party on, whipping up their horses to a gallop.

Looking ahead, Brielle understood. Though it was still early afternoon, 'twas hard to see clearly more than a few yards ahead, and even as she looked, the snow came thicker in the gray air. She clutched the reins of her young mare firmly and settled herself in the saddle for the ride. They would be lucky, she thought, if they didn't lose their way.

As if he had heard her thoughts, Adam touched her shoulder and thrust his thick arm forward, pointing at a silver glimmer. She looked and knew what it was: the Thames. The Thames would guide them home. She drew an easier breath and smiled at him, nodding, pulling her hood closer around her face. He smiled back, his teeth shining in his frosted golden beard, his gaze locked on hers, and for an instant it was as if they were alone in the whirling snow, as if they knew each other's thoughts. Then he turned to look ahead again and left her wondering if the moment of closeness had been real or if she had only wished it so.

They galloped on, the sound of the horses' hooves muffled, their smooth flanks steaming, melting the snow that fell on them. The other riders, Brielle thought, were like huddled haystacks balanced in saddles, their heads obscured by the hoods they pulled forward. Covered with snow, it was hard to tell one

rider from another, though Isabella was small enough
to identify as a woman; as she, too, must be.

The city gates flashed by, hooves clattered on the old
bridge that topped the dry bed of the River Trent. They
were out of London now and nearing the sharp turn
that took the Thames looping its way around Westminster Hall. The knights in the vanguard picked up the
pace again, galloping ever faster toward the palace.

They were in the turn, Brielle concentrating on the
movement of the horses before her, guiding the little
mare in the same tracks, when a stallion in the van of
the knights threw up his head, squealed, and blew, and
through the falling snow another unseen horse challenged, a shrill war cry.

Bursting through the thick-falling snow from the
hump of the riverbank, dark knights in full armor bore
down on them, snarling mouths roaring, mailed arms
brandishing swords.

"Detruiere! Detruiere! Tout a coup!"

Brielle's scream died in her throat for lack of air.
Destroy! Destroy! All at once! These assassins meant to
kill them all! Horses reared up around her as Edward's knights drew them in, frantic beasts that
squealed and fought the reins, came down, and
whirled into a circle around the Black Prince and his
cowering sister. But not all of them, for three plunged
forward to do battle, swords drawn, one huge haystack
in the van, two turning out to the sides. A strong, familiar voice rang out: "To me! To me, for the Black
Prince!"

'Twas Adam's voice. Brielle's heart lurched. *Why?*
'Twas not his duty! She tried to call out, to stop him,
but no sound emerged from her fear-frozen throat. Beside her the prince barked out an order, and four more
knights leaped toward the fray. Brielle moaned invol-
untarily, twisted her hands on the pommel of her sad-

dle, and mumbled a prayer. On her other side, a small, warm hand topped hers and squeezed.

"'Tis a known fact," Isabella whispered, "that no man alive can best Adam Dunbarton."

"Oh, *don't* say that!" Brielle cried out, forgetting to whom she spoke, and snatched her hand away. "Don't, please! You might tempt Fate to turn against him!" She was trembling, afraid to look yet straining to see, her face a mask of anguish. Isabella made a sound in her throat, half sympathy, half chuckle.

"You do love him, then. The hangers-on at court say there is no affection between the two of you—that yours is a *mariage de convenance* only. But they were wrong, I see."

"Oh, no," Brielle babbled, "oh, no—they were right. We—" She shrieked in horror as Adam's broadsword sliced through steel mail, flesh, and bone, and a helmeted head fell to the ground, dyeing the snow red. The spurting body followed with a clattering thump. She looked away as hot blood showered the snow, and she felt her stomach turn over. Still her ears were assailed by the cries of fury, the clang of sword on steel. An English voice rang out hoarsely: "Adam! To your right!" Brielle tensed, and then heard the solid thunk of a broadsword again, followed by a long scream of pain, shuddering into silence.

"*Mon Dieu,*" she whispered, afraid to look again, "keep him safe."

"The cowardly fools!" Isabella shouted beside her, loud and scornful. "Surely they know they're beaten! Ah-ha! They do! They are running away."

Brielle raised her head, and relief as sharp as pain ran through her, giving her life again. She saw that the battle scene had turned into a rout, leaving five bodies in the bloodied snow. "There are some foolish Frenchmen," she answered Isabella shakily, "who will die for honor as willingly as any Englishman."

"Oh? Well, some have, but the rest are leaving fast enough. And Adam is only a little bloody. But Andrew Mackenzie has a bad wound, and so does John Harley. Both good men. Damn the French assassins!"

Adam, kneeling in the snow beside the wounded men, motioned for the others to go on. "Send back two litters and men enough to carry and protect the wounded." His face, the ice-whitened beard flecked with gouts of blood, turned toward Brielle. His eyes met hers and held, searching the amber depths and seeing only what he expected to see: her fear, her horror of what he had done. He looked no longer, only turned away, his face hardening.

"Get the women to safety," he said. "This is not a place for them."

11

Brielle did not see Adam that evening, nor the next. But then all of the king's favorites were pressed into constant service, settling and protecting the late-arriving guests, escorting them to the tower or finding other accommodations in the town. With only days left before Christmas, noblemen and their families were pouring into London to attend the traditional King's Festival, held on Christmas Eve.

"You will enjoy this celebration, Brielle," Philippa told her on the final day. "There is much to see and hear. I think of it as the gayest and most heartwarming time of all."

They were at breakfast and, as often happened, alone. Isabella refused to rise so early every day, and the prince was usually preempted by the king. The arrangement suited Brielle. She loved this hour of solitude with Philippa, when she need make no effort to hide her real thoughts and feelings. Philippa, with her calm nature and her affection for her, was like the mother she'd never had.

"When do we gather for this event, and where?" she asked the queen, beginning to wonder what she would wear and whether the King's Festival was held indoors or out. The weather was bitter cold.

"We gather just before the evening mass in Westminster Abbey, across the way from the hall, and take part in the service." Philippa said. "Once the service is over, there will be a huge crowd outside, in spite of the hour. They will be carrying torches to light our way to Westminster Hall, and for their king to follow." She

shook her head, as if even after the years she had seen
them do it, it was still hard for her to believe. Then she
went on, her rich voice deepening with emotion. "'Tis
not only a sight for them, 'tis a sight for me. It makes
me happy to see how the people of England love Edward. They will stand for hours in the snow just to
cheer him and see him wave to them and smile."

"I believe you," Brielle said softly. "I have seen it in
their faces. I will like seeing it again."

That evening the royal family and their guests—the
Knights of the Garter and as many of the noblemen
and their ladies as the nave of the old abbey would
hold—crossed a snowy field and road that separated
the hall and the abbey and heard the visiting Archbishop of Canterbury pray first for an end to the war,
and then for an hundred years of peace.

Watching the progress of the king as he strode down
the aisle to kneel for his blessing, Brielle fancied she
could see a brightness about him as from some inner
fire, but his eyes were humbly cast down, his handsome face serious, as befits a man coming to his God.

She smiled a little, unconsciously, as he drew
nearer. That pious expression was the only humble
thing about Edward. His fair hair gleamed on wide
shoulders covered with an ermine cape; his cloth-of-
gold tunic was banded with pearls. His crimson robe,
made of English wool and powdered in a design of
England's golden leopards, fell gracefully over his
muscular body. His head was bare; a young page followed with the heavy crown on a velvet pillow, jewels
gleaming in the mellow light. He wore his ceremonial
sword in its jeweled scabbard, and spurs of gold shone
on his heels. He knelt on the low bench provided,
kissed the crucifix held out to him, and listened soberly
to the long and halting speech that served to bless England's king. Then he rose again and turned, head up

and smiling, to walk back through the crowd of wor-
shippers and join the Knights of the Garter in the rear
of the abbey.

"Next to fighting," Isabella's amused whisper came
silkily to Brielle's ear, "my father loves to parade
about and dazzle his subjects. He does it well, don't
you think?"

"Enough." Philippa's voice was calm, but Isabella
glanced at her and said no more. Brielle was pleased
she needn't answer, nor talk. She absorbed the ancient
abbey, the old stone walls deeply shadowed yet rosy
where the candlelight reached; the gentle and worn
statues of the saints and the stained-glass windows
high above the altar. And always her gaze returned,
secretly and from the corners of her eyes, to the
twenty-four Knights of the Garter, resplendent in their
official costume of sky blue woollen, the surcoat and
hood with the emblem of a garter embroidered in silk
and powdered with gold.

Most of the favored knights were unknown to her,
but she recognized Henry of Lancaster, Sir Walter
Manny, and Sir Henry Eam, all three of them among
Edward's favorites; the last two of Flanders. This was
the first time she'd seen all the members of the order at
once, and judging them one by one with Adam, who
stood in the center, she found them all wanting. Even
the king. The king, she thought, flashed like a diamond
in the sun, but Adam owned a deeper strength and a
warmer glow, at least to her mind. And to her heart.
She knew now that she wanted him as her husband.
Facing the altar again, she silently asked for guidance.
There had to be a way around the barriers between
them, a way that would let her keep her pride. That
was essential.

The Archbishop of Canterbury spoke on and on, until
the restlessness of his congregation became too plain

to ignore. Then, though he clearly wished to continue, he ended in a hurry, blessing everyone seated in the nave with a wave of his golden shepherd's staff. He came up the aisle in the wake of his young acolytes and a cloud of sweet-smelling incense, and stood at the door as the noble families passed through. Outside, the bitter cold air vibrated with a roar of voices as the huge crowd waiting saw the Parade of Lords begin.

Brielle turned to Isabella, her eyebrows rising. "I thought surely the king would lead the march to the hall, and we would follow."

Isabella shook her head, looking serious. "'Tis the one time the king must show humility. Our Lord taught his disciples that in the kingdom of heaven, the first shall be last." Her impish face turned merry again. "'Tis fair enough, is it not? Though I suppose my father will argue even with God after his first few centuries of being last. . . ."

"Isabella!"

Turning to her mother, Isabella bowed her head. "I beg pardon, *ma mère*. But it does seem possible to me."

Philippa was trying hard not to laugh. "And to me, I admit. However, your levity is not appropriate this night. Come now, we must take our places." She paused, noting that the crowd was thinning fast, then looked at Brielle. "You may choose, cousin. As a relative of mine, you are very welcome to walk with us, or you may choose to follow the Knights of the Garter. There will be perhaps a dozen wives proudly walking behind them."

"I shall join them," Brielle said. Was this an answer to her prayer? "That is my place."

Philippa nodded, well pleased. "Then go, *mon enfant*. They are gathering in the transept."

Brielle nodded, swept her cloak around her, and went rapidly down the crowded nave, slipping in and out of the slow-moving, chattering nobles and their ladies. She passed the waiting Knights of the Garter with only a quick glance over at Adam, who seemed to be staring straight at her, a look of wonder on his bearded face.

Arriving at the clearer space of the transept, she looked both ways. On her right were the ladies of the knights, easily recognizable because three—no, four— of them had the sky blue wool of the order made into cloaks and embroidered with garters. She went to them diffidently, smiling but not daring to speak. One, a handsome young woman with a look of Flanders about her, gave her an open smile.

"So you chose us, Lady Dunbarton. Not many would give up the right to walk with our gracious queen, though I have no doubt you're as proud of your knight as the rest of us are of our own."

"I am, my lady. And you—why, I know who you are! By the sound of your tongue, you are from Hainault and are therefore the wife of Sir Walter Manny."

Lady Margaret Manny laughed, her high color deepening with pleasure. "Indeed I am. You have caught me out. Oh, there! The first of the knights are marching through. We must gather behind them as the last of them pass."

Fastening their cloaks, the wives moved forward as the men marched through the transept and into the passage that led outside. Slipping into place, the women followed, and behind them came the darkly handsome Black Prince with his sister, Isabella. Last in line were King Edward III and his queen, Philippa.

Because she was small, because she could not see past those who marched before her, Brielle was at first aware only of the roar of voices and the flaring red light of what seemed to be a thousand torches reflecting from the lazily falling snow. Then the column turned east, and she saw on either side of the column the huge crowd that had waited to cheer the king.

It was easy to tell when the king came into sight, striding along at the end of the long column, head up, his bearded face alight with joy, his crown glittering with its constellation of sparkling jewels. He waved an arm, and the cheers were a roll of thunder, shaking the air.

Brielle glanced back and thought how the king always seemed to grow larger, seemed to give off sparkles of light in his glory and excitement. Beside him Philippa was attracting a share of cheers, but her attention stayed on her king, her dark gaze loving and proud. When he put an arm around her and swung her gaily toward one side and then the other so everyone could see her, the crowds went wild, waving their torches and sending up a deafening roar.

It seemed to take forever to get across the snowy field and lane that separated the abbey from Westminster Hall. Most of the delay was the fault of the king, who kept slowing his pace to enjoy the adulation of his subjects. Even as the last of the wives following the knights disappeared inside the huge arch of the hall entrance, Edward turned on the top of the shallow steps and flung out both arms.

"May God bless all true Englishmen," he bellowed, "and confound their enemies! Pray for our success in battle!"

Inside the door, standing in the entry room of the hall, Philippa laughed and clapped her hands over her ears at the thundering agreement. Brielle left her milling group long enough to squeeze Philippa's hand.

"It was wonderful," she whispered. "The king is not the only one loved by those faithful citizens outside. I heard many cheers for Good Queen Philippa."

"'Twas a courtesy, that is all," Philippa said, but she

smiled. "Go now, *mon enfant*, and find a place near Adam. The entertainment will be worth a close look."

Brielle followed Lady Margaret Manny and the other wives, staying close in the press of the tight-packed crowd. This was the first time Brielle had seen the inside of the two-hundred-year-old hall, and though she had known it was large, the grace of the towers and the double arched windows seen from the outside never hinted at the tremendous open space within. As she inched along, sheltered by Lady Margaret's tall figure, she saw that the thick ashlar walls rose a good twenty feet before they reached the deep window embrasures, and the dark, hammer-beam ceiling was another twenty or more higher. As for the length and width of the hall, she couldn't hazard an opinion. She simply stared, and the amazement in her eyes brought another chuckle from Lady Margaret.

"Don't try to count the guests," she advised. "The hall seats two thousand, and it is safe to wager that every seat will be filled and some will still be standing. Come, there are our men." She grasped Brielle's hand, so as not to lose her in the press, and moved on.

Three levels of wooden platforms had been thrown up at the south end of the hall, and there were festively dressed acrobats working on one, adeptly stringing rope from side to side over their heads and fastening it securely. On the highest platform musicians were tuning their instruments, tightening the skins on the kettledrums and the strings on the lutes and crwths, and since the trumpeters had nothing to tighten or tune, they spent their time polishing their trumpets. Then, as she watched, a slender gypsy girl whirled onto the stage, danced across it, and disappeared again in a flurry of bright-colored skirts and a kicking of bare brown legs that brought a wave of laughter from the milling audience.

"A rope dancer," Lady Margaret said, pleased. "I

love to watch them, and I wish myself half as graceful. Look, there is your husband, waiting for you. Oh, and there is Walter." She was gone, hurrying toward the large, genial man who was motioning to her.

Adam's expression, Brielle thought as she approached him, was unreadable, at least to her. He smiled a smile proper for the occasion; he put forth a chair and assisted her into it. He sat down beside her. All of those things reassured her—she had feared he would offer nothing in the way of a welcome. Still, he was not a man to be rude, and she was his wife.

In name only. She looked around at the other Knights of the Garter welcoming their wives—though in these plague years there were many who had no wife to welcome—and wondered if any other man in England who had been married for nearly two months had not yet slept with his wife. She glanced upward at Adam's bearded face and saw that he was looking down at her.

"You surprised me," he said, "again."

She drew in her breath. He had surprised her! His tone was not censuring nor harsh; 'twas more amused. She studied him, wishing she could read his mind. "How have I surprised you, my lord?"

"I would have wagered you'd walk the distance with the Queen of England, not behind a strutting player in fancy embroideries."

She took in his description of himself and thought she should have expected it. He wore his clothing well, but what he chose for himself was never startling in fashion nor fad. Perhaps he felt foolish in sky blue and embroidered garters.

"The clothing fits you and the occasion well, sire." She kept her head down, her hands busy smoothing her skirt, pleating a ruffle back into place. Still, she knew he had settled back in his chair and was watching her instead of the stage, where musicians were beginning to play. "Are you not proud to be seen as a Knight of the Garter?"

"There are others who defend England better than I, yet have not been rewarded. But yes, I am proud to be one of our king's protectors. 'Tis seldom such a true and honest man takes a throne."

Brielle was silent; she was not convinced that any of that was true. To her, Adam had become a knight without equal, and Edward, though she believed him wonderfully able as a king, had a taint of the actor about him. Or was she inclined to criticize Edward because he played Philippa false with Alice Montagu? Or, yet another thought: Perhaps she had lost faith in him when he offered her the Arabian mare, and she had seen in his eyes why he offered. She still wasn't sure she'd convinced him that her virtue was unassailable. She sighed and sat back as the entertainment began, with a wild blast from the trumpets and a roll of the drums. It didn't matter that the talk with Adam had ended. There was no way to speak of those things to him, nor to ask him, as she would like to ask, if a man false to his good and loving wife might not, under the weight of hard decisions, be false to others. In mind and heart, Adam was the king's advocate. He would listen to no questioning of Edward's character.

The music began, lighthearted and rhythmic, and hearty cheering burst out. Gaily dressed tumblers came onto the middle stage in a series of springing somersaults and comic pratfalls, tossed each other about with yipping cries, and built a tower of jiggling, awkward, sometimes upside-down bodies in harlequin patterns of yellows and reds, green liripipes flying from their tight caps. They were in constant movement, swinging on the lowest of the overhead ropes, standing on them, falling off, grabbing the rope on the way down, laughing like fools when the audience gasped.

A company of mummers, some dressed as gaudy lords, some as courtesans, one as a king with a tin crown flashing bits of glass, appeared on the lower stage and began a comic dance with exaggerated bowing, scraping, and sexual byplay. It was so close in its parody of nobles and their ladies that the laughter of the audience was sometimes forced. It was clear that some of them felt they were being ridiculed.

Then, drowning the faint rumble of disapproval, came an uproarious welcome to three gypsy girls flashing across in front of the musicians on the upper platform. The gypsies whirled and kicked and called invitations to the men in their strange language. First one and then another kicked off their shoes and stepped out from the boards onto one of the high ropes and danced, holding their skirts high, showing their shapely brown legs. Brielle trembled for them. A fall from that height could kill or break a back. . . .

"'Tis safe enough," Adam said beside her. "The tumblers catch them when they fall. They are all one family."

She turned to him, meeting his blue gaze, asking herself how it was that he so often knew her thoughts. Again it was as if they were alone in the noisy crowd, together in a moment of wonder. She was breathless when she answered him.

"How did you know I was worried about one of them falling, sire?"

He grinned without humor, a savage glint of white teeth in the neatly trimmed golden beard, his eyes still holding hers. "You have a face that mirrors your feelings, my lady. 'Tis easy enough to read, though at times the meaning may be unwelcome."

She felt heat rise rapidly to her cheeks and knew she was giving him a blush to peruse. "I'm sorry to hear it," she snapped. "There are times a woman would keep her thoughts to herself." She turned back to watch the entertainment, or at least to pretend to watch, while her resentment grew. She thought of the night de Rohan came into her room. It would have been much to her credit and good reputation if Adam could have read her thoughts correctly then. He would have seen the truth. Angrily she faced around to his large and impressive presence again.

"Ah, but I have known you to be wrong!"

His thick brows rose, his gaze centered on her quizzically. "It may be so. Still, you were hiding something from me that night. I saw it in your eyes."

She turned away with a soundless gasp. She *had* been hiding something—her stupidity in believing the whispering de Rohan was Adam. So 'twas neither a hazard nor a trick; he knew to the letter what her feelings were. He had just proved it, for she had said nothing about that night. Frowning, she wondered if she could learn to hide her mind from his. . . .

She saw that Margaret Manny was looking at her with an expression of concern on her charming face. Immediately she smiled and straightened in her chair, raising her chin and giving a nod toward the rope dancers to indicate she liked them, too. Satisfied, Lady Margaret turned back to watch.

Brielle kept her face forward, avoiding another encounter with Adam's penetrating gaze, and kept the smile. There was more entertainment, more music, more bawdy plays by the mummers. The great hall rocked with merriment. Then came the jongleurs with their stunts and magic, with their long and wonderfully descriptive stories of adventure in the Saracen lands. The crowd listened, fascinated, and applauded loud and long. It was a time to enjoy, to leave troubles behind. 'Twas Christmas Eve, a night of happiness, a night of wondrous meaning and hope.

They parted at the end of the entertainment—Adam going with the other knights, Brielle with the queen,

Isabella, and ladies-in-waiting—but at midnight they came together again, this time in the palace chapel to celebrate the birth of the Christ child. The king led in the three of his sons who were present in the palace: the Black Prince, John of Gaunt, and Edmund of Langley, the last two only ten and eight years of age. Following the king and his sons were the Knights of the Garter and the few menservants who were not busy cleaning the hall. The queen led her daughters: Isabella, Mary, who was five, and Margaret of Calais, who was close, now, to three. Following the queen, Brielle brought Honoria and Leone with her, and the women servants came, headed by the chatelaine, round and smiling Adrienne. Men sat on the benches at the right, women on the left. No one spoke nor lifted a head to look around. Hands played ceaselessly along the beads of rosaries, and lips moved silently in praise of God's great generosity to the world.

The chapel, a small jewel of a room, had been built at Philippa's request for a place of silence and calm and prayer. The murals of the Holy Family were painted by an Italian master, the crystal candleholders were French, the altar and benches carved from the finest woods, the tapestries woven especially for these walls. The place had become a favorite with Brielle, who felt its calming influence and needed it. Now, waiting in the silence for midnight and the Christ Mass, she prayed not for triumph but for understanding.

By simply sliding her downturned gaze to the right, she could see Adam's strong, sternly carved profile; past him, the same though softer outline of forehead, nose, and golden beard belonging to the King of England. Past the king, a younger and darkly somber look identified the Black Prince.

Brielle returned her gaze to her clasped hands, reflecting on how often the three of them sat together, almost, she thought, as if Adam were part of the family. What was it Philippa had said? Something about the king thinking Adam was part of him—his judgment, or conscience. But Philippa had laughed at the notion herself, likening it to superstitions of the early days, even before King Arthur. . . .

Around her the women were easing to their knees, and she saw that the old priest had come in, ready to begin the mass. She knelt quickly and put the concerns of the world out of her mind. It was time to thank God for the gift of His son.

12

On Christmas Day, King Edward gave a royal pardon to men in debtors' prisons and, for the benefit of the poor, distributed food from the supplies that came into the city as tribute to him. He was happy to do these things; he was not happy with the constant stream of ambitious men who took advantage of the open audience to ask for favors, complain of taxes, or beg for revenge against an enemy. Therefore he appointed the Black Prince to deal with them.

Isabella, accustomed to the protective company of her brother and tied to the palace without a reliable escort, was bored and not a little headachy after the long night and much wine. She went to Brielle's room, seeking a solution. Sitting down on the bed and looking about, she asked where Adam was.

Brielle was sitting in the light from a small window, embroidering. Her needle flew faster at the mention of Adam's name. "He never tells me of his plans," she said quite truthfully. Isabella gave a little grimace.

"But I need to move about in the fresh air! Let us find him and have him ride with us. 'Tis too dull to stay inside all day."

"I would not object," Brielle said, her eyes still on her work, "but I truly don't know where to look for him."

Isabella perked up. "You have quarreled?"

"No."

"In that case," Isabella said, jumping up, "I shall find him myself. He is probably with my father."

Less than a quarter hour later Isabella walked back

into Brielle's suite and knocked again on her door. Receiving permission to enter, she came and sat down on a stool at Brielle's feet, looking her in the eye.

"The first person I questioned was Adrienne, and she said Adam was conferring with the king and the other Knights of the Garter. Then she told me the meeting was being held in Adam's bedroom because they wanted no interruptions. Put down that silly embroidery and tell me why you sleep here and Adam sleeps elsewhere."

"'Tis a private matter between us," Brielle said stiffly. "You need not concern yourself."

Isabella put on her air of royal command. "I have chosen to concern myself, Lady Brielle. Particularly as I have seen a look of unhappiness on your face whenever Adam is mentioned. Tell me what is wrong."

"No." She looked up, catching a quick flicker of temper in Isabella's eyes. "I mean: no, Your Highness."

After a long, waiting silence, Isabella sighed. "I see 'tis of no use to try to help. I shall go and find someone more amusing to ride with—and commandeer my brother's guards for myself."

Brielle nodded, relieved. "I think it a good decision. The weather is fine."

"Well—you know you are welcome to join us," Isabella said, and waited again. Brielle only nodded. Turning away with an angry flounce of hips, Isabella took a parting shot: "No matter what happened between you, Adam landed in clover. This suite is fine for servants, but he has the luxury of the royal blue chamber. You've seen it, I know. Adrienne said she took you there, for the king said to give the best room to Adam Dunbarton and his wife. But Adrienne said you refused to stay in it because you preferred the company of your companion and your maid to that of your handsome husband."

Isabella was gone in an angry flip of skirt and a toss of head. Brielle laid aside the embroidery with trembling hands. Now she knew why Adam had turned from friendliness the first evening here to cold irritation the next morning. He believed she'd refused to share that beautiful room with him! It was clear that she'd made a terrible mistake—again.

In the next few days Brielle devised a dozen ways of telling Adam why she had refused to stay in that room, but none of them possessed even a hint of truth, so she discarded them. She couldn't imagine telling him—or anyone else—that she'd thought the King so enamored of her that he'd tried to put her in a special room he could visit—oh, she could never say it! She could hear Adam howling with laughter!

She needed someone—not Philippa, not Honoria. Those motherly women would be so pained at what she had done that it would be too cruel to tell them. Nor did she dare talk to Isabella, who had forgotten her pique in an hour and was as friendly and gay as ever. Isabella might have advice, but she could never keep such a rare tale to herself.

Finally, she chose the one woman who she was sure would keep the secret a secret and understand how she felt. She chose Leone, and sitting together in Leone's room, Brielle told her the whole story.

"As you see," she concluded wearily, "I have been a real fool. This was a chance to give in gracefully to the king's command that we share that room. As it is, I've made my husband even more angry by seeming capricious."

Leone nodded. "You must go to him," she said, "and tell him the truth."

"I cannot!"

"You can, my lady. Trust him; he is a fine and honorable man, and I believe he has a *tendresse* for you. It is time you showed that you can be humble when you should."

"I'm not a humble woman! I have pride and temper!"

"Those are the words of a child," Leone said rather dryly. "Neither pride nor temper will keep you warm at night."

"But—he has a caustic tongue. He bests me in every argument."

Leone smiled. "Then leave off the arguing, my lady. There are better ways to win a man over. If you want a husband, then offer him his husbandly rights."

Brielle was silent. She *had* offered, and Adam had spurned the offer. He wanted her humbled. But there might be a way. . . .

"I believe I must find him alone and explain that no one told me we were to be in that room together. I— well, I can say that I thought the room much too grand for one woman."

"Such a tale would not convince me," Leone said, "but perhaps he is more gullible."

"But he is not," Brielle said despairingly. "He has but to look at me, and he knows if I am hiding something. Never mind. I shall think it over."

Brushing her hair that evening, Brielle made up her mind. She knew which room was his, and she would go to him as soon as all had retired. But she would not go in her nightclothes. She would be fully dressed, and she would tell him she had come only because she owed him an explanation. Perhaps, if she managed to be very charming, he would ask her to stay. . . .

Wearing a thick black cloak with a deep hood, and under it a velvet tunic and wool skirt, for the halls in the palace were freezing cold, Brielle set out when the palace grew quiet to find her way to the blue bedroom. Candles flickered in sconces along the halls, casting deep shadows in the corners. She swept through them like a small wraith of the night, looking for the turn into that single corridor. Then a large, dark figure loomed up and turned into the hall where she was, his face lit for an instant by a candle set at the corner. The instant was all that was needed for Brielle to know it was Adam. She drew in her breath and stayed in the shadows until he had passed.

Her heart pounding, she watched him as he turned into the main upstairs hall and started toward the steps. Where was he going? It was very late—even the servants had finished in the kitchens and gone to bed. Curiosity overcame her, and she slipped along the hall to the opening he'd passed, and heard the soft sound of his feet going down the stairs. He too was dressed in black and moved quietly.

A woman! It could be nothing else! He was going to an assignation. Hot with instant anger, she forgot her vow to be sensible. Pulling her hood forward to hide her angry face, she followed. She would first see this woman whom he preferred to her, and then—*then* she would ask for an annulment!

From the top of the stairs she saw him swing around the newel post and head toward the rear of the entry hall. By the saints, 'twas some servant, not even a lady! Brielle's whole furious intent was to discover the woman's face and name, and she scurried down the steps, a heel catching once and making a soft thump. She crouched, peering through the railing as Adam stopped and turned, looking. But then he went on, and, gathering courage, so did she.

Turning again as he reached the end of the hall, Adam disappeared from her view. She ran lightly and soundlessly along the carpeted hall and stopped, her hand flying to her mouth, as a wide door opened and bright light streamed over her, bright as day. In the doorway was King Edward himself! And beside him was the Black Prince, and beyond them was a roomful of armored men, several of whom she recognized and who recognized her, from their startled looks. Kiernan Comyn, Walter Manny, and the Earl of Lancaster all looked dumbfounded. Then the king glanced past Adam and saw her.

First amazement, and then anger swept across Edward's regal face. "By God's teeth, Adam," he swore, "this is no place for a woman!"

Adam swung around. His jaw dropped as he saw her standing there.

"Brielle! How came you here?"

She flinched. "I—I started out to find you, for I had something to say. Then I saw you l-leaving . . . and followed. I am very sorry." She turned to leave, but Adam reached out and caught her arm in a cruel grasp.

"Why didn't you speak to me? What are you hiding?"

Brielle's face was red. "I wanted to know where you were going."

Adam spoke through clamped teeth, his voice a growl of anger. "You thought I was meeting a woman, didn't you? Well, now that you've satisfied your curiosity, go back to bed."

"Yes, sire." With relief, Brielle turned to flee.

"No," the King said shortly, stopping her in her tracks. "She'll go with us, Adam. She's a woman, and she's French. Remember, our success is possible only if our arrival is kept secret."

Adam frowned. "She knows nothing of our purpose."

Edward looked grim. "But she knows we have gathered, and by morning she would know we were gone— and that alone would put the enemy on guard. Women talk. I'm afraid your lovely bride must taste the perils of a night crossing on the Channel. Bring her inside before the servants see her."

Adam took her arm again. "Come into the room," he said gruffly. "Take that chair, and be silent."

Seated in a corner of the room, her gaze on the tips of her leather shoes, Brielle tried to ignore the low-voiced conversation going on amongst the men. At once she knew they were planning a sortie against the French, and twice she heard the name Aimery, the man in charge of Calais Castle. The king, she thought, was right to keep her with them. There could be traitors among his own servants, and a word of their plan would fly from the castle to enemies who would attack the party before it ever left England. She was no spy nor would ever be, but King Edward had no way of knowing that, nor could Adam argue that she wouldn't betray her husband. He might even believe she had betrayed him already—with that bestial de Rohan. She sighed, wondering if he'd ever believe her again, and shut her eyes, trying to doze in the chair.

Within an hour they were on their way, all the men in dark woollens and chain mail, galloping north from London and then east toward a bay at the southern end of East Anglia, where there was little chance of being seen by men who favored France. They carried no torches, but a half moon sailed in drifting clouds and lighted their way. No one spoke to Brielle, who, muffled in her dark cloak, rode a strange black horse. The speed kept them all breathless.

Exhausted by the time they arrived, Brielle was glad to discover that the trip across the Channel would take place the next night—and they would spend this dawning day resting at a small inn. She took off her outer clothes as soon as she was shown into a room, and crawled into bed in her shift. She was asleep when her head touched the pillow, but in early afternoon, she awoke and was instantly alert. Adam was asleep beside her.

Scarcely able to breathe for fear of waking him, she

slid from the bed and put on her outer clothes again. She was smoothing down her skirt, rumpled from the saddle, when his deep voice, laced with irony, made her jump.

"I see you remember what I said in Dover, my lady. You are prompt to act on the advice I gave you then."

Her mind fled back. What had he said? *Put on your clothes. I'll not take an unwilling woman.* She gazed down at herself in horror. He had been in her bed, where she wanted him, and she'd been fool enough to crawl out and put on her clothes! She moistened dry lips with the tip of her tongue.

"But, sire, I—it wasn't that. It was that I feared to waken you with my tossing about, and then, once I left the bed, I was cold."

Adam stared. Her small face looked utterly miserable. Was she truly afraid of him, or was she trying to fool him into sympathy? She could not be so innocent as she pretended. No grown woman he'd ever known would have misinterpreted his reason for getting into her bed. But—why would she lie?

"That last remark," he said, closing his eyes, "is undoubtedly true. There is food on a tray by the window, and a garderobe past that screen in the corner. Do not attempt to leave this room. I shall beat you if you do."

"Yes, sire." Her tone was so respectful that Adam's eyes flickered open, stared at her in disbelief, and closed again. She waited, surprised that he hadn't beaten her before, after the trouble she'd brought him. Finally a slow, even rise and fall of his massive chest told her he slept. She turned away, went to the tray of food, and sat down. She was hungry in spite of her fears and embarrassment, and she made a meal of meat and bread, finishing with a cup of hippocras.

Sipping the warm spiced wine, she found her gaze constantly going back to the huge man on the bed. He had removed his light chain mail and the steel kneeguards, had taken off the heavy wool shirt and the stiffened leather that protected his thighs. What was left was a shirt and a pair of chausses, both knit of the finest wool. He had not bothered to get beneath the covers, but he did not look cold, nor did he huddle up as a cold man does, hoping to contain his own body warmth. He sprawled, she thought, like a young boy who had flung himself down in a soft summer meadow.

But Adam was no boy. The soft knit material clung to every part of his superbly muscled body and offered stirring evidence of a mature male. It was her first chance to study him without his caustic gaze on her, and she took full advantage of it, her eyes moved over him inch by inch until she felt the warmth of desire come singing into her blood. Half ashamed, for she had no wish to want a man who didn't want her, she turned and stared through the window.

It grew cooler as the day waned, and shivering a little herself, Brielle rose and draped her cloak over her shoulders. Then, picking up a blanket from a chest at the foot of the bed, she laid it carefully over Adam and went back to her chair.

An hour later there was a soft knock on the door. Adam sprang from the bed and went to open the door a crack. "Who is it?"

Kiernan's voice was soft, answering. "The night is coming, cousin. We've but a half hour."

Adam shot a glance at the window. "'Twill be full dark, then, when we pass into the Channel. Thank God." He shut the door and went to the pile of clothes and armor. Beginning to dress, he looked around at Brielle and nodded.

"'Twas a kindness to cover me, my lady. I awoke warm, not shivering, as I would have in this evening air."

Surprised, Brielle inclined her head, acknowledging his gratitude.

"We will go to the boat now?"

"Boats," Adam said laconically. "Three of them. They are small, belonging to Channel fishermen. Since they believe it will be a rough, stormy night, they refuse to overburden the boats." His glance at her was tinged with sympathy. "I am sorry you must endure it, my lady. 'Twill be hard enough on men."

Brielle's chin went up. "I will endure it as well as any other. I do not fear the sea."

Buckling his heavy metal belt, Adam laughed, amused by her prickly pride. "Nor do I. But I am not looking forward to this night. Come then, my brave wife, and see what you think of the weather. We walk, for the horses are stabled."

Leaving the shabby inn at twilight, the party of some thirty or more men looked like a bevy of immense crows, winging their way home against the wind. They all wore cloaks as black as Brielle's, and clothes as common as any soldier, even the king. The wind caught at them, set the cloaks to flapping, and shook the trees overhead.

"A wild night," the king said, and laughed. "We'll have the Channel to ourselves in this weather." He clapped Sir Walter Manny on a broad shoulder and quickened the pace as if he were eager to meet the storm. "'Tis well you learned the tricks of sailing in strong wind, Manny. You will need them all tonight."

Manny's deep, calm voice rumbled in assent, the words flying away as the wind gusted. Brielle's heavy cloak billowed out, dragging at her, and she slowed, grabbing the edges and wrapping it tight. Adam's thick arm went around her shoulders and brought her along. The feel of how small and slight she was dissolved his anger and brought a sudden pity he couldn't deny. He bent and spoke to her.

"Do not be afraid, wife."

She glanced up, her face pale in the growing darkness, the amber eyes dark with foreboding. "I will not disgrace you, my lord. If I feel fear, I will not show it." She felt the arm squeeze approvingly and then fall away.

"There is one thing I must say, my lady. Now that you will be aboard a boat with strangers—for the fishermen are unknown to us—you will not address the king by rank. He travels as a common knight, and we are all named as Admiral Walter Manny's men, headed for Hainault."

"Oh! I see 'tis a wise move. But—Admiral?"

"'Tis Manny's true title: Admiral of the North. He is renowned as a boatman and has spent a great deal of time on the Channel, often ferrying the royal family across."

She nodded, and the wind whipped her dark hair across her face; she turned and swept it back into her hood, looking up at him again, drawing strength and confidence from him, for she realized now that she faced real danger. "I will remember, sire."

"Good."

They were at the docks, a series of wooden platforms stretching into the bay, soaked by the rough water that shot up through the spaces between the boards. Three cogs, small fishing boats with lateen sails furled tight against the wind, were tied there, rocking violently. The lanterns on their masts swung a near half-circle in the night, made blacker now by rain. A half-dozen men stood about, as if to watch the crazy nobleman and his men embark on a raging sea. Their eyes widened as they spotted the small woman in the midst of the armored knights, and a mutter of disapproval ran through their midst.

The knights ignored them. They had made their

plans, and now they separated into three groups and
headed for the cogs.

Three fishermen broke away from the crowd of
watchers and followed, their steps lagging, their faces
grim but determined. That large fool, Walter Manny,
had offered them enough gold to buy their craft and
services on a trip to Hell, and not one would cry off
and lose his pay.

Brielle stepped out briskly between the Black Prince
and Adam, but the first wave that spurted up between
the planks of the dock sprayed her feet with icy water.
She gasped, and Adam swung her up in his arms.

"That little wave was a warning," he said, and inclined his head forward to indicate the dock ahead.
"See? That lovely fountain that burst there in front of
us would have drenched you to your waist."

Brielle was silent, her arms around his shoulders.
He was quite right, and spending the rest of the night
in icy wet clothes did not appeal to her. When he
stepped agilely from the dock to the gunwale of the
rocking boat, she was sure they would both end up in
the bay. But big as he was, he balanced neatly and
stepped down safely onto the deck.

"Now," he said, putting her down, "you go into that
forepeak cabin there and stay in it until I call you out.
Use whatever you can find to make yourself comfortable."

"Yes, sire." She said it meekly but tarried to see how
many of the few men she knew had come to this boat.
Bracing herself, grasping a rope threaded through
rings that ran around the whole boat, she managed to
keep her feet while the cog rolled in the heavy seas.
Not all the faces were familiar, but the king had
climbed in, and the Black Prince behind him, and
among the strangers in the dark she recognized Sir
Eam of Flanders, Henry of Lancaster, and another she
had seen about the palace. Then she saw Adam's gaze

on her, his thick golden brows lowering and pulling
together, and she turned quickly to make her way
down a small step into the cabin.

A faint gleam from the swaying lantern above helped
her find a cot. It had a stout frame fastened to a bulk-
head and an odorous, filthy woollen pad. She sat on it,
her cloak clutched around her, half frightened yet intensely curious, alive to every shouted word, every order given. The men called back and forth to the other
boats to see that all had boarded and were settled.
Then came the call, echoing from one craft to another:
Away! Away!

Suddenly the sturdy cog in which Brielle rode was
free of restraint, the lines to the dock loosed. At once it
ceased its constant jerking, seesawing, plunging from
side to side, and caught the howling northwest wind.
To her it seemed that the little craft whirled away from
the dock gladly, its upthrust bow breasting the waves
with relief. There were hoarse shouts and curses, a
rattling and snapping as the sail was unfurled, and,
when the sail filled with wind and the lines were
drawn tight, it snapped again like the crack of a whip,
loud enough to be heard over the roaring storm. She
felt the boat leap forward and lean to the wind, heard
the dashing spray on the cabin top over her head. A
sudden excitement filled her. She was tired; she was
embarrassed at being caught out spying on her husband, and she couldn't deny she was at least a little
frightened. But still, she felt her spirits rising high.
They were heading for Calais in secrecy and danger,
and it was suddenly a fairy tale, a mad but brave ven-
ture, and she was part of it!

The three cogs bent a course south by southeast, passing the mouth of the Thames and staying out of the
rushing tide by sheltering as long as possible behind
the outthrust bulk of Sussex and Dover.

Manny left the steering to the fisherman on this leg of the trip. "We're making good time," he said to Adam. They stood near the opening of the makeshift cabin, and Brielle could hear his words, though not Adam's reply. In a moment Manny laughed, though without much humor. "Unless this wind has turned the current at Dover, which I pray to God it has done, we'll be fighting for yards, not miles, once we pass into the rage. That's the time to keep an eye on that new man of mine—he'll be heading for the gunwale."

Brielle listened, not understanding a word of it, and watched, her golden eyes shuttered by lowered lashes but missing little. The men stood, for the most part, with one hand on the rope that ran around the gun-wales and balanced as well as they could on the rocking deck. She looked for the king and found him by the flickering of light on his yellow beard. He stood calmly in the middle of the others. She studied him, for she knew that this time no one could see her staring, and she thought again how much Adam resembled his liege lord. But if she were to stay wed to Adam Dunbarton, she decided, she would pray constantly that he would be a more honest man and faithful mate than Edward of Windsor.

In another few moments Brielle yawned and felt behind herself to see if there was room enough to lie down on this rude bed. The sleep she'd had at the inn hadn't cured the weariness of riding hard and fast all through a long winter night, and the sway of the boat was making her drowsy. There was room, so she pulled up the hood of her cloak to protect her hair from touching the greasy pad and lay back. In minutes she was sound asleep, in spite of the rough sea and howling wind.

Some time later, she roused to a touch on her cheek and saw the shape of Adam's broad shoulders and bearded face leaning over her in the darkness.

"I am sorry to wake you," he said with an odd gentleness, "but we are approaching the worst of the seas. You might be thrown to the deck. Sit up and brace yourself."

She did as she was told. From where she sat she saw a bit of the night sky, the ballooning sail, and a fatter moon than she had seen the night before. With the clouds gone, the moon gave light enough to make out the faces of the men; most of them were still standing, still braced, still holding on with one hand.

Then all at once the bow of the boat where she sat rose up, rose up twice as high as it had before, and still rose, hesitated, and plunged. Down, down, and down, into the sea, and rushing water covered the top of the little cabin and fell like a curtain over the doorway. She gasped and struggled to her feet, only to be thrown into the cot again by the rising bow as it climbed another high wave. Fear clutched her throat, she clamped her jaws shut on a shriek of terror. But the next time, the bow climbed a lower wave and came back down without taking on water. And outside the door she heard Manny's shout of triumph.

"'Tis a tide rip, thank the good Christ! The high wind has turned the current at Dover!"

Brielle stood, her feet in cold, sloshing water, and grabbed the edge of the opening to look out. Past the huddled men, past Manny at the steering rudder, past the peaked stern of the cog, she saw the wild, foaming rip where the waves leaped high from opposing currents and fought each other. One of the other two cogs had come over the rip, off to the right, and as she watched she saw the third one come through, spray flying in the moonlight.

A hand came down and grasped her arm. "Come up," Adam said gently. "You're standing in water there."

She looked at him, her eyes a dark, burning gold

from excitement, her smile wide and brilliant. "At last," she said, her voice as exuberant as the wild waves, "I'm proud of my English blood! What courage and skill these Englishmen have to bring us through that mad race! But where is our king?"

Adam smiled wryly. "In the stern, his head over the rail, his stomach emptying itself. Edward suffers from *mal de mer* and always has."

Brielle shivered, as much from excitement as from her freezing feet. "Then he is even more courageous than the rest—he could stay safe and well at home and send his men."

Adam laughed. "Not Edward! He wouldn't miss the fight." He turned, leaned against the doorway of the cabin, and opened his heavy cloak. Drawing her slim back against him, he wrapped the cloak around them both, holding it closed with one arm and holding on to the boat with the other.

"'Twill be an easy run now, my lady, and a fast one, with both wind and current in our favor. Lean on me; with those cold, wet feet, you need my warmth."

Silent, she leaned. Her head fit neatly just beneath his bearded chin, the arm around her crossed just below her breasts. She could feel his heat even through the light chain mail that covered his chest, and the heat of his woollen-clad thighs and loins enveloped her whole lower body. Stiff at first, she gradually grew accustomed to the comfort and solid strength of his support and rested against him in perfect confidence.

Pushed by the high wind and riding the hard current, the three cogs came up to the port of Calais long before sunrise. Warping in at the side of the long stone piers, they looked up and saw men coming toward them hurriedly, carrying hooded lanterns. The man in the lead stopped at the side of the first boat and swung the lantern up to look into the men's faces.

"For Lord Aimery?"

Sir Manny frowned and stepped forward. " 'Lord' Aimery? Has the captain of the Calais galleys become a nobleman?"

The servant lowered the lantern. "No, but he demands the title from us because of his position in the castle. Are you the men he sent for to help him defend Calais?"

A rumble of laughter ran through the crowded deck. Releasing Brielle, Adam came close to the dock and looked up at the men with their lanterns, pushing back his hood.

"Enough. Take us to the castle."

One of the men on the dock gasped and stepped back, bowing awkwardly. "Your Majesty! Your pardon, sire."

Clambering to the dock, Manny laughed. "Your mistake, my man. But many have made it. 'Tis the king's own champion, Lord Adam Dunbarton of Northumbria. Come now, all of you. After this crossing we can do with a day of rest."

Moving forward with the others, Brielle glanced through the darkness toward the king and saw the glint of a grin inside a deep hood that hid his yellow beard. For this sortie, King Edward of England was hiding behind another identity. As well he might, she thought suddenly. If the French knew he was here with this tiny force of men, they'd bring an army to capture him for ransom. The English would scrape up every gold piece in all Britain to pay for their king, and that would end the war. How could Edward take such a foolhardy chance?

13

As they disembarked, Adam swung Brielle up into the center of the group and stood between her and the men from the Calais castle. In the darkness no note was made of a woman's presence, and as they were led to the postern gate of the town where flaring torches might have identified her as a woman, Brielle kept her hooded head down, her thick cloak around her skirts.

Until the guards at the gate were well behind them and the few people in the silent streets left off their staring, Brielle continued to stay well in the middle of the crowd of men. But as they entered the great stone hall, dim and smoky and lighted only by a roaring fire, she stepped aside from the others and sank down wearily on a bench near the huge fireplace. There she pushed back the hood that covered her head and watched a man who hurried down the stone stairs to greet the newcomers.

Walter Manny signed the group to stay back and went forward, maintaining the appearance of being the highest-ranking member of the force.

"Captain Aimery?"

Aimery, a thin, scurrying little man in a cut-velvet tunic too big and far too fine for a man of his station, clasped his hands together and bowed deeply.

"Sir Walter Manny! England has indeed sent me her finest. And Lord Dunbarton! *Mon Dieu!*" His face turned pale as he looked about at the company of huge men. "I—I asked only for a company of common soldiers to help me hold the castle."

Manny's voice, usually calm and pleasant, was icy

cold. "Calais is England's prize stronghold on the shores of France. We'd not leave its fate to your judgment, Aimery."

Aimery's white face broke out in patches of red. "I did my best, my lord, when the bribe was offered. As important and strong as Geoffrey de Charny is, I could hardly refuse to listen to him. Certainly with the small force the king has given me, I could not have withstood him if he besieged me."

Adam broke in. "At the moment," he said in a dangerously mild tone, "we need baths, beds, and food—not hasty excuses for cowardice."

Listening, Brielle was astounded at what Aimery had said. Even she knew Calais could have held out for far longer than it would have taken England to send help. This Aimery must be a coward indeed. Suddenly, the truth burst in her mind. She knew Geoffrey de Charny, the always-scheming Governor of Saint-Omer and a favorite of King Philip of France. No doubt he and Philip had got up a princely sum to bribe Aimery into surrendering Calais, and Aimery had agreed. Then, having played the traitor to King Edward and perhaps afraid of being found out, he'd turned about and played traitor to de Charny by informing the English king of the plot. She stared at the fussy little man with his weak, red-mottled face and felt a distant pity. One way or the other, the traitor Aimery had little time to live.

Later, in the barren tower room allotted to her, Brielle slept until full daylight. Then she rose and bathed herself, sending her clothes to be cleaned by the thin and shabby maid who attended her. The maid, an English bowman's woman, chattered with her eagerly, explaining that she'd been widowed when her man was killed during the fight for Calais.

The maid, who took it for granted that the Lady Brielle's luggage had been lost overboard in the storm, searched through the no-longer-used wardrobes left by the Montgomerys and found clean cotton shifts and a simple gown in crimson wool that had been made for the Montgomerys' young daughter. Brielle was grateful for it and for the stew of venison and rough herbs the maid also brought. In the light of a clear day, even the shabby room, warmed by the sunlight, took on a feeling of comfort. At least, she thought, it didn't roll and toss in icy waters.

Adam, who had told her on no account to leave the room, had also told her to sleep as much as she could during the day, adding that no one could sleep during a pitched battle. She tried but excitement kept her awake. Though barren, the high tower room was large, with two sets of windows. One gave her a view of the city itself and both sides of the Boulogne Gate, where travelers moved in and out. The opposite view allowed her to see the sun-bright, busy courtyard below. She leaned on the wide sill, looking. She could see the postern gate they had entered on their way in, though the piers and the water were on the other side of the tower and therefore out of her sight. Still, there was much to see and to remember, for the courtyard and the city's every tree and brick were familiar to her, and she was filled with nostalgia for the days here with Honoria and her father.

"My lady."

She whirled, dashing sentimental tears from her eyes, and gazed at Adam almost with alarm. She had heard nothing.

"My lord?"

Adam's face softened as he saw her tears, but he knew her well enough now not to mention them. "We've heard part of the plan," he said, "and we know when de Charny strikes. 'Twill be at midnight. The man fancies a good blow for France to usher in the new year of 1350. Perhaps he is superstitious and believes the hour will favor him."

Brielle came close, her eyes questioning. Since Adam had held her on the boat, keeping her safe and warm, she felt much more at ease with him.

"What do you believe, my lord?"

Adam's faint smile crinkled his bronzed cheeks. "I say he's put his faith in a false man and a soothsayer's lies."

She nodded. "And the king?"

"He feels the same. We have questioned the main force of English bowmen and guards, and none of them had been warned by Aimery to expect an attack. This smells more and more of high treason."

Brielle nodded again, her face pale. "I saw treason when Aimery showed fear at sight of Sir Manny and you. I was glad that our king was hidden in his cloak. Aimery would betray him to de Charny, I vow."

Adam's brows rose in surprise. "So you saw that, my lady? You notice much more than I would expect from a woman."

She shrugged and turned away, going back to her window. She thought it rude to expect less from a woman than a man, but she knew most men felt the same as Adam. In all her life, no man except her father had given her credit for a good mind. But she said nothing, not wanting another quarrel, and after a moment Adam followed her, standing behind her and peering out.

"If you are awake at midnight," he said, "you will have a good view of the beginning charade. Yon postern gate is well lit at night, and 'tis where Aimery intends to let de Charny's emissaries in, disguised as merchants. They are to bring him twenty thousand gold crowns and collect his young son as a hostage."

Brielle turned and stared up at him. "This Aimery would risk his own child?"

"Indeed. Until we came, I suspect, he had no fear for his son. Now he quakes in his boots."

"As well he might," Brielle said, "and for himself, also. It proves he's meant all along to surrender. Strange that he sent word to England."

"He hoped to cover his treachery. He asked the king only for a company of common soldiers he could command. So—with a few careful mistakes—he could lose the battle to France while appearing loyal to England."

Studying him, Brielle saw the glimmer of amusement in his stern face and understood it. Her lips curved in a smile, her eyes danced.

"And then our king sent his best! 'Tis no wonder at all that the man Aimery broke out in spots when he saw you and Sir Manny. Two more difficult men to lead into a major defeat, I cannot imagine."

Adam laughed out loud, surprised by her quick humor. "True. Both of us intend to see England win tonight, as we always have."

She nodded, her face resuming its serious expression. "You will sleep first, I trust. Have you eaten?"

"I go now to eat with the others, plan, and then sleep. There is much to be decided yet." He paused. "I regret I must order you to stay in this room until de Charny is repulsed and the city safe again."

She inclined her head, accepting the decision. She had expected nothing else. Watching him leave, hearing the latch click as he shut the heavy door, she felt happier than she had in days. She had not expected his visit, nor his friendliness. Thank heaven he was not a man who held a grievance long. In time, she thought, they might come to some sort of mutual trust—though never to love. That last, sudden thought saddened her, and she pushed it aside. Only a giddy fool would expect love in an arranged marriage.

Still standing at the window, she looked about the

room. There was a chair with a high back and a pillowed seat near the bed. She went to it and dragged it to the window. With no embroidery nor any book of verse or advice to read, the window and the activity below must serve to pass the hours.

Late that night, the same maid, whose name, she said, was Arabella, brought up a tray of food for Brielle—meat, bread, thick, fresh goat milk, and pasties full of dried fruit. Setting the tray on a table, the maid lighted a lamp and set up a spirit candle beside the bed to be lit later. Then she came to Brielle and stood between her and the window.

"They say, my lady, that there will be hard fighting here before dawn. Some stranger has reported that a company of French knights have taken the bridge at Nieulay and hold it against all comers. Next, they say, there will be men storming the Boulogne Gate of our city. Best you stay out of sight. There's nothing a soldier likes better to capture than a pretty young woman."

Brielle smiled and thanked her. Then she saw her to the door. Afterward, she put the lamp on the floor behind a screen, took the tray to the wide window ledge, and sat down in the darkness to watch while she ate.

She was through with the meal and had left the tray and dishes beside the door when she heard muffled voices below. Rushing to the courtyard window, she saw a dozen big men, familiar to her in their long black cloaks, emerge from the hall below and go quickly across to the huge keep of the castle, open the heavy wooden door, and slip inside. The last one to enter, pulling the door shut till it showed only a small crack, was Adam. She knew him by his size and by the quick glance he cast toward the window where she sat. She smiled, knowing he couldn't see in the gloom but glad he'd thought of her.

Moments later, Aimery left the hall, going toward

the postern gate. The lantern he carried flickered over
a fair-haired lad with him; a boy of perhaps ten years.
Brielle's throat tightened. How could a man offer his
son as surety for treason? What if the enemy—cheated
of his purpose—took his revenge on the child? Her
heart felt squeezed by a giant hand, thinking on it.
Drawing her thoughts together, she prayed for the
boy's safety as he and Aimery reached the gates.

"Open up," Aimery shouted to the guards. "There
are merchants outside with goods."

Men rushed to do his bidding. The gates swung in,
and with them came a half dozen armored men on
horseback, carrying bundles. The leader swung down
from his horse and took a weighty leathern bag from
the hands of a man behind him, turned, and offered it
to Aimery. As Aimery took it, the leader grasped the
young boy and lifted him into the empty saddle, motioning for one of the other dismounted men to lead
the horse with their hostage.

In her window, Brielle watched, nauseated. It was
done; gold had been traded for treachery, a child
traded for his father's safety. The men's stern faces
were lighted by the burning torches, and she recognized Sir Edward de Renty, a landowner with vineyards as great as those at the Le Fontin Château. De
Renty, she remembered, was known as an honorable
man.

There was a dead silence in the courtyard now, for
the castle's serfs and servants had let their voices die
away, so interested were they in what was going on.
Aimery turned from de Renty, went to an iron-doored
lockup in the walls of the old keep, tossed in the bag of
gold, and slammed the iron door.

"No time to count gold pieces you've probably
counted a time or two yourself, Lord de Renty."
Aimery's voice shook with either fear or excitement.
"Now let me show you where we plan to put the

wounded. Since this old keep is warm and dry, 'tis suitable for injured men." He stopped at the heavy door and flung it wide. From the darkness inside, King Edward's voice roared forth:

"Manny to the rescue!"

A dozen knights, swords flashing, faces disguised by darkness and black hoods, poured out beneath the fluttering pennon of three chevrons sable. They surrounded the Frenchmen, forcing them to drop their weapons and shields to the ground. Edward was laughing, but he kept his hood over his head. "Into the keep, you traitors!"

"'Tis not our men who are traitors," de Renty shouted. "We came to take back what the English stole!" He lifted an arm and pointed at Aimery. "There is your traitor, Englishmen! He swore on the sacrament of Jesus that he would help us. He has betrayed both England and France—and God!"

A man in the midst of the enemy suddenly drew a hidden knife and whirled toward the young boy cringing in de Renty's saddle. The youth screamed in terror, and Adam leaped forward, knocking the man to the ground and disarming him.

"Enough," he growled, "of war on children." He grasped Aimery's son and swung him off the tall horse. "Go, boy. Find your mother." The youth ran awkwardly toward the castle, sobbing with wild relief. Watching from above, Brielle saw Adam's tall body shimmering like magic through her own tears. She could nearly believe she saw the fabled hero light shining around his head.

At the door of the keep, Kiernan was cheerfully bowing the French noblemen into the gloomy interior. "Fear not, my lords, there are comfortable cots and food and water waiting for you—enough to last you until the battle ends."

Stung, de Renty sneered. "And then we'll be freed by

our own men! You fooled me with your lying tongues,
but de Charny will prove a different foe." He turned,
his angry face steel hard, staring at Adam in the dim
light. "I thought I heard the voice of Edward of Windsor, and I see him now. Once de Charny knows the
English king is here, he'll bring an army and break
down the walls to take him captive."

Above them, listening to every word, Brielle drew in
her breath. Then into the silence came Kiernan's quick
laugh, light and merry. He reached up and pulled back
Adam's hood, exposing his face and golden hair to the
light of a lantern.

"If this be the King of England, de Renty, he has
grown an inch or so and regained his youth!"

De Renty retorted with embarrassed fury. "I see
that. However, he undoubtedly has the same blood.
Another of Edward II's bastards, I vow."

Their voices were loud, the words distinct in the
frightened silence of the courtyard. Above them,
Brielle gasped as Adam made an involuntary movement toward the Frenchman, his hand going to his
sheathed sword. She could almost feel his tensing
muscles, his rising rage. Finally his hand fell away
from the jeweled handle and clenched at his side.

"When you are armed and not my prisoner, de
Renty, you will beg for pardon or answer with blood.
Lock them up!"

Behind Brielle, the door of her room creaked open
and the excited face of the scrawny maid peeked in.
"My lady! Go to the other window and look at the
Frenchmen gathered at the city gate, waiting to be let
in!"

Brielle ran across the room and threw open the
shutters she had closed against a cold wind. With a
muffled squeal of excitement, Arabella came pelting after her to watch. There, close together outside the Boulogne Gate, scores of steel helmets glittered in the fitful

light of torches; suits of mail and the steel tips of
lances gleamed. As Brielle searched the darkness, she
realized the French knights were all on foot, their
lances shortened for close infighting.

A moment later she remembered and realized why
they'd left their horses behind. The Calais pale, that
section of land set aside for the main gates, was a hellish trap for horses. Swampy along the edges, full of
holes, it caused more sprains and broken legs than any
other battlefield in France. Would the English know
that? When they won Calais, Edward had attacked
from the sea and fought in daylight hours. Her heart
contracted, squeezed by an awful fear. She whirled to
the maid.

"Run, Arabella! Find the Englishmen and warn
them of the treacherous bogs that will break their
horses' legs!"

The maid gasped and was gone like a hare for cover,
her skirt held high so as not to trip on the stair. She
was back in a quarter hour, panting but smiling.

"The Englishman I found was glad of the news and
will tell the others. He said"—she hesitated and gig-
gled—"he said to tell Lady Dunbarton she'd make a
true Englishwoman yet."

Brielle was startled and a trifle angry. "Who said
that? What did he look like?"

"Handsome, my lady. Enough like your husband to
be his older brother, but much more overbearing in his
manner."

The king. Brielle turned away to hide shocked
amusement. She could imagine Edward's thoughts
when a chambermaid grabbed him close and whispered in his ear. 'Twould take a supreme act of will to
keep him from ordering her dragged off to a dungeon!
But 'twas good. The king would remember it.

"What else did you hear?"

The maid shrugged. "Only that a party was sent off

to take back the bridge at Nieulay, and that the attack here would come at midnight. 'Tis another half hour yet."

"Not long." Brielle shut the windows again, shuddering from either cold or fright, thinking perhaps 'twas both. She paced the long room, peering into the courtyard again, seeing the bowmen filling their quivers with arrows and silently mounting to the towers and walls. The longbows gave her confidence, but still the men would need more light to aim well—and, *mon Dieu*, there were all those armed and bloodthirsty men outside, just waiting to kill!

'Twas past midnight when a blare of trumpets beyond the wall startled Brielle up from her chair, and an answering cry came from inside: *For God and England!* Her heart hammering, she rushed to the windows again, though all she could see was masses moving, like storm waves in a dark sea, and all she could hear was hoarse shouts and rallying cries.

The French drove hard against the gates with battering rams, hoping for entrance, but the English knights mounted the French horses inside the wall and rushed out the opening sally ports on either side, forming a pincer move toward the center. Swords drawn, they drove off the Frenchmen trying to smash in the doors.

Brielle gasped and ran across the room to throw open the other windows and peer down at the scene outside the walls. But the English had, after all, listened to her warning, for after the first hard attack they dismounted to fight on the ground, giving and taking tremendous blows. The noise of clanging steel and hoarse cries made pandemonium in the cold night air. Shivering, her hands over her ears, she watched and tried to recognize Adam by his size, by the occasional glint of yellow beard. . . .

"I cannot *see*," Brielle mourned as Arabella came

flying in again and to the windows. "I can only hear."
And as they stood together and listened, the well-
known war cry of the English king came roaring
through the air:

"Ha! Saint Edward!" *Clang!* "Ha! Saint George!"
Clang!

"Oh, no," Brielle whispered. With every blow of his
broadsword, Edward of Windsor called upon his saints
to witness the strength they had given him and how
well he used it.

Then an answering roar came from the man who led
the French, Geoffrey de Charny: "'Tis the English
king's war cry!" he yelled. "He's here! Capture him!"
The French flung themselves toward the sound, yelling
hoarsely, pressing hard.

Brielle groaned. Her face in her hands, she sank into
a chair. "Listen to our king! Such careful planning to
hide his presence, and now in his excitement he shouts
the secret to the world! God help the men who must
protect Edward!" She meant it for all, but she thought
of Adam.

Arabella crossed herself. "Our *king*? He's here?"

Brielle nodded sadly. "'Twas he you gave my message to."

"That man was the king? Oh, Jesus save me! May
sweet Mary and all the saints bless him and hide him
from the French," Arabella babbled, "an' then hide me
from him! Oh, m'lady, I grabbed the king by the seat of
his chausses and spoke as to a common soldier! 'Tis
likely he'll have me beheaded!"

Brielle held in an hysterical laugh. "He will not
blame you, I promise. Pray for him now and for England."

Total confusion reigned below; the cries of the
wounded and shouted curses wove together in a rising
and falling howl. Some of the French broke away and
rushed in another direction, disappearing in the black

night; in a few minutes a new contingent ran toward the walls again. From every quarter the king's war cry sang out—in varying English voices. The night went on, the cries and shouts never diminishing. Finally, Brielle shut the windows again and turned to Arabella. "We must gather supplies now. No matter who wins, there will be wounds to tend and bodies to ready for the grave. We will be needed."

14

In the first pale light of a winter dawn, the raging battle was resolved. The English bowmen's eyes narrowed on their targets at last and ended the squabble with a shower of yard-long arrows, powerful enough to penetrate mail. Once more the powerful six-foot bows and the men who could pull them had won a battle for the English.

Weary and injured Frenchmen dropped their weapons and cried peace. Peasants with carts came to gather the dead, and all the French who could walk were sent to the dungeons. The badly wounded— French or English—were brought into the great hall and laid on the long tables for bandaging and setting bones.

Brielle had seen a bloodstained but triumphant Adam come into the courtyard before she had left her room, and she had called down and waved to him. He had swept off his helmet and bowed, white teeth shining in his golden beard. He had looked wonderful, like the hero he was. She had felt her heart lift high, and a quick warmth flood through her. Life was sweet.

Then she'd seen Geoffrey de Charny being led to the dungeons in company with many of his knights. She was well acquainted with the Chevalier de Charny; he'd come often to Le Fontin Château and in fact had once offered for her hand. Her father had been diplomatic in his answer, but it had still been no. De Charny was known for his sneaking ways, and her father had disliked him. It was while she was having these thoughts that she realized that since the danger was over, the enemy vanquished, Adam would undoubtedly allow her to leave her room. She turned away from the window and faced Arabella.

"Come. We will go down and help with the wounded. I know a little from binding the wounds of the château's vineyard workers; I am sure you know much more from battlefields."

Arabella was more than willing. She provided them both with full-length aprons, with cloths to wind around their hair, with scissors and soft white rags, with a box of herbs and potions kept there at the castle for the injured. Then they went down and into the great hall. The noise of shrieks and groans was indescribable. Blood ran from the tabletops to the stone floor as men bled and died of the bleeding. At first Brielle wanted to turn and run, to shut out the horrid noises, the stench of blood and entrails, the hovering death. But a hot flood of anger and pity stiffened her spine. These men had fought for England and for France; they were now fighting for their lives. 'Twas only right for the women to help them. She reached out and grasped a man screaming with pain and held him, muffling his gasping cries against her shoulder.

"Cleanse his wounds and bind them up," she said to Arabella, "before all his life blood leaks out. He is already weak; I can hold him."

Together they moved around the room, finding the ones they could help. When the less injured men saw what they did, they helped, holding the men down while the women washed and sewed and bandaged.

Adam, who was on the battlefield identifying the French dead, heard what his wife was doing and came to see for himself. He came in frowning. He was used to the grisly aftermath of war, but for a young delicate woman to be exposed to such sights and sounds seemed wrong to him. He expected to find her either crying or fainting, nothing less. Instead, she was leaning over a table, carefully cleaning a gaping wound while an already-bandaged knight held down the injured man.

Adam stood quietly and watched her pack the wound with clean rags and bind it tight. Then, as she moved to another, he touched her arm. She turned quickly, looking up at him.

"My lord! Are you wounded?"

He looked into her amber eyes, burning with purpose in a white face. "Only a scratch or two, already tended. This is too hard for you, Brielle. Let the others do it. See, the men who have experience in such matters are coming in—"

"Yes, I do see. And they are finding men alive who'd be dead if they'd waited for them. Arabella and I will keep on while we're needed."

He saw determination and a surprising strength behind it. "Then I will help you. I have no duty elsewhere."

Hours later, as the last of the moaning wounded were carried on litters to the old keep where there were cots and warmth, Brielle motioned to Arabella.

"Come. We must bathe and dress. My lord tells me the king will honor the bravest of his enemies with a dinner tonight." Her eyes met Arabella's with a gleam of pure amusement. "Who but Edward III would do that? I hear he's anxious to honor Sir Eustace de Ribemont of Picardy, whose mighty blows knocked our king to his knees twice last night."

Arabella laughed out loud. "I'll offer to help with the serving, m'lady, so I may see our king do that."

A little the worse for salt stains and grime from the fishing boat, the silk and velvet gown Brielle wore when she crossed the Channel had been sponged and steamed. In the firelight and the glow from a few candleholders on the tables, the gown looked almost new. After all, she thought, smoothing the velvet, it hardly mattered what she wore. Only women were interested in other women's clothes, and tonight there were no other women. Aimery's "wife" was no more than a common bawd, and no other noble had brought his lady to a battle.

King Edward was at his Arthurian best during this victory feast. All was chivalry at its finest. By his order, the Black Prince and young members of the Garter served the first course to the captives before joining the king at the high table. And then, after the wine and sweetmeats, the king himself moved down amongst his guests. He had no words for de Charny, whose wounds had been tended by his own physicians, but when he came to Sir Eustace de Ribemont, Edward took off the pearl chaplet he wore on his head and bowed, presenting it to Sir Eustace.

"Show it to the ladies, de Ribemont, and tell them how you came by it. Nor must you pay ransom, as these other French nobles must do, though I bested you in the end. Your skill and bravery in the field won both my favor and your freedom."

The king also rewarded Sir Walter Manny, giving him land near Bordeaux and in Scotland; Adam, who owned more than enough land, was given a generous annuity. All the knights were honored, and toasts drunk till near dawn.

Brielle's eyes were drooping with weariness as Adam took her to her room. Still, she turned at the door and asked him if he'd come in. After all, it was an opportunity. . . .

"You need sleep, my lady, not company."

She couldn't deny that. "'Tis over, then, and the battle won. Must we return to England in those fishing boats?"

Adam smiled. "No secrecy is needed this time. But

. . . are you so anxious to leave France? I thought to see your château again and make arrangements for the vineyard workers before spring arrives. A good time, now, with the Black Death frozen out."

Brielle gasped, thrilled. "Could we?" A new thought —a desperate measure to gain what she wanted— sprang full-blown into her mind. She grasped his hand with both of hers. "What a wonderful thing to do!"

He smiled. "'Tis done, then. We leave tomorrow for Picardy. We can sail to England when we please."

Calais, full of horror and pain when they had traveled through in the fall, was lovely now, the old stone buildings touched by the winter sun. A thick fall of snow covered the narrow streets, hiding every flaw and muffling the sound of the horses' hooves. Kiernan Comyn and several of the young knights without sponsors rode with Adam to see the French countryside. For female companionship, Brielle took Arabella, whose thin cheeks burned crimson with the wild hope of gaining steady employment with this kind young noblewoman.

They left early, and by noon they were on Le Fontin land, under a brilliant blue sky. Brielle gestured off to the south.

"The largest of the vineyards is just over that rolling hill, my lord. Perhaps you'd like to see it."

"I would." Huge in his trappings of red velvet and wool, his thick dark cloak and hood, he looked back to the others, throwing up an arm to signal a turn to the right. Jostling, blowing out clouds of steam, the still-fresh and playful horses plunged from the road and into deeper snow, leaping like deer until they found the upward slope above the drifts. At the top of the rolling hill Adam drew up his horse, and the others followed suit, eyes widening at the snowy fields stretching away into the distance. Row after row of pruned vines followed the contours of the land, crooked dark sticks frosted with snow, thin skeletons promising to live again next spring and bring rich harvest in the fall. Adam drew in his breath, knowing he stared at a fortune in wine.

"How many plantings on the estate, my lady?"

"Eight, all told. No other as big as this, but . . . none are small. Claude Poirtre, our chief in both vineyard and winecellars, can tell you what you need to know. He knows the land, the vines—and the wines." Joyous amber eyes peered at Adam over the soft wool scarf wrapped to cover her nose and mouth from the cold. "Claude's wife, Anne, does the cooking for the vineyard workers—and will for us, while we are here. Oh, but I am looking forward to seeing my home again!"

His head turned, his calm blue gaze dropping down from his towering height to the small woman. "This is your childhood home, wife. Your true home you have yet to see. 'Tis in Northumbria."

She smiled and was glad her scarf hid it. So he was more possessive of her now than he had been before. An encouraging sign. His trust in her was growing. Now, if only her pride could live through the plan she made. . . .

When they came within sight of the old Le Fontin Château, one of the elderly kitchen maids was sweeping drifted snow from the steps that led up to the front entrance. Left there all night in this weather, the snow would turn to uneven ice and someone might slip and fall. Since it might be she, the maid took on the task willingly.

Shaking her straw broom to rid it of the sticky snow, the maid's eyes were caught by the approaching train. She squinted into the glare for a moment, then whirled and ran up the steps into the hall, screaming with joy and excitement.

Brielle, who was wiping her eyes, saw nothing but the beautifully carved towers and the sloping wings of rooms on either side, like welcoming arms. When the courtyard gates swung open, it seemed to her that the château itself welcomed her in.

They were all waiting there; the Poirtre family— Claude and Anne, their four grown sons, their two young daughters. The stable boys, the master of the horses, the woodcutters. There was the elderly maid, Geneva, still crying a little, and the scullery maids, two beaming village girls. Brielle flung herself from her saddle, laughing, hugged the old ones and shook hands with the new. Then, after the horses were led to stalls, they made their way into the kitchens, where everyone gathered to keep warm. Anne Poirtre's hurried instructions sent the two young maids running to make up beds, roused young boys from before a fire in the kitchen to bring in wood for the great hall and the small fireplaces in the bedrooms on the second floor. In the middle of the preparations, vineyard workers brought in two fat and squealing pigs, along with a double brace of flailing, squawking chickens, and asked Anne if she needed more.

"A banquet," Kiernan said, and laughed. "Reminds me of our first visit, Adam. The food was good."

But the squawking had been louder then, Brielle thought, remembering her own furious, screeching voice. She felt her face grow hot. Was that truly only two and a half months ago? It seemed a year. . . .

Anne Poirtre excused herself to begin the cooking, and Brielle turned to Adam.

"I'll see to the rooms, sire. Tomorrow you have time enough to talk to Claude about the grapes. Oh, and wine—will you bring wine from the cellars, Claude? You'll know the best." She was gone into the great hall and on to the wide stairs, Arabella panting at her heels.

"We will make up the solar for Lord Dunbarton," Brielle said, taking sheets from a press in the upper hall, "and a nearby smaller room for me. Those young maids can take care of the others. Oh, they'll work long hours satisfying all those men. They'll all want baths and their clothes cleaned, and . . ."

Arabella filled in the pause. "My lady, they seem very pleased to have the men here. You'll hear giggling in the corners, believe me." She laughed. "And likely babies crying nine months hence."

And one of them may be mine. Brielle smiled and was silent. Perhaps Arabella's light remark was a portent of success.

15

$\mathfrak{A}$nne Poirtre was determined to set a grand table for Lord and Lady Dunbarton. Ever since Brielle Le Fontin had married the English lord, Anne had dreamed of the time when Count Henri's daughter would return to her homeplace, perhaps to set up a permanent ménage for seasons in Picardy. Of a certainty, Anne told herself, she herself would be chosen as chatelaine, now that Honoria Woolford was living in England.

By late afternoon, the great hall had been swept and garnished, strewn with sweet-smelling rushes saved for that purpose, lighted by tapers and the glow of the center fire. The high table was draped with the whitest of linen and set with the finest of silverware and dishes. As for the food, the two suckling pigs were roasted to a golden brown, and the meat of the chickens simmered in a wine sauce thickened with cream. Oatcakes, cheese, and pasties filled with preserved fruits were served with the meats, and a cask of chilled wine set on a sideboard kept the goblets filled.

Once seated and served, the young knights fell to. Conversation came to a standstill as they ate. Brielle was pleasantly surprised by Anne Poirtre's skill. The subtle flavors of Picardy had never been better. Across from her, Kiernan Comyn lifted his filled goblet to toast the cook. "You have an artist in your kitchen, Lady Brielle."

Adam had eaten little and said nothing. He had been to his luxurious room and had been assisted in a bath by one of the older maids, and after she left, he'd found

only his own belongings put away in the wardrobe.
He'd been sure Brielle would relent and join him if he
brought her here. He knew now he'd been wrong to
refuse her offer to receive him in her room at Windsor
Castle, but he couldn't go begging her favor. Ever
since then, she seemed to have the pride of the Devil
himself. If he didn't take matters into his own hands,
he might well wait forever. Moodily, he ate little but
drank much wine, his goblet filled and refilled. When
Kiernan made his toast, Adam frowned. Then he held
out the goblet to be filled again by one of the young
maids. When it was full, he rose to his feet, wavering,
and held it high.

"To my *wife*, the Lady Brielle Dunbarton!"

Brielle was amazed as she noted his drunkenness.
Still, she was pleased by the honor. She smiled around
at the young knights as they leaped to their feet and
raised their glasses to her.

"Thank you," she said, for once humble. "Thank you
very much. But I believe Sir Kiernan had the right of
it. 'Tis Anne Poirtre who deserves the praise. Sit down,
gentlemen. There is brandy to end the meal. I'll leave
you to enjoy it."

She left, going to the kitchens to give Anne her
praise, and then to climb the narrow back stairs that
led up to the bedrooms. Her skirts rustled as she
moved, and the silk she wore felt lovely against her
skin. She had almost forgotten the clothes she had left
here. This primrose satin with taffeta silk layers beneath the skirt was the most becoming gown she had
owned before going to England. The low-cut neckline
was edged with pearls that flattered her ivory skin and
the shining dark hair that flowed down her back. She
had left off her wimple and bound her hair with the
simple gold filet she always wore. She knew she looked
her best; she hoped Adam approved. His eyes on her
had seemed almost angrily possessive.

In the small bedroom off the solar she took off her gown and put on a *chemise de nuit*, also of silk, and a wool robe. Sitting before the small, flickering fire, she brushed her hair slowly, going over the plan she'd decided on. She intended to stay awake and listen until she heard Adam enter the solar to go to bed. Then, when the rest of the house was silent and no one was in the halls, she would take her pride in her hands and offer herself to him, as he had insisted.

When she came to that point in thinking out the plan, she became breathless. It would take courage and a great deal of poise to say to Adam what she had to say. But if she said it well, she might possibly save her pride.

She went over and over the words, trying to memorize them. "My lord," she whispered, practicing, "being here in my own home has made me more aware of my duties. This land, these fertile fields, and the workers dependent on them have shown me I am failing in my life's purpose. My father counted on me to pass along his blood and his estate to an heir. It is my duty to do so. So I've come to you, as you told me I must, to begin—uh . . . I mean, to . . ." Frowning, she let the whisper die away. The man wouldn't need to be told what she meant. She might not know all there was to know about mating, but surely he did. . . .

An hour passed. Feet stumbled up the stairs, trod along the hall. Laughter broke out and was quickly stilled. More feet, and Kiernan's soft Irish voice coaxing some giggling girl. Why hadn't she realized there would be footsteps other than Adam's? She couldn't be sure he'd even passed her door, for the sounds were blurred and continuing. She must wait, then, till all was quiet.

Later, dozing in her chair, Brielle awoke with a start. The small candle she'd lighted was guttering in its holder, so she knew it was very late. She rose and got another candle, lighting it from the old one, and carrying the small flame, she made her way out and to the door of the solar, slipping through and closing it silently behind her.

Heart pounding, she went soundlessly across the thick Saracen rug to the enormous bed and the huge figure sprawled in it. The faint light she carried was the only illumination, for Adam had not lit the tall spirit candle. She lit it now with a shaking hand, wondering if he'd be angry when she woke him. Leaning down, her fascinated gaze on his bearded face, she whispered his name.

A quarter hour later, she knew that the smooth Le Fontin wine had conquered Adam Dunbarton. She had kept asking him to wake, she had stroked his hair and his bearded cheek, and the most she had gotten as a response was a humming sound of pleasure deep in his chest. She should, she thought, go back to her room and sleep, for tomorrow would be a busy day. But staring down at his strong face, smoothed by sleep and half smiling, she told herself he might awaken later, and she could talk to him then. After tomorrow, they'd be going back to Calais and back to England. The same strain would be between them, and her chance gone.

Shivering in the chill air, she made up her mind. She moved around to the other side of the bed, stripped off her robe, and climbed in, inching over to the warmth of his big body, pulling a pillow along. The comfort was irresistible. She snugged herself close and shut her eyes.

Brielle dreamed that after a long, cold time and much sorrow, she was rested and warm. She was lying in the soft valley behind the Le Fontin Château, and the leaves of the gnarled apple trees brushed against her skin, stroking and soothing her like fingers, bringing a

wonderfully pleasant feeling that sang in her blood
and ached with an exquisite tension in her breasts.

Caught in the dream, she wanted to stay. When her
eyes tried to open, she kept them shut; when she felt a
moan of pleasure rising in her chest, she kept it silent.
Nothing must be allowed to enter this dream, to break
this spell. . . .

Adam's big hands cupped her head. Warm, and gentle in spite of his great strength, they held her still
while his soft beard brushed her face, while his mouth
touched hers and his tongue licked her lips apart. And
in her dream Brielle opened her mouth to him. Then
she put her arms around his strong neck and opened
her thighs, dreaming that they were making love at
last, that soon she'd know whether he had a great affection for her—except—except he was *hurting* her!
Her eyes flew open and blinked up at the bearded face,
hard and flushed with passion, the eyes a hot midnight
blue.

She stared, frightened and bewildered. Her arms left
his neck, her hands pushed at his heavy shoulders.
"No! Oh, no, no! Stop at once! You're hurting me!"

"Shh," Adam whispered hoarsely. "'Twill soon be
over." His mouth covered hers, his beard soft and
musky on her face, his heat burning her breasts, her
belly, her tender thighs.

She arched and tried to squirm away from him,
from his crushing weight, from the scalding pressure
against her most vulnerable spot. Her struggles only
seemed to inflame him, to make him increase his pressure. His mouth muffled her cry as she felt the first,
searing tear of her virginal barrier. She broke away
and dragged air into her throat.

"Stop, for God's sake—" Tears squeezed out from
her tightly shut lids, and she felt his hot tongue sweep
her cheeks and lap them up, as if the tears excited him.

"I will not," he said hoarsely. "I must go on. The pain will not last. Bear it bravely."

She drew in her breath, hearing the animal growl in his deep voice, feeling the savage unleashed passion in his powerful body. He meant that. He knew well he was hurting her, and he would not stop. She gritted her teeth and reached for her pride. Damn him to Hades! She would not beg. She would bear the pain. . . . Tears sprang to her eyes again and seeped out as he increased the pressure, making her whole body tremble with tension. He paused, panting, staring down at her.

"You hurt yourself, wife, by fighting me. 'Twill be easier for you if you give a little."

She was silent. But the hot golden eyes that came up to him spoke for her, saying back to him what he had said to her.

I will not.

Adam held the rebellious gaze while his own eyes darkened even more, while his jaw set hard, rippling beneath the shaggy beard. Then he arched his back and took her challenge. He used his strength at last, driving his loins against her, penetrating, filling her with searing fire. He let out his breath in a great gust of relief and pleasure and flexed his hard buttocks, burying himself deeper.

Brielle came back from the jagged edge of pain, tasting blood from a bitten lip, dizzied by the spiraling stars that had pierced the darkness of her closed eyelids. The pressure was gone, the sharp pain subsiding, stinging but bearable. She felt him moving within her, huge and hard, felt her traitorous flesh accommodating him, giving way, fitting around him. Her wet eyes opened, seeing the light of a rosy dawn striking through the silk curtains and turning Adam's wild mass of hair and beard into a red-gold glory. He smiled down at her, bringing the pace of the mating to a slow and sensual rite, his face soft now with heat and desire.

"It's done," he said, and slid his hands beneath her. "You'll soon forget the pain. Move with me, now . . . like this." He rocked her with him, thrusting gently, looking into her eyes. "You'll like it once you learn a little, I promise. Come, make me a warm welcome, my lady."

She shut her eyes against the scorching passion and possession in his. Damn him! Damn all selfish men! She would *not* like it! But deep inside she sensed an insidious warmth, a tingling glow that made her catch her breath. She stiffened, willing the feeling away. He had tricked her. He had taken advantage of her desire to be alone with him, to talk to him, and had caught her in her sleep! And if Honoria spoke true and a man who had affection for his wife was gentle to her, it followed that Adam cared nothing for his! He'd hurt her, and he refused to stop hurting her, just for his own pleasure. She gritted her teeth as the warmth grew, as the temptation to move with him nearly overcame her.

"Brielle"—Adam's deep voice shook—"Brielle . . . my little love . . . come up to me."

She steeled herself, keeping her eyes shut, pressing herself flat on the bed, trying to lie absolutely still, though the memory of his passion-flushed face and the scent of him were making her feel half out of her mind, and inside her the swelling flesh he was stroking clasped him and pulsated with pleasure. . . .

"Come up, my love, my darling . . ."

Quivering, breathing fast, she clamped her teeth together and refused to move. Oh, she knew what to do. She had heard the stories from Leone, the jokes about passionate women that the vineyard workers told. And there had been nights full of erotic dreams and fancies for these last two months while she had waited for

Adam to come to her. She knew, but she was angry now. Never, she thought, *never* will I give in to him. . . . Then Adam's hands moved frantically beneath her hips and lifted her high. His first full thrust broke through her resolve, sent her past thought, past vengeance, into rolling, beating, thrumming sensation. She heard herself moan, felt her arms tighten around him, her legs wrap his muscular flanks. She was swinging with him, her body hot and undulating, her eyes closed in ecstasy. Climaxing, Adam felt her shudder and her flesh lock around him. They cried out together, sank into the rumpled bed, and let the storm waves roll over them.

Later, rising to call a maid and ask for an ewer of water, Adam lifted the curtain of silky chestnut hair that hid Brielle's face and found her cheeks wet. Puzzled, he stared. He knew she'd had her pleasure.

"Tears, my lady?"

She sat up, tossing back her hair, and looking at him. He looked . . . triumphant. He'd won, and he knew it. She hadn't had the chance to tell him why she was giving in and save what little pride she could. She hated the weakness of her body. Whatever he wanted from her now—be it tears or kisses—she was bound he'd not have it. She spoke coldly.

"'Tis nothing, sire. A moment of weakness, only. Hadn't we best be starting our day?"

There was much in his heart but nothing that came easily to his tongue. He nodded and turned away, going to the door to call the maid. 'Twould only be insulting to tell her how pleased he'd been to discover her virginity, to realize she hadn't lied to him. And to find that under all that cold pride lay a warmly passionate bedmate. All in all, he was content at last with his wife and felt—had always felt—that talk was unnecessary as long as everyone was satisfied.

* * *

The day went well. The weather had moderated; the sun shone brightly. Claude Poirtre proved as well versed in the business of the vineyards as his wife was in cooking. He took both Adam and Brielle on a tour of the cellars and on a snowy ride to the farther ends of the estate, where he and his workers had begun a new planting of *vin noir* grapes during the fall.

Adam, whose opinion of the Le Fontin estate had been formed in adverse circumstances, was pleased and impressed by Poirtre's good management.

"Raise his salary," he told Brielle later, as they rode back toward the stables. "He's too good to lose."

"You do it, then. You are the sire, my lord." Her tone was careless, even haughty. Adam studied the calm ivory face, the lowered lashes that hid the hazel eyes, the stubborn set of the chin. She had been either silent or haughty the day long, as if they had quarreled. His own expression hardened.

"I am the sire, indeed, and I gave you an order."

Her eyes met his, surprised, and flicked away angrily, her lips thinning into a straight line. She kicked her young mare into a gallop and left him, heading for the château. Adam watched her go and smiled grimly, thinking of the night ahead. In time, he thought, she'll sweeten. First he must conquer that pride.

They were to leave in the morning for Calais and the trip back to England. Again the dinner was superb, the wines better than any Adam knew. But this evening he drank sparingly, though he ordered two casks of the best wine to add to their luggage for the trip to England.

Again Brielle left the table to the men when the brandy was served. Upstairs, she went into her own room and told Arabella to arrange for a hot bath, pleading aching legs from the day-long ride around the vineyards. Then she sat down to wait. After a time, she heard the two young maids, awkward and giggling,

dragging the large wooden tub up the stairs and along
the hall. She rose and opened the door for them, but
they only smiled and curtseyed and dragged it on,
heading for the solar. Following along behind them,
Adam looked at her and grinned.

"We'll share it, my lady, once they fill it."

She stepped back and shut the door in his face.
Then, trembling with rage, listening to his soft laugh
and departing footsteps, she latched it and sat down,
fuming. 'Twas *her* home, not his. Her orders should be
obeyed by her maids. She'd turn those girls out to
work in the vineyards instead of the house!

Well, no, she wouldn't. She understood their awe of
Adam Dunbarton, huge and foreign and yet the sire
here, by virtue of her father's choice. Her temper
turned to grim acceptance as she listened to their hurrying footsteps going back and forth with the pails of
water to fill the big tub. So it was no different here
from England. Adam was still her master. Frowning,
she thought how foolish she had been to think she
would make the decisions about the château, its people, and its wine. Or even herself. She rose quietly and
fetched from her wardrobe her nightdress and robe,
some drying linens, and a scoop of soft soap, which
she placed in a bowl. Then she donned an apron and
unlatched the door, going out and toward the solar.
There had to be ways to better her lot, but childish
defiance was not one of them.

The maids had placed the tub in the center of the
solar and were pouring in the last of the pails of hot
water. When Brielle came in, they bent a knee and
scurried out, taking the pails with them, shutting the
door. Adam, standing near the blazing fire, looked
around and saw the things she brought and the apron
over her gown. His hard face softened into a smile as
she nodded to him.

"I will bathe you now, sire."

"First I will bathe you. I am more used to cold water."

She started to answer and thought better of it. It was chivalrous indeed, and he was undoubtedly right. She was not in the least used to cold water. She put the bowl of soap down beside the tub, hung the drying linens on a chair, and went across the shadowy big room to the wardrobe, turning her back to take off her clothes. Methodically, she began with the gold filet from her hair, the embroidered slippers from her feet.

He watched her, though it was hard to see clearly in the shadowy light from the fire. His hands knew every curve of her body, but his eyes had yet to learn them. She had worn again the satin gown with the taffeta layers beneath, and it took some time to unfasten and drop each layer. Gathering them up, she put them over a chair. Then, holding her voluminous woolly chemise clutched to her breasts, so that it covered her from shoulder to ankle, she came back to the side of the tub, shivering. Adam eyed the chemise curiously.

"We have enough drying cloths here."

"This is my nightdress, sire."

"Ah? Then lay it over that stool where the fire will warm it, and get in the tub."

She did as she was told. He watched her walk away from him, her wealth of dark chestnut hair covering her shoulders and hanging halfway down her bare back, nearly black in the shadows. Still, she was outlined by the fireglow, and he noted her tiny waist, the feminine flare of rounded hips and firm buttocks, the surprising length of her legs. Then, as she laid the gown on the stool and turned to come back, he let out his held breath in soundless appreciation. Clothes, no matter how becoming, could not add to this beauty. She was one of the rare ones, a woman without physical flaw, a woman proportioned by angels, kissed by Fate. Firelight gleamed on skin like ivory satin, glowed

on the curves of small, rounded breasts, ruby-tipped;
sheened the satin texture of her belly and touched off
lustrous light in the midnight-dark curls between
curved thighs. Small, he thought, yes, very small. But
perfect in every line; in her coloring, in the texture of
hair and skin. Like a work of art, like a lovely jewel
beyond price. And his. His *wife*. His loins tightened as
he reached for her hand to steady her as she stepped
into the tub.

"You are very beautiful," he said, and was surprised
at the hoarseness in his voice.

Brielle sat down, careful not to splash water out,
and wrinkled her brow. He seemed to be courting her
at last, now that he'd taken her by trickery and brute
strength. Perhaps, she thought, he'd realized that he
hadn't been fair.

"You flatter me," she began sweetly, and stopped,
spluttering as he poured a pitcher of warm water over
her head. She saw him reach for the soap and closed
her eyes.

"I do not flatter you," Adam said, still with wonder
in his voice. "I am very pleased. Every man wishes for
a truly beautiful wife." He smiled a little as she turned
and looked up at him, wiping the water from her eyes.
Strangely, he thought, she seemed to feel no shyness
about her nakedness. She had instead a rather cool,
considering look.

"Do you think me truly beautiful, sire? Or did you
mean to say, kindly, that for a dwarf I do quite well?"

Adam threw back his shaggy head and laughed out
loud. "I'm damned if you didn't look like some strange
little creature that day. You swept along your gallery in
enough black silk to drape a king's funeral bier, all
fluttering skirts and flying cloak and a tiny white face
in the midst of it. But I was wrong, then. The beauty
was there, and the pride. Here—let me soap and rinse
your hair."

His praise warmed her; his gentle hands in her hair seemed those of a dear friend, and when he poured the clear water over her, it was like a benison, healing the hurts to her heart and pride. She was smiling as she washed the rest of her, and he washed her back, his hands as easy as Honoria's. She stood and accepted the length of soft material.

"Take off your clothes while I dry myself," she said, "then I will assist you." She could hear the tremor of excitement in her own voice and tried for dignity, stepping out and wrapping the cloth around herself, turning away as he stripped off his clothes and got into the tub. Dry, she put on her chemise and the apron over it and took an extra bucket of fresh water to set aside for rinsing. Dousing him well, she took up the soft soap and began. Scrubbing, she found both hair and beard teasing her, the curls clinging tight to her fingers. Close like this, she was intensely aware of his firm skin and masculine features. His dark gold lashes were thick, framing the bold blue eyes, and the muscles that rippled sleekly across his shoulders fascinated her. Before she'd finished rinsing the soap from his head and face, she was shaky and warm and rattled, afraid to start on the rest of him. Adam sensed her nervous reluctance and took the soap and cloth from her hands.

"Enough," he said. "Sit by the fire and dry your hair. You'll not want it wet in bed."

She was glad enough to move away, to find an ivory comb, and sitting on the stool in front of the fire, to unwrap the towel from her head and comb out her long damp hair, raising it and letting it fall, so the heated air dried it. The warmth was soothing, the long, slow movements of her arms as she combed calmed the disturbed pulsing of her blood.

Leisurely washing himself, Adam studied her. The fire lent its own color to her gleaming hair; the glow on her cheeks rivaled the reddest of roses. Fair-faced indeed, and his memory eagerly supplied the perfect body beneath the voluminous gown. His own body grew hot in spite of the rapidly cooling water. By chance alone he had married the most beautiful woman he had ever seen, and though her overweening pride and lack of humility might bother a lesser man, he was certain that neither fault would conquer him. He had never known a woman, not even amongst the proud and obstinate beauties at court, who would not bend gracefully to his will once he'd made love to her. At least, not until now. . . .

He rose from the tub, his body in quivering readiness, and wrapped a drying cloth around himself. It was Brielle's duty to call the maids, who would be waiting in the hall, and see that they emptied the big tub and dragged it away. But she looked so soft and warm, dreaming there in front of the fire, that he spoke to her gently and told her to get into bed.

"I'll get the maids in," he said, "to empty the tub. They'll move quickly for me."

Brielle rose from her seat near the hearth, swept her hair back, and yawned. "'Twas a long day of riding the hills," she said, "and 'tis true I'm tired. Thank you, sire." She went directly to the canopied bed, looped back one curtain near the spirit candle, lit it, and crawled in. Snuggling down, she smiled. She'd seen his readiness for love and wondered. If he thought her truly exhausted, would he assert his rights or let her sleep? He wasn't entirely without sympathy. . . .

Adam opened the door of the solar and saw the maids whispering together at the end of the hall. They saw him at the same moment and came rushing with their buckets, eyes widening as they took in the huge half-naked man and the telltale bulge beneath the drying cloth that wrapped his loins. They scooped up water and ran back and forth, dumping the water in the garderobe at the end of the hall, coming back for

more, whispering and giggling. Adam watched them
with a lenient eye, amused himself, knowing gossip
would be bandied about belowstairs but not caring.
Once they'd emptied the tub and propped it against the
wall to dry, they gathered up the drying cloths, bobbed
him a curtsey, and left. He latched the door, from
habit, and banked the fire. Then, unwrapping the cloth
and hanging it over a chair, he went naked and silent
to pull back the bedcurtain and look in.

Immediately he was reminded of the first night at
Dover. Once again the candlelight fell on a pillow
strewn with lustrous chestnut hair. Once again the rebellious golden eyes were closed and long black lashes
lay like silken fans on velvety skin. Brielle's lips were
slightly parted, her face still and quiet. She looked to
be fast asleep and perfectly content to sleep the night
through.

But she was not asleep. His eyes sharpened on the
soft white skin of her neck, seeing a fluttering throb
there, like the wing of a snared bird. A fast-beating
heart could mean fear, but Adam knew she wasn't
afraid of him. Excitement, then. A game. A desire to
thwart him. Perhaps her pride still demanded payment
for the night before, when her frightened pleas were
met by denial. In some ways, he thought, his little wife
was still an arrogant child. Amused, he lifted the covers and slid in beside her, curving his massive body
and gently easing her close.

She was very good at pretense. He felt the nearly
imperceptible stiffening, but that was all, and that
gone in an instant. He sighed and settled, his bearded
face in the curve of her neck, his hand cupping her
round breast, his aroused body cradling her hips.
When she still didn't move, didn't—except for the ac-
celerating beat of her heart—in any way acknowledge
his presence, he thought it might seem a very long
night for both of them. Still, having begun this com-

edy, he was determined to see it through. Somehow, she must be taught to want his lovemaking—and to admit it.

Brielle wondered how long it would be before he fell asleep. He was always so warm. His heat and the clean musky odor of his skin surrounded her. His hand, loosely clasping her breast, sent jolts of sensation shooting down through her, and the feel of his soft beard against her neck was strangely exciting. She tried to stay lax in his arms, tried to imitate the slow, even breathing of deep sleep.

"So beautiful," Adam said in a whisper, softly caressing her breast. "So perfectly formed." She stiffened again as his hand moved away and long fingers slowly loosened the tie that held the chemise together at her neck. Carefully, lightly, he folded the sections back and bared both breasts to the dim glow of the spirit candle. Then he rose on one elbow and loomed over her, descending slowly until the soft curls of his beard brushed the silken skin of a breast. The nipple reacted to the touch, to the warmth, and drew up into a tight bud, waiting. . . .

Agonized by the fear that she'd give her feelings away, Brielle risked a glimpse through her lashes. But Adam drew back, the silhouette of his head against the faint light again like a huge mane, his shoulders and wide chest a darkly gleaming wall. Brielle forced herself to shut her lids and stare only at darkness. Perhaps now he would settle down and sleep. Instead, he whispered again.

"How lovely she is. The angels themselves must be jealous of that skin, that shining hair, those ivory limbs. . . ." His hand slipped beneath the rumpled hem of her chemise and stroked upward, warm and calloused, curling about the soft flesh above her knee, squeezing it gently.

Brielle gritted her teeth and choked down a small sound that rose in her chest. Sensation ran away with her, so warm and tempting she could hardly resist. Feigning restlessness, she pretended to toss in her sleep, rolling away from him. The hand held and went with her, ending up almost beneath her. She felt the bed give to his weight as he inched closer, drew in her breath soundlessly as his hand slid farther up, cupping the mound of dark curls below her belly. She lay still, her heart in her throat, and she knew she must lose again. Somewhere there might be a woman who could ignore those gently questing fingers, the heat of that cupped palm, that passionate man pressing ever closer. She couldn't. She was on fire. After only one night, her body had learned its destiny.

Slowly, then, she let out her breath in a sigh of surrender and turned back, reaching up and fastening her fingers in his thick hair, dragging him down to her opening mouth, accepting the hot thrust of tongue, wanting it, wanting him, ready to beg for his lovemaking if she must. . . .

"Damnation." The word came from her throat in a soft growl. "Damnation! Are you never satisfied?" In truth, she didn't know if the question was meant for him or her. In any case, he didn't answer, only kissed her again.

He hummed his deep pleasure as she touched him. His arms gathered her in, his mouth took hers gently and wandered on, taking her breasts, suckling them hungrily, then moving over her inch by inch. Her hands touched, marveled, stroked, and her little sounds of helpless desire were sweet to his ears. The air around them seemed charged with a strange power neither hers nor his but belonged to them both, controlled them both.

They mated once, with none of the pain she expected and all of the glorious, thundering excitement and ecstasy; then again, slowly, taking time and luxuriating in each touch, each teasing caress.

When it was over, and they returned to being two instead of one, Adam fell immediately into a deep, satisfied sleep. Brielle, surprised and chagrined to realize that desire could overcome her will, lay drowsily studying the strong profile outlined by candlelight. She had counted on his desire for her as something she could use when needed; she wondered now if he might turn the tables on her. Ah, well. When each owned the same weapon, the fight was fair. . . .

16

two days later, accompanied by both Honoria and Arabella, Brielle entered the queen's chamber at Westminster Palace and dipped a knee to the imposing figure seated at her desk. Philippa rose quickly and greeted Brielle like a long-lost daughter, throwing her arms around her and kissing her cheeks.

"You gave us anxious moments, dear Brielle. Honoria and I suspected that you'd managed to join the sortie, if only for the excitement. But not until Edward sent a message were we able to conquer our fears. I thank Our Lady for her answer to my prayers." She glanced past Brielle and Honoria, who was all smiles, to Arabella, standing at the door. Dressed in one of Brielle's gowns from the château and with her hair neat, Arabella made her a deep curtsey, standing afterward with her head bowed. She was speechless with awe before the queen.

Brielle explained. "I chose an English bowman's widow to take Leone's place as my maid, Your Highness. Honoria has told me that Leone wishes to remain in your employ if you agree. She has an intention to wed one of your guards."

Philippa bent a penetrating gaze on Brielle. "Certainly I shall be glad to keep Leone—she is an excellent maid. But if you are not staying, I will miss you sorely."

Brielle met her gaze with a sudden brightness in her own eyes, an open smile. "I travel with Adam, dearest Philippa. We leave for Castle on Tyne on the morrow."

"Ah? Are you telling me more than the words I

hear?" Philippa's handsome face glowed with expectancy.

Brielle glanced at the others; Honoria, trying to act as if she were deaf, Arabella fascinated by her conversation with the queen. Turning back to Philippa, she was pink-faced.

"Indeed. There is, ah, much reason to hope for the best, though the troubles may not be over."

Philippa's eyes widened and she laughed. "Wonderful! But only a young wife would say that, my dear little one. Troubles can drift away, troubles change, troubles become easier to bear. But troubles are never over."

Before the Dunbarton company set forth, King Edward made a gift of a fine black leather saddle, trimmed in silver, and a padded red silk saddle blanket for the white Arabian mare he'd given Brielle. He took pains to present it while Adam was standing beside Brielle, as if to prove he had no underhanded motives. Brielle was delighted. She named the mare Angelique, a name she felt took in both the mare's disposition and her light-footed pace that seemed more like floating than riding.

Leaving the courtyard of Westminster Palace a day later, turning north, Brielle glanced up at Adam and found his gaze on her, warm and possessive. She smiled, feeling excitement leap up and ease the sadness of leaving Philippa behind.

"How long will it be before we sight Castle on Tyne?"

"The weather will let us know. The trip measures the better part of the length of England, and the snow is deep in the valleys. With the two wagons we'll have when we leave Windsor Castle we will have delays."

"Two wagons? Only Honoria and Arabella are in the one we have now."

Adam laughed, his eyes crinkling at the corners. "And the gifts and supplies that Philippa thrust upon us. Another pound added would sink it in the first deep snow. Adding your cook, your majordomo, and the baskets Berthe will bring would cause it to disappear."

Brielle laughed with him. To see him so lighthearted made her feel the same. And her excitement kept growing as she thought of the end of this arduous trip. She had not forgotten the glowing picture of Castle on Tyne that Kiernan Comyn had painted for her the day after she'd wed Adam so unwillingly. She watched Kiernan now, riding at the van with a company of the king's soldiers, and wondered if he'd made the prospect more beautiful than reality just to lift her spirits that day. 'Twould be like him to be kind. . . . She caught his eye and smiled as he turned his handsome face to look back, and his grin broke out, merry and irrepressible. She'd ask, she decided, when she had a chance.

They arrived at Windsor Castle in midafternoon and were greeted with both envy and pleasure by the four Dunbarton knights who had been left behind to spend the holidays quietly. The news of the Calais coup had preceded them to Windsor Castle, for three of the French nobility had been imprisoned there, waiting for their connections in France to find their ransom money. In the meantime they were fed and amused in comfortable quarters, as was proper.

That evening, bathed and in their best finery, they dined in the great hall and the noble captives with them, also gaily dressed and conversing pleasantly. Geoffrey de Charny was among them, and after the meal he asked Adam if Aimery was again in charge of the Calais fortress. Adam's thick brows rose at the question.

"Is another try in your mind, de Charny? Put it aside. Sir John Beauchamp controls the defense there now. You'll find him hard to bribe."

"Nor would I try," de Charny said, his face suddenly dark with hate. "I'm no fool. But when that weakling that now sits on our throne pays my ransom, I will find Aimery, whether he's hiding in England or in France." He rose from the table, and his guards sprang to his sides for the walk back to his cell. De Charny ignored them and went on: "I have a dream that keeps me warm in my cold prison cell, my lord. I know I'll not see my twenty thousand pieces of gold again, but when I find Aimery I will take from him a full twenty thousand small pieces of flesh before he dies, and I will laugh in his screaming face."

Brielle shuddered as de Charny turned and, still ignoring the guards who walked beside him, went from the great hall into the cold night.

"He will," she said to Adam later, when they entered the bedroom she had used for so many lonely nights. "I know him. He is one of the cruelest men in France."

"Second only to the poisoner Charles of Navarre," Adam said, assenting. "But then Charles may be the most evil of all evil men."

"My father would agree," Brielle said absently, her eyes scanning the room, which held a warm fire and a freshly made-up bed. "He spoke of him as an incarnation of the Devil." She turned and swept her cloak from her shoulders, draping it across a settle near the fire, then sitting down herself to enjoy the light and flames. Adam watched her, his mind on the night ahead, wondering if she felt tired after the long ride. To his own amazement, he could barely wait to get her in bed. His body ached for her.

Slowly he turned away and took off his cloak, hanging it up. Then his leather half boots, his tunic and knit shirt. In his chausses he came to stand at the fire and look into the glowing coals, still thinking, trying to decide if he should demand his marital rights from a woman who, though she looked wonderfully well, might be tired and sore.

Brielle watched him from under lowered lashes, fascinated as the firelight played on the red-gold thicket of curls on his massive chest and gleamed along the breadth and thickness of his bare shoulders. As always, the clinging knit chausses that covered his hips and muscular thighs drew an exact image of the man within: the long, sturdy legs, the tight buttocks, the flat belly, the rampant masculinity. He was already more than half aroused. She felt a sudden heat, a pooling of sensation deep in her belly, and wrenched her gaze away from the telltale bulge straining against the soft knit.

"We'll need our rest," she got out, standing and turning away. "'Twill be a long journey that starts tomorrow."

A heavy arm snaked out and caught her waist, pulling her around and holding her close. "Are you tired, my lady?"

The fine, springing hair on his chest was thick and soft beneath her cheek, his odor exciting. She swayed closer, rewarded by his heat and hardness pressed against her belly. She sighed soundlessly and ran her hands around his waist and down over his buttocks, kneading and caressing. She'd promised the truth between them, long ago.

"I am tired, yes. But . . . I am hungry for you. Take me to bed."

The flare of desire in her amber eyes, her warmth and her bold words inflamed him as no other woman ever had. He crushed her to him and kissed her deeply, his hands trembling as they ran down her back and urged her closer, tighter. She gave a little cry as his aroused loins ground hard and hot against her, then tilted her hips to take full advantage of the searing sensation.

"Adam," she whispered, "Adam . . ."

They were on the bed, her skirts up around her neck, his chausses down around his feet, his entry swift and strong. Arched over her, his strong face flushed with passion, his eyes like blue flame, he drove into her yielding flesh. She cried out softly, and her slim legs embraced him, her small body swung with his, frantic with desire.

"Oh, Adam—more. More! Oh-h-h-h . . ."

He could not resist her. He could not hold back. It was over in seconds. Her throbbing release brought him instantly past control. He reared into his final thrust, leonine head back, a hoarse sound of pleasure rolling like thunder from his throat, quivering in ecstasy as his life-force spent itself.

Finally he sank down, edging away to keep his chest and shoulders from weighing heavy on her breasts. Lying there, his blood taking its time to cool, he marveled at the power this small woman had, at the passion she felt and made him feel, at his own inability to control the mating. She had seemed so cold and bitter in the beginning, and now . . .

"Adam?" A whisper, a light touch that smoothed along his thick arm.

He raised his head and looked at her, at the dim oval of her face, the firelight reflected in her amber eyes. "You have bewitched me," he said. "I would take you slowly and sweetly, not like a wild beast. But when you touch me"—he shook his head—"no, 'tis not fair to cast blame."

She stopped his words by pulling him down again to her lips. She licked his mouth open and opened hers to him, luxuriating in an intimacy she would never have dreamed of until now. Then, softly, she answered him.

"Then cast no blame. We have too much now to disagree on. Let this part be as it is. We've plenty of time to mate again in whatever fashion you choose."

* * *

They emerged from their room at first light to begin
the final preparations for leaving. Bundled to the nose,
Brielle came out into the courtyard to see that all was
in order. The day was bright and cold, promising good
traveling weather, without snow. The four knights who
had been left at Windsor—Charles Eastham, Philip
Tournard, John Worth, and Marsh Nelson—were more
than ready to ride again. They had finished an early
breakfast and brought the wagons up to load before
the sun rose.

This day the frost rime was thick on the uneven cob-
bles, adorning each stone with an edge of bristling
white. The patient carthorses, their big bodies steaming in the cold air, blew heavily through their nostrils
to clear them of frozen crystals. A scene, Brielle
thought, in winter dark and frozen white, enlivened by
bright colors of red and purple wool, of russet and
green and blue, as the servants ran back and forth.
England was a cold, cold place in January—yet there
was cheer.

Arabella had packed Brielle's clothing with particular care; now she brought it forth and sat on guard
beside it in the wagon, dressed in layers of wool and a
cloak with a hood, daring anyone to put foodstuffs or
liquid near the neat bundles.

Berthe, half wanting to stay at Windsor but choosing
to go, sent the kitchen serfs to the stoutest wagon with
basket after basket of food; none would starve in this
train. Skinny old Jacques, fair bursting with pride,
again had a seat as the driver of one wagon, though
there was a young man beside him in case he tired.

The sun had climbed over the high walls by the time
they were ready to leave, the first bright ray striking
gold in Adam's beard as he settled his rearing
warhorse. Illumined by the sun, he looked at Brielle
and his broad mouth widened into a slow smile.

"At last, we're going home."

Seated in her comfortable saddle on eager Angelique, Brielle was struck by the happiness in his strong face, the unconscious yearning in the deep voice, and was aware for the first time of what his north country castle and his family meant to Adam. Most men who had the ear and the deep regard of a king would have to be pried away from court, but it was clear that Adam had stayed from duty alone. She smiled, saying nothing, for he was already signaling to the castle guards at the gate, and the knights who would ride in the van of the train were gathering around him. The gates swung open and the horses came together in orderly procession, heading out. With one long last look at Windsor Castle, where her sore heart had been mended by a queen, Brielle urged Angelique on, into the sharp wind from the north. She felt excited, yes, but her feelings were mixed. With two older noble families behind the same walls, she wondered what her position would be at Castle on Tyne. Whatever ensued, she meant to be the mistress of her own home, not just Adam Dunbarton's lady.

17

the weather held, cold and dry. Adam set a grueling pace to take advantage of it. Staying at night in an occasional inn or abbey, eating on the road, they passed Coventry and Chester, passed Scafell Pikes, highest of England's mountains, and arrived at the city of Carlisle in the afternoon of the fifth day. Riding in through the high city gates, Brielle was thankful for the biting wind and hard flurries of snow that promised the first storm since they had left Windsor. They were due a rest; the storm would see that they got one.

A good-sized and prosperous city, a short distance from the Scottish border, Carlisle offered a chance to buy more provisions for their depleted supplies. It was also the site of Scudder's Inn, one of the most comfortable hostelries in Britain. They were brought into the warm, massively beamed, and smoky common room and greeted by Scudder himself, a short man nearly as wide as he was tall, his stained tunic stretching across a monumental belly. He bowed and smiled and promised the best of the private rooms upstairs for Lord and Lady Dunbarton and their party.

White with fatigue but thankful for the warmth and security against the storm, Brielle was silent, looking around: stone walls and floor, roaring fires, rough wood tables and benches, and the pervading odors of roasting meat, wet wool, sweating men and the tang of spilled ale. She saw that Kiernan was watching her with concern in his green eyes. He had quietly become more and more protective of her in the last few days, like, she thought, the older brother she'd always wished for. She smiled at him, warmed by his concern.

"I'm only tired," she said, keeping her voice low as Adam talked to Scudder. "A night's rest will cure that."

Kiernan nodded, edging closer. "You were very pale all day," he murmured. "Too many hours in the saddle for a bit of a young woman." He was suddenly conscious that Adam had stopped talking to Scudder and was listening to him. He flushed and went on: "But still you did well to push us hard, Adam. Certainly this is the best place to spend the next two or three days— and I suspect 'twill be that long before the weather lets us ride again."

Adam's hard blue gaze searched Kiernan's face, then dropped to Brielle.

"Are you tired, my lady?"

She let go of his arm and straightened. "No more than the rest of you, my lord. 'Twas a hard day, today."

His expression gentled. "True. But there will be time enough and more to rest before we can start out again, and Kiernan has said it—there is no better place along our way than here."

The landlord saw that a table was set for them before the fire and loaded with food and wine. Spirits began to rise as they ate, and rose higher as Adam announced they'd not risk traveling on until the storm was well away.

"I'd not want my lady nor her female companions to face this weather on the high barrens," he said to Scudder. "You'll have us here until the storm abates."

Scudder bowed and smiled, rubbing his hands together.

"The house is honored," he answered. "We now have two noble parties as guests. Sir Marc de Rohan and two of his knights arrived this morning, on their

way south. Since he, too, is from Northumbria, perhaps you know him."

"Too well," Adam answered dryly. "We are enemies." He watched, sardonically amused, as Scudder's
round red face went redder and frightened. "However," he added, "you need not fear trouble between
us while we shelter here from the storm. I have women
to protect, and de Rohan will not start a fight he knows
he cannot win."

"Thank the good Christ," Scudder said, examining
the tall and muscular man in front of him. "I'd not like
seeing a battle between the two of you in my common
room."

Later, upstairs in the room set aside for Lord Dunbarton and his wife, Arabella and Honoria gossiped
with Brielle in her bath while Adam saw to the food
and comfort of the horses, stabled behind the inn.

Honoria was full of advice. "If you see that dishonorable de Rohan, you must look right through him, as
if he were not there. You must show no fear nor revulsion nor recognition."

Intrigued, Arabella listened and asked questions.
Honoria told her of de Rohan's savage attack on
Brielle, more as a warning than as gossip. "They say,"
she concluded, "that Sir Marc does not confine his at-
tacks to noblewomen—he has been known to leave a
servant girl unconscious and bleeding in the hall she
was sweeping."

"Come now," Brielle broke in. "While Adam is with
us, none of us need worry about the coward de Rohan.
He may be the madman they say, but he'll not be mad
enough to rouse my lord's anger." She stood, indicat-
ing to Arabella that she wished to be rinsed with a
bucket of clear water. The maid complied, lifting the
bucket high and giggling at Brielle's strangled yelp as
the cold water cascaded down. Behind them the door
of the room opened and closed softly.

"Here," Adam said, coming close, and picked up the
nearest linen drying cloth to hand to his wife. "Wrap
yourself and go nearer the fire." Flinging down his
cloak, he turned to Arabella and raised his arms, bending to allow her to remove his hauberk of mail, then
taking a chair and extending a booted leg to the maid's
competent hands. Once the boots were off, he waved
her to the door.

"My wife will manage the rest," he said. "Sleep well
and late if you wish—we do no traveling tomorrow."

Honoria was already slipping out as Arabella
bobbed a bow and followed, shutting the door softly.
Adam threw the heavy bolt and turned, planting his
feet wide, thrusting his arms high, shaking his tangled,
tawny hair back, glad of the freedom from heavy boots
and mail. He settled then, gusting out a long breath,
and looked at Brielle.

"Go on with drying your hair," he said. "I'll take off
my own clothes and begin my bath."

She hurried. She put up her hair half damp and
threw on a shift and apron. There had been little time
for baths or rest on the trip so far, and no private place
for husband and wife: just hard riding, quick meals,
and exhausted sleep in chilly common rooms. Now her
pride compelled her to take on her wifely duties.
Clothed, she took a washcloth and went to him where
he sat in the still-warm water.

He'd drenched his head, and the mass of hair and
beard hung in wet, dark gold waves. She soaped and
scrubbed and rinsed, her small hands energetic, her
brows drawn down in concentration. She began again
at his brawny shoulders and thought of the centaurs,
half man, half animal, that once inhabited the earth.
This man seemed to have that same kind of strength;
no softness, no weakness, no puny human failings. She
thought again of that morning in Dover, when she had
been so frightened of him and had actually envisioned

him as an animal from the days before God. Slipping
now to her knees, she washed the thick pelt that covered his chest and struck down a path to his loins. The
curls twisted around her fingers like tangled silk and
led her on, exploring. . . .

Adam leaned forward, nipping her earlobe with his
strong teeth. "Careful," he breathed into the ear, "you
may excite me. The inn maids will not like finding water on the floor."

She flushed pinkly. "'Tis foolish to blame me for
your own thoughts," she said, and went on with what
she was doing.

"'Twas your mighty leap at me that slopped the water out," she told him later, after he'd stripped her and
carried her to bed. Adam lay back and laughed at her
prim tone.

"And 'twas your hands that drove me wild, my love,
as you well know." He lifted her, his big arms making
play of holding her in the air above him. "By the
saints," he added, his voice dropping into a soft growl,
"my father's choice was fortunate for me. Not only do
I have the most beautiful of all wives, but she has a
passion as hot as mine own. 'Twill be easy to be faithful
to such a wife."

Brielle's dark brows rose questioningly. She wanted
him faithful, yes—her pride demanded that—but what
he said puzzled her. "Are not all women much the
same in their feelings, my lord?"

He laughed out loud and lowered her to his broad,
golden-furred chest. "They are as different as the dead
of winter from a June day, my lady. There are wives
cold enough to freeze a man's shaft, I have heard, and
others who cry and bemoan the night if the husband
steps a foot toward their bed. The same wives, my little
one, are those who daily berate their men for inconstancy."

She rose on an elbow and looked at him curiously.

"Have you ever made sport with one of those unfeeling women?"

"Never! Nor would I try."

"Then you cannot be certain they exist."

"The men tell."

"Perhaps the men lie."

Adam sat up, shaking his head. "Why would a man lie when the lie makes him look a fool? No, I am of the opinion that a man is more honest and true than a woman. He has the stronger nature, the better understanding of honor."

She straightened, sitting erect beside him. "I am of the opinion that where honor and truth are known, there is no difference between man and woman. 'Tis merely a matter of courage enough to hew to what is right."

They sat looking at each other, the firelight playing over their naked bodies. Then Adam smiled, caught by what she had said. He thought it unusual for a woman to think so nobly. He reached for her.

"There is no better way than this for a man and woman to learn each other well," he said, drawing her close. She gave herself into his arms, it seemed willingly. But when he bent over her to look into her eyes, he saw the gathering chill, the resistance that was always there until her passion flared and took her over. He smothered his disappointment. He didn't understand it; it was enough, he thought, to know he could conquer her strange unwillingness if he took his time. He laid his palm softly on her slim belly and left it there, warm and heavy, while he kissed the wary eyes shut and licked her lips apart, coaxing her tongue to play with his.

His body was like a breathing wall pressed against her, half over her, his thatch of golden hair soft and teasing on her smooth skin. It was warm in the room; the fire roared and shone red on the stone walls, red-gold in Adam's hair. Flames leaped in the cavern of the fireplace; in the cavern of her body. In her imagination she could see the flames inside her, stretching high, leaping wildly, yearning upward toward the hand that lay so quietly atop them.

Twisting away from his kisses and plundering tongue, Brielle drew in a ragged breath and lifted her lashes far enough to glance down at another firm weight that lay on the top of her slender thigh. His throbbing, engorged shaft was like a living being, smooth and silken, pulsing as the firelight flickered over its shining length. She sighed, letting the breath out, and shut her eyes.

"Please . . ."

Adam waited, but when she said no more, he went on with his lovemaking, mouthing her breasts, taking the pebbles of nipples into the heat and wet, rubbing them gently against the roof of his mouth. A rush of confidence flooded him as he felt her hands touch his head, her fingers tangle in his hair and hold him close. And then came the slow, sensual rise of her body against his quiet hand that lay low on her belly. He moved it lower, questing with long fingers, and felt her tremble, felt her widen her thighs to give him room to play. He let out his breath then, in a gusting growl of pleasure.

Her answer to that was to curl a hand around the back of his neck and bring him close to look into his eyes. "Why do you tease me, my lord?"

He smiled in the dim light, caressing her softly. "I would teach you the many pleasures along the way, wife."

There was neither doubt nor fear now in her dreaming face; 'twas all desire in the half-open golden eyes, the parted lips, the shallow breathing. "I would learn them, sire. But now . . . now it has been too long. I want you in me."

His hand told him she spoke the truth. She was hot
and ready, her quivering flesh sucking at his fingers.
He swung over her and placed himself to be enveloped
in her heat, his hands beneath her hips. Carefully he
pressed upward, the thick, hard weight sliding into her
swollen flesh with agonizing slowness, a pleasure so
intense that her legs trembled and she cried out. This
time she was swept away, caught in a torrent of nearly
painful ecstasy that went on and on, shaking her to her
depths. In the final release she felt tears running down
her cheeks.

They had made love half the night, yet when Adam
woke and saw Brielle, fully dressed and sitting in a ray
of sunlight from an east window, he hardened again.
Still, he would not ask for more. He wanted her willing, and, he reasoned, had she wanted more herself,
she would have remained in bed.

"Have you eaten?"

Brielle put down the torn shift she was mending and
shook her head. "I am waiting for you, sire. I would
not go down alone, knowing that de Rohan may be
about."

He'd forgotten. The night had driven any unpleas-
antness away. Still, he should have remembered. He
clambered out of the comfortable bed, pulled on his
soft wool chausses and shirt, and went out and down
the hall to a garderobe. Coming back into the room a
few minutes later, silent and angry at himself, he finished his dressing, even to the chain link hauberk.

"I want no knife in my back," he said in answer to
Brielle's inquiring look. "De Rohan is not a man to
trust."

"Philippa told me that in the beginning," Brielle
said. "Had I understood all that it meant, you'd have
no enemy now. I am sorry my foolishness put you in
danger, sire."

Surprised, Adam stood still, Strange, how she managed to apologize without sounding humble. 'Twas in the voice, he decided. This small female managed to be proud even while admitting a fault. He smiled faintly.

"We were never friends, my lady, nor ever could be, but 'twas right to say you are sorry." Hesitating, he thought this was as good a chance as he'd ever have of learning the truth of that night. He went closer to study how the question would strike her. "I've wondered often," he went on carelessly, "how de Rohan talked you into opening your door." He watched the tide of red blood come up her neck and turn her face crimson. She picked up the mending again and began to pluck at the threads, keeping her eyes down. Somehow his question had brought the pain and horror back, worse now than it had been then, when shock had numbed her feelings.

"I"—she swallowed—"I thought—I mean, I was convinced that . . ." She lowered her voice to a mumble he couldn't decipher and haltingly finished the sentence, adding after a moment: "Of course, I was wrong."

"You mumbled," Adam said sternly. "You hid your words behind a garbled noise. Is that what you call telling the plain truth?"

Her head shot up, her eyes blazing, her face redder and more furious than he had ever seen it.

"When he knocked and whispered, I thought 'twas *you*! I thought you'd given in and come to my room at last to begin our marriage! But no! You were still waiting for me to humble myself to you! Don't you see? 'Twas you and your insufferable pride caused me the worst hurts and fears I ever had in my life!"

Remembering, she shuddered and put her hands up to hide her face. "I was so glad, opening the door for you. . . . And then, and then, that devil was on me, ripping my nightclothes, biting my breasts—it was *aw-ful!*" She burst into tears, keening in her throat.

He believed her, but he made no move to comfort her. He was stunned by the furious anger in her golden eyes. He hadn't known she blamed him for that night. Now he knew why she had chosen to sleep with Honoria and Leone at the palace, why she had continually wanted her own room. She was dutiful in wanting a child; she was passionate by nature. But underneath it all, she hated him for humbling her. He swallowed, feeling a strange, terrible sense of loss.

Moving away, he stood by the window and waited for her sobbing to quiet. "Wash your face," he said then. "We'll go down to eat."

They met de Rohan and his knights on the stairs. Elaborately courteous, Sir Marc drew aside and bowed. Brielle, a hand on the rail and her eyes straight ahead, went past him. He ignored Adam; his eyes clung to Brielle's slight figure in rose velvet and floating cream silk as long as she was in sight. Adam's eyes darkened and grew dangerous, watching de Rohan's lustful stare. De Rohan caught the look and leered at him, amused.

"You've naught to fear, Lord Dunbarton. While you go home, I leave tomorrow to fight the French. 'Twill be many a day before I return to Northumbria and flirt again with your lovely wife." He saw Adam's hand move toward his sword and ran up the stairs, laughing shrilly.

Two days later, rested and with new provisions, the party began the trip up the narrow Eden Valley and so north to the pass that led east.

"The hardest part of the trip lies before us," Adam remarked as he and Brielle led off the train. "But the distance is short. One night in a primitive shelter, and then Castle on Tyne."

Brielle's heart soared and then dropped. She felt like a thief going before a judge, thinking of facing Adam's mother.

"I will wager," she said, her eyes on the high, frozen drifts of snow lining the valley, "she will think me a miserable little creature."

"She?"

"Your mother. Philippa told me your family takes great pride in being tall and strong, even the women. I am strong, truly I am. But I am not tall."

Adam shrugged. "Lady Martha Dunbarton believes everyone in her great circle of family is perfect. Put your mind at rest. My mother will love you. Whatever you may think of the rest of my family will matter very little. We will live in our own house, and you will have your own servants around you. There can be no trouble."

That thought kept Brielle's spirits up, though Adam's gloomy silence worried her. She rode with the knights, who stayed ahead of the wagons to break down the drifts, and rode back often to see that Honoria and Jacques were warm enough and feeling well. It was impossible to worry about Arabella, who smiled at everyone and remained in the best of spirits. She was clearly happy with the prospects of being a part of the Dunbarton fold.

Had there been a road, Brielle thought, it had long since disappeared. All around them were high rolling hills, swept clean of snow by the constant wind. Below them in the shallow valleys the snow lay in deep drifts. They traveled now toward the northeast, and the way seemed smoother than she had expected. She mentioned that to Adam. He turned to her, his heavy golden brows and moustache glistening with ice crystals.

"'Tis a way hard packed by use and many lifetimes old, my lady. Look beyond that tumbled pile of rock ahead, and you will see part of the wall built by the Roman Emperor Hadrian, to separate his dominion from that of the wild and quarrelsome Scots. We follow the way made by his workmen and traveled by the Roman soldiers who once owned and guarded Britain."

"So the other side of this wall is Scotland?"

Adam shook his head. "'Tis now England. The Romans grew greedier and took more, building another wall that has gone to ruin. But from here Scotland is less than a half-day ride. From now until we see the towers of Castle on Tyne, we must watch for trouble."

Brielle nodded, shielding her face from a swirling wind that came as they topped a rise. Now the jagged wall showed clearly, built of stone, of varying heights, at times eight to ten feet high, then sloping down to no more than four, only to rise again. It ran east in a rising and falling pattern that suited the stony, rolling land it followed. Then running in and out along the south side of the wall was a wide and shallow depression in the earth. They avoided it, turning and going directly east along the higher ground. With a few words Adam now sent Charles Eastham and Philip Tournard galloping ahead and motioned John Worth and Marsh Nelson to the rear.

"We need no Scottish surprises," he said to Brielle. "They will keep watch."

The day wore on, colder as the wind strengthened. They didn't stop for a midday meal but continued on, silent, only their eyes showing above woollen scarves wrapped within their hoods, until finally they came upon a large and peculiar tower against the wall. It was then close to dark, and Adam told Brielle that here was the place they would stay the night.

Brielle stopped Angelique and sat still, studying the building in some wonder. It was built of ancient stone,

irregularly patched with new, to the height of two tall
men, then continued with rough logs above that. It
was circular and very large, with a wide entrance on
the south side. On the north it embraced the old Roman wall as part of itself. Seeing arrow slits above,
Brielle thought it might be part of the protection
against the Scots—unless, she amended, the Scots arrived first and took it for themselves.

"Come," Adam said behind her, his tone impatient.
"Don't dally. The sooner we're hidden inside, the better. We need no wild Scotsmen coming down on us
when we have women to protect."

She followed him meekly. All day, and even yester-
day in the comfort of the inn, he had seemed a
stranger again. There was a flatness in his eyes when
he looked at her, a curtain that hid his thoughts. She
wished mightily to see the usual amusement, the teasing admiration she had seen before. It was gone, but
she was hopeful that once the strain of the trip was
over, he'd be the same again. She had begun to feel at
home with that Adam.

Ahead of them the wagons disappeared into the
wide entrance of the old fort. They rode behind them
into a huge, shadowy space lighted only by the arrow
slits, a large smoke hole in the ceiling of the big room,
and far above and dimly seen, another smoke hole
through the roof. The men before them had already
dismounted and were taking their horses off to one
side, removing the bridles and tethering them to rings
in the stone wall. Adam did the same, lifting Brielle
from her mare and taking both animals to the rings.
There were hayracks there, and the drivers, excepting
exhausted old Jacques, were carrying armloads of hay
to each horse. Two men had begun bringing wood
from a pile beside the wall and building a fire below
the roof openings. Everyone knew his duty and was
anxious to get it done.

Brielle turned to Adam, who was taking off his cloak. "Should I make up pallets with the blankets we have in the wagon, sire?"

"'Tis not needed. There are pallets aplenty above, and we sleep in our clothes." He waved a hand at the ceiling. "'Twill be warmer up there, by far."

She looked about for stairs and found only sections of logs, thrust into the wall on a slanting line that led to a corner and a hole in the ceiling. Warmer? Yes, she thought ruefully, it would be warmer, and full of swirling smoke.

"I see," she said, and shrugged. "We will not be cozened and made so comfortable as we were in Scudder's Inn."

Adam gave her a sharp look. "Northumbria has never been at its best in winter," he said, "but Northumbrians are. You won't hear the men and women who live here complain of rough living. They pride themselves on their fortitude."

Brielle turned away, embarrassed. She had complained; she couldn't deny it. But she hadn't expected Adam to be curt. It seemed to her there was enough to complain about. But it was something to remember. If she was to be a part of his family, she must have great fortitude.

The knights Eastham and Tournard had been waiting here when the party arrived, and now the rear guard, John Worth and Marsh Nelson, rode in and dismounted.

"We saw no Scots," John Worth said, "which is not to say there were none around. But 'tis likely the weather has kept them huddled by their fires."

Brielle drifted away, leaving the men to talk, and joined Honoria by the fire. Berthe had come from the wagon with a huge iron pot and with Arabella's help was making a stew of beef and barley, enlivened by herbs. There was plenty of bread and ale, and a crock

of butter. No one would starve. Brielle went to the
wagon and began getting out bowls and spoons. Coming back, she saw Kiernan warming himself at the fire
and smiled at him. Putting the bowls down, she went
to stand beside him, laying a hand on his arm.

"I have been wanting a word with you," she said,
"and this is my first chance. Remember how you saw
my sadness as I left my home, and you undertook to
cheer me with a description of Castle on Tyne? I have
not forgotten a word of what you said, nor how well it
mended my grief. Now—since I no longer need visions
of beauty to look forward to—tell me if you told me
true. I will forgive you if you painted only dreams."

Kiernan's green eyes warmed. He covered the hand
on his arm and spoke softly, his gaze on her face. "Not
one word was untrue, Lady Brielle. I could not have
praised the place enough in so few words. You will
soon see the biggest and best of north country castles.
Castle on Tyne would be the envy of lesser kings."

Brielle laughed. "Wonderful! I've dreamed of it,
often, and it's very hard to wait—" Then, behind her,
someone grasped her arm firmly. She turned, still
smiling, and looked up at Adam. "Oh! What is it, sire?"

Adam gave her a cold stare. "I would like some ale.
Bring it to me."

Her smile wavered slightly. He sounded rude, yet
what he said was a simple request she could hardly
refuse. She looked down, knowing her uncertainty
would show in her eyes. "Yes, my lord," she said, and
moved away as the grip on her arm eased. She saw his
anger and was bewildered by it. Going to the cask in
the wagon, she drew a mug of ale and brought it back.
By then, Kiernan had left the fire and joined the group
of other knights. Adam stood there alone, the firelight
accenting his deep frown.

"Why did you seek out Kiernan, my lady?"

Brielle blinked, surprised. "I did not seek him out. I

simply saw him and went to ask him more about Castle on Tyne. He described the place to me as we rode away from the château that first day." She smiled, remembering. "I believe he saw how unhappy I was and sought to ease my sorrow."

"I see." Adam was silent a moment and then added: "You have much to learn. My cousin Kiernan is very fond of women, and women are often very fond of him. He is noted for his success with them. And I have seen from the first that he is attracted to you."

Brielle gasped, outraged. "Why, that is not so! He has made no attempt at a flirtation, nor has he tried to engage my interest, sire. He is only friendly."

Adam shook his head. "Talk to him only when you must, and stay a good arm's length away. Not that Kiernan would force his attentions on you, but for appearance's sake. My men will wonder if you seem too friendly with Kiernan, for they know his weakness. Remember that as my wife, you must not appear to be attracted to another man."

Brielle's temper was rising. There, she thought, is the crux of the matter: I am no longer myself! I am only Adam Dunbarton's wife. His humble servant, the receptacle for his seed. Damnation! She choked down anger and answered him coolly.

"I am an honorable woman, sire. You have no reason to fear for your good name."

His expression didn't change. There was still that flat look that hid his thoughts. But he nodded.

"I believe you. But I know my cousin, and I've never seen him as taken with a woman as he is with you. You must be on guard, my lady. 'Tis not only our good name in danger, 'tis also Kiernan's life. He is like a brother to me, yet I will kill him if he seduces you."

18

that night, shocked and angry because of Adam's suspicion, which she felt reflected on her honor as much—even more!—as on Sir Kiernan's, Brielle used her two women like the walls of a fortress. *If he seduces you*, indeed! As if her honor would melt away under Kiernan's charm!

Grumbling and sharp-tempered, she spent the evening staying between the two women while they ate and while they climbed the rough steps to the floor above, then swooped down on a pallet like a small, angry hawk between two plump hens.

Nothing Honoria could say had the least effect on Brielle's bad temper and in fact made it worse, for Brielle wouldn't listen to words that bade her be gentle and give her lord his due, which was the advice Honoria always dispensed. Nor did the night's rest and a good breakfast seem to ease her resentment. In late morning, when Adam assisted her to mount Angelique for the rest of the journey, her manner was as cold as the frosty air. Swinging into his own saddle, Adam gave her a long and enigmatic stare, then ordered her forward, to ride with him at the head of the column. She dared to argue.

"I prefer to ride near the wagon," she said harshly, "if I am allowed to choose."

"You have no choice in this matter," he said. His tone was quiet, but his eyes were like blue steel. "Nor in any other matter, once I have told you what I want."

There was no one near them, so Brielle felt free to

answer him with bitter sarcasm. "'Twould seem to me that a man who questions his wife's honor could not desire her close company."

Adam set his jaw hard. Silently, he motioned her to follow him. Angry as she was, Brielle didn't dare to disobey that mailed fist. She followed at a fast trot, Angelique's small hooves sure on the rocky ground. Adam glanced down from the superior height of his warhorse and saw her slender figure swaying gracefully in the saddle, her face calm and proud, disdaining a show of her feelings. Inwardly, he smiled, feeling better. He still liked her pride, even when it was directed against him. The time would come when he must teach her the proper humility a wife should show toward her husband, but that could wait until they settled into their own home. It was more important now that she understood what he had meant last night. They were now well ahead of the others, and he slowed the pace so they could talk. Staring ahead, past the clouds of warm fog that came from the nostrils of his huge horse, he opened the conversation bluntly.

"I had no thought you meant to dishonor me," he said. "You have not gone so far past simple friendship as to earn my suspicion. My real concern is Kiernan. As I told you last night, he is bewitched by you. By my oath, I have never seen him so besotted by a woman."

Brielle stared, amazed by his implied flattery, her anger dying away; her face showed uncertainty and an effort to understand. "But you were angry with me, sire, not with Kiernan."

Adam shrugged. "He is a man. He cannot be blamed for wanting a woman who attracts him so strongly. Were you older and more experienced, you would realize how he feels and be more careful. Still, people say he has a great power over women, and indeed I have seen it." He glanced over at Brielle and added deliberately: "And, I believe you have felt it. You have never laid your hand on any other of the knights, yet you often come close to Kiernan, touch him, and smile. You are giving him thoughts and hopes he should not have."

Stung, Brielle did not trust herself to answer. Instead, she raised her chin and looked away from him, waiting to gain control over her anger. Adam watched feelings chase each other over her expressive face, first shock and then a fierce and resentful anger, and as the anger faded into reasoning, a wave of embarrassed color. She kept on, riding easily, scanning the bare and inhospitable hills around them, until when she turned back to him her face was a normal color, her golden eyes clear.

"What you say about my actions is true, sire," she said gravely. "Kiernan, alone of your knights, has been friendly to me, and I do have affection for him. But while my attentions to him may have been unwise, they were not meant to inflame."

"But the fact is that they do inflame," Adam said flatly. "For a hungry man takes a crumb as a banquet and calls the merest touch a caress. I know that in such things between a man and woman you are an innocent, but I have now warned you. I do not expect to see you lay your hand on Kiernan with affection again, nor show him more consideration than you show my other knights."

He waited, watching her while she thought about what he had said. A pale sun had emerged from the gloom overhead, putting a golden wash of light over her ivory face as they rode east. Daily she seemed more beautiful to him, and he wasn't at all sure that pleased him. A beautiful wife was a great joy, 'twas true, but a man could grow tired of fighting off rivals. Still, he thought, he was able and willing in the lists. Let them come.

"I shall not touch him in that way again," Brielle

said at last. "I promise you that, though 'tis hard to
believe he truly thinks I caress him. But since he is
your cousin, I cannot neglect to show him consideration."

"As my wife, you will show consideration and care
to all of my knights alike. They are brave and loyal
men, as close as family to me, and naturally they will
live in our home. Our servants will care for them as
they do for us, as to food and clothes. If they are
wounded in battle, you will bind up their wounds and
nurse them. No doubt you'll need instruction in managing these duties, but my mother will be happy to
teach you. The care of our home can be left to our able
staff."

"I was chatelaine of our château for six years,"
Brielle said stiffly. "I can manage all those things myself."

Adam turned to keep her from seeing his amusement. If she thought her experience in the quiet château, with only her father to care for and a staff of a
half-dozen servants, could prepare her for the brawl-
ing life and the endless tasks of Castle on Tyne, she
would soon find out she was wrong.

They rode on, and though the way still rose and fell,
the rising ground was gentler, the downward paths
longer, and snow covered the few tangles of briers and
small trees appearing along the windswept path.
Brielle realized they were gradually coming down
from the high ground of the night before. She started
to mention it to Adam, but as she turned toward him,
she saw him suddenly rise to his feet in the stirrups,
drawing his sword and thrusting it high, turning to
shout back to his knights.

"To me! To me! Scots attacking Hugh below!" He
was gone in a thunder of hooves, his bright blade flickering in the sun, the fleeting sight of his face within the
hood frightening in its grim ferocity.

Hurriedly, Brielle pulled her mare off the path, into a spot well out of the way of the knights galloping past, their swords drawn. Then she urged Angelique to the top of a rise and stared down the hill. There in the distance was what Adam had seen from his height above her on her little mare—a scene of violence. Four knights on horses, attacked by a swarm of stocky, bare-legged men wielding clubs and huge axes. Now she could hear the echoing cries, see the swinging, murderous blows. Even as she watched, one of the horses went down and the knight on his back leaped free, brandishing his sword. Two of the stocky men closed with him, their axes glittering in the pale sunlight. And there, rushing toward the melee, far ahead of his own knights, was Adam on his huge warhorse, his bright gold hair and beard clearly recognizable. Brielle turned her face away, swallowing hard, thinking her throat would close with her dreadful fear for him.

"'Tis not a large band, my lady. Sir Hugh and his three well-trained knights could best them alone, I vow."

Brielle whirled at the first word, staring in disbelief at Philip Tournard, calmly sitting his warhorse behind her.

"Why are you not fighting with the others?" Her tone was full of outrage, her pale face reddening with anger. "Had I a sword I would fain be with them, not skulking about up here!"

Sir Philip smiled. "My lady, had I left you alone with no other champion but old Jacques, our sire would have had my head removed from my shoulders."

"*Why?* The enemy is down there!"

"Indeed, the ones you can see are there. 'Tis the Scots you cannot see that fall upon the train, kill your servants, and steal away your goods and women." Philip's smile was a bit mocking. "Trust our sire, my lady. 'Tis his home land, and he knows its dangers well.''

The advice was wasted on Brielle, who had turned back and was watching the melee again, beginning to breathe more easily as she saw the Scots begin to break and run, overtaxed by the added number of mounted knights rushing into the fray.

"The Scots have no horses, then?'' she asked.

"Not these raiding Scots. They haven't the money for horses, the cunning to capture one, nor the ability to ride. They are like our meanest serfs, save they are free—free, that is, to steal or starve." Looking behind him, Philip motioned Jacques to start up again. "The wagon,'' he added to Brielle, "will be handy. I see two men down.''

Brielle, who had watched no one except Adam, gasped and scanned the scene below, seeing two men on the ground, with others bending over them. She touched her heels to Angelique's sides and sent her cantering down the rocky path. Like other women who lived on busy country estates, she had some skill with wounds. Now, she thought, she could be of some value. The thought gave her a feeling of kinship with the men.

Those wounded were Kiernan and Marsh Nelson. Kiernan had a cut from an ax, still bleeding, on the side of his leg below the knee. Marsh had a broken arm, caused by a blow from a club.

With a quick look from one to the other, Brielle dismounted beside Kiernan, knowing the bleeding must be stopped. She looked back and saw the wagon rumbling onto the field and threw up an arm to wave Jacques to her, for the wagon held the healing ointments and the cloth she used for binding up wounds. Then she knelt on the icy ground and looked into Kiernan's pale face. The brilliant green eyes, glazed with pain, warmed into near adoration.

"My lady," he said softly, "do not disturb yourself. My wound is not great. The men will take care of it."

Brielle was touched. But this time she recognized the infatuation in his gaze, and she knew she must cure him of it. She held out her hand with a show of impatience. "Your knife," she said. "I must cut away the cloth. I am not disturbed, Sir Kiernan. To tend these wounds is my duty as Adam's wife."

Kiernan drew his long knife from its sheath and offered her the hilt. "Do not be angry with me," he said, even more softly than before. "I would never shame you. But I cannot change the wish in my heart."

Brielle kept her eyes on the cloth she cut while she thought of what to say. She was glad of the opportunity to speak her mind, and sad to think she might cause pain. But better pain than such trouble between Adam and his cousin.

"If you speak of love to me, Sir Kiernan, you shame yourself. I am your friend, as you well know, but that is all. Remember your oath of fealty to Adam Dunbarton."

Kiernan's pale face went paler yet. "You are right," he said after a long moment. "Forgive me, my lady."

Within a quarter hour, refusing help from a white-faced and frightened Honoria, Brielle had Kiernan's wound cleansed, packed tightly, and bound, and she had shown John Worth and Charles Eastham how to stretch Marsh's broken arm so that the split bone straightened into place, and then to hold it there while she and Philip Tournard strapped it between two thin wooden strips taken from the back of the wagon seat.

Rising from her knees as the men helped Kiernan and Marsh into the wagon, Brielle pushed back her tangled hair and swept it into the hood of her cloak again. Her eyes were full of sympathy as Marsh relaxed his clamped jaws and cursed his pain. She turned to Jacques, who had climbed down from the wagon to offer advice on bone-setting.

"Some of the brandy we brought would not be amiss, Jacques. Tell Honoria to give the two wounded men a good portion, and more if they want it. 'Twill deaden the pain." She looked up as a shadow fell across her path and saw Adam, seated on his warhorse. He was calm, unruffled, and smiling. Her eyes ran over his huge form, and into her mind came the Greek myths her father had loved. There had been a golden god who conquered earthly virgins with his love, and his enemies by tossing thunderbolts. He was never injured. She frowned at the foolish fancy. Certainly Adam Dunbarton was no god!

"Are you wounded, sire?"

"Not I, my lady. No mark on limb or horse. What of Marsh and Kiernan?"

"Their own good health must heal them now. I have done all I can."

"You have done well, then. Here—raise your arms." He leaned far down, caught her up, and swung her into her saddle in front of him. He held her against his mailed chest and took her across the wide space to three knights who sat their horses and awaited them. One, more richly clothed than the others and nearly as large as Adam, brought his horse a few yards closer to meet them. Dark where Adam was light, his broad face gentle instead of stern, still the man bore a true resemblance to him. 'Twas Hugh, then, and older than she expected, Brielle thought, seeing silver-gray streaks in the dark hair showing below his leathern helmet. Her eyes met his, and his smile came slow but genuine as he studied her.

"My brother has found a prize, I vow," he said. "A small but perfect jewel."

Adam laughed, and conscious of her bedraggled appearance, Brielle had to smile at such arrant flattery.

"That was kind, Sir Hugh, but far from the truth. Are any of your men injured? I will see to their wounds."

"One only," Hugh Dunbarton replied, still studying her, "and I saw to him myself. He is able to ride." Hugh's soft brown eyes shifted to Adam, full of approval.

"The Lady Martha will be pleased."

"True." Adam's grin glinted. "I am married at last. She can now omit me from her daily prayers."

Hugh threw back his head and laughed out loud. "Nay, Adam, our mother would never do that. She has only changed her prayer to asking for more grandchildren. She also watches constantly for your arrival."

"Then by all means let us ride." Adam glanced around, seeing the knights waiting patiently, the wagon drawn up in line. "Lead off, Hugh. I'll take my lady to her mare and follow."

Wheeling away, Adam rode to the tree where Angelique was tied. Sprawled on the ground nearby were two dead men in rags of worn furs and filthy rough wool, their feet covered by pieces of hide tied at the ankles, their long hair and beards matted around raw, chapped faces and staring eyes. Brielle shuddered, glancing aside. The bodies seemed less than human to her.

"The Scots are like animals," she said. "How could they be allies of the French?"

"These are wild men from Scotland's southern uplands," Adam said. "Outlaws to decent Scots as well as to us. There are many educated and noble families within the country, and many honest burghers. But these"—he glanced at the bodies with scorn—"these are scum, no different from the scum of any other country. They would rather steal and kill than work." He grasped her again in his arms and lowered her to the ground so she could untie her mare. Leaning on his saddle, he watched her mount Angelique and turn her to travel east again.

"You have come here from a far gentler country," he said, wheeling to ride beside her, "and now must study ours. Philip tells me you were angry with him for staying to guard you. Now, having seen our enemies, perhaps you understand why we never leave our women unprotected."

Brielle nodded glumly. It was beginning to dawn on her that the freedom she had enjoyed in Picardy was over. There she could ride through the valleys for miles without harm; here in this bleak land one must travel in armed groups. She looked behind, seeing now only one knight riding between them and the wagon, and behind the wagon two more leathern helmets bobbing along, leading two horses with empty saddles. As Adam had said, Picardy was a far gentler country, yet —and this was strange—at this moment she had no great wish to return there. Instead, she found herself watching the great spread of rolling valley land ahead, hoping to catch sight of a dim tower, a bright, waving banner—some view, no matter how distant, of Castle on Tyne.

19

the first sight of her new home came to Brielle's eyes like something imagined in a dream. The outline of an ancient donjon appeared, soaring into a misty sky. It seemed to float there, airy as the red banner above it, lifting slightly in a faint breeze. For a moment she wondered if 'twere only illusion, if she imagined what she wanted to see. Then the knights made it real by sending up the halloo for a first sight of home.

Brielle laughed and glanced quickly at Adam. He was smiling, sitting straighter in his saddle. His home, she thought, and her home, though she knew nothing of the place, nor the others in it.

Silent, she watched the eastern land unfold as they came over a rolling hill, and saw the high curtain walls of a great castle in the shallow valley below. The walls rose from a wide moat of dark water, and in the walls were rounded towers with arrow slits for defenders and turrets blazing with bright, fluttering banners. Another donjon had appeared, not so high as the first, darkened by age. There seemed no end to the wall, no final curve to show 'twas completed, even from the vantage point of the small hill they traveled. Brielle knew nothing of English castles, save the ones they had seen along the way from London, but some memory of what Kiernan had told her of Castle on Tyne now came back. She looked at Adam again.

"How long has your family made their home here, sire?"

Adam pointed at the smaller, ancient donjon. "The first Hugh Dunbarton built that keep over two hun-

dred years ago, beginning work in the year of our Lord
1128. Since then, the family has continued to thrive
and build." He glanced down at her and laughed.
"Have no fear. Our place will be much more comfortable than that old pile of stone, which is used now as a
dungeon for men who break our laws."

"And the other keep?"

"'Tis warm and dry in any weather. Grain is stored
in the top, and quarters for our men-at-arms take up
the second level. An infirmary for those who are injured in tourneys and battles is on the first level."

"I see." She wanted to ask more, but when he volun-
teered no other details, she held her tongue. She
would find out for herself all she needed to know.

Hugh Dunbarton, as the heir apparent of the castle,
had ridden before them with his three knights. Now,
within sight of home and with the path they traveled
widening into a road, he dropped back to ride on
Brielle's other side, his knights joining the others who
rode behind the three.

"It is good to see you return with all in good health,"
Hugh said to Adam. "We have heard many stories—no
doubt embroidered with fancy—of the horrors of the
plague."

"The plague needs no embroidery," Adam replied
shortly. "The truth is horror enough. We have been
fortunate." Adam's glance at Brielle's suddenly somber face caught Hugh's eye, and Hugh asked no more,
only commented that the family at home were also
well.

"Except for Royce," he added, his own face falling
into a patient acceptance. "My son is weaker, I fear,
though Candida points out, and 'tis true, that cold
weather has always been hard on Royce's chest. She
believes he'll mend with the coming of summer."

"So it has been before," Adam said. "Don't give up,

Hugh. Many a healthy man has outgrown a sickly childhood.''

Hugh's expression was oddly tender for a large and powerful man. "I wish I could agree. But I think you'll see the difference in Royce this year. I dread to think of how Candida will react when she realizes how little time he has.''

The brothers went on talking, seeming to forget there were others with them. Brielle was shocked and sorry over Hugh's sadness, but warmed by the brotherly feeling between the men. A rare thing, she knew. Rivalries between the first and second sons of a rich family often erupted into bloodshed and murder.

Then, still staring ahead as she rode and marveling at the continual unfolding of the curving wall, she thought of the law of primogeniture, by which the first-born son of a nobleman inherits title, privileges, castle, and all important lands, leaving nothing but a dower house and daily monies to the nobleman's widow and even less to other sons. That law encouraged envy and jealousy—and therefore violence. She glanced again at the two men and felt more comfortable about meeting the family than ever before. Adam, she told herself proudly, would never be without land or income. Due to her father, he owned an important estate in France.

She sat straighter, her pride in what she had brought to the marriage suddenly growing. There would be no envy in Adam's feelings about his brother in their later lives, no hidden hate. 'Twould be a better life than most, and for the first time she realized this was what her father had planned—a safe and comfortable life for her and for her children with a younger son, who would appreciate his good fortune. Yes, safe and comfortable, she thought, but never truly happy. 'Twas sad for them, as for any couple forced into union with strangers and told to make the best of it.

The way they traveled had become a wide way be-

tween the small hills; the hills on the right had become
an old forest of large trees, some evergreen, some winter bare. On the left the rocky ground gave way to
meadows covered with frost-browned grass. Woolly
coated sheep wandered and grazed there.

Now they turned and rode south, in line with the
curving wall that reared less than a quarter mile away.
The height of the wall and the width of the huge moat,
glittering in the long shafts of afternoon sunlight,
struck her mute. Such a castle must be impregnable.

"Why so quiet? Have you nothing to say now that
you draw near the walls of your new home?" Adam's
deep voice was amused. Brielle looked up at him, seeing his love for the old castle shining in his eyes.

"I can say that once inside, the Dunbartons can have
no fears nor foes. Who could cross that moat and
breach those walls? 'Twould be impossible."

Both Adam and Hugh laughed. "Our forebears
planned well," Hugh told her. "That moat was long in
the making, with hundreds of men digging and placing
stone to strengthen the sides. But once done, and the
River Tyne diverted to fill it, it became a defense from
our enemies and a road for trade, for when we open
the iron gates, boats can come into the barbican with
their goods to sell. Look south, my lady. Soon you'll
see the Tyne."

Brielle stared south. Far in the distance, there was a
shimmer of light on water, showing through a break in
the trees. "I believe I see the river," she said. "But 'tis
all a wild scene to my eyes. Those bare rock hills we
passed, these long, untilled valleys, and the mighty
trees of your forests are strange to me. In Picardy all is
farmland or vineyards. Still, something here calls to
me."

Hugh's gentle smile broke through. "Perhaps 'tis the
soul of your mother, Catherine of Pembroke. She loved

these wild lands, and it may be she returns to roam them."

"My mother! Surely, Sir Hugh, you were too young to know her."

"Indeed not. Catherine was only a few years older than I, and as a boy I worshipped her. She was very beautiful and as wild as Northumbria itself. She rode as well as a man and liked to play at jousting." Hugh smiled down into Brielle's wide eyes. "And I also remember your father, for he often visited mine. He was a handsome and gentle Frenchman, who nevertheless fought like a tiger. You carry the blood of two of the best, my lady."

Hugh's lined but kindly face blurred in her sight, for her eyes had filled. Not only had Hugh made it possible for her to picture her mother, he had also given her reason to feel at home on this land. "You have told me more than I ever knew of my mother," she said. "My father never spoke of her because of his grief."

Adam tightened his gloved hand on her shoulder in a gesture that seemed to say he wanted her attention on him. "No tears from you, wife, as we approach our home. Look there, where the wall curves east, and see the barbican." He turned, glancing back at the tired knights carelessly slumped in their saddles, and he raised his voice. "What now, friends? Will you be killed by a crossbow? I see no banners flying to show we are for Dunbarton."

There was laughter and two red banners came up, unfurling as all the party quickened their pace, breaking into a canter. Angelique whinnied and tossed her head, jingling her bridle. Brielle soothed her with a pat even while she eagerly stared ahead. Now the glistening river showed plain to the south, and to the southeast the causeway and barbican in the moat.

Past that, on both sides of the cut that let the water of the moat pour back into the River Tyne, were win-

ter-bound fields and, on the far side, the outlines of
many small houses and a number of larger buildings.

The village of Turnbull, then. Le Fontin Château had
been some miles from the nearest town, and even so
the town was tiny. This was wonderful. Then her attention went back to the castle. The dying sun glinted
flame red on the creamy walls, on the donjons, on the
tip of a graceful white steeple inside. The fresh dark
water of the moat swirled and lapped against its
banks, driven by the river current. Brielle felt a sudden, tremulous joy that tightened her throat. Castle on
Tyne shimmered and again seemed to float, magically,
on the swirling water, on the hot tears brimming in
her eyes. She was awed, for the feeling she had was
the feeling of coming to her true home at last. . . .

They had been seen. Trumpets blared out from the
wall walk above, the drawbridge crashed down before
they could signal, and the portcullis between the two
towers that guarded the entrance to the outer bailey
went up, the chains creaking and straining. Then the
inside drawbridge came winding down to allow a
troop of men-at-arms to march out and line the stone
causeway that crossed from barbican to castle entrance. Hugh led the way, the hooves of the horses
echoing on the wooden drawbridge, clattering through
the barbican and onto the causeway. They passed between the lines of cheering men, and Brielle had her
first sight of the outer courtyard of the castle. Her eyes
widened and then shot to Adam's bearded face. He
glanced down at her and smiled.

"Our people are quick to make holiday of any
event," he said. "They have gathered to see my bride.
Toss back your hood so they can see you well. 'Tis what
they want."

Her cheeks red, Brielle did as Adam ordered, throwing back her hood, shaking out her mass of lustrous
hair, trying to smile brightly as cheers went up from a

mass of serfs and men-at-arms lining their path. She was only vaguely aware of the many buildings crowded in this large space. Besides the two ancient donjons there was a church, an armorer's house and open shed, the stables and mews. She glanced at them, but the number and noise of the celebrating people had her attention. Some two to three hundred were crowded along the way through the outer bailey. From white-haired old men to waving, noisy children, all were bent on greeting the bride. Brielle felt the warmth and saw it in their smiles, and she thought again of Calais, where the eyes had gleamed with anger and hatred and the children lay dying in the gutters.

"Pray God," she muttered, suddenly overcome by the memory, "the Black Death will never find Castle on Tyne."

Adam leaned down as they slowed in the crowd. "What did you say?"

She looked up at him again, her gold-flecked eyes still shining with unshed tears. She would not ruin this day with a mention of the plague, nor the trouble in Calais. "I but asked a blessing on this place, sire. There is so much happiness here."

He smiled and reached his gloved hand to smooth her hair. "'Tis always so," he said carelessly, "and will always be." Looking past her, he laughed and added: "Turn, wife, and take your gift."

She turned and saw a big, yellow-haired woman, dressed in a dark red fustian gown and a blue woollen cloak, walking along fearlessly between Hugh's horse and Angelique, holding out a sheaf of dried golden wheat and dark barley tied with a tangle of bright ribbons.

"For you, my lady, from all of us," the woman said, and smiled. "My name is Linnette, and I was chosen to give this to you because I have eight children."

Laughing, for she knew the gift of stored grain meant she would be as fertile as the woman who gave it, Brielle took it and held it high so all could see.

"I thank you for your good wishes," she called out, "and pray I may fulfill your expectations."

Laughter sprang full-throated from the crowd, and then they came to the gates of the inner bailey and the crowd moved back, respectful of the noble Dunbarton family waiting inside to meet Adam's new bride.

Here the heavy portcullis was drawn up in preparation for their entrance to the courtyard, which was partially paved with brick and the rest laid out in small gardens. The main mansion could be seen through the open gates, a large two-story and gabled home with arched windows decorated with insets of stained glass. The other two mansions were at opposite ends of the large space, facing each other and set apart from the smaller buildings used as kitchens and breweries, laundry, and storerooms. But at first Brielle saw only the three people waiting for them.

Standing together, dressed in velvets and fur-trimmed wool cloaks, the two adults and a tall young boy were waiting with smiles and outstretched hands. The man and woman had to be Adam's parents; the boy Hugh's son. Brielle had time to decide that as they entered the gate, and time to wonder where Hugh's wife might be. Not ill or hurt, she thought, for they were all smiling and pleasant. They were also tall, all of them, as Philippa had said. The Baron Bruce Dunbarton's luxuriant iron gray cap of hair looked as high as Adam's head, and even the boy was tall for the age of ten. And the baroness—oh, very tall, she was, and very dignified. And beautiful in her velvets and furs and snow-white hair. Brielle raised her chin. Travel worn, her hair tangled, her face reddened and wind-scoured, she still must hold her own. But thinking of her hair, she fumbled for her hood to pull it up again and hide the tangles. Adam's hand reached over and pulled it back.

"Such beauty," he said calmly, "should be seen. Leave it down."

She smiled at him; how could she not? Then they were reining in, coming to a stop before the group. Adam slid from his horse and lifted her down. She straightened her shoulders and lifted her head, walking proudly on the frosted bricks as he led her to the tall woman in the ermine-lined cloak.

"My mother," he said, "the Lady Martha Dunbarton."

Brielle had time to note that the woman's hair matched the ermine in color, that her face had tiny wrinkles all over it, delicate as lace, and then she was enfolded in the woman's arms, conscious of warmth and a delicate scent and a soft voice that welcomed "my new daughter." Then she was passed to Lord Bruce, who grasped her shoulders and leaned far down, kissing her on each cheek, then holding her away to look her over.

"I see my beloved friend Henri in your eyes, Lady Brielle, and welcome you as his daughter as well as ours. Allow me to present you to one who has waited impatiently for you to join our family"—he turned to his side and smiled at the youth who stood there—"our grandson, Royce Dunbarton."

Brielle turned to the boy, who was regarding her with curiosity and a dawning pleasure.

"You are Royce, then," she said, smiling, and extended her hands. "I am very glad to meet you." The boy was tall, yes, and handsome, but pale and extremely thin. His eyes, a true violet blue, were huge in his white face, but there was a touch of childish triumph in them as he took her hands.

"I am honored," he said formally, and then laughed

with childish glee. "You are no bigger than I, my lady."

"Royce," Hugh said warningly, "be careful in what you say."

"'Tis but the truth," Brielle said, laughing with the boy, and kissed his cheek. "And I fear he'll soon outstrip me. He looks much like you, Sir Hugh."

Stepping down from his saddle, Hugh came forward and put an arm around Royce's shoulders. "Where is your mother, Royce? Surely she isn't ill?"

Royce shrugged. "Shopping, sire. She meant to be home before you came back." He looked back at Brielle. "I am sorry *Maman* was not here to greet you, Lady Brielle."

"Never mind," Hugh said quickly. "She will meet her tonight at the welcoming feast. We will all be together then."

Adam had waited, impatient but courteous. Now he made their farewells and accepted his father's command to attend dinner, and as his parents turned toward the entrance to the main manse and Hugh drew his son toward home, he placed Brielle's hand on his arm in the formal way and turned her toward the courtyard again. She saw the wagon pulled up before the entrance of the mansion on the west wall, with Jacques, Arabella, and Berthe busily unloading baggage and baskets.

Brielle lifted her skirts with her free hand, far enough to keep the hem from dragging over the muddy bricks, and stared at the building.

"So," she said, unable to keep her pleased satisfaction out of her voice, "that is the home you have for me. It is—quite impressive."

"'Tis beautiful in spring and summer," Adam said. "'Tis barren and cold now." He had forgotten formality and was sweeping her along with an arm around her waist. "But inside 'tis warm enough. As you see,

there are two entries, one into the great hall, and one
—the smaller one to the side—into a private hall and a
staircase to the gallery. Which do you choose?"

Intrigued, Brielle smiled. An hour ago she had felt
exhausted by the rigorous traveling; now she was full
of new spirit and strength. "The smaller, sire. We'd
best stay out of Honoria's way as she directs the unloading."

They passed through a winter-frosted garden space
in front of the mansion, onto the flagstone rectangle
that formed the entryway, and turned to the side. The
heavy door swung open at Adam's touch, and he
ushered Brielle inside with a flourish.

"Your home, my lady."

Brielle was silent, looking around, gazing up. The
walls in this staircase hall were some twenty feet high,
though the balustraded staircase before them disappeared only ten feet above, through a doorway cut in
the south wall. On the east, the wall had three long and
arched windows. There were chairs against the high
west wall, and carved chests, with ancient shields em-
blazoned with the Dunbarton falcon hanging over
them on the polished paneling. Turning slowly, Brielle
absorbed it all. This entry was used as a waiting room,
she realized, for those who came to sell or came with
messages. It was private, away from the usual noise
and confusion of the great hall.

"Come," Adam said, and took her hand again, leading her up the staircase. "You will have years to study
these walls."

They went through the upper door into a scene familiar to any who entered castle domiciles. Just past
the door the hall became a gallery that on the one side
gave access on the south and west to the upper rooms,
which were private to the noble family and their personal servants, and that on the other side gave a full
view of the spacious, reed-strewn great hall below.

Disordered now as the servants bustled back and forth with bundles from the wagon and the heavy helmets and mail shirts removed by the knights, it was still impressive with its long tables and the piles of pallets along the walls. It looked as if it could house a hundred souls or more.

Brielle nodded slightly, glad to find arrangements here that were familiar to her, even though they were much larger. She surmised that one could go down the gallery steps and find many more doors hidden beneath the gallery, for there would be other rooms, some for the favored knights, and some for storage of certain foods, such as wine, herbs, and the rare Eastern spices. And then there would be the locked wardrobe room containing the nobles' valuables—linens, Saracen rugs, all the rare tapestries, silver utensils, gold and silver coins, and bejeweled containers; and last, always on the cool north side, the buttery, where the supplies of milk and butter, the gallons of ale, and the huge rounds of cheese were kept. This much she knew from the château, where all was the same. But instead of a fireplace in the middle of the hall and a matching hole in the roof, as in the château, there were two large hearths on the north wall, hooded to lead the smoke up stone chimneys and so outside, as the fires were in Windsor Castle. She turned to Adam.

"Without the smoke, the cleaning will be cut in half."

He laughed, his blue eyes gleaming. "Your mind is hurrying ahead to domestic duties, I see. Come with me, for I am thinking of better things." He grasped her hand again and leaned over the thick, carved railing of the gallery.

"Seneschal!"

Old Jacques leaped, startled but pleased. He had not been at all sure of the post, though he had known he would be given the stewardship of the domicile if Lady

Brielle had any say in the matter. *"Oui*, sire! Your pleasure?"

"Tell the cook we wish for hot water and soap. There are young, strong maids in the scullery who can bring the tub and pails."

"Oui! Tout de suite!"

Adam frowned. "Speak English."

Jacques bowed. "Eet weel be don now, sire." He scurried off, and Honoria, sending a fleeting look of reassurance up to Brielle, was close behind him. Brielle looked after her with a faint smile. Jacques would do well. Honoria would keep after him until he settled into English ways.

Adam led her back along the gallery to the southeast corner of the upper floor and swung a door wide.

"Ours," he said, and strode in, hurrying her steps with his grip on her arm. "I have decided that I prefer sleeping with you to the privacy of a room alone. Therefore, the lady's room connecting with this one will be left empty until filled with a cradle and child."

Brielle gave him a swift glance, her lips compressed, and then bent her head slightly, acknowledging his right to choose. "As you wish, sire." She turned away, studying the large room, the fireplace, the already-lighted fire, the deep, pillowed embrasures of the leaded windows, the luxurious Saracen rugs, and the satin- and sendal-draped bed with its fine linens and furs. Barbarians the English might be in many ways, she thought, but they were civilized enough in their homes. "How many souls, sire, are in our household?"

Adam shrugged. She noted again how different he seemed here. He had always shown an air of confidence and command, but now he seemed to take on an added luster, as if he, not his father nor his older brother, were the supreme lord of this domain. It puzzled her; she meant to study this until she understood it. She noted that he answered her question carelessly, as if it didn't matter.

"I know not. Perhaps a score or more, since you have added four of your own. 'Tis still less than those needed in the usual households, since my family shares a great number of serfs, a priest, and a physician amongst the three households. Also, we hire our minstrels and mummers from the village for amusement. Why do you ask?"

"Why, so that I may know what amount of foodstuffs and clothing to buy and store."

He laughed and reached for her, swinging her slight body into his arms and kissing her lightly. "We have knowledgeable servants who will manage that, my lady. You will take care of me. I need cosseting and warm encouragement in my primary duty."

"Duty, sire?" She was conscious of his soft beard against her face, the firmness of his lips, the laughter in his blue eyes. He was nothing like the cold and angry man who had come into the Château Le Fontin to claim an unwanted bride, yet she knew that that man still lurked inside and would come out in battle array when Adam was displeased with her. She swayed against him, urged by the big hands that ran slowly down her back and cupped her small buttocks. "What duty?"

He kissed her again, taking his time about it. She felt her passion awaken and begin to simmer deep in her belly. It angered her to be so easily swayed by this man, and she pulled away. He pulled her back, closer.

"'Tis the primary duty of every loyal English noble," he answered, and though his eyes still held laughter, his tone was serious, "to breed loyal English sons. You, my love, have made that duty into the greatest of all pleasures."

Behind the laughter, behind the serious tone, there was a softness, a note that asked for an answering tenderness from her. She knew what he wanted; she could have satisfied the want easily, but she saw no reason to build his pride. *Le bon Dieu* knew that Adam Dunbarton had more than enough pride. Enough for two men. Besides, he needed no more power over her than he already had; why should she confess the wild pleasure she felt in his bed? There was no real love between them, nor tenderness. Only passion.

"You flatter me," she answered coolly, deciding once more that she must rid herself of the desire he was able to make her feel. 'Twas one more rope around her neck; one more iron bar to her cage. Unless she took care, she would lose all of her independence. She pulled away at the sound of footsteps in the hall, approaching the door.

"That will be the maids," Adam said briskly, "with the tub and water. I will send Arabella to you, my lady, while I see to my wounded knights below. Kiernan's cut must be cleansed and bound again. This time I will do it, so you may make ready for the evening."

Brielle nodded, relieved. "I will put on my finest gown for the dinner with your parents," she said as he opened the door. The four maids came in, two of them bringing the big tub, two of them bearing large buckets of steaming water.

"They will appreciate your trouble," Adam said absently, thinking of something else. He stepped aside as the maids set the tub in front of the fireplace and began to fill it. "What did you think of Royce?"

Standing near the fire, Brielle had begun to remove her outer clothes, beginning with the long, warm cloak. "He is a handsome, well-mannered lad," she said thoughtfully, "but I see why Sir Hugh is concerned. The boy does not look well." She looked up, catching the look of pain in Adam's eyes. "Surely," she added softly, "you could see that yourself. Anyone could. He is very weak."

"I know," Adam said abruptly. "But Candida refuses to see it. The time will come when she must face his illness honestly. But I warn you, do not speak of it until she does."

"I understand, sire. I'll not mention it to anyone."

Satisfied, Adam left her with the maids, who then rushed to help her disrobe. Brielle asked their names. One of them, clearly the oldest, spoke up.

"My name is Anna, my lady. I have some skill with dressing hair, having been a tiring woman for Lady Candida whenever her own maid is ill. These others are but kitchen maids. The dark one is May, the stout Saxon girl is Ginnie, the thin one Vernah. Shall I wash your hair?"

Greeting them all, Brielle stepped into the tub and explained to Anna that she had brought her own maid along and that she would attend her. Anna sniffed.

"She'll not know the styles here, my lady. Mayhap she'll burn your hair with a French frizzing iron."

Holding back laughter, Brielle thanked her. "I shall watch her closely," she said. "It was good of you to warn me."

20

Night still fell fast in January, and this night brought snow. Fires roared in Lord Dunbarton's great hall as Adam and Brielle, accompanied across the dark courtyard by servants bearing torches, came into the wide entry passage.

Two huge hounds rose from their places near one of the fires and came to meet them, friendly but curious. Rough-coated, muscular beasts with long, powerful jaws and vicious teeth, they were brindled with tan and gray. Brielle stroked them and exclaimed at their size. The male had only to lift his head to swipe her chin with his tongue. She laughed, but Adam pushed him away and ordered him to lie down. He slunk to the fire again and crouched, the female with him.

"Wolfhounds from Ireland," Adam said. "Good hunters and trackers. Druid there can put down an armed man, and Witch can catch a deer. They will think you a friend coming here with me, so you have no reason to fear them."

"Nor did she," Lord Bruce said, coming up to them. "She seemed well pleased with their attention." He gazed down at Brielle with amused approval. "You have had dogs yourself, I vow, and have learned to trust them."

Brielle smiled, allowing a maid to remove her heavy cloak. Honoria and Arabella had worked wonders with her rumpled clothes, so that her best silk gown had a sheen to it, emphasizing her slenderness and providing a contrast for her ivory skin. Over the pale pink of the silk was a long form-fitting tunic of rose velvet, slit on the sides to show the graceful silk skirts and cut low at the bosom, where a froth of lace half revealed the swell of her breasts. Her dark hair was drawn up to the crown and fastened there, allowing a few waving locks to cascade down her slender neck. She had left off her wimple, and except for the ring Adam had given her and her own cross of gold and rubies that lay in the hollow between her breasts, she wore no jewels.

"I like dogs, Lord Dunbarton, and trust them also. I believe they know I do."

He laughed and offered her his arm. "Indeed, they are harder to deceive than is a man. They know their friends. Now come you and satisfy my dear Martha's burning desire to know everything at once."

Brielle took his arm and walked between the two tall men across the flagstone floor, impressed by the size and luxury of the principal manse. The stone walls of the immense hall soared some thirty feet high and bore hanging tapestries and panels of embroideries, done in brilliant colors and edged with gold. The gallery that gave access to the rooms above was enclosed, though there were many arched openings, decorated with carving and columns, where guards lounged and watched the crowd below.

Tonight, Brielle noted, there were many to watch. Lord Bruce led her through a maze of trestle tables and benches where an hundred or so roistering men-at-arms and castle servants—all those who neither cooked nor served—were already seated and drinking honeymead and fermented cider. Talk and laughter stilled as Lord Bruce neared the closest tables, curious eyes swept the trio of nobles, and talk swelled again in excited waves as they passed.

Chin up, a faint smile on her face, Brielle gave no hint of her surprise at how many men and women were there. She went on, her hand lightly balanced on Dunbarton's arm, toward the dais that stretched

across the room at the far end. Seated there at the
long, linen-covered high table, reserved for the nobles
and their families or guests, were the Baroness
Martha, Sir Hugh, Hugh's son Royce—excitement
burning inside his huge violet eyes—and beside Royce,
one of the most beautiful women Brielle had ever seen.
She looked to be extremely tall, but slender, and her
hair was pale blond, waving back from a face like
white velvet tinged with rose. Her features were delicately formed, her eyes the same shade of violet as
Royce's eyes, identifying her as his mother. The Lady
Candida sat beside her son, and on her other side was
a nobleman with a mass of red curls on his head.

Looking along the table, Brielle noted three empty
places, one on the Lady Martha's left for Lord Bruce
and two on her right, where she and Adam would sit.
The rest of the table was filled with knights in their
holiday finery. She recognized Abel Southers and
Henry Eastham, the two men sent ahead to inform
Lord Bruce of Adam's plan to stay at Windsor. All of
Adam's knights were present except for Kiernan and
Marsh Nelson, who were still recovering from their
wounds. The three who had been with Sir Hugh and a
half-dozen unfamiliar to her finished the table.

In a full year's time, she thought, there would not
have been this many people inside her father's château. And a good thing, too, for they hadn't the servants or room to entertain such a multitude every day.
Some of her confidence wavered and faded. It would
take time to learn the English ways—for her as well as
for poor Jacques. But they *would* learn. She would
make sure of it.

As Lord Dunbarton handed Brielle up on the dais,
everyone at the high table rose and stood without
speaking, their eyes on Dunbarton. Adam, Brielle
noted, moved quietly away from her to stand near one
of the empty seats. Gradually silence came to the rest

of the great hall as even the giggling maids became quiet. Then Dunbarton spoke to them all.

"This day we have met the Lady Brielle Le Fontin, daughter to the Comte Henri Le Fontin of Picardy and now the wife of my son Adam. We have welcomed her to our family and to Castle on Tyne. I bid you now to look upon her and to fasten her image in your memories, for as a Dunbarton she must receive from all of you the same respect you give to me."

He took Brielle's small shoulders in his large hands and turned her first to the left, then center, then right, so that all could look at her face. "Any of you who cannot see her plainly enough to know her tomorrow may now come forward and study her features." He smiled broadly. "'Twill not be hard on your eyes, I promise you."

From the entrance hall came a sudden shout and an explosion of color as three mummers, wearing scarlet tunics and yellow chausses, their pointed hats, arms, and legs covered with jangling bells, danced into the hall and whirled around and through the crowd, shouting questions, pretending to look everywhere, even under the tables, for the new lady.

"I see her not! They say she is as small as a fairy! How shall we know where the lady is hiding?"

"How will we know to bow to her? We may make a mistake and bow to the cook!"

"We must find her and stare! We must study her nose, her eyes, her hair! The great Lord Dunbarton will have us flogged like dogs if we dare to scorn his new daughter!"

Laughter rose higher as they whirled up to the dais, peering at Brielle, laying a finger against a nose and nodding at each other. "'Tis the Lady! Bow, you fools!"

Sweeping off their pointed caps, they bowed in jingling confusion to each other, all three heads cracking together. They sprawled on the floor as cheering became pandemonium. Brielle wiped tears of laughter from her eyes and returned the compliment, bowing with exaggerated grace to the sprawled bodies. From behind her, Adam reached forward and took her arm, raising her up again.

Then from the tables hidden minstrels sprang up with their beribboned lyres and began to play and sing, each taking a different ribald song so that laughter and bells blended and made a roar of gaiety. On the dais everyone was laughing and sitting down again. Lord Bruce beckoned to Adam and Brielle and led them around the table to the opposite side so to sit facing the crowd. Lady Martha patted Brielle's hand as she slipped in beside her and motioned to one of the servants for wine. When the crowd grew quieter and the minstrels changed their tunes to the soft songs of love, Lady Martha spoke and introduced her to "the Lady Candida, Hugh's wife and Royce's mother."

The Lady Candida reached across and took Brielle's hand in hers. "My son has spoken of nothing else but the charming Lady Brielle since I returned from the village! I am so glad to meet you at last. If you need a guide in Turnbull, I will be happy to take you along on my visits there."

Brielle smiled. "Thank you. You are kind to offer. No doubt I will need help. All of you have been so good to me."

The baroness broke in.

"We are all enjoying it, my dear. The castle servants and guards have been looking forward to this ever since Adam left to fetch you. They love the festivals, and I see you like the mummers, as I do. I am so glad you are here at last. Candida and I have been lonely for another woman, and Adam has needed the gentle influence of a wife."

Brielle flushed with warmth and pleasure, feeling

the sincerity in Lady Martha's voice. "My home in France was empty to me after my father died, and had it not been for my English companion, Mistress Woolford, I would have been miserable. Having a large family around seems wonderful to me. I hope to prove myself worthy of such good fortune." She tried to include Lady Candida in her appreciation, but the blond head had turned, leaning toward the man with the red curls, and Candida was carrying on a spirited conversation of her own.

Lady Martha beamed. "Well said, for humility becomes a woman, my Lord Bruce has always told me." She laughed and winked, tapping again on Brielle's hand. "Not that I ask you to believe such manly words. But I have no doubt you will prove much more than worthy. I have seen by my son's face that he feels the good fortune is on his side."

Brielle could not resist a quick sidelong look, catching Adam's blue eyes resting on her with undeniable warmth. She reached for her goblet of wine and pretended to a thirst she did not feel to cool her aroused blood. Catching his eye, she had been pierced by desire so strong, she was afraid it would show on her face. She was still uncomfortable with her feelings for this man who seemed to want nothing from her but a son and a hot body for his lust.

No, he had never mentioned a son, but all men wanted one. And perhaps men who protested great love were only sweetening their chances. No, not all men. Her father had *loved*. He had loved Catherine of Pembroke so well, so thoroughly, so much, that when she died he never looked at another woman. She was suddenly sorry she had thought of her father's love for her mother and his eighteen years of faithfulness to her memory. At this point, Brielle turned up her wine goblet and drained the contents. How sweet it would be if Adam loved her like that. Or . . . loved her at all.

Now, staring at her empty wineglass, she decided she must never allow herself to become a slave to her own lust. If she could not love Adam Dunbarton, she should not want him so much. Her father had told her once that love was all; that in the breeding man was no different from the animals if he had not love for his woman.

"Let me serve you," Adam said, startling her. He grinned as she turned to look at the dripping chunk of rare beef he held. "You were far away," he added, putting the meat on her plate. "Possibly you were visiting Picardy?" He chuckled as her expression confirmed it. He picked up a loaf of still-warm bread and broke it, handing her half. "Eat well, my lady. This is no sleepy château in France. You will need your strength in the days ahead."

Hours later, they emerged from the still-noisy great hall, pulling their cloaks about them and shivering in the sudden chill. Servants carried flaring torches on either side, lighting the dark, snow-spangled night and showing the way to their own domicile.

Content, Brielle held lightly to Adam's arm and thought how wonderfully friendly everyone had been, how amusing the entertainment.

"I have never before seen such an occasion," she said, stifling a yawn. "Though I have heard of such at the French king's court. I feel greatly honored."

"Had Candida her own way," Adam said sourly, "there would be mummers and singers and her red-headed slave at every meal. As Hugh says, Candida is a devoted mother, but she is also a frivolous woman. There are many things to do here besides eat and watch and laugh."

Brielle, conscious of the men carrying the torches and aware that she herself was still a stranger here,

said nothing. But in their room, with the fire burning
brightly and no one else around, she dared a question.

"What is the name of Lady Candida's friend—the
one you called her red-haired slave?"

Adam had relaxed as they came into the comfortable
room and shut the door, but the question brought back
his sour look. He had removed his long, belted tunic of
black velvet, revealing his massive shoulders and
chest, and was busy untying his cross-garters. He
looked up, frowning.

"Sir Eric Fieldham, of Barnstowe Castle, a demesne
some twenty-odd miles from here, owned by his uncle,
Baron Terence Fieldham. Eric is a fool; his thoughts
are constantly fastened on the newest fashion, the
prettiest woman. He idolizes Candida, and Candida is
flattered."

Brielle was silent with surprise. Adam looked disgusted, but that was all. He seemed to bear no real
rancor toward Fieldham, who had done nothing all
evening but dance attendance on Adam's brother's
wife. She thought of Philippa's words about courtly
love and pardonable dalliance.

"Sir Hugh takes this in good part, then?"

Adam shrugged. "He has reason to trust Candida,
even if not Sir Eric. And Hugh is well known to be
difficult to anger." His frown had smoothed out as he
went on removing his clothes and dropping them to
the rug. Brielle, who had learned that a good English
wife hung up not only her own clothes but those of her
husband, came to take them, averting her eyes from
his now-naked body: not from shyness, but from
knowledge of how the sight would affect her. Adam
caught her and whirled her around into his arms. Lifting her off her feet, he stared into her startled eyes.

"Do not believe that I would allow an admirer of
yours to hang around your skirts and kiss your hands,

my lady. I have not Hugh's sweet nature, nor his confidence in his fellow man.''

Calming, Brielle studied his stern face, the thick brows lowering over the darkening blue eyes, and the wide, sculptured mouth set hard in the golden beard. She sighed, and then leaned away, though her impulse had been to lean forward and put her mouth on his.

''I know. Yet I am sure that someday you will have confidence in me. I have been taught to be true, and I promise you now I will be true to you, if only because I have sworn to God that I will.''

Adam's face softened. Letting her slide down his body, he clasped her head in both big palms and kissed her, his tongue gentle, insinuating, stroking suggestively. ''A pretty speech, wife, and I pray you'll never forget it. Here, let me help you.''

''I can manage.'' Watching his hands, she marveled that his big fingers could make such quick work of unfastening her belt, her lacings, her ribbons. Glancing down, she saw that his reason for helping her was becoming very clear. She averted her eyes again. Didn't he know it was past the middle of the night and the end of a tiring journey? They were home. She was exhausted. She was also trying to keep bounds to her passion for him, though that was something she couldn't use as an excuse. But she could say her head ached from too much wine, her legs from all the riding —Sainted Mary! He was in such a hurry he was tossing her good silk gown and her velvet tunic to the floor. . . .

''Adam!''

''Yes?'' Pulling her shift off over her head, he bent and looked at her emerging face and the shining, tumbling hair that fell to half cover it. He lifted the darkly gleaming strands aside and brushed them back tenderly. His eyes, glowing and soft, moved over her nude body. ''Have I done something wrong?''

Slowly, Brielle's indignant expression faded. His hands were not yet clasping her breasts, but she could almost feel them there. He was not yet inside her, but her body was warming, wanting, inviting him in. She thought of how it would be when they came together, and suddenly the warmth spread and turned into raging fire. She gasped with it, shuddered, and reached up, grasping handfuls of his thick golden hair and pulling his bearded face down to hers.

"You have put a devil's spell on me," she whispered. "You've made me a wanton. . . ." She heard her voice as if it came from someone else; she felt herself sway, pressing against him. "Hold me, Adam. Take me, let me feel you moving inside of me. . . ."

Adam groaned, his huge body springing into instant readiness, his arms lifting her again, crushing her to him. He strode to the bed, pushing aside the sewn furs that covered the linen sheets, and sinking down with her. "My Brielle—my little firebrand . . ." His hands were feverish, running over her, kneading, rubbing, exploring her small body. He laid her down beside him and hovered over her, and his hands beneath her brought her breasts up to his lips, then her belly, her loins. His hot mouth licked and sucked and bit, gently at first, and then hungrily, and she cried out, grabbing his crisp hair and holding him to her, knowing they were sliding into madness yet wanting him to go on and on. Adam growled deep in his throat and seized her thighs in his strong hands, parting them, smoothing his hands up the soft inner flesh, probing the nest of dark curls, and finding the heat, the wet, the swollen and throbbing flesh he wanted.

"I ache to know you," he whispered hoarsely. "I want all the mysteries of your body open to me." He felt inside, gently, wonderingly, and felt her velvety flesh clasp his fingers and draw them in. He shuddered with passion and bent his warm, bearded face to her loins, drawing a line upward with his tongue to the apex of her smooth folds. There he felt the jolting surge of her desire shake her and leave her trembling, whispering incoherently.

"Adam, please . . . please. Oh, damnation . . . must I want you so much?"

He was heavy with his own wanting, his own urgent need. His entry was swift, his thick shaft scalding hot as he thrust into her, filling her. Immediately he felt her tighten hard around him, felt the strong, rolling waves of completion begin, heard her moaning in the greatest of pleasures. Awed, he tried to hold himself still, knowing instinctively that 'twas her body begging his for seed, and wanting to feel it, to glory in it. In an instant he knew 'twas of no use, no use at all to try such denial when she asked so sweetly—and so agonizingly well! One more long thrust, and he flung back his head and bellowed out his triumph, his passion, his ecstasy.

21

Within a week, Brielle had fallen into the order of the days in Castle on Tyne. In the mornings the nobles gathered informally around nine and walked in twos and threes together through the opened portcullis and lowered drawbridge to services in the small but lovely chapel in the bailey. Father Mordain, who had been the Dunbarton priest for years, urged them all toward constant prayers for virtue and mortification of the flesh by fasting, a penance Brielle thought, rebelliously, he could use himself and profit by, for he was fat enough to butcher.

But she absorbed the quiet beauty of the chapel, the wavering sweetness of incense, and the chiming of the bell in the reverent silence during mass. It made her think of Father Abelard and realize that she missed him sorely, here in this strange place, in this strange life of duty and passion.

After the services, Adam joined Lord Bruce in his solar for talk, and if it were one of the days when Royce felt well, Hugh took his son riding for a short time, and Brielle was left to walk back to the mansions with Lady Martha and Candida. The walks were brisk in this weather, but during them Brielle discovered several open secrets of Castle on Tyne.

One surprise was that Candida left all household duties to her servants and was quite certain it was proper. She said her constant care of Royce and her own comfort and amusement were more important than domestic tasks any servant could do. Hugh agreed with her, always. Another was that Lord Bruce,

who looked strong, was in uncertain health and did
very little. And the last, a conclusion Brielle made
alone, was that of the three noblemen inside the castle
walls, there was only one to whom the serfs and men-
at-arms looked for guidance, and that one was Adam.
No matter that the winter season was an idle time for a
demesne based mostly on sheep, cattle, and coal, there
was still something to be decided or acted upon every
day—from the hunt for whatever animal was suspected of killing the sheep, to the health of the horses
in the stable. And 'twas always Adam who decided or
acted.

Then she thought it must be her pride in her husband that caused her to think he was acting as lord of
all Castle on Tyne. The more she thought, the more
convinced she became that she was wrong. Lord
Bruce was the master here, and Hugh the firstborn
son. The orders she heard Adam give to men must
have first come from Lord Bruce.

She left off thinking about it and left it to the servants to handle the misguided serf or captain of the
guard who came asking for Adam to settle disputes,
and she began to go about her own business. But the
more she tried to pick up the reins and take over the
management of the mansion, the more puzzled and
anxious she became. It seemed that no servant, not
even her own, listened to her. Honoria, Jacques,
Berthe, and Arabella had been caught up in the regular order of a well-run household and seldom sought
her out to inquire about anything, even for judgment
in a case of disagreement.

Yet it wasn't a matter of disrespect. She couldn't
complain about the way she was treated. All the servants in the household rushed to serve her, bowed
deeply, and smiled often, but they never inquired
about their duties. True, they did them well and properly, but Brielle was not content. She looked for the

reason and found it in the ample person and smiling
face of a middle-aged woman named Hester, whom
she found conversing with Adam one early morning.
She watched and listened until the conversation ended
and then followed Adam through the passage to the
great hall, stepped outside, and asked him into the private hall on the southeast there, where they could be
alone. Everything seemed clear to her now.

"You are robbing me," she told him firmly. "You
have taken my work from me and given it to that
woman."

He stood looking down at her with a half smile on
his wide mouth, his eyes open and clear as a summer
sky. He was wearing a fur-lined cloak in a deep blue,
and beneath it a wool tunic in bright yellow, orna-
mented with chains of gold and rough medallions. His
cream-colored chausses were cross-gartered in russet,
his shoes of russet leather. Beside him, Brielle felt very
dull in her white wimple and the simple gown she
wore for domestic duties.

"No, my love. I have taken away only your drudgery.
Hester has been the chatelaine of my house for years,
and I don't want my wife mending linens, making lists,
and counting jars. I have servants to do that."

She frowned. Why couldn't he understand? "I did
not want to do those silly things," she said shortly. "I
want to run my own house. I want to know 'tis being
done with care and without waste. But you have taken
away all my usefulness."

"You have one useful thing to do," he said, and
grinned, his teeth very white within the golden beard.
"And you do it very well. Everyone within the castle
walls is the happier for it."

She stared at him suspiciously, her throat tight. She
was almost afraid to go on, for she thought she knew
what he meant from the teasing look in his eyes, and if

she was right—her hot temper stirred even as she
asked:

"Just what is this magical thing I do to make everyone happier, sire?"

Adam laughed. "You keep my temper sweet. And all
know it—'tis many a man has said to me that I have
improved wonderfully since my pretty little wife is
keeping me busy in bed. They say they are very grateful to you, my lady."

Brielle was too angry to speak. How *could* he talk of
their lovemaking to others? She could almost hear the
coarse laughter, the bawdy remarks—she whirled
away and ran up the steps to the door that gave into
the gallery, twisted it open, and slammed it shut behind her, running for their room. She was in, shutting
the door and locking it, when she caught sight of herself in the glass that hung on the wall. An old gown;
loosened, trailing hair; a white and contorted face. She
looked like a demented witch. She clenched her fists,
angrier than she had ever been in her life—at herself.
It was her stupidity that had been leading her astray,
making her hope that Adam's lust was turning into
love, that he respected her as chatelaine of his home.
Why, if all the Dunbarton men wanted was a woman
willing to spread her legs so he could pleasure himself
and beget an heir, then why should they get more?
Damnation! She marched to the rows of clothing behind a corner screen and snatched out a warm cloak.
She would go a-visiting. Candida would know who to
find to make new gowns. Gowns in velvet and satin,
gowns in rich russet, in leaf green. And yellow! A yellow like Adam's tunic. . . .

"You are being very sensible," Candida said approvingly. "A bit of gay color is cheerful on a winter day,
and you will want new gowns for the warm weather to
come. Here, try this cream velvet gown of mine. 'Tis

tight on me, and more flattering to your coloring than
ever it was to mine."

They were in the solar of Sir Hugh's home, and the
westering sun of afternoon shone in on an array of
gowns and materials greater than Brielle had ever
seen. Candida had brought them out at the first mention. Draped over beds and chairs, they tempted
Brielle with colors and textures far finer than she had
ever seen. But the admiration in Candida's eyes did
even more for her.

"I vow," Candida said when Brielle disrobed, "'tis
hard to believe a woman your size has a body like that.
I wondered at Adam's contentment when he brought
you here, but I see he has reason. I would say he uses
you often and with great pleasure."

Brielle bit her lip. "I would rather not speak of such
things, Lady Candida. 'Tis a subject that pains me."

Candida's perfect eyebrows went up. "So that's the
way of it. I understand, my dear. I too am cold. I have
not slept in Hugh's bed since Royce was born, nor will
I again sleep with him or any other man. But in company I truly enjoy having men fawn over me. You will,
too, once we dress you properly."

There was no answer to that, Brielle thought, and
she remembered Adam's words: *Hugh has reason to
trust Candida*. Now the reason was plain—Candida
would want no lover. She was one of the cold ones
Adam had told her about; all she wanted from a man
was admiration and frustrated desire. Embarrassed
and silent, Brielle pulled the cream velvet gown over
her head and let it drop. It fell heavily to the floor
without stopping, so she stood within the circle of the
low-cut neck, staring down in surprise. Candida burst
out laughing and rose from the padded bench where
she sat.

"'Tis big enough for two of you! But the color and

texture are lovely for your skin. I'll summon Celestine
—she is an excellent seamstress."

At twilight Brielle made her way home through several inches of snow, glad for the high boots Candida
had lent her. She still felt painfully disillusioned, even
more so after seeing through Candida's sweet exterior,
but her temper was gone. She was able to smile as she
saw Adam coming toward her, huge and dark in his
heavy coat and hood, his beard frosted with snow. He
smiled back at her and took her arm, turning toward
his house.

"Honoria said you'd gone visiting. Did you enjoy
it?"

In a way, she thought, Adam had become himself
today, and a stranger to her. The man she had thought
she knew had been made of her own wishes; therefore
her disappointment was none of his doing, nor was her
pain. He had never asked her to dream of being respected—and loved.

"I did," she answered calmly. "Candida and I
talked, and she advised me on clothes. I am having
some gowns made."

She glanced up at him and seemed to see doubt in
his eyes. "The gowns I ordered," she added deliberately, "are colorful and costly. I hope you will not be
angry at my extravagance."

He shook his head. "'Twill be pleasant to see you
dressed in new finery. 'Tis a shame for a beautiful
woman to hide herself in plain clothes."

They had come to the entrance of their own place,
and Adam slowed his step. She looked up at him in-
quiringly.

"You were angry with me this morning," he said,
pleasantly enough. "Why?"

She turned away. "I had no good reason, sire."

"But you had a reason, good or poor. I'd hear it."

Whirling to face him, she felt the tightness of tears in

her throat. "Why? If I asked you not to tell of our love-making to your friends, would it not spoil your jokes?"

He grasped her arms and held her still, staring down at her. "I told them nothing! All men gibe at a bridegroom and make tales about how weary he looks, how satisfied! What ails you, woman? Do you believe I go about bragging like some young cock with his first conquest?"

"But—you said—" She stopped, staring back at him. "You *said*," she burst out again, trying to loosen her arms from his grasp, "that it was the one useful thing I did! How dare you talk of me as you would a castle whore?"

His grip on her arms tightened like a vise, and his face went red. "I did not class you with a whore! I said —damnation! What I said was praise, you little fool! You please me, by God. What else is a woman for?"

What else is a woman for?

She went on staring at him for a long moment, her golden eyes bleak, her face pale in the evening light. Then she shivered and stepped back, and with a long breath of relief he let her go, opening the heavy door for her. Inside their hall was warm and noisy, the fires roaring, the knights gathered at the high table, talking and drinking wine. They raised a glass to Adam and Brielle, who acknowledged it with nods and then shed their heavy outer clothing and went to the lavers, washing their hands before sitting down, Adam at the head of the table and Brielle on his right, to have their evening meal.

Glancing along the table as the servants brought in food, Brielle saw that Kiernan Comyn had joined the group again. She had been told his wound had healed rapidly. He was talking to Abel Southers about some deer they'd seen in the woods, and his head was turned away from her. But his color was good and she judged him well, if a pound or two lighter, and she was glad he'd suffered no inflammation in his leg. She wondered sadly if Adam would consider the care she had given Kiernan and Marsh Nelson as a useful occupation, or brush it away with the thought that anyone else could have done it as well. Still, Marsh Nelson's arm was straight now and would be as strong as ever, not bent and paining, as a badly set arm might be. And Kiernan was healthy, without a draining and suppurating wound—she glanced at him again and caught his gaze turned toward her face, his green eyes full of a helpless longing. The others were all looking at Henry Eastham and roaring with laughter over his droll tales.

Jolted, Brielle snatched her eyes away and rose from her seat. Adam's gaze swung to her, coolly inquiring. She tilted her head toward the stairs, asking permission, and when he nodded she quietly excused herself, making her way up to the gallery and their rooms.

She did not look around. She was shaken by her reaction to Kiernan's gaze and fearful of Adam's anger if he realized why she had left the table. The look in Kiernan's eyes had struck into her like a sword, and— God help her!—her heart had swelled until it nearly burst. She had wanted to put her arms around him and ease his longing for love—and hers, too.

A week later—a week filled with disturbing thoughts and acts of penance—Brielle walked with Adam toward the chapel in a freezing dawn, wearing a yellow velvet tunic over a flowing russet wool skirt, a hooded sable cape with pouches for her hands, and new russet boots on her small feet.

"We near the end of January," Adam said, his breath a foggy cloud. "Time will run fast toward spring." He hesitated and then went on, asking Brielle if she had any good knowledge of household accounts. His tone was careless, but his eyes swept her face thoughtfully as she answered.

"My father thought me quite able to keep his," she said shortly.

"We have few to keep," Adam answered, still off-hand. "We share the costs of foodstuffs, hay, and oats for the horses and wood for the fires with my parents and brother. Those accounts are all done together in the loft of the main kitchen, where most of the grain and dried fruits are stored. A knight named James Spencer has always done them, and done them well."

"Who oversees him?"

The sudden interest in her tone made Adam smile. "I do. I also oversee Hester's accounts, which are falling behind. They are, of course, only of wages for our servants, the linens and soaps and utensils and such that we use, but the additions to our household have strained Hester's time, and, well—I have been wondering if you could take on the task."

Her face inside the fur hood tilted up to his with an expression of surprise. She swallowed and looked down again, placing her boots precisely on the snowy path. "Why, I wouldn't mind, sire. It would help fill these gloomy winter days—and—and Hester surely needs her load lightened."

He could have laughed at her attempt to hide her pleasure, except that something caught in his throat and stopped him. He was truly amazed at her glad acceptance. No gift he had given her had seemed to please her as much as being given work to do. He slowed his steps as they neared the chapel to ask her an amused question.

"Why does the thought of poring over accounts make your eyes shine so brightly?"

"Oh!" She laughed, gazing up at him and squeezing his arm with both small hands. "Surely you know? You have given me my rightful place in your home. I have become a wife at last, not just a—a—"

"A what?"

She frowned, looking away. "No matter. I am a wife now." She reached and pulled him down, kissing his mouth in spite of the icy frost on his beard and moustache. "I thank you, sire. I will do the work well."

Candida's light laughter came as she swept past them, hurrying Royce to the chapel door with an arm around him. "What a gift Adam must have promised you, my dear Brielle, to make you break through his icy beard to kiss him in gratitude! Did you see that, Hugh?"

"I did, and I envy him."

Laughing, they all crowded into the chapel, Lord Bruce and Lady Martha coming along behind them, stiff with the cold but smiling at their high spirits.

The winter winds dropped during the next week, and the sun shone from a near-cloudless sky. Seated at an oak table in the solar, her account book open and a quill in her hand, Brielle stared through the deep embrasured window seat where Honoria sat embroidering and swore to herself that she could feel the warmth. The morning was like a promise, like a blessing. You could believe in summer again, even with the ground frozen hard as rock.

"A false spring," Hester said direly, coming into the solar with a marked counting stick, "is the Devil's trap. Make sure Sir Adam takes a heavy cloak when he ventures out these days. Such weather can change in a twinkling." She handed the counting stick to Brielle and turned to leave. "'Tis the number of whole sheets, my lady. Another half dozen or more could be mended. I'll set Anna to it—she's handy with a needle."

"'Tis a good thought, Hester. We must be ready for company when spring arrives and people begin their travels to London and back. I wonder who will visit here first?"

Hester grinned. "Sir Eric of Barnstowe, for one.

And Baron Robert Bellenden of Bellenden Castle, a day's ride north of here. Both are forever seeking rich wives, my lady, and hope to find them languishing in neighboring castles."

Brielle laughed, picking up her pen again. "Castle on Tyne would seem the wrong place to start, with no young maidens either rich or poor."

"Yes, m'lady." Hester's brown eyes were guileless. "Perhaps they only come here to enjoy good food and practice their manners before leaving for court. But come they will, for they always do."

Brielle nodded, but absently, for her eyes were on the courtyard again. Adam and Lord Bruce had come out of the big house and now stood talking in the sunlight. Adam drew her eyes as no other person did, and always she felt that certain surge of warmth, the quicker beat of her pulsing blood. She was disillusioned in her hope for real love, but her body dreamed always of passion. She felt it now and yearned after him as he strode toward the outer bailey and the stables. Their lovemaking seemed more tempestuous, more exciting every time, and last night . . . catching Honoria's penetrating glance, she realized her thoughts were showing. With a shake of her head and a compression of her lips, she looked down at the account book again.

"We shall be ready for them, then," she said to Hester belatedly. "But I would speak to Lady Martha before we make any plans."

"Aye, m'lady." Hester bobbed her head and was gone, looking satisfied. Brielle smiled faintly and went on writing down the number of various linens in the wardrobe. Not only Hester but all others in the house had been relieved when Adam gave the household accounts to his wife. Brielle could admit to herself now that Adam had meant well in keeping her idle—but it worked better this way; the servants had expected it, and she was happier.

"Young Royce is coming across the courtyard," Honoria said, her needle pausing as she looked out again. "He is early for his lessons. I have noticed he often is. He must like learning his French from you, Brielle."

"He is bored," Brielle said, and pushed away the sheets of numbers. "Even lessons are better than his empty hours. He is not strong enough to ride now, and for that matter Candida keeps him indoors constantly in bitter weather." Looking at Honoria affectionately, she thought how much happier this English woman was, now that she had returned to her homeland. Honoria's blond hair was now touched with silver, though pleasingly so, but the lines of loneliness and grief had left her smooth face. The days in Picardy during the ravages of the plague and Henri Le Fontin's death had been as hard on Honoria, Brielle thought suddenly, as on herself. A warm and sympathetic woman, Honoria had suffered more than Brielle had expected. It was good to see she had mellowed into contented happiness again. "Wait," she added quickly, seeing Honoria gather her materials and rise from her seat, "you needn't go on Royce's account. He likes to have you here."

"I know. But I, too, tire of empty hours. The Lady Martha would have me visit often, and—well, 'tis a good time for me to go there." Honoria hesitated at the door. "Is there aught you would have me ask or say?"

"Only to give her my love, and ask about her health," Brielle said absently, studying Honoria's pinkening face. Then she smiled broadly. "Oh, yes— you might inform Lord Bruce's handsome steward of the amounts we need of dried fruit and grain. Inquire of Hester before you go."

"Aye," Honoria said with scarlet-faced dignity, "that I will do, if Sir James is not occupied. He is not just a steward, you know—he has the rank of a knight, with many duties." Back straight, she left the room quickly.

Brielle sighed, her smile fading. She had seen the middle-aged James Spencer looking at Honoria like a youth stunned by love, and it didn't surprise her that Honoria was responding to him—Sir James was a gentleman and quite good-looking. How fortunate they were! If only Adam would look at her like that, just once. . . .

"My Lady Brielle!" Royce burst into the room, his pale face alive with excitement. "My mother has sent me to say that since the weather is beautiful, we are going into Turnbull and visit the shops. I am not to have my French lesson, but if you care to go with us, she would be—would be delighted, I believe she said, to have your company in the carriage." He stopped, breathless, and beamed at her. "As I would be, myself. Very delighted!"

Brielle laughed and gave him a quick hug. "And I, also, will be delighted. I will go, you may tell your mother, with the greatest of pleasure. 'Twill be my first trip to Turnbull, and I've wanted to see it."

"Good!" Still breathless, Royce whirled to go back, putting out a hand to steady himself as he wavered and nearly fell. Brielle was quick, catching his hand and holding on, alarmed by his weakness. "Here, now—not so fast."

"I'm not sick!" Royce said defensively. "I'm *not*. Just a little dizzy . . ." The dark eyes looking directly into hers were blurred and fearful. "The trip will do me good. My mother said so."

"Indeed it will," Brielle said comfortingly. "You will be comfortable in the carriage, and warm. You need not overdo."

Royce grinned. "I have money in my pocket, Lady Brielle. I can't spend it in the carriage." He was gone, laughing a little, spots of hectic red on his thin cheeks.

Going to the wardrobe to fetch a warm cloak, Brielle felt tears well up in her eyes. Poor Royce! Inside he was the same as any boy, wanting excitement, wanting play, wanting to test his young strength in contests with his peers. But he had no strength, and he knew it. It was past time for him to be sent to another castle, to be made a squire and taught how to be a true knight. Lessons in swordplay; lessons in horsemanship; lessons in honor. She wiped her eyes and tried to forget the time when he asked Hugh when he would go to be trained. Hugh had said, gently—for Hugh was always gentle—that he would go when he was strong enough.

"And that will be never!" Royce had blurted out, and turned away. "I'll not be a knight, will I, father? I'll not even be a man." The heartbreak and fear in his huge eyes had haunted Brielle ever since. He *knew*.

22

the winding streets of prosperous Turnbull were more like narrow country lanes, each small hut with a garden plot lying fallow beneath the snow, each with a plume of wavering smoke sifting through the holes in the peaked, snow-laden roofs. Children, their faces chapped red from the cold, their stocky bodies bundled in grimy woollens, played in the icy streets without fear, skipping aside and laughing as the carriage came slowly along, bucking over the frozen ruts.

Candida, though she had been cheerful enough as they left the castle walls, grumbled as they drew nearer the sparse line of shops along the icy riverfront.

"I dream of London," she said, "and pray every night that the plague will not come this spring so we can travel there again. It is hard, Brielle, to stay in this God-forgotten place and dream of the wonderful London shops."

Brielle nodded but was silent. She too prayed for the plague to cease, but not for the same reason. Royce, looking first at his mother and then at Brielle, spoke up.

"My father says we are most fortunate to live so far from the large seaports, for the plague seems to be carried by foreign ships. He also says that according to some, it is safe enough to travel through a town where there is plague, but not to stay there even one night. I wonder at that."

Candida patted his hand. "Don't trouble your mind, son. 'Tis God's will who is to suffer the illness, not man's. There, Brielle, there on the corner is the

weaver's shop! Now we will see lovely fine-woven
wools from our own sheep."

The driver from their stables and the man-at-arms
who had accompanied them as a guard took their
purchases of woollen cloth back to the carriage and
then drove behind them as they walked along the
riverfront road to other shops that Candida knew, one
for furs and one where hides hung from a rack.

For many years Turnbull had prospered by tending
the large flocks of Dunbarton sheep and the herds of
Dunbarton cattle, the stocky breed of the Highlands
brought down a century before by Lord Bruce's great-
grandfather. At first, they had traded in bales of wool
and bundles of tanned hides; now, encouraged by Lord
Bruce some years ago, the skillful among them had
become members of the weavers' and leatherworkers'
guilds. Fine woollen cloth and boots, helmets and even
saddles traveled the Tyne to the coast and buyers.

A genial leatherworker sold all three of them fancy
dyed and carved belts and, for Candida, fine soft shoes
with bits of rough rubies sewn on the toes. Royce, fascinated by the cunningly worked leather, bought a
coin pouch with the outline of Castle on Tyne's walls
and donjons worked on it in silver.

"I shall give it to my father," he confided to Brielle,
laughing. "I may as well! I used all of my coins to buy
it, so it is of no use to me."

Royce's face was flushed with excitement, his eyes
too bright, his manner almost feverish. But, Brielle
saw, he was truly enjoying the day. Now, if it could be
a short day, he might not be the worse for it. She mentioned that to Candida as they left the shop and started
along the street, their cloaks beginning to billow in a
sighing wind. Candida frowned and looked at Royce,
tagging behind them.

"Are you tired, my son?"

"No, my lady mother," Royce said, and laughed again, breathlessly. "I am feeling wonderfully strong."

"There," Candida said, turned back, and walked on, smiling with satisfaction. "I knew it would be good for him to get out in the open air. After all, he is a growing boy and 'tis right for him to stretch his strength. Come, this next place is a spice shop, and I wish for something to brighten the dull winter meals."

"There are plenty of spices in our jars," Brielle said, glancing again at Royce. He looked exhausted, and she no longer trusted the weather. "I think I'll wait in the carriage, for the wind is cold and becoming colder as it gains strength. Do not dally, Candida, for it may storm. I'll take Royce to keep me company while we wait."

An hour later, when they were leaving Turnbull, the rising wind had become a snowstorm and people were seeking shelter. The roof of the carriage was little protection with the wind blowing the snow in; they could only huddle together beneath the lap furs, which were soon covered with snow.

"There is no real danger," Candida said crossly. "Even I can see the walls of the castle there before us. For that matter, the horses know their way back to the stables."

Brielle nodded, pulling the furs higher around Royce's pale face, rubbing his icy hands in hers. Candida was right, of course. But it was a slow trip, and cold, an intense cold Brielle had never felt before, colder than ever it got in Picardy, a cold that seemed to enter the bones and freeze the marrow. Still, huddled together in the open carriage with Royce in the middle, they endured the freezing wind without more complaint and breathed sighs of relief when the carriage finally passed through the inner portcullis and stopped at Candida's door.

"Thank God," Candida said, and put an arm around

Royce. "Come now, dear boy. There will be a great fire and hot soup, waiting for us."

Royce's eyes were fever-bright, his thin white cheeks now splotched with patches of frostbite. He struggled to rise, his long, gangling legs giving way. Stricken with sudden fear, Candida cried out and tried to lift him.

"Tired," Royce whispered, his eyes closing. "Let me stay here and rest."

Grasping his wrist, Brielle tried to help him up. Beneath her fingers, his pulse slowed and then raced erratically. She let go of him and flung open the other door, leaping out into deep snow, looking up at the two men huddled on the driver's seat beneath a wool blanket. "Come down and help us, for God's sake! The boy is ill and freezing cold!"

They were down, lifting Royce out, when Hugh and Adam came galloping from the outer bailey. Sliding from his horse with a look of agonized fear on his face, Hugh took his son in his arms and carried him inside, followed by the others, who left the driver and the guard to see to the carriage and their horses as well as the others. Hugh laid Royce on a pallet in front of a blazing fire and went for blankets. Candida, calling loudly for hot soup, ran for the chatelaine.

Kneeling beside the boy, rubbing his icy hands, Brielle was as cold with anxiety as she had been in the icy carriage. Royce's heart was fluttering frantically, his breathing shallow. She prayed as she warmed his hands, her lips moving silently, and finally his pulse settled into a steady beat, and his eyes opened and looked at her with recognition.

"Thank you," he whispered weakly. "It was . . . foolish of me to go. But I so wanted to . . . while I could."

"He will be fine," Candida said later, once Royce had taken a little soup and had spoken again and

smiled. She said it firmly, like a vow. Her eyes were
like the eyes of a fanatic, wide and blank. "'Twas only
the shock of that awful wind and snow that came on us
so quickly, like an evil curse. But do not be frightened
for him, dear Brielle. He'll be up and around again in
a matter of a few days. He's been like this many a time
before and come out of it."

Brielle embraced her, wishing for a miracle to bring
Royce into a full and healthy life. She was determined
to pray for it and to do all she could to help. In the last
few hours she had discovered she truly loved the gal-
lant boy.

"If you need me," she told Candida, "I will come at
once. I have some skill at caring for the sick."

"I will remember," Candida said slowly, "and I
thank you. But Royce is not really sick, you know. He
is only a little weak, a little tired. Rest and good food
will cure him."

Huge and silent, blue eyes impassive above his
golden beard, Adam waited near the outer door until
the women had finished their talk, then moved forward to put Brielle's heavy cloak over her shoulders
again and pull the hood close around her face. His
expression was stern, his mouth set hard as he took
her to the door and out into the blowing snow again.
The wind was howling from the north, strong enough
to make her stagger. Adam moved to block it off, grip-
ping her against his side and holding her in the lee of
his wide body. Her feet barely touched the snow as he
plowed across the courtyard and into the entrance of
his own manse.

Inside, before the fire, they took off their snowy
outer clothes and handed them to Hester, who had
been waiting hours for word of Lady Brielle.

"Did I not say to you this morning, Lady Brielle,"
she babbled excitedly, taking the heavy cloak, "that a

false spring was the Devil's trap? Why, you could have been lost and frozen to death in that storm!"

"Not likely," Adam said stiffly, "as long as they had the carriage. Horses have sense enough to come back to the stables, once the winter wind begins to blow." He looked down at Brielle angrily. "'Tis plain that women do not have the same wisdom. Surely you must have felt the wind come up and seen the sky darken. Why didn't you insist on coming home?"

Was he always to be so angry when some mishap occurred? Brielle hardly knew how to answer without sounding as if she blamed Candida for the dangerous condition Royce was in. Silent, she shook her head and hoped he would realize in a moment that 'twas Candida's carriage, Candida's choice to stay or go. When he said no more, she shrugged and moved away and noticed that Hester left them rapidly, her round face alarmed. Adam's hand shot out and grabbed her shoulder.

"I asked you a question, woman!" he shouted. "Answer it!" Hester broke into a frightened trot, and across the room the knights and Honoria, sitting at table, turned and stared.

Fury flashed through Brielle. Her head came up, her golden eyes glared, she tossed back her tangled hair and set her hands on her hips defiantly. "I have a question of mine own, sire. Why do you humble your wife in company?"

Looming over her, wide as a wall and strong as a bear, Adam let go of her arm and dropped his voice as well, though he was still angry. "Humble you?" he asked savagely. "No one could humble that devilish pride of yours! All I hope to do is keep you safe from harm. From this day on, if you go outside the castle walls, you go with me, and with me only. See that you remember it."

After another long moment, she inclined her head.

"Yes, sire. And now may I retire?" Her tone was as cold as the snowstorm outside. Adam bared his teeth in a travesty of a smile.

"As soon as you've eaten."

"I am not hungry, thank you."

He raised his brows. "Oh? Then I suppose it will take a little longer. I'll not have you go without food after that ordeal. Wait by the fire until your appetite returns."

It was almost laughable. Not quite, but her eyes were no longer icy. He had not hurt her; he had lowered his voice to spare her feelings, and now he was thinking of her well-being. And also, he was making sure she obeyed him. But that much she had promised in her marriage vows. *Promised.*

"In that case," she said, taking his arm formally, "I will give in to your tyranny and eat now. I am too tired to stay up all night."

His other hand covered hers on his forearm, a warm, possessive gesture that he used without thinking. "Tyranny?"

"Do you object to the word? Then of course I must change it. I give in to your superior size and strength."

He shook his head, his eyes cold and steel-blue again. "You have a sharp and acid tongue, my lady. And too little respect for your husband, which you may be learning from Candida. Take care, or I will forbid you her company."

Brielle drew in her breath. He *could*. He could isolate her from the companionship of other women; he could make a prison of the new home she was beginning to enjoy. He had but to open his mouth and say it, and her freedom to come and go was gone. She was finally more uneasy than angry, and silent as he led her to the table. Honoria's worried face relaxed when they sat down and began to eat.

"We feared you snowbound," Honoria said after she

judged Brielle had simmered down. "I am happy to
see you well. Are the others well, also?"

Brielle's mind fled back across the snowy courtyard
and a pang of sorrow tightened her throat. "Not
Royce," she said, and saw all the faces at the table turn
toward her. "Royce is not well at all. The cold wind
was too much for his chest." Her voice shook, and
tears came to her eyes as she thought just how dangerous this day had been for the boy. The mildest winter
wind caused Royce to wheeze and strain for breath,
and 'twas a miracle he'd lived through the storm. She
stared at the food remaining on her plate and knew
she could not eat more. She glanced at Adam and saw
that his expression was serious but softened, his eyes
full of sympathy. He gave her a short nod.

"We will all pray for him, my lady." He turned to
Honoria, who had pushed her plate aside. "Find Arabella, Mistress Woolford, and say my wife is retiring
early. She is exhausted from the storm."

Every day now, Brielle spent an hour at Royce's bed-
side, giving Candida rest and amusing Royce with stories, keeping him at his lessons, which he enjoyed
almost as much as the tales, and watching him drop
off to sleep. It was little enough, she thought, to do for
a friend. Two friends, she amended, for Royce still
thought of her as a magical woman who had secretly
stayed a child inside, for wasn't she the same size as
he? He teased her affectionately for her grown-up airs
and, one day when she sat with him in his sunny room,
looked at her with feverish eyes and insisted that when
he was well, she must still come to play with him. She
smiled and nodded, but that wasn't enough for him.

"Say it!" he commanded imperiously, "Say you will.
You must promise me, Brielle."

She promised and pushed away the thought that he
was not getting well. "I will come until the day you

don't need me," she qualified, and suddenly death
loomed in her mind and frightened her. Upset, she
added crossly: "You shouldn't be so demanding and
disrespectful to me, Royce. I may be small, but I am a
grown woman and I guard my dignity."

"Ha!" Royce closed his eyes, his emaciated face
cracking into a grin. "You may fool the others—but not
me. You act the haughty lady very well, but . . ." He
was gasping for breath, and Brielle put her fingers
gently on his mouth.

"Shhh, dear Royce. Please, do not tax yourself."

He opened his violet eyes and stared at her. "I will
say it yet, Brielle. Inside, you are afeared . . . that the
others will find out . . . that you love us all." His slow
smile was as sweet as Hugh's. "'Tis safe with me, you
know. I . . . won't tell and spoil your dignity."

Brielle laughed, but there were tears in her eyes as
she leaned to kiss his cheek. "So you have found me
out."

One morning as Brielle was readying herself for an
early visit to Royce, Adam told her that the Lady
Martha had called off the usual festivals given for their
Northumbria friends before the Lenten season.

"Because of Royce," Adam added. "My mother said
last evening that she was certain no one in the family
would want the usual mummers and plays and foolish
gaiety."

"I agree," Brielle said sadly. "Royce is weaker. He
sleeps a great deal now but still must be watched. If he
slips from his pillows and lies flat, he cannot take a
breath. Candida is like a wraith, thin and white, floating in and out of his room and speaking constantly of
how much better he seems. If he dies, I fear for her."

Adam held his tongue about Candida. He was sure
Royce would die, for Hugh's description of his son's
frail hold on life was even more convincing than

Brielle's. Hugh, who spent the long night hours with Royce, knew he was losing his son. Adam, considering how he would feel in Hugh's place, wanted to tell Brielle he took great pride in her for the selfless care she gave the boy, but there never seemed to be a time for sentimental words. He turned away instead, remarking that she must be on her way and asking if it were time for him to take a look at her accounts.

Her hand at the door latch, Brielle turned back and blushed. She looked suddenly much younger and far less sure of herself than usual. The golden eyes were shy, asking for understanding.

"The morrow would be better," she said. "I'll have them done by then, truly I will. I—I've fallen behind, sire. I will do better."

Adam smiled. His little wife was always beautiful to him, but with the stiffness of her pride gone and the charmingly flushed cheeks, she was even more appealing. "There is time enough for the accounts when you are not needed in other ways," he answered. "'Tis no great fault to fall behind."

She smiled back, surprised and touched by his kindness. "Thank you, sire. Still, I will order my days so that I do not neglect my duties." She was gone, leaving Adam with a feeling of simple happiness and the thought that perhaps it was as they had once said—in time they would know each other in every way. He had never dreamed that there would be such strength of purpose and respect for duty inside that small head. Nor, he thought, so much passion in her heart. If he could learn the secret of controlling her, he told himself, he would be truly fortunate in his wife.

January faded into a blustery February, and still Royce lived, though the harshness of his breathing could be heard along the hall, and his paroxyms of coughing were terrible to hear or see, for the bright red of blood stained his pillow. Hugh now slept beside his son, wanting to be with him when death came, and Brielle came every morning to take over and allow Hugh time to rest and to comfort Candida.

Stepping from her own threshold into bright sunlight, Brielle decided that though the cold was still bitter in mid-February, the day was one as beautiful as the one Hester had called a false spring—the day they had stayed far too long in Turnbull. The thought sobered her, but as she entered Hugh Dunbarton's manse, Candida came to greet her with a happy smile. She was very thin, the bones of her face showing beneath her translucent skin, but today she had conquered her despair and gone back to her meticulous grooming. Her hair was cunningly looped and braided in a becoming fashion, and her gown was new, a pale blue corded silk bound in silver and gold and embroidered with silver falcons scattered on the wide skirt. She took both of Brielle's hands in hers in greeting.

"I have been waiting for you, my dearest friend! I have wonderful news to tell you! Royce is much, much better, and Hugh has gone to the Convent of the Blessed Child that lies north of here, and has promised to bring back the mother superior. She has great power over any illness, it is said. I feel she will strengthen Royce wonderfully, don't you?"

Surprised and doubtful, Brielle stared at the thin but beautiful face, the strange violet eyes that now seemed to see through Brielle to something far away. She made herself smile. "I pray that she will, Candida. Is Royce sleeping?"

"Oh, yes, sleeping soundly and well, and Lady Martha is watching him. Come, while we have few moments alone, and have a friendly talk. I am hungry for conversation."

There were knights in the great hall, a large number of them, which puzzled Brielle. The group included Sir

James Spencer, Lady Martha's steward who must be
waiting to see her home. Had he come forward, Brielle
would have spoken to him, but he turned away quietly,
like the others, which she thought odd. But Candida
led her on, repeating her news and saying again how
happy she was. They went up the steps to the solar,
which was at the rear of the west-facing house to catch
the early sun. The room was bright today, and warm.
They settled down in a window seat together, and
Candida went on talking.

"I am so relieved, Brielle. During the night, Hugh's
somber fears nearly had me convinced that Royce was
dying. Hugh has always been like that. From the beginning I have recognized that Hugh is weak and easily
frightened. "Why, I recall a time during a tournament . . ."

A strange fear took Brielle as Candida chattered on.
She put a hand on Candida's arm to stop her. "Dearest
Candida, let me ask—are you sure Royce is all right?"

Candida laughed. "I am sure, dear friend. He will
live to see himself as lord of Castle on Tyne yet, in spite
of his silly father." She leaned forward, her smile
bright, but her eyes the same, full of distant visions.
"You see, Royce *has* to live. He knows that, and he will
not fail me. I have planned carefully."

Suddenly Candida left the window seat and began to
pace back and forth, words tumbling from her lips.
"Even Lord Bruce knows Hugh is not strong enough
to rule, and I've pointed out to him often that Adam is
sometimes too lenient with the serfs." She stopped in
front of Brielle and nodded firmly. "But *I* can rule,
and rule well! Once our dear Lord Bruce is gone, I
shall ask Hugh to step aside for Royce, who is next in
line. And Hugh will! He has never wanted to rule this
castle. And then, Brielle, you'll see Castle on Tyne become the richest and most envied demesne in all north
England! Royce will be the ruler, but he'll never argue

with my decisions." She hesitated, staring at Brielle, suddenly anxious. "You do understand, don't you? No one else must know. I will be his regent and the power behind him!"

Brielle's blood ran cold. God help the poor woman! Her worry over her son had disturbed her mind. Her eyes . . . her eyes were too wild, her lips trembled. Slowly it came to her that behind the crazed talk was a woman in fearful agony. *Why?* And why had the knights gathered? To be ready for a death watch? Oh, dear God, please—Brielle leaped to her feet and whirled to the door. "I—I must go, Candida. I must see Royce—I must see him *now.*"

"Oh? Why, there is no need. . . ."

Brielle heard, but she paid no attention. She was gone, skirts flying, running along the gallery to the room where Royce lay, stopping at the open door and catching the edge of the doorway for support as her legs went weak.

There was no need to hurry. Royce was at peace at last. His thin body, dressed in the finest of black velvet laced with silver, lay on a shrouded bier, and candles burned in tall silver stands at each of the four corners. Standing guard, in full battle dress and drawn sword, Kiernan Comyn stared straight ahead, honoring his young cousin for the hour of the death watch allotted to him. His green eyes never wavered, yet tears came into them as Brielle tried to smother her sobs.

The Lady Martha knelt on a velvet-covered prie-dieu near the door. Seeing Brielle's white, contorted face, Lady Martha crossed herself and rose, coming to take Brielle's hand and draw her in to the side of the bier. Royce's face was calm and pure, the lines of pain gone.

"I would have called you in the night," Martha said softly, "but Hugh was with him and comforted him. Hugh said Royce was tired and ready to go. Do not grieve, my dear."

Brielle leaned against the tall old woman and wept.
Not for Royce, rid of his pain-filled and disappointing
life and now in God's arms, but for Hugh and Candida.
For this kindly old woman, losing her only grandchild.
For her own aching heart.

"I loved him," she whispered. "I loved him."

Across the room, Kiernan stood motionless, still as a
statue, tears tracing paths down his rigid cheeks.

The Convent of the Blessed Child was located in an old
priory on the Tyne River some ten miles west of Castle
on Tyne. The nuns there served their God by taking
care of orphaned and deserted children, and also the
occasional travelers who fell ill along their way and
needed nursing. When Hugh saw Candida's hysterical
madness, he had called in his mother to sit with his
son's body and see to the preparations for a death
watch by all the castle knights. He then set out immediately to speak to the mother superior of the convent,
who was noted for her calm acceptance of nervous
madness and her ability to bring a victim back to reality.

Hugh far preferred her way of dealing with the sickness to that of the Bishop John Frederich of Turnbull
Abbey. Instead of the bishop's method of using severe
beatings and purges to rid victims of the evil spirits
that caused madness, Mother Georgina trusted in
prayer, counsel, and time. She agreed immediately to
Hugh's request for haven for his wife but advised him
to placate the bishop by asking him to officiate at his
son's funeral.

"Monsignor Frederich," she added delicately,
"could, if he wished, take your wife from my care and
treat her himself. But he is not likely to do so if he is
asked to officiate at such an important event. The funeral can be held here, so that your wife can be pres-

ent. It may help her return to the sad reality she flees
now.''

Hugh thanked her and said it would be as she
thought wise, and he stopped at the abbey in Turnbull
on his way home to make arrangements. The funeral
was set for two days hence, but Hugh decided to send
Candida to the nuns as soon as he returned home. It
would be kinder by far than to let her go on with her
mad denial of Royce's death.

Each decision Hugh had made was supported by his
parents. Four of the knights who served Lord Bruce
and Candida's own chatelaine, Mary Danforth, set out
immediately with Candida for the convent and returned without her the same day.

Because of Candida's madness none of the neighboring noble families were asked to brave the frigid
weather and attend the rites. Even so, when the time
came for the funeral march, a long line of carriages,
wagons, and men on horseback gathered at midnight
of the day before. Somber and grieving, the Dunbartons made ready for the long ride.

The night was black, no sliver of moon, no faint star
shone. Dozens of flaring torches were lighted and carried high along the sides of the procession as it wound
through black woods toward the distant priory. The
sounds of hoof and wheel were muffled by the thick
snow, the silence broken only by the hissing of the
torches, the creaking of wagons, the fluttering sound
as a horse blew out his warm breath to ease his icy
nostrils.

Brielle sat straighter. The scene had brought her a
strange comfort, for she knew Royce would have delighted in the drama. He would have been fascinated
by the serpentine trail of ominous figures pacing
slowly forward, a dark face suddenly gleaming in the
red light of a torch and then disappearing. He would
have noticed that overhanging branch silhouetted

against the fiery lights, like some giant's hand. He would have broken the silence with his laughter, disdained the freezing cold. Yes, he would be fascinated—and immensely proud of the many stalwart knights come to do him honor. His greatest desire had been to be one of them—a skilled and armored knight, defending Castle on Tyne.

At last the pale sun of winter rose and showed them the old stone priory where the bishop awaited them. Riding toward it, for she had chosen to ride Angelique and give up her carriage space to one of the older women of the households, Brielle hoped she would be able to see Candida before they left. Adam had warned her the mother superior wanted no early intervention by the family, so she had little reason to think she could. But she knew she would try. If not today, then soon.

As they approached the priory, bulking large against the pale western sky, people stepped out from the woods around it and stood in the light snowfall, watching and respectful.

"The villagers, or most of them," Adam muttered, "with nothing but those few fires they tend for warmth. They have come a long, cold way to do honor to a Dunbarton son."

Brielle nodded. "A shame there is not shelter enough inside. But if they are like our peasants in Picardy, they will make do. I am glad they came. Royce would be proud."

Once inside, she was surprised by the number of villagers waiting there. The priory had been built well and boasted a large interior space with a fine but ancient altar, carved by an unknown artist. Bishop Frederich, a strict and silent man who held sway over the convent, liked to conduct marriages and funerals here, for the space held a large crowd; twice as many people could attend than at the abbey. Besides, it was fitting, all said, to have Royce Dunbarton's funeral there and his remains, sealed in a marble casket, buried beneath the altar. For one thing, he was still a blessed child; for another, it had always been the Dunbarton family that supported the convent and the work of the sisters.

Filing past the marble casket, already sealed and held by great ropes over the uncovered pit in front of the altar, the family found seats on either side of Lord Bruce and Lady Martha and settled down, their eyes on Bishop Frederick as he said the funeral mass and then began a long and threatening sermon on death and the hereafter. Heartsore, Brielle endured, taking no comfort from the funeral ritual, nor fright at the description of hell the Bishop deemed necessary to keep others as pure and sinless as "this poor, innocent child, sent but to show us the vanity of the flesh and the failure of riches when God's hand strikes."

That last phrase brought on a moment of rebellion for Brielle, whose wet eyes shot to the bishop and glared. Her firm belief was that the bishop had maligned God. She was certain the Almighty would never lift His hand against a child, though He would gladly open His arms now to receive him.

Candida sat between two strong young nuns, near the altar and the casket. Brielle felt that Candida was beginning to accept the reality of Royce's death, for she was mournful and silent all through the service, instead of talkative and cheerful, denying any trouble, as she had been at home. When the service was over, the two nuns rose and helped Candida to stand, then led her out while the rest of the family kept their seats. To Brielle's eyes, Candida seemed dazed by grief. When she passed Hugh, who sat near the aisle, she seemed to falter, as if she wanted to speak to him, perhaps to beg to come home. Still, Hugh gave no sign that he saw her. Arrangements had been made to leave her at the convent until she was fully recovered, for it was generally thought that she would come to her full senses more readily if she joined in the constant prayers of the nuns and therefore received the help of God.

Brielle failed to get close enough to speak to Candida, for the nuns whisked her away—and outside, Adam bade her to mount her horse at once and start for home with him.

"The others can dally away the day. I am needed at Castle on Tyne."

Brielle persisted. "Stay but a little while, my lord. I wish to speak to Candida. She seems to have realized her loss, and I'd not have her feel we have deserted her."

Adam froze her with a look. "Candida will be better served by Mother Georgina's rules than by your interference. Here—" He swept her up in his arms and set her on Angelique, handing her the reins. "Keep in mind 'tis Candida's stupid pretense that prevented us from making Royce's funeral a dignified and worthy occasion. Kind as he is, Hugh wants her away from home at this time. He says the nuns want no family members to visit her except for him."

"*Pretense?*" Brielle stared at him, shocked. "She is not pretending! She is mad with grief, Adam."

Swinging to the back of his horse, Adam gave her a cold and rebuking glance. "Do you question my judgment? I have known Candida well for many years. If she is mad, she is mad with disappointment. She lived for the day her son would be the Baron of Castle on Tyne."

Brielle gasped. "That is a despicable thing to say. Have you no heart, Adam? No sympathy?"

"My sympathy lies with Hugh. Ride on, wife, and be quiet. I tire of your continual sorting and picking."

* * *

The sun was setting behind the walls of Castle on Tyne as Adam wound his horn and brought the outer draw-bridge down. They rode through the gateway and stopped inside the barbican until the inner drawbridge was lowered and the portcullis raised. Waiting, Adam scanned Brielle's taut face, an ivory cameo wrapped in fur, topping a small tent of dark woollen.

"'Tis amazing," he said, "what a large temper can be confined in such a small body. You have not spoken to me since we left the convent."

She swallowed the impulse to scream a curse at him and stared ahead, silent. The man felt nothing, saw nothing except what mattered to him. Her heart was breaking for Candida, driven mad by the loss of her only child.

Adam smiled. "Have you nothing to say, my lady? 'Tis a rare thing, your silence."

A wave of heat went up over Brielle's face. She grit-ted her teeth.

"You are right as always, my lord." Her tone was heavy with scorn, and Adam's smile faded. Neither of them spoke again, only watched the drawbridge creak slowly down over the ice-crusted moat and then rode on in silence.

Passing through the bailey, Adam motioned for one of the stablemen to follow them to their door. Dis-mounting at the manse, he lifted Brielle from her mare and gave the reins of both horses to the stableman, took her arm, and went inside.

Brielle wondered at that, for it was Adam's custom to see to it himself that his horses were well taken care of after a long ride. But she kept the wonder to herself, anxious only to escape his company and ease her trou-bled spirit. Inside, she loosed herself from his grasp to go in search of Honoria, but even as she drew away, taking off her cloak, Adam ordered her upstairs to their room: not angrily, yet with authority. She stood, holding her cloak, and looked up at him.

"I am not tired," she said clearly. "And I have plans of my own."

Adam smiled slowly, and in the smile she read his intent. He had taken off his leathern helmet and let loose the mass of golden hair that fell near to his wide shoulders. His great, glowing beard, untrimmed for long winter weeks, curled against his strong neck and framed his wide mouth and white teeth. He looked more the lion than ever, and as always when he looked and smiled like that, she felt a hot, treacherous flame leap and grow in her belly.

She said no more. She might have tried to deny Adam, but not the flame that seared her, made her weak. Her will failed against it. When Adam reached for her hand and clasped it, she went with him through the great hall and toward the steps up to the gallery. He stopped there, long enough to order Hester to bring them brandy after their cold ride and to send someone to fill the tub in the solar. Then he went on, still firmly holding Brielle's hand.

Someone had seen their arrival from the upper story, for a hastily laid fire was burning in their room. Adam poured a small glass of brandy for each of them, and they stood near the blaze to drink, watching the hurrying maids with their buckets of water splashing them into the big wooden tub. Hester, mindful of the small size of her mistress, came to Adam and lifted off his heavy mail, looking at it critically.

"'Tis rusted in spots," she said. "'Twill need a good rub to shine again. Your boots, sire?"

Adam sat on a bench by the fire and let her pull off his boots. When she offered to take his thick woollen shirt, he shook his leonine head.

"My wife will manage the rest. We would be alone now."

Hester bent a knee, beckoned the maids, and was gone, closing the door quietly behind her.

The strong brandy, on top of the long ride and torn emotions, had dissolved all of Brielle's restraints. After the week of watching Royce slide toward death, after the horror of Candida's madness and the bitter sorrow of a child's funeral, her mind wanted forgetfulness and her body was ready for warmth and passion, for the promise of life. When she came to Adam, when her hands touched him, taking off his shirt, he knew she'd put aside her bitter anger. His hard face softened, his blue eyes lost their wariness.

"We'll use the tub together," he said, and began undressing her, tossing aside the heavy layers that hid her beauty from him, touching her gently. Brielle responded to him with downcast eyes, with her yielding flesh, her offered kiss. In the tub she soaped and rinsed him from neck to knee, then encircled his narrow loins with her legs and eased herself down on his upthrust shaft to move against it, giving, taking, and ending by lying against his broad chest, shuddering with the intensity of a throbbing climax. Yet when her spasms faded and she sat straight again, she found him still as hard as a rock within her. She felt suddenly shamed.

"My lord, I'd not have taken my pleasure without you, had I but known."

Adam laughed softly. "'Twas a hard-held victory, my love, held only because I wanted more. Tonight I want to revel in your passion and drink my fill of your caresses. Come, let us to bed."

He dried her slowly, carefully, with soft linen and soft strokes, kissing here and there with his hot mouth and the cool, damp beard around it. Brielle was afire again before he finished. Crawling between the linen sheets under the heavy winter furs on their bed, they came together in a sliding tangle of warm skin, reaching arms, low laughter, and kisses.

"A man needn't seduce his own wife," Brielle whispered later, and Adam kissed her open mouth, his raiding tongue smoothing into the corners, curving around her tongue in a thrusting dance.

"I want your pleasure to equal mine."

She marveled at him, her fingers stroking into the thick mass of his golden hair, her palms measuring his immense shoulders, stroking down the iron-hard body she now knew so well. "Perhaps I have already surpassed it."

"The night is not over."

"For either of us," she taunted, her voice betraying the excitement she felt. "If all goes as well for me again, I shall be the victor twice."

Adam laughed, knowing this was one place where his little wife would never give him a real argument, one place where she gave him his due, full and running over. He lay back and stretched his full length, tossing the covers back in the now warm room.

"The battle is on," he said. "See if you can bring me to my knees."

She sat up, her hair falling around her like a dark veil, her golden eyes gleaming in the light of the spirit candle.

"I vow," she murmured, bending over him, "you shall cry mercy." She nuzzled into the soft haze of dark gold hair on his chest, breathing in his musk, then found the hard, flat nipple. She scraped it with her small teeth, then licked the pain away as it hardened. "More?"

"More."

Slowly she moved down, tonguing his navel, feeling the involuntary tensing of his buttocks. She drew lines down the creases of his groins, her fingers warm and slow, and then circled his straining shaft with both caressing palms, stroking and squeezing gently.

"More?"

"If you will . . ." His voice was husky, uncertain. She smiled and swung her lithe bare body between his thighs, leaned over him, and let her hair fall to hide her face. He felt the magical softness of her lips enclose him, the heat of her tongue. For an instant he lay motionless, and then, with a strangled roar, he grasped her, pulled her up beside him and surged over her.

"Tantalizing witch," he growled, and lifted her to his thrust, taking her with tender violence. Brielle closed her eyes, wanting to intensify how he felt inside her, the way their bodies swung and rose, the way she seemed to spiral upward, farther than ever before. Far enough, she felt in her dream, to touch the winter stars and feel their fire in her palms. Then slowly, they reached and found an ecstasy that shook them both and left them limp.

"Wonderful," Adam whispered. "Bliss borrowed from heaven . . . who could have believed it possible. . . ."

Slowly drifting down from that peak of fulfillment, Brielle became aware of an eerie feeling of change in the air, as if the life she had lived until now had shattered and come back together again, shaking itself down into a new form.

For a long time after Adam's deep breathing told her he slept, Brielle lay still, her eyes on the flickering flame of the spirit candle beside their bed, and wondered at the feeling. She felt she had shed some part of who she used to be. As if the love she had felt for a dying boy and the pity she felt for Candida had changed her forever. At this moment, her heart felt full and running over.

A month went by before Brielle spoke to Adam again about Candida, though there hadn't been an hour in any of the days when she hadn't thought of Candida and of her grief. The whole castle seemed steeped in the gray winter gloom, as if Royce's death had taken away all merriment, all laughter and jokes. Perhaps, she thought, Candida would be no happier here than she is in the convent; indeed, she might be better there, where naught would remind her daily of her son. But at least someone should visit her, let her know she was not forgotten. Finally, she dared to broach the subject to Adam one morning in their room, as he donned his heavy outer garments to visit Lord Bruce.

"Has Hugh said aught of Candida? Has he been to the convent?"

"He has, for he went that way some days ago and carried with him a number of barrels of barley and a bale of carded wool for the sisters. But he has said nothing of his visit, nor will I ask. Candida is his wife; when he wants us to know something of her, he will say it."

"She is my friend," Brielle said, turning away, "though she must doubt by now that I am hers."

Adam stayed her with a hand on her shoulder. "I know you want only to comfort her, my lady. And so you will, when she returns. But first she must conquer the willfulness that caused Hugh to send her there."

"The English way of treating a woman half mad with grief is strange to me," Brielle returned with biting sarcasm. "To call her willful, give her silent nuns for company, and leave her there for weeks alone. To my mind 'tis more likely to make her lose what reason she has. Is Hugh hoping she will become truly mad and a magistrate will then set him free?"

"That will be enough." Adam's expression had gone from gentle to thunderous as she spoke. "You overstep yourself. All know that Hugh is the kindest and most dutiful of men, and you are a fool to think otherwise."

After he was gone, Brielle prayed for guidance. The thought of Candida's terrible grief and loneliness and her own inability to comfort her weighed on her mind constantly. She had been sure Hugh would bring her home by now, yet the man had gone there and back again without a word. She also noted that if Hugh was lonely himself, he had managed to hide it. He went about his few winter duties with a calm and pleasant expression, much as he had before. In this world, Brielle told herself bitterly, it was much the best to be a man, whose God-given dominion over the beasts of the field evidently included the women of his household.

Adam returned to the manse at noon. He sought out Brielle, finding her in the window seat of their room, busy at her accounts. Surprised at his early return, she noted a new gleam of anticipation in his blue eyes, quickly explained by his news. The dullness of winter life had lifted.

"My father has been summoned to Bellenden Castle for a meeting of the border lords, and I am to ride with him. We will be gone for upward of a week, perhaps longer if the weather permits a tournament."

"I see. You will enjoy that, sire." Her pen still in her hand, she suddenly brightened. "Is not Bellenden Castle just past the convent by a half day's ride? Could I not go there and stay with Candida for the time you spend at Bellenden?"

Adam's eyes darkened, his golden brows drew down. "I vow your interest in that woman is greater than your interest in your husband. 'Tis enough, Brielle. Let there be peace in our home instead of this eternal wrangling over a selfish, play-acting woman. I'll not have you tagging along as far as the convent just to cosset and spoil Candida."

Brielle's mouth opened and then snapped shut. Adam's remarks were utterly unfair. Her request was eminently sensible; the idea of visiting Candida a Christian one. She had done no wrangling about it at all this time. She laid down her pen and rose from her seat.

"I will see to the clothes you will take with you," she said with frozen dignity. "When do you leave?"

"Before day breaks tomorrow."

"I will have everything ready for you, my lord. What of your knights?"

"I take only four, and they will be John Worth, Marsh Nelson, Charles Eastham, and Abel Southers. My father will be taking four also; we'll not burden the Bellenden staff with too many men."

"I will have Hester see to the provisioning and packing." She swept toward the door, her heavy gown swirling around her, then stopped and looked back. "You meet with the other border lords? There is not another war brewing, Adam?"

Adam smiled slightly. "Not a border war. Perhaps a war of sorts in London, when we travel there in the spring. King Edward is calling us in again, and 'tis rumored he intends to double the amounts we must pay this year for the war with France. The barons may well refuse."

"'Tis a foolish thing," Brielle said stiffly, "for a small country like England to try to conquer France, which is many times England's size and much more civilized." She went on, closing the door firmly behind her, not waiting for his reply. 'Twas bound to bring a dispute, in any case.

It was that night, lying sleepless again beside Adam, that Brielle suddenly saw that her prayer for guidance had been answered. She knew the way to the convent herself; she needed no escort for less than a day's ride. Once Adam was gone, there would be no one left to gainsay her decision to go alone. Of course, she must obey Adam, but if she did not ask, he could not refuse. She curled against him, sleepy at last, satisfied that she was being eminently sensible. On their trip to and

from the Convent of the Blessed Child, they had seen
no beggars, no thieves, no enemies at all. The woods
were safe, and Angelique a fast but gentle mount. She
would go alone, and Candida would know she had a
friend.

the day after the Dunbarton lords left for Bellenden Castle began with a bright, windless morning, ideal weather for a long ride. Brielle hurried through her preparations, gathered the baskets of small cakes and comfits she'd ordered through Hester, put on the warmest of her clothes, and sent a manservant to the stables to bring up Angelique. She was happily excited, laughing at Honoria's dire predictions of Adam's fury. Still, Honoria's frightened face touched her with pity.

"Forget your fears, dear friend. Adam has not ordered me to stay home. Therefore I am not disobeying him."

"He would not think you foolish enough to ride alone!"

"Perhaps. But—oh, Honoria, think of the distress and sadness Candida must feel! Not only has she lost her son, but she is kept from her home, her husband, and those who love her. I am certain Hugh believes it best, but to my mind 'tis torture worse than an enemy could devise. Surely, she'll be happier knowing she has a faithful friend."

Following Brielle's quick steps down the stairs, Honoria was inclined to argue, even though she saw how useless it was. "There could be reasons why the Dunbartons have put the Lady Candida in seclusion, Brielle. Reasons they have not told you. Go to Lady Martha. She will explain, I am sure."

"I know the reason," Brielle said, stopping at the foot of the stairs. "Everyone knows she was driven mad by grief. But she must recover, and I must try to help her."

"Then," Honoria said, giving up, "since I cannot stop you, send for a gentle horse. I shall go with you."

Brielle kissed her cheek. "I go alone. I will be traveling fast, and you cannot sit a galloping horse. Stop fretting. I will be back two days hence, safe and satisfied. Perhaps my lord Adam will never know I went."

She motioned to the groom who had brought Angelique, and he bent, clasping his hands for her foot and boosting her up. She reached down, took the baskets from Honoria's hands, and hung them on either side of her saddle. She was wearing a voluminous red cloak that spread to cover the baskets and most of Angelique's snowy hindquarters.

"There," she said, laughing down at Honoria's worried eyes. "Does this not bring back the days at the château? Don't you remember how I rode out with baskets for the sick? You never worried then, Honoria. Perhaps you are getting old."

Honoria reddened. "I am old enough to have some sense," she said tartly. "This is not the château, nor is the convent as close as our workers' huts in France. Besides, the woods in Picardy are not full of wolves and dirty Scots."

Brielle was still smiling. "True, but on the other hand, neither wolves nor Scots can catch Angelique." She was gone through the open portcullis of the inner courtyard, and through the crowded bailey, where men and women stopped what they were doing and stood smiling as she passed through. She glanced at the small chapel there and crossed herself, breathing a prayer for Candida's happiness. Then she threw up a hand to signal the watchman at the outer portcullis. Unmoving, he gazed at her in disbelief. She rode closer, frowning.

"Are you blind, Thomas?"

"No, my lady! But—are you riding out alone?"

"Indeed. Unless you intend to keep me prisoner."

"Oh, no, my lady! But—"

"Either you raise that maze of rusty iron now, or I shall report you to Sir Adam. I am late in following him, and he is not a patient man!"

With a sudden creaking of chains, the portcullis screeched upward.

There had been no snow since the Dunbarton lords rode west. Once across the stone causeway, Brielle had but to follow the path beaten down by the hooves of the heavy warhorses. She gave Angelique her head, and in less than an hour they were in the thick woods.

In the woods she slowed to a fast trot because of the uneven ground and the big rocks, some covered with slippery moss, that lay in the path. She was guiding Angelique between two of the rocks when she heard a deep, belling howl behind her, followed by an excited yipping.

Wolves! For a long moment she couldn't breathe. Then, turning Angelique away from the rocks, she kicked her sides. She had heard that hungry wolves sometimes pulled down a horse as well as sheep, and she took no chances. The wolves would have to catch her.

Minutes later, racing across a clearing, she looked back and gasped. Two enormous gray and tan animals loped along behind Angelique's heels, tongues lolling from open jaws full of sharp, vicious-looking teeth, their eyes on her. She brought Angelique to a stop, her held breath whooshing out in a great sigh of relief.

"Druid! Witch! You've come to see me through my trip, then! Good dogs."

The two wolfhounds lost their dignity at her pleased tone, and cavorted, kicking up snow and pouncing at each other. She laughed and turned Angelique toward

the convent again. Undoubtedly Honoria had gone to
Lady Martha, and the two of them had had the dogs
loosed on her trail. The wolfhounds had been taught to
follow and protect; without an escort, she might have
asked for them herself, had she thought of it.

At noon she stole three of the rich cakes in one basket, eating one and tossing two to the hounds, who
snatched them in the air and swallowed them in a
gulp. An hour later, she saw the crenellated tower of
the old priory, the cross dark against the bright sky.
Almost there. Another half hour, and she would be
with Candida, comforting her.

An old man came to meet her in the cobbled courtyard of the priory, a gentle man showing no fear of the
huge dogs.

"I see ye come from Castle on Tyne," he said, grasping Angelique's bridle and giving the mare a pat. "I
know Lord Dunbarton's alaunts. 'Tis handsome beasts
they are, and well behaved. Have ye news?"

Dismounting, Brielle petted the eager dogs, scratch-
ing their ears. Druid was a favorite of hers, and Witch
a close second. "Nay, no news. I come to visit a day or
so with my friend, the Lady Hugh Dunbarton."

The kind look in his faded eyes sharpened. "Ah, yes.
The woman who lost the power of speech. A pity, that.
The mother superior says 'tis a Devil's spell and takes
time to cure."

Brielle gazed at him with questions tumbling
through her mind, then shook her head. He'd not
know answers for her, only gossip.

"Will you look after my mare and the alaunts?"

"That I will, my lady. The stables are clean and
warm; the dogs more than welcome to share."

"I thank you." Taking the baskets as the old man
handed them over, Brielle gave him a packet of the
comfits and then picked her way across the slippery
stones to the priory entrance, her chest tight with un-

certainty. It was hard to imagine Candida unable to speak. Was her grief overpowering enough to possess her whole mind? Oh, if only she can hear and comprehend! Surely, if she could convince Candida that she was loved and wanted . . .

A young girl, wearing the white gown and plain headdress of a novice, opened the tall door and came out, startled as she saw Brielle coming toward her. She curtseyed quickly and stood back to allow Brielle entrance.

"Shall I tell Mother Superior she has a noble caller?"

"Take me to her, please. I am Lady Brielle Dunbarton."

The Dunbarton name worked magic, as Brielle had supposed it would. The novice asked no questions, only led her through the echoing stone hall and along a dark passage behind, coming at the end to a half-open door. Looking through, Brielle saw a room cheered by the warmth of a fire and the golden light of afternoon.

Mother Georgina, dressed in her usual gray and white habit, came to the door when the novice tapped it timidly and, seeing Brielle, opened it wide.

"Welcome, my lady! 'Tis an honor to have you visit us." She motioned to the novice, who was backing away. "Wait, Serena. I'll want to send you to Sister Louise so she can prepare rooms." She turned back, beaming, to Brielle. "How many are in your party?"

"I traveled here alone, Mother." She smiled at Mother Georgina's expression. "Except for two large dogs. They are already comfortable in your stables, along with my mare."

"Alone? Your husband permitted you to ride here from Castle on Tyne without an escort?" Georgina was horrified.

Brielle raised her chin. "I arrived safely, did I not? I

was protected by Lord Bruce's pair of wolfhounds."
She was careful not to answer the mother superior's
question but hurried on. "I need only a bed in Lady
Candida's room, for I've come to keep her company
for a day or so. I hope that won't disturb your daily
life." Watching the elderly woman, she saw a shadow
cross the usually amiable face; a look of sorrow in the
deep-set eyes.

"I'm afraid you've made your trip for nothing, Lady
Brielle. Lady Candida has lost the power of speech.
Nothing rouses her from her grief, not even the presence of her husband. Lord Hugh stopped here yester-
day, on his way to Bellenden Castle, and tried once
more to talk to his wife. She only sat there like a
statue, staring past him."

A tremor of dread struck through Brielle's chest, a
feeling of imminent pain and sorrow. She pushed it
away, hunting for courage.

"Take me to her at once," she said, and handed the
baskets to Serena. "We have been close friends. Perhaps she will recognize me."

Mother Georgina hesitated and then nodded. "It can
do no harm, I suppose. Come with me."

They went out again into the dark passage, lit by an
occasional candle stuck into the crevices between the
stones, and then another passage, leading away from
the sanctuary and the altar, toward the shabby but
comfortable living quarters of the nuns and the rooms
where they kept and fed and taught the orphan children. They walked quickly, Serena trailing behind, until they were past the cheerful sounds of children and
came to the rooms set aside for the sick and dying and
those suffering from spells or possessed by evil spirits.

Approaching these last rooms, located in a wing at
one end, the mother superior slackened her pace. Her
glance slid to Brielle's questioning eyes.

"I must warn you," she said, "you will find Lady

Candida much changed. She eats very little, and though her health seems good, she is thin. God alone knows what terrible spell holds her in its grip."

"It may be simple grief," Brielle said, "and the loss of all she loved. Still, 'tis strange that her husband cannot rouse her to speech. He is a gentle and loving man."

Georgina nodded. "He seems so," she agreed, stopping before a closed door. "But she does not recognize him."

For a moment Brielle's determination faltered. If Candida failed to recognize her husband, how could she recognize a woman she'd known for such a short time? Perhaps she'd made this trip and risked Adam's anger for naught. . . .

Mother Georgina was unlocking the door, opening it wide. "Come," she said, "she is sitting up in her chair, almost as if she waited for you."

Brielle stepped inside. It was true; Candida sat in a pillowed chair, her long blond hair hanging in gleaming swaths that covered her shoulders, her brilliant violet eyes fixed on space. She was thin, yes, but still eerily beautiful, with a delicacy of bone and paperwhite skin that frightened Brielle with its fragility. She went forward and dropped to her knees before Candida, grasping one of her large hands, holding it in both of hers. The hand was lax and cold.

"Candida, dear friend!"

For a second the violet eyes flickered and deepened, as if some deep emotion stirred inside. Then the pale, perfectly formed lips moved and a hoarse voice whispered words.

"You . . . came. I prayed you would."

Behind Brielle the mother superior gasped audibly. Tears came to Brielle's eyes. She lifted Candida's hand to her warm cheek and held it there.

"Yes," she said, choked. "I am here, Candida. I want to help you. I'll stay as long as I can."

"Good. I wanted you—not Hugh. He doesn't know. Nobody knows but us. . . . You and I, Brielle. . . . We know what happened."

Mother Georgina had gone to her knees at the prie-dieu against the wall. Her fervent prayers of thanksgiving for a miracle grew louder as Brielle got to her feet, still holding Candida's hand.

Awed and wide-eyed, the novice Serena stood in the doorway, clasping the baskets in her arms. Now, knowing from the odors that the baskets contained sweets, she came forward with them, eager to help.

"Perhaps Lady Candida would eat these delicacies you brought," she whispered. "She eats very little, and it would be good for her."

When Mother Georgina rose from her prayers and came to the small group, Candida was holding a small cake and taking bites of it, finishing it all and licking her fingers like a child. Looking up, she frowned at the mother superior.

"You are not to take Lady Brielle away from me," she said. Already the disused, hoarse voice was coming clear again. "She must remain with me."

"And she will, my lady. But first we must bring in a bed for her and find the linens. Also, I must talk to her in my retreat. But I promise you she will return, and soon."

Later, after Mother Georgina had sent Serena and a young nun to take a cot to Candida's cell and spread it with linens, she spoke with Brielle in her own room.

"I am ashamed to say that I had given up on curing Lady Candida's soul. I believed I saw a dark shadow in her eyes, as if a demon possessed her. Yet the sight of you, her friend, worked a miracle! 'Tis strange that her husband never mentioned the friendship between you

and his wife. But then, a man can never fully understand a woman's heart."

Brielle nodded. That was a statement with which
she wholly agreed. Thinking of how pleased Sir Hugh
would be at Candida's recovery, she felt a flicker of
selfish triumph. Adam, too, would have to admit she'd
been right to help Candida. Rising, she smiled at
Mother Georgina.

"I'll find my way back," she said. "I want to be with
her as much as I can. I'm hoping for a full recovery
before her husband comes this way again. Surely he
will be pleased to have his wife at home once more."

That night Serena brought full trays of food to
Candida's cell and took away empty ones. Candida
said very little but ate with a will. Brielle praised her.

"'Tis good food you need, Candida. It gives strength
and health." She wanted to add that with her mind
and body restored, Candida could have another child.
She was still in her thirties; a healthy child would give
her purpose in life. But she said nothing of children,
fearing to intensify Candida's grief over Royce.

Candida's pale mouth flattened in a small smile. "I
may look weak, but I have the strength I need, dear
Brielle. Remember, I am much bigger and stronger
than you are."

The next day Candida insisted on going to the great
hall to pray at the altar, and she walked there without
aid. Mother Georgina saw tall Candida pass her door
with her tiny friend beside her for support and went
with them, her old face soft and thankful as they came
into the echoing room.

"I will give thanks to the Mother of God," Georgina
said, her voice trembling. "She is always a woman's
advocate when God turns His face away."

Candida frowned, fingering the gold crucifix she
wore. "Pray as you will, Mother. I myself will pray at
my son's tomb. 'Twill give me the courage I need." She

pulled away from Brielle's arm and went quickly to the front of the altar, kneeling at the graven silver plate let into the floor. Brielle started to follow, but Candida raised a hand to motion her away. Kneeling in her gauzy white silk gown, her pale blond hair floating around her beautiful face, she leaned to trace the words engraved on the plate, speaking them in a whisper.

" 'Here lies the body of Royce Ainsley Dunbarton, son of Lord Hugh Dunbarton and Lady Candida Ainsley Dunbarton, born on June 23, in the year of Our Lord 1339, died on February 25, 1350. The Lord giveth and the Lord taketh away. Blessed be the name of the Lord.' "

Kneeling herself beside the bulky body and gray habit of the mother superior, Brielle had not begun to pray. Instead, she watched Candida fearfully, afraid she'd overtax her strength. But as the whispered words died away, she saw Candida straighten on her knees and lift her face to stare at the vaulted ceiling. She raised her hands heavenward, and her lips moved again, soundlessly. Watching, Brielle felt a sudden profound shock. She could read the lips almost as well as if Candida spoke aloud.

"Now damned to hell be the Lord who stole my son from me. Lucifer, Lucifer, hear my plea. . . ." The rest was lost as Brielle leaped up and went swiftly to Candida, reaching down and grasping her arms, bringing her upright. Hearing Mother Georgina scrambling to her feet, she spoke quickly.

"I am sorry to disturb your prayers, Candida, but you seemed faint—"

"I am not faint! I—I . . ." Her hands had come apart, and there was a glint of gold inside. From behind Brielle the mother superior reached and snatched the crucifix she held.

"Sainted Mary preserve our souls! 'Twas good that

Lady Brielle stopped your prayer, Lady Dunbarton! In your confusion you were holding your crucifix upside down! Good Christian though you are, that sign would bring the Devil to you had you continued to pray."

Fear and love for her friend warred in Brielle's heart. She knew Candida had tried to pray to the Devil, though she knew nothing of Lucifer save his name and the story of his blasphemous pride that had made God drive him from Heaven. She had never feared Lucifer, for she knew God Himself protected His people from that Dark Angel. But if Candida called a curse on God—no! Candida was held by a demon, and the demon must be blamed. She put an arm around Candida, who was white and weak. "Come," she said gently, "we will pray in our room."

For an instant the violet eyes defied her. Then, leaning heavily on the offered arm, Candida nodded. "Perhaps you are right. Prayer works best in secret."

All day Brielle talked to Candida and asked her to join in prayer. But Candida, who had quickly regained her confidence, only smiled.

"I have my own gods," she said. "I pray to them, and they answer. My gods brought you here."

"Nay. The true God brought me here. He knew you needed me. Now, pray with me. Cleanse your heart of pain and false gods. I must leave tomorrow."

"You will not leave here, Brielle. I know." Candida's voice was sure, though her thin face showed strain. "You will stay with me forever."

Brielle sighed and gave it up. Late in the day, she left the room they shared and went to talk to Mother Georgina.

"I have failed," she said, her voice full of sadness. "Perhaps I have even made her worse. She cannot grasp the truth and insists I must stay with her forever. When I leave, she may go back into silence again." She said nothing of Candida's "gods," and certainly nothing of Lucifer. If it were known that Candida prayed to the Devil, she would have to be handed over to Bishop Frederich for punishment.

"You have done your best," Mother Georgina said. "Have no regrets. We may be able to bring her out ourselves, now that you have shown us that it can be done. We are grateful for your help."

Brielle returned to the room in the company of the nun who brought their suppers. During the meal, which they ate at a table by a window, she talked of Castle on Tyne and the people there, hoping to interest Candida. But Candida was lost in thought, her violet eyes wide and blank, her mind elsewhere as she toyed with her food.

Later, as Brielle prepared for bed, Candida became talkative. She spoke of Royce, calling to mind his handsome face, his tall body. She recounted his jokes and tricks, and she praised his good nature. Brielle, sitting up in her bed, leaning against the thin pillow provided by the nuns, listened and agreed, hoping to ease Candida's heart.

"He was a joy to us all," she said softly. "Everyone loved him."

Candida sprang to her feet. She still wore the voluminous white gown she'd worn all day, but she'd added a full black wool cloak that covered her from top to toe. She seemed distraught, her hair disarranged, the violet eyes glittering in her white face. "Come," she said, "I would pray in the sanctuary, near my son. This time that old woman will not be awake and prowling around. This time I will say a proper prayer!"

Brielle was doubtful. "To God? To the Holy Trinity?"

Candida laughed. "If you wish. Even to doleful Mary! Does that please you?"

Brielle slipped from the bed and flung on her cloak.

"Indeed," she said, smiling, and put an arm around Candida's waist. "'Twill do us both good."

They took candles, for the guttering stubs in the halls would not last another half hour. The whole priory was as quiet as the grave; the children were asleep, and the nuns who prayed the day through had gone to bed. They went swiftly along the cold halls and into the sanctuary. Teeth chattering, Brielle lit all the candles behind the altar and turned to find Candida staring at them and the figure of Christ on the cross. In the flickering light the figure seemed alive.

"Mother Georgina will not like so many candles used," Candida said, her voice trembling. "Blow them out."

Brielle shook her head. "I will give her money for more. She will understand that we needed them." Stepping down past the altar, she turned and bowed, making the sign of the cross. Then she went to Candida and stood, looking down at the silver plate that identified Royce's tomb.

"Shall we pray now?"

Candida didn't answer. She still stared at the Christ, her eyes wide and blank, the candles reflected in the violet depths as in a mirror. After a long moment, she whispered.

"Royce was all I had. My life. My future."

"I know."

"I loved him."

Brielle winced, feeling the sting of tears in her eyes. "And I. I loved him, too." She sensed the tension in Candida's tall figure beside her, heard her indrawn breath. She looked up and saw that the violet eyes had left the figure of Christ and were fixed on her.

"You hated him," Candida said hoarsely, "and you killed him. Didn't you know I'd find it out?"

Brielle gasped and shrank away, staring in horror at

Candida's glittering eyes, her twisted face. When she found her voice, it came out in a choked whisper.

"How can you say that to me?"

Candida stepped closer. "I knew you were jealous of me. You wanted to be the baroness someday, you wanted your son to rule instead of Royce. You gave yourself away when I told you Royce was better. You became agitated and ran to his room. When I went there later, he was dead. You killed him!"

Brielle burst into tears. "Oh, Candida! Surely you can't believe that? I was there every day, helping to nurse him, praying for his recovery."

Candida's lip curled. "More likely praying for his death, hoping you wouldn't have to commit murder and lose your immortal soul to Hell!" Suddenly, she thrust her hand beneath her cloak and drew a bejeweled dagger from a hidden pocket. She laughed as Brielle stepped back, frightened.

"You'll have no children, Brielle! You die now!" Raising the dagger high, she lunged forward, her eyes wild, the blade glittering in the wavering candlelight.

Brielle screamed at the top of her voice. Frail Candida still was far larger than she and possessed of a madwoman's strength. The knife slashed the air as she dodged to the side and ran toward the dark archway that led into the passages. She heard Candida's pounding feet behind her, her shriek of rage—dear God, 'twas too close, too loud—and felt the tug as the dagger caught in her billowing cloak, heard the rasp as the cloak split. She swung around, seeing the mad fury in Candida's contorted face, the swinging, shining blade. She swayed, half fainting from fear, and put her hands out as if to stop the knife.

"No, Candida! I am not your enemy!"

From the archway, like an echo, came another scream, another voice, hoarse and terrified. "No! No! Stop, in the name of God! Put down your weapon!"

"Murderess!" Candida hissed, and flung herself forward, her foot catching in the front of her swinging cloak, tripping her. The descending dagger wavered from its target as she fell, missing Brielle's breast and heart by inches, then burying itself in her upper thigh. Falling heavily to the stone floor, Candida loosed her grip, leaving the quivering blade embedded to the hilt.

Brielle's eyes widened, staring down at the glittering handle, and then closed. She slumped in a faint, never feeling the arms that caught and eased her down, never seeing Serena's young eyes full of fear and pity, nor the horror in Mother Georgina's face.

Lying before them, eyes immense and wild with fury, Candida screamed and beat her closed fists against the stone. "Lucifer, Lucifer! I pray in the name of the Dark Angel, take the soul of this woman to Hell!"

By now, the archway was crowded with a half-dozen frightened nuns, roused by the screaming, horrified by what they saw and heard.

"Bring a litter," Mother Georgina commanded. "Be quick about it! Then waken old Jonas and have him send a stable boy to Bellenden Castle to tell the Baron Dunbarton and his sons what has happened here.

"And mark this, all of you! Do you not look at the Lady Candida's face again, not in the eyes, nor listen to her words. She is possessed by a powerful demon. You could lose your immortal soul!"

24

Brielle opened her eyes, seeing through a haze of pain the elderly sister who set the bones and bandaged the wounds of the injured who came to the convent. Sister Lorraine was leaning over her where she lay on a litter, removing the dagger. Brielle gave a quivering groan as the blade slipped out from the puffed flesh and blood welled up, sliding bright red over the ivory skin of her thigh. The sister's faded eyes, full of sympathy, went to her frightened face.

"'Tis wise to let it bleed freely for a moment or two," she said. "It washes the wound with your own good blood."

"It hurts, sister." Brielle's voice shook. "Truly it does."

"Naturally. 'Tis a deep wound." The old woman swabbed the thigh with a clean linen rag, watching the flow carefully. "Ah! Our God has been merciful to you. Cuts like this can pump out all a heart's blood, but this one is only welling up and will soon stop. The danger is over, though you must suffer the pain. Bring me more cloth, Serena."

Serena came forward, bringing folded white cloth, and helped as Sister Lorraine stanched the bleeding and bound the wound. Mother Georgina, her face greenish white, stood in a corner and watched until it was done. Then she came forward and, in a pitying gesture, put her cool hand on Brielle's forehead.

"'Tis precious little sleep you'll have tonight," she said, "but you are safe. We have locked the Lady

Candida into a cell at the other end of the priory, and
Serena will stay in your room to keep you company."

Brielle's eyes filled with tears. "Poor Candida," she
whispered. "Will she regain her senses, mother?"

"Perhaps. But in some cases many demons come to
fill the empty space only one left behind. 'Tis a matter
for Bishop John Frederich now."

Brielle gasped. "But—he beats his prisoners with
rods! Keep Candida here, please! When I am gone,
there will be no trouble. 'Tis only I she hates!" Brielle
winced with pain as she tried to sit up. Failing, she
reached a hand and clutched Mother Georgina's arm.
"She may die if you send her to Bishop Frederich. She
is too frail for cruelty."

Georgina shook her head. "I too am sorry she must
undergo such treatment, Lady Brielle. But I heard her
myself when she prayed to the Evil One. Bishop
Frederich is hard, but he is often successful."

Later, when she was alone in the room she and
Candida had shared, tears came to Brielle's eyes. She
had not helped Candida at all; she had caused her even
more pain by defying Adam and coming here. She
thought of what Adam might say to her tomorrow
when he arrived, and she bowed her head. He would
be harsh, this time. Worse, he would be right.

At sunrise, Adam stood in the small room where
Brielle slept, looking down at her wan face and wondering if he would ever be able to handle the willful
and imperious nature inside that small body. He knew,
for Mother Georgina had told him, how close Brielle
had come to death. His first anger was gone, swallowed up in an immense gratitude for her life. He
would have another chance to make a life with her.
Turning, he glanced at Serena, who had brought him
here, and spoke softly.

"Did the wound bleed overmuch, sister?"

"No, my lord. Sister Lorraine allowed the blood to flow long enough to cleanse the wound, then bound it well. 'Twas an even flow that soon lessened."

"But she is pale, and she seems very tired."

"Indeed she is, sire. Pain and fright kept her awake until less than an hour ago. She is concerned about Lady Candida."

He made a gesture with one hand, a gesture that seemed to consign Candida to her fate. The same hand was gentle, smoothing back the strands of hair clinging to Brielle's pale forehead.

"She is ever too concerned about others," he said, "and too sure she knows what to do. Yet I cannot fault her for loving her friends."

Young as she was and seriously thinking of giving her life to God, Serena was still woman enough to admire the superb physique and rugged looks of Adam Dunbarton. Besides, the unguarded look in his eyes as he stared down at Brielle stirred her romantic heart. He loved his wife too much, Serena decided, to punish her for her reckless disobedience.

Moving away to leave them alone, Serena wondered if Brielle knew how fortunate she was. She doubted it. Brielle had confessed last night to Mother Georgina that her husband hadn't known anything about her visit and likely would not have approved if he did. The mother superior had been frantic with worry—and still was—thinking the Baron Dunbarton might withdraw his support of the convent if he thought she had taken in his son's runaway wife. 'Twas time to ease the fears Mother Georgina felt, and after listening and watching Brielle's husband, Serena knew the fears were groundless. She left the room quietly and went to find the mother superior.

Something soft and warm brushed Brielle's face, then lips she knew touched hers. Her eyes opened and

stared into infinite blue. 'Twas Adam, and he had just
kissed her. It was hard to believe. She struggled to
speak without trembling.

"My lord."

"Somehow," Adam said, straightening to his full
height, "that term of respect seems sadly out of place."

She shut her eyes again. It was always easier to say
what she knew she must say if she couldn't see him.

"I was wrong to come here. I humbly beg your pardon for being stupid."

Adam sighed. "I share the blame, Brielle. Hugh had
told me that Candida accused you of killing Royce and
warned me never to allow you to visit her. I should
have told you."

She opened her eyes, staring at him. "Why didn't
you?"

Adam pulled up a stool and sat. "I thought 'twould
make you all the more anxious to visit her and assure
her that her suspicion was groundless—because of
your great love for her and for Royce. Was I right?"

Brielle squirmed and then winced from the pain in
her thigh. "'Tis likely I would have wanted to try,
sire." She watched him from half-closed eyes, seeing
the stern face washed by concern as he looked around
the small room, noting the two beds, the two chests
and chairs.

"Did Candida sleep here, in this room?"

"Yes, sire. I asked to share her room, to comfort
her."

"Good God! She could have murdered you in your
sleep!"

Brielle nodded. "I thought of that last night. I believe she wanted to first let me know of her hatred."
Tears came to her eyes again, tears for a lost friend. "I
loved her, sire. And even more, I loved Royce. I will
pray for Candida's full recovery."

"And I," Adam said dryly, "will pray for yours. In

the meantime, you will stay here with the sisters until
your wound heals. Hugh and I have been called to
London for a meeting of the English barons. It seems
our king has annoyed them by asking for more tribute
to continue the war.''

London. All of England would lie between them. Her
eyes met his.

"Must you go?"

He rose from the little stool and turned away, going
to the window that looked out on the bare countryside
and the dark gleam of the Tyne. The river was frozen
along the banks, but the rippling center was clear of
ice. Spring was not far away.

"I must," he said, clearing his throat, staring outside. "I had hoped to take you with me."

The words twisted her heart. Standing there, his
shaggy hair and beard bright gold in the light from the
window, his muscular body seemed to give off a comforting warmth she could feel even across the room.
And he was leaving her.

"Sire—perhaps within a few days I will have healed
enough to travel."

He turned back and came to the side of the bed, his
face stern. "We leave tomorrow. My father and your
servants will come for you when you are mended and
take you back to Castle on Tyne. I trust you will remain
inside the walls until I return."

"Yes, sire." The pain in her heart vied with her
wound. "How long will you be gone?"

"I have no way of knowing. Edward, as you know,
can be stubborn and willful. And the barons are angry
at what they believe is a waste of their gold. But somehow England must hold together against the French."

'Twas a measure of her new humility that Brielle
nodded and let the reference to the French go. "While
you are gone," she said slowly, "I will give you no

cause to become angry, sire. Nothing will draw me outside the Castle walls alone."

As March ended and April brought buds and small green leaves, the Baron Bruce Dunbarton and a company of knights brought a wagon driven by Jacques, with Honoria and Arabella riding along, to the Convent of the Blessed Child. They had made a soft nest in the wagon with pillows and thick piles of blankets, where Brielle could lie at her ease, and tied Angelique to the rear. The wolfhounds had been taken back to Castle on Tyne long since.

Brielle came out and got into the wagon without a hint of favoring the leg that had been stabbed. It was healed and only needed to be used to gain its strength again. She laughed at the elaborate nest and sat in the middle of it, so happy to be going home that tears kept coming to her eyes. But she was afraid to ask about Candida and how she fared. Arabella told her, not waiting for the question.

"They say the Lady Candida has been cruelly used, and her demon driven out. The bishop insists on keeping her for a time to make sure no incubus lies with her and impregnates her with an imp. They say the bishop prowls the locked cells at night, searching for manifestations of the Devil."

Brielle's happiness faded. She had been diplomatically silent, but she'd never believed these tales of demons. To her mind, Candida had been mad with grief, not possessed by evil spirits.

"The man is mad himself," she said angrily. "Someone should beat the Devil out of him!"

Arabella blanched. "Shhh! If others heard your words, my lady, you might end up in the abbey yourself. Don't try again to rescue Lady Candida. Next time, she might succeed in her purpose."

"Hush," Honoria broke in, annoyed. "You make too

much of Candida's plight, Arabella." She turned to Brielle. "Sir Hugh has made arrangements to have Candida returned to the convent and Mother Georgina, now that her demon has been routed. She will remain there until fall, helping to care for the orphans. She herself has asked for that privilege."

"Then she will recover," Brielle said, satisfied. She leaned back in the pillows, content. "'Tis the children she needs, Honoria. They will heal her heart and mind."

For the last hour of the trip, Brielle insisted on riding Angelique. "I'll not have our serfs thinking I'm badly injured, for I am not. And to be truthful, Angelique is a softer ride that this jouncing wagon."

Silver-haired Lord Bruce laughed and gave in. Once she was mounted, he invited her to ride beside him at the head of the procession. "If you tire," he added, "tell me. I'd not have Adam blame me for a setback."

"He would know where the fault lay," Brielle retorted, smiling. "He has learned well. Have you news of him, my lord?"

"Indeed. We can look for his arrival within the next two weeks. He sent word by a wool-buyer that he intended to return in the last half of April."

Gladness ran through her, flushing her cheeks. "I am happy to hear it, my lord. Thank you for telling me."

The small community of craftsmen, stable boys, armor makers, and other artisans who lived in the bailey of Castle on Tyne had gathered with their families to welcome Lady Brielle home again. Always these people who lived within the curtain walls of the castle knew everything that happened in the three noble families—sometimes before the other nobles. Candida had not been well loved by the serfs and other workers, for she ignored them as she did the stones in the walls. Sir Hugh was admired for his generosity to the poor and

ill, but none thought he'd make a good master, for the
men had seen that he handed over every castle problem to the baron or Sir Adam.

It was said in the bailey that if the Dunbartons were
to keep their lands and dominion, the younger son
must rule. However, it was also said by the old women
that his tiny but proud wife, the Lady Brielle, over-
stepped the bounds of a noblewoman. As in the case of
Thomas Neill, for instance, whom she had forced to
raise the outer portcullis so she could ride out alone.
Poor Thomas had taken a lashing from Lord Bruce
and lost his position.

Looking up as they rode through the gates and into
the teeming bailey, Brielle noted the strange face in
the gatekeeper's shelter. She had wondered now and
then if there had been trouble for Thomas; now she
knew. Her heart dropped. The gatekeeper was envied
by all, for the pay and the esteem were high due to the
skill and judgment needed. She turned to Lord Bruce.

"I see you have appointed a new gatekeeper, my
lord."

His sidelong glance showed hidden amusement.
"True. We discovered Thomas Neill had poor judgment."

Brielle looked away. As she had suspected, the man
had lost his favored position because of her. It was
something she must try to mend. She pushed down
embarrassment and spoke.

"The day I left here to visit Candida, Thomas Neill
was loath to let me through the gate alone. Therefore I
threatened him by saying I'd report him to Adam. I—
well, I think he believed Adam was waiting for me
along the way."

Bruce raised his bristling gray brows. "Did you give
him good reason to believe that?"

She forced words out. "I did."

There were cries of "Good health, my lady!" and

"Welcome home!" as they rode through the bailey. Brielle was glad of the distraction. She smiled and waved, calling out her thanks. Lord Bruce waited until they passed through the inner portcullis and into comparative silence before he answered her.

"Thomas Neill will be given the post of gatekeeper again, then."

Brielle let out her breath and smiled. "Thank you, Lord Bruce! I would not like knowing I caused him to lose it. I'm sure you can trust him to fulfill his duties."

Bruce grinned. "Indeed. Now that I think of it, more so than any other man. He'll not listen to a devious female again. We Dunbartons will know where our wives are, with Thomas on guard."

Brielle turned red but managed to hold her tongue.

It was wonderful to enter her own home again. Brielle burst in through the entrance, trailed by Honoria and Arabella, and found Abel Southers, John Worth, and Marsh Nelson waiting to welcome her. One at a time each came up and bowed, taking her hand and bringing it to his lips. Each wished her good health; each offered to attend her if she wished to visit Turnbull Village. She cocked an eye on them and laughed.

"'Tis a trio of prison guards I have here, I see. However, 'twill be pleasant to have strong arms to carry my purchases. Where is Hester?"

"Here, my lady."

Brielle swung around. Hester beamed at her from an open doorway. "Is there anything we need from Turnbull?"

"No, my lady."

"Good! Then send Anna and the maids to see to my bath. 'Twas naught but cold water and harsh soap at the convent, and I would fain take my comfort now." She turned toward the steps that led up to the gallery, her step light.

"Anna is gone, my lady. Sir Adam sent her away."

Brielle swung back, her brows rising. "She gave him cause for such action, I am sure. Then send the maids to heat the water, and come with me long enough to tell me how Anna angered my lord."

Hester reddened. "I do not know the whole of it, but the Lady Martha can tell you. I must see to your hot water." She wiped her hands on her apron and disappeared toward the kitchen.

Brielle stared, then turned to Honoria. "Come. End this mystery."

"I cannot, dear child. Only the Lady Martha knows. Have your bath and I'll fetch her. She'll be anxious to see you once she knows you're here."

Later, in a solar bright with late-afternoon sun, two women sat together at a table placed in the pillowed embrasure of a big window. The light shone on the Lady Martha's sweet, serious face as she spoke to Brielle.

"One of Hugh's knights told us all that Candida had put Anna into your house so she could listen to what was said between you. She knew it had been decided some years back that Adam would take over as baron when Bruce died. You see, Hugh never had interest in the land or sheep, and we all knew Royce would die before he grew old enough to rule. Also, Hugh recognized Candida's strange weaknesses and was determined not to have another child."

"But *why*? What did Candida expect to learn from Anna?"

The Lady Martha's mouth trembled. "Anything you said about Royce. Candida meant to see that he lived, and that he inherited. And—Anna was wicked. She was earning two salaries, and she wanted to continue earning them. So she made things up and told Candida you were plotting to kill Royce. She would take a few words she'd heard you say and twist them into a threat. We knew 'twas all lies, and 'tis no use at all to repeat them."

"I would hear it, my lady. Tell me the truth. Did she poison Candida's mind against me?"

"She did. She said on the very first night you stayed here that you and Sir Adam discussed how sickly Royce looked and laughed about it, saying 'twould be easy enough to see that he died."

Brielle well remembered the night, remembered the words that had been said, and the sympathy she had felt for the ill boy. She shuddered. So much trouble and sorrow caused by a lying, grasping woman.

"Thank you," she said, and meant it. "Now I know why Candida attacked me. Perhaps someday 'twill all come right again."

25

Expected daily through the rest of April, Adam and the two knights he'd taken with him—Kiernan and Charles Eastham—arrived in midmorning on the first of May.

Alerted by the noise of cheers and laughter in the bailey, Brielle ran to a window and peered out. She was just in time to see Adam, wearing leathern chausses and a loose, sleeveless tunic, riding into the courtyard. To her eyes he was still like a god, his strong face alight with laughter, his muscular bronze arms shining, his thighs clamped on the huge and excited black stallion.

She stared down at him, enthralled. England's golden lion, home again. King Edward's hero champion—and *my* husband. For a moment she was jealous of both country and king, but then Adam looked up, saw her, and grinned. He spread his arms wide, as if to take in his house and his wife together and hold them against all comers.

"I'm home!" he shouted. "Come to me!"

She ran down the stairs as if her feet had sprouted wings and rushed from the door. Adam swung from his horse and met her with open arms, snatching her up and whirling her around, bruising her lips with his kiss. She didn't care.

"You stayed overlong in London," she said when she could. "Your place is here." The words and even the tone of voice were prim, but the look in her eyes was of longing and wild passion. Adam looked into hot, glowing amber and laughed.

"Here," he said, and tossed his reins to Kiernan.
"Take my horse to the stables. My wife has told me my
place is here, and so it is!"

Brielle gasped as he swept her up in his arms and
strode inside. Those waiting at the door to greet him
scurried to get out of his way, laughing, exchanging
knowing glances. Adam grinned wider but never slackened his pace. Mounting the steps to the gallery, kicking open the door to the solar, he went in. With a swift
backward thrust of a heel, he slammed the door shut
again and headed for the bed.

"Never," he said, dropping her in the middle,
"never again will I leave you behind when I must
travel. 'Tis plainly unnatural for us to be apart. . . ."
While he talked he was kicking off his boots, skinning
out of his tunic, unwinding his cross-garters. She
watched him for an astounded moment and then un-
fastened her belt and started flinging away her own
clothes. Hadn't she waited long enough? Hadn't her
dreams at night been feverish with visions of—of what
she now saw? Wasn't it right to offer herself to an
aroused husband? She pulled her shift off over her
head and shook out her hair, smiling at him, pausing
as he paused, wondering. . . .

Slowly he reached out and touched her cheek, his
hand hard and calloused, his touch as gentle as a drifting wind.

"You are more beautiful than ever, my Brielle."

She caught his hand and held it there, moving her
cheek against his palm. Tears of happiness glistened in
her eyes. "I . . . have missed you overmuch, my lord.
Come, lie with me now."

Silent, he eased down and pulled her into the curve
of his big body, caressing her, kissing her open mouth
and tasting her tears. His own throat was thick, his
heart full. When she reached up and buried her fingers

in his great mane of golden hair, urging him over her, he made a sound deep in his chest.

"Wait," he whispered hoarsely. "Wait. I would not hurt you. I would give you time enough to let your passion rise." He began to caress her in all the ways he knew, his hot mouth within the soft beard moving over her breasts, her belly, her loins. He kissed and kissed again the pale pink, silvery scar on her thigh, laving it with his tongue. Though he trembled with the effort of holding back, he continued until she stopped him with her own impatience, catching at his beard, bringing his face to hers.

"You are driving me mad," she gasped. "I will wait no longer. 'Tis cruel to—" She drew in her breath as he swung up and arched over her. He was glorious, all bone and sinew and clean bronze skin rippling with smooth muscles. All potent masculinity, his male parts tight and hard, shining in the sunlight that came in through the wide windows. She sighed and reached up with her slender legs to embrace him, draw him down as she arched to meet his thrust. "Now," she whispered, "Oh, now. . . ."

To be in Northumbria in May was no bad thing, Brielle discovered. 'Twas a time of flowers, of lambs, of riding the fields of barley and oats, of fishing in the Tyne. Of making love. The month sped by without a cloud of trouble and turned into warm and giving June. Brielle, now confident in her own household, often helped Hugh's chatelaine, Mary Danforth, with her records and purchases. She felt a fine confidence in her own worth and was happier than ever before in her life. Recognized by every merchant in Turnbull as one of the rare noblewomen who knew and demanded a fair value for a fair price, Brielle walked the streets proudly, though she never walked alone. That part was due to Adam. He took no chances.

But as Honoria always said, there is no season without a dark day. In early July Brielle went shopping for pots of fruit preserve and bags of early oats, accompanied by both Charles and Henry Eastham on the street and followed after by Jacques, driving a wagon. Rounding a corner, she came face to face with Marc de Rohan and a pair of his hangdog knights.

Instantly Charles Eastham was between them, his hand on his sword, and Henry dropped behind, protection against a sneak blow from the rear. Brielle, her ivory face icy with contempt, passed without breaking her stride.

De Rohan, knowing from the past that Brielle would not acknowledge him, stepped aside and bowed, his dark face twisted in an unpleasant smile as he called after her, "A good day to you, my lady. May we meet again—alone."

Sir Charles Eastham was angry enough at the implied threat to see Brielle off in the wagon with Jacques and Henry, then return to search the streets and taverns for de Rohan. He failed to find a sign of him or his ragtag followers.

"'Twould be best to hunt him down," he told Adam that night as they sat to dinner, "and end his chance to annoy Lady Brielle. The man is dangerous."

Adam shook his head. "Within a few days my wife will leave with me for London and the security of Queen Philippa's guard. There are plans afoot that will please you, Charles. Another of Edward's wild schemes—promising amusement. This time we will all be in it."

"But there will come a time," Kiernan broke in, "when one of us will be forced to kill de Rohan." Kiernan, who had lagged behind Adam by a month, had only just arrived from London with secret news from the king. Now he was visibly upset about the meeting and de Rohan's words. "I will seek him out and undertake the task," he added angrily. "'Twill give me no more regret than killing a snake."

Adam shook his head. "No. To kill a man apurpose when he is not threatening your life is a danger to your immortal soul. We can surely prevent harm to one small woman. In time, de Rohan will tire of the game."

"So I believe, also," Brielle said, but neither Charles nor Kiernan looked convinced. Diplomatically, she changed the subject, turning to Adam.

"Tell us the news Kiernan brought and our king's plans."

Adam grinned. "As always, Edward's plans are secret. But I can tell you that Charles de la Cerda of Spain would be even more anxious to learn them than you are. De la Cerda seems confident that his mighty Castilian fleet will help Spain best by winning the war for France."

"And well it might," Kiernan said dourly. "He now ranges the Channel as if 'twere his, running down and robbing English wine ships leaving Bordeaux. Even worse, he came close to capturing Henry of Lancaster and his men on their way home from Aquitaine."

"Then thank the good Christ for Henry's escape," Charles Eastham said. "We need him if we are ever to conquer France. Is that why Edward is making plans? To teach de la Cerda a lesson?"

"Partly, perhaps," Kiernan said. "Edward does not like to have his best men attacked by Spain when 'tis France we fight. But even more aggravating is the last bit of insolence from the Spaniard—the man has sailed the whole fleet to Sluys and stolen English wool cloth made in Flanders! We hear the huge carracks are loaded with it and will soon be carrying it back to Spain." He looked at Adam and grinned suddenly. "The contentment of your summer is over, my friend. Our king has called for his champion."

Brielle sighed, soundlessly. Would it be ever thus? No settling of family life, no notion of when Edward would call on Adam? All England between them, always? But no. She sat up, remembering. He would take her along, for the day he came home he had said they would never be parted again—and he had sounded as if he meant it.

In three days' time the travelers, Adam with his seven knights and Brielle with Arabella, had gathered their stores and bundles of clothing. They planned to dispose their baggage on three stout mules instead of taking a wagon.

"'Twill shorten the trip wonderfully," Adam said, "if we aren't held down to a wagon's pace. Can your maid ride well?"

"No doubt she will by the time the trip is over," Brielle said. "She is a strong and determined woman."

"Good. And you? Have you regained all your strength?"

"Indeed. I'm looking forward to the ride." To be truthful, she still felt rather weak at times and dizzy, but she put that down to the weeks abed while the deep wound in her thigh healed. The ride, she thought, and the fresh summer air would undoubtedly put her to rights.

She had gone the day before to visit Lady Martha and give her a parting kiss and hug. Druid and Witch met her at the entrance to the great hall and paced solemnly beside her, their shoulders higher than her waist, as she went through and up the wide stone steps to the gallery and solar.

"They think you a child," Lady Martha said, laughing at the strange tableau. Brielle had draped an arm over each pair of hairy shoulders and the wolfhounds looked ridiculously pleased. "'Tis your size, I believe. They've not been so protective of anyone since Royce was small. Go now, you silly beasts! I'll not have your hair on my good rugs."

They went with dignity and took up a spot on the gallery to wait.

"Good dogs," Brielle said in fond farewell, and came to sit on a tapestry-covered stool at Lady Martha's feet. "They are, you know," she added. "They followed me faithfully to the convent, and I felt safe."

Martha smiled and put down her embroidery. "We have half-grown pups in the kennels. When you return, you may have your choice of them."

"Thank you. I'll be pleased to take one, though Honoria may growl louder than he. I am leaving Honoria here, by the way. I know she prefers it, and I thought perhaps you would, also."

"Indeed I do. She is wonderful company for me. I've been worried how I'd go along with no woman to talk to."

Brielle's gaze dropped. She picked up the embroidery and studied it, wondering how to say what she had come to say. "That makes me think of Candida," she said finally. "I am sure there were many times when you depended on each other for friendship and understanding. Now that she has come to her senses, perhaps 'twould help her to talk to you."

There was a long silence. Finally, Martha spoke.

"You have a forgiving nature, Brielle. More so than mine, I believe. I find it well-nigh impossible to forgive Candida for her murderous attack on you, nor, for that matter, for the years of unhappiness she gave my son Hugh. When you have children, you will realize my feelings. Now come, give me the kiss of kinship and allow me to ask a blessing for you."

Returning to her own home, Brielle was subdued. She had meant to go on, to suggest that while she was in London, Candida should be brought back to Castle on Tyne and her own house. She was sure the change would be wonderful for Candida and less lonely for Lady Martha. She had even thought that when she came back from London, 'twould be safe for them all. Surely, once Candida had realized Anna had been lying, she would lose all enmity. Ah, well—perhaps later.

Stopping in the small garden beside the entrance to her own home, she pulled a number of brightly colored rose hips from the still-blooming bushes. Steeped in boiling water, the rose hips made a fragrant tea, used to soothe irritated throats and painful chests. 'Twould be well to carry a supply of it to London. They must be in good health while they stayed there—'twas summer, and time again for the Black Death.

In less than a week the entire party of Adam Dunbarton's ménage rode into London and were greeted at Westminster Palace. Philippa welcomed them as family. There were tears in both the queen's eyes and in Brielle's as they embraced. Philippa herself escorted Brielle to the royal blue bedroom at the end of the private hall.

"This time," she said, smiling, "there will be no mistake. Adam will share it with you. Since you are with child, you must put any differences aside."

"We have no differences," Brielle began, and stopped, staring at Philippa's glowing face. "Nor am I with child, Your Highness. I have put on a bit of weight, that is all."

Philippa sat down on a window seat, laughing. "I have put on that kind of weight eleven times, little one. I know it well. Some months from now, 'twill leave your belly and lie in your arms."

Gazing at the halo of red evening light misting the queen's shining ebony hair, Brielle believed her immediately, as if an angel had spoken. She dropped into a chair, her knees weak, and a tremendous excitement swept over her.

"I must tell Adam!"

"Oh, no. Let him find it out for himself. A man about to become a father first becomes a jailer. Adam likely will be one of the worst. He will wrap you in pillows and keep you safely inside walls."

"He'll not!"

Philippa chuckled. "Still the little firebrand. Take my advice, cousin. Men are all the same. They think nothing of casting their seed in any woman who attracts them, but let one take root in their lawful wife, and they become as watchful as a guard in our dungeons. You have something of value that belongs to them, and they can't quite trust you with it. Don't give up your freedom until you must." She turned to look as Adrienne came again to the doorway, peered in, and curtseyed.

"Shall I send in the maids with the tub and hot water, Your Highness? Lady Brielle's maid requested it."

"Indeed, Adrienne. 'Twill rest her from her trip."

Later, alone, Brielle hugged the knowledge to her heart. She should have known. But she'd blamed the lack of courses to fright and nervousness, to the long stay in bed with her wound, to many things, like fear and worry. Thinking back, she decided that the night when they'd come home from Royce's funeral and quarreled and cried and made passionate love was the night she had conceived. She remembered feeling that life had changed. She smiled, knowing Adam would be excited and, as Philippa had said, would undoubtedly go charging about setting rules and demanding instant obedience for all the days and months ahead. So her secret must stay hidden for as long as she could manage.

At dinner that night Brielle wore the necklace of diamonds that Adam had chosen for a bride gift in the

Street of the Jewelers. Coming into the huge dining room on Adam's arm, she felt as if she were coming to the house of friends, a feeling that grew as Princess Isabella came running to fall on her neck and kiss her cheek.

"How I have missed you, Brielle! And Edward"—she turned and motioned gaily to the Black Prince—"Edward said we should never have allowed you to leave London. You two are mad to stay in the dreary north."

"The north," Brielle said, amused, "is not always dreary. But I am glad to be with you again."

"And at such an exciting time! Did you know that next month the whole Spanish fleet will be invading England's waters?"

Coming up behind Isabella, her brother reached around her great mound of crimped hair and put a hand across her mouth, pulling her back against his chest. "I told my father he'd made a mistake in telling you his secrets. What do you want, Izzy? To have the King of England's plans cast to the gossip winds?"

Isabella wrenched herself away from the Black Prince and glared at him. "All I said was—"

"Say nothing! 'Tis always better than spreading rumors or fear."

"'Twas neither fear nor rumor, as well you know. And you insult our dear friend. Brielle is not a spy!"

"She's half *français*," Adam said, coming up beside them. "Who knows what she will do or say?" But his look at Brielle put the lie to any intent to hurt.

Brielle linked arms with Isabella. "And who knows what will happen? De la Cerda may come to his senses and pass us by. The English Channel is always partial to England, *n'est-ce pas?*"

"Indeed, my bright little friend." Usually somber, Edward was often smiling when in company with

Adam and Brielle, and he was now. "'Tis almost always so, which you learned one perilous night. Come, let us sit together at table and listen to the others. It may be we will learn more."

26

Gradually, by listening and putting things together, Brielle began to understand what King Edward planned. The knowledge chilled her blood.

"How impossible!" she said to Adam in the privacy
of their room. "No one could go against Charles de la
Cerda's tall ships with no more than cogs and fishermen's wherries and a few pinnaces! Why, all the Spaniards need do is rain down iron bars from their high
decks and sink those tiny boats! The English will
drown before they have a chance to engage the men.
Please, do not enter this fray."

But Adam only laughed, as if it were nothing. And as
the gay round of parties and amusements went on,
Brielle began to believe the foolish plan had been discarded. Even the king, who truly believed God was
always on his side and therefore that all things were
possible, must have seen the dangers.

But on the tenth of August the English archbishops
ordered public prayers for the success of the king's
battle with Spain. It was termed a Tournament at Sea,
with the king in charge of the royal event instead of
one of his admirals. That alone, Brielle thought, was
terrifying. King Edward was brave and he fought well
—but his tactics were strange and often dangerous, in
her opinion.

Two weeks later, King Edward made the trip to Win-
chester surrounded by family and close friends. His
queen and her cousin, the Lady Brielle Dunbarton; the
Black Prince, who had his admiring ten-year-old
brother, John of Gaunt, with him; and the entire mem-

bership of the Order of the Garter, including Adam
Dunbarton, and many knights who aspired to the order came along. Everyone cheered when on the very
day of the fight, Robert of Namur, a nephew of Philippa's, arrived from Hainault. Edward gave him the
Salle de Roy, his flagship, for the king intended to sail
in the small cog, *Thomas*, a lucky charm for him ever
since he bested the French with it years back in a fa-
mous battle at Sluys.

Philippa and her ladies, including Isabella and
Brielle, were installed in an old abbey on the Winchel-
sea Downs, which gave them a broad view of the sea.
But during the waiting hours Philippa and Brielle rode
down to the shore of the port and watched the preparations. A motley fleet of some fifty small sailing boats
were manned with enough fishermen to handle the
sails and fitted out with shields of oak planks to protect
the full load of English bowmen who marched aboard,
their quivers full of arrows. Philippa smiled.

"I believe I see the battle plan," she said to Brielle.
"De la Cerda will not relish it. Come, we'd best get
back to the abbey. 'Tis coming on late."

As they turned to leave they saw the king on board
the tiny *Thomas*, dressed in a black velvet jacket and a
hat of beaver fur. He had evidently asked his musicians to play a German dance and ordered John
Chandos to sing to it, for they heard it faintly. Then, as
they watched, they saw Edward strike a graceful pose
with his shapely legs and begin to dance, holding his
wine goblet high as he kicked.

"Always the actor," Philippa said, only half amused.
"Oh, there is Adam going aboard. Good. Thank God he
sails with Edward."

They lingered, watching, until an excited cry from
the lookout on the tallest mast rang out.

"A sail!" A moment later he burst into the count:

"Yes, Yes! I see two, three, four—so many that, God help me, I cannot count them!"

Philippa and Brielle urged their mounts into a full run. They would be able to see the ships from the abbey much sooner than here.

'Twas a spectacle, Brielle thought as they watched from the abbey, bound to strike fear in a woman's heart. Their men in their tiny boats frisking out to harry and anger forty-four huge carracks, proud ships with sheer sides and towering war castles bristling with men-at-arms. One by one, the Spanish ships burst into sight, great sails bulging, pennants streaming; one by one the English longbows picked off the invaders. Figures ready to catapult rocks and iron toward the little boats fell overboard with arrows stuck through them, and others fell on their own decks. Nor were the great ships allowed to draw back to deeper water; the little cogs and pinnaces nipped at their heels and drove more than a quarter of them aground on shoals in the harbor. Then, arrows flying, they coursed back and forth around the giants until after dark.

At midnight the noble sailors came into the abbey, all telling their tales at the top of their voices. In his enthusiasm, King Edward had crashed head-on into the leading Spanish ship, as if in the lists. He made no great impression on the ship, but his own prow split and began to fill with water. He and his crew, including Adam, scrambled aboard another enemy, disarmed its confused and bloody crew, and flung them all in the sea.

The Black Prince, who was accompanied in his boat by his brother John of Gaunt, had his boat holed by a stone from a trebuchet, and was sinking fast when rescued by Henry of Lancaster, who had boarded the enemy from the other side. There were some English dead but few compared with the Spaniards. And they'd captured nearly all the Spanish ships.

"Once more," Adam said as they celebrated with wine and cakes, "the English won with the gray goose feather that guides the arrow and the ash longbow that sings of death. However, we were also aided by the Spanish habit of overfilling their ships. A blind archer could not loose an arrow without killing someone in the crowd."

Edward flung back his head and laughed. "'Tis true my archers won the day," he said. "'Tis true the Spaniards always overload their ships with men. But the day was won because we fought against the odds. 'Tis always so, my friend. He who dares, wins."

Henry of Lancaster, seated between Brielle and Isabella, raised his glass. "True, sire! And now I dare to prophesy: Within a year, King Pedro of Castile will be on our side, and the Channel ours forevermore."

The high spirits stayed high for another day, while the royal family and their friends made the trip back to London. But riding through the mean streets along the waterfront, they came back to grim reality. There again were the blotched bodies put out along the gutters, the tolling bells, the death carts rolling. Again they must brace themselves for the sight of horrid death, the sound of grief, the odor of rotting flesh.

That night in the royal blue bedroom of Westminster Palace, Brielle whispered to Adam her deepest wish.

"I want to go home."

It was too dark, even with the spirit candle, to see the expression in her shadowed eyes. Adam was curious.

"'Twould suit me, also. But why? I thought you'd like to stay with our queen for a time."

A shudder ran through the small body he held close. "I—I fear the Black Death."

"You?" He sounded incredulous. "You've never feared it afore."

But now I have reason. The thought was chilling. If she died, Adam's child—*her* child—would never be. She was silent, not sure of what to say. Then Adam chose.

"Whether from fear or superstition," he added, easing her closer, "it suits me. We will leave tomorrow."

"Tomorrow?" She smiled in the darkness. "Wonderful!"

He chuckled, staring up at the glisten of candlelight on the velvet canopy. " 'Tis no great favor from me. The king and his family are no fonder of the plague than you. They also leave London tomorrow. We'll travel to Windsor with them, spend a day of rest, and leave from there. Or if you like, we'll stay for a time. Windsor has always been free of the plague."

She knew that, but she shook her head. "No, I want to go home. I want to be at Castle on Tyne."

He drew her closer, caressing the breasts that every day were heavier now, filling his hand. The hand moved on, circling the gentle bulge of her abdomen.

"Then you shall be, wife. 'Tis a woman's privilege to choose her nest when her babe is born."

Brielle gasped. "You know! Who told you?"

He laughed out loud. "Why, you did. When your body changed to this soft luxury, when your voice gentled and sang like a dove, when your amber eyes dreamed, I knew. You've given me yet another reason to love and care for you."

"But . . . I thought you'd—I mean, you haven't said a word about—" She stopped, wondering how to say it. "You haven't ordered me to be careful! Philippa said all men were the same when their wives carried their seed. Always setting rules and keeping their women indoors."

"Many do. But I believe a woman has a deep knowledge of her own and a deep desire to keep her babe safe. In this particular matter, I trust you."

After a long moment, Brielle answered him. Her voice was cool but courteous. "Thank you, sire." She turned away from him, her hair sliding to hide her face, and settled down to sleep. *In this particular matter*, I trust you? Well, perhaps it was a beginning. . . .

Traveling, even the first few hours of the first day, Brielle felt her yearning for home growing like a lump in her throat. Castle on Tyne shimmered in her memory, seeming again to float in the air or on the waters of the Tyne that surrounded it. She was quiet, glad for the last warm days of August, wondering at the movement of the babe within her. He changed position often, she thought, as if he were impatient in his prison. Surely, she thought, surely he'd be in her arms by Christmas.

Philippa, riding beside her, chided her for dreaming. "You've not spoken a word in the last hour," she said, "nor heard one, for that matter. What are you thinking?"

"He knew," Brielle said, and smiled. "Adam knew. And he says he'll not confine me. He believes women know how to keep their babes safe."

"Adam has learned much from you," Philippa said, unexpectedly. "He was as arrogant as any prime fighting man before he married. He's different now, and I enjoy him more. Are you two staying at Windsor for the rest of the summer? I know Edward has asked Adam to put off going back to Northumbria. There's a meeting of some sort planned for fall. A secret meeting between Edward and one of the French pretenders."

"Oh?" Brielle glanced around, but there was no one near enough to hear. She was flattered that Philippa deemed her safe as a confidante for startling news.

"Indeed," Philippa went on. "Now that King Philip is dead and foolish John the Good sits uneasily on the French throne, Charles of Navarre is making a final effort to have his right to be the French king recognized. His mother was the daughter of Louis X, you know, and she was never given her due. She should have been queen, but France doesn't believe in women inheriting.''

"That I know," Brielle said, a tinge of bitterness in her voice. "'Tis the reason I had to marry Adam—not that I regret it now. But if Charles becomes king, I pity the French. He well deserves the name they gave him —Charles the Bad.''

"Truly? I have met the man but once, when he was more a handsome stripling than a man. He was delicate in stature and bone, but a competent swordman, quick and daring. His manners were excellent, his presence debonair and charming.''

"'Tis true, ma'am. My father called him all those things and more, and if he'd been chosen as the true King of France, instead of having his rightful claim pushed aside, he might be as charming now as you thought him then.''

"Ah," Philippa said, looking interested. "He is different now?''

"Inside he is different. He has grown bitter and savage. He is always conspiring against his enemies, and if someone he knows needs help to dispose of an enemy, Charles is always glad to help them. He's known as an expert in the Italian art of poisoning. 'Tis said he's always successful.''

Pale, Philippa looked away and swallowed, her strong hands clenched on her saddle. "A poisoner! Would Edward know this? Or are you alone privy to Charles's secrets? Did you or your father know him well?''

"My father did, though I did not and certainly never will. Nor am I privy to his secrets, for secrets they never were in France. He bragged on his potions, knowing there was no danger unless he named the men who paid for his talent.''

"Then you believe he would make a bad king and a poor friend for us in France?"

"I do, for he cannot fool the French. If our king became close to him, many of the noble French who would help the English now would turn away."

Philippa rode in silence for a long time. Then, as they came in sight of the great round tower at Windsor, she brightened again.

"I shall tell Edward what you have said," she told Brielle. "And remind him that we do have one true friend from France. Perhaps that is all we need."

Early the next day, as Brielle and Adam prepared to leave Windsor, Brielle saw for the first time a frightening show of King Edward's legendary temper.

Arriving on the scene as the Dunbarton party gathered before the castle, Edward's handsome face was reddened and set. He strode through the milling horses and piles of bundles to catch Adam by the arm as he started to mount his horse. Whirling him around, the king glared at him.

"Do you desert your king, Dunbarton?"

Adam's heavy brows shot up, his calm eyes met Edward's angry ones. "Never, my lord. 'Tis but a time I must give myself and my wife. We travel home and will stay there until our child is born."

"The child can just as well be born at Windsor! I told you I wanted you here for decisions that must be made in the next few months. You are playing with both your freedom and your life when you flout one of my orders."

Adam's face went pale. He knew the power this man had, and how a whim of his could ruin a life, or take it. "You gave me no order, Your Majesty. And in all fairness, you won't now. If I am truly needed, I will come when you send word, as I always have."

"Until now," Edward sneered. "You've let your French wife cloud your judgment, Dunbarton."

Adam glanced at Brielle, puzzled. "In what way, sire? My lady has made no judgment for me."

"Has she not, now? Think a bit, my friend. She has been extremely free with her opinion in talking to my queen; surely she must have spoken with you on her strong dislike of Charles of Navarre."

"No, sire. She has not." Adam's tone was pleasant and unhurried. "I was not aware she knew of the man nor his reputation. However, there are many of the French who dislike Charles the Bad—and with good reason."

Edward's red face swelled with anger. "We will speak of this in private," he said harshly, and motioned with a sweep of arm to a group of men-at-arms gathering near them. "You and your party are now under guard. Meet with me in an hour at the tower hall. I mean to get to the bottom of this disagreement!" Turning away, he strode back into the castle.

With a clatter of hooves and a clashing of shields, the Dunbarton knights surrounded Adam and Brielle. Kiernan's green eyes glittered in a pale and angry face, but his voice was calm when he spoke.

"We await your order, sire."

"We will, as always, obey our king." Adam said evenly. "Our entire party will attend his audience an hour from now." His eyes went to Brielle, perched in her saddle on Angelique. Her face was stiff with shock, her eyes guilty and frightened. Adam pushed through the ring of knights and came to her side. Reaching up, he caught her around the waist and swung her down.

"Perhaps you'd better tell me what you said of Charles to Philippa. And why."

"Only the truth," she said, half choked with fear for him. "Which is bad enough. I should have kept quiet.

The king may have set his heart on Charles becoming King of France."

"Come, we'll go to the tower now and talk this over while we wait." He took her arm and started through the courtyard, stopping long enough to put Kiernan in charge of stabling the horses again and storing the bundles of baggage.

"Whatever comes of this," he added, "you are in charge. If I am held, you will see that the Lady Brielle arrives at Castle on Tyne safely."

Kiernan flushed red. "Yes, sire. But I do not believe these walls and these few hirelings of the king can hold you here if you wish to leave with us."

Adam's face settled into stern lines. "I am sworn to follow Edward in his every honorable effort to advance England's good and to obey his commands. He has ordered me to an audience in the round tower. Would you have me break my sworn word?"

Kiernan stared down at him, and suddenly his devil-may-care smile broke out. "No, sire. But mine own allegiance goes first to you. If I see you in danger, 'twould be my duty to abduct you, would it not?"

Adam laughed, his stern expression creasing into humor. "Pray that it does not come to that, then."

Walking alone with Adam across the cobbled courtyard, Brielle was cold with apprehension. There had been fury deep in the king's cold blue eyes, the look, she thought, of a man itching for a fight; and, in his absolute power, a man well able to destroy any of his subjects, including Adam.

Climbing the covered steps that led up to the tower, she related the conversation she'd had with Philippa.

"I should never have said any of it, true that it is," she ended painfully. "I have put you in disfavor. Perhaps I have put you in danger. I'll not blame you if you punish me for this stupidity."

"I told you long ago I preferred the bitter truth to charming lies, wife."

"And I, also. But 'twas foolish of me to say anything that might affect the temper of the king. I shan't be so careless again."

Adam was silent. She had been careless, but her relationship with Philippa led her to speaking her mind without thought. She had learned from this.

"Did Philippa say what part Charles of Navarre would play in France?"

Brielle sighed. "I believe from what Philippa said that he is Edward's choice as king."

Adam's jaw snapped shut. After a long moment, he spoke. "I see. Then you were right to say what you did."

They entered the great hall of the tower in silence, bowing toward the altar. Adam took her arm and led her to the Chapel of St. George, dedicated to the Order of the Garter.

"We will wait here," he said, "and hope the king joins us. We can hope he'll be influenced by memories of honor."

Brielle glanced at him quickly, wondering at his dry tone, at the implied need for a good influence for Edward. But she held her tongue, thinking it was time she learned to do so.

Next came Adam's knights, and with them the company of men-at-arms that had been set to guard them. They took seats in the hall where they could see into the chapel and were then silent except for whispers, coughs, and a shuffle of boots, echoing hollowly in the large space.

When Edward strode in, he came directly into the chapel and took a place opposite Adam. The king was accompanied by the Black Prince and, following determinedly behind them, Queen Philippa. Her black eyes sought Brielle's and warned her of trouble with lifting

brows and a shake of her glossy dark head. Brielle
gave her a barely perceptible nod and settled back to
listen.

The king had put on an air of authority he seldom
used with his friends. Now he looked at Adam and
spoke.

"If there is an even-handed adviser you trust
amongst your knights, Sir Adam, you may call him in."

Adam smiled, his teeth glinting white in the shadowed chapel. "Thank you, sire. But I fear they are all
unduly prejudiced in my favor."

"As you will." Edward was frowning, looking down
at a paper he held. With a quick, uncertain movement,
he handed it to the Black Prince. "Read it," he commanded, "and then pass it on to Adam. 'Tis the bones
of a plan offered by Charles of Navarre, a contender
for the French throne."

The prince, his dark eyes and calm face so much like
his mother, read the paper with little change of expression except for a fleeting grimace halfway through and
a cocked eyebrow at the end.

"Charles promises much and guarantees nothing,"
he said as he finished, and stood, walking across the
aisle and handing it to Adam.

"'Tis the best plan we've had offered," the king
growled, frowning at his son. "And the only one this
year. John the Good is still sure he can pull France
together and hold it all. And I—I am tired of war and
war's debts."

Adam read the paper with a gradually reddening
face. When he finished he stood up, bowed to the king,
and offered the paper. Edward took it, folded it, and
laid it down.

"Do you agree to the plan, Adam Dunbarton?"

"No, sire."

"Will you carry out your part of it if I so order?"

Adam's face flamed. He fixed his eyes on the eyes so

like his own and shook his golden head. "No, sire. I am a man of honor and I'll not be a party to assassination."

"There is not one word in that paper concerning an assassination!"

Adam stretched out his hand. "Let me read to you the final passage, sire."

Grabbing the paper, Edward thrust it toward him. "Read it then! Damnation! Am I wrong to want you to help me finish this cursed war?"

Silently, Adam opened the paper again and held it to the light. "This last paragraph is clear, which is more than I can say for the flattery and lies that precede it. Listen," and he read it aloud.

Then, since your champion Adam Dunbarton has married into the Le Fontin family and now owns the château and winery, King John will want to make a friend of him. I suggest Dunbarton make a visit with me to court, and we bring along a cask of Le Fontin wine as a gift to our new king. This mark of favor from a man well known for his honor and honesty will lull John into believing England will accept him and his meager offers of French land. In the meantime, I promise to quietly deliver France from the hands of this idiot well before the cask is empty. France will be ours.

Adam handed the paper back to the King and sat down again. "I have ever been ready to die for England and for honor," he said. "But this time my strength goes to honor alone. I will not take any part in such a foul deed."

Edward leaped to his feet. "You need not! Making a gift of wine to a king is a gesture of goodwill, and that is all I ask of you! As for Charles's part in it, neither you nor I need know his scheme. Lending our strength to friends of England is part of our duty. No one would dare to say we encouraged a treacherous act."

Adam gave a short laugh. "Would *you* drink the wine after the cask has been secretly handled by Charles of Navarre?"

There was a dead silence. Then Edward spoke angrily.

"I now order you to honor my agreement with the future King of France. How say you?"

Sweat glistened on Adam's forehead. Behind him, Brielle was white and still, watching him, knowing what he would say.

"I say nay, sire."

The king moved jerkily, clasping his hands together. He had expected the answer. "Because of your former faithfulness, Dunbarton, we will give you time to think on't. But you will spend that time in Colehous prison. Guards!"

In the hall the men-at-arms stood up, and Adam's knights leaped to their feet, drawing their swords and turning to face them.

"Wait!" Rising from her seat behind the king's chair, Philippa of Hainault waved the men down again and came out to stand between the king and Adam. She faced her husband silently and bowed. "I demand the queen's right of pardon," she said calmly, and went to her knees.

"Damnation!" Edward said, furiously red. "Stop that, Philippa!"

She ignored him. The queen's right of pardon had certain rules, and she followed them to the letter. From her knees she slid forward till she lay flat on the floor in all her finery and jewels, her hands grasping Edward's feet, as if abasing herself to a god.

"For the life of your champion Adam Dunbarton," she said, "I prostrate myself at your feet. Pardon him for all charges and release him unharmed, for my sake."

"I do so grant you his pardon," Edward muttered the words prescribed by custom and sat down, looking dazed. Glancing around, he looked at the Black Prince.

"Clear the place, then," he said. "Everyone out but Adam and his wife. I've something more to say to them."

There was a great clatter and rush of feet. The place was empty in minutes, and Brielle was wiping her eyes and staring at Philippa, who had gotten to her feet and was brushing dust from her gown.

"I am forever in your debt, ma'am."

"And I in Adam's," Philippa said, and reached a strong, wide hand to grasp Adam's shoulder, "for he holds England's honor high."

"Enough," Edward said grimly. "Adam needs no praise from you. The man has ended my last hope for peace this year." He turned and looked Adam in the eye. "It seemed to me you could shut your eyes once, my friend, to win this hellish war."

"And make a new friend who someday would happily poison us both and take England, too?"

Edward fought an unwilling grin. "One needs a long spoon to sup with the Devil. Perhaps you are right." He stood and came to Adam and gripped his hand, looking into his eyes. "So I've lost my champion. But not my friend, for Philippa has seen to that."

"True," Philippa said. "And I've won you a man you can trust to watch the Scottish border. You need Adam at your back while you play with the wolves from France." She turned and held out her arms to Brielle, who came into them in a rush.

"I will never forget your kindness, my queen. And I will miss you sorely."

"And I you, *mon enfant.* Send word when the babe is born."

"'Tis late," Adam said. "We must go if we go today."

Brielle took his arm and turned toward the door. "We will go today, my lord. 'Twould spoil a miracle to dally."

27

The Dunbarton train arrived in Castle on Tyne the evening of September fifth, along with a cold wind and a gray sky. Tatters of dark clouds sailed in from the north, promising either rain or sleet. But the fires were lit inside the manse, and the odors of good food filled the great hall. Hester had been alerted an hour or so past by a watchman on the taller of the two donjons. He had seen the straggling line of tiny figures wending their way over the last hill and down into the valley.

Lord Bruce and Lady Martha came to the smaller manse to greet them, and Lady Martha's eyes took note of Brielle's condition. She smiled.

"I thought you *enceinte* when you left," she told Brielle in private. "Now I know I was right. When do you expect the child?"

"'Tis hard to say. But I believe 'twill be November. The queen thinks earlier."

Lady Martha laughed. "She should know." Studying Brielle again, she grew serious. "I must tell you now that Candida has prevailed on Hugh to bring her home. She is here, and though she seems to be much happier, there is still a look in her eyes—"

"But that's wonderful, my lady! Is she well?"

"Well enough in body. She rides a good deal now and spends many a day in Turnbull, shopping." She paused. "Candida speaks often of you, and says she was horrified when the nuns told her what had happened between you. She says she can't remember any of it. I—hope that is true. But there is something strange in how she says it that worries me."

"Believe her," Brielle said instantly. "If you had seen her that night, you would have known she wasn't herself. Her grief and Anna's lies had driven her mad."

Martha gave her a searching look. "Perhaps, and perhaps not. She is still a bitterly disappointed woman. 'Twould be best if you were not alone with her until her goodwill is proven by her actions."

Brielle nodded obediently. She was not frightened, but she could hear Martha's deep concern in her voice, and she wanted to reassure her. "I shall be careful, Lady Martha. But still I am glad she's come to her senses. The ordeal she went through at the abbey must have been horrible."

"Perhaps," Martha said again, and rose from her chair as Lord Bruce came toward them. Looking down at Brielle, who had risen also, Martha's eyes were still worried. "She bears no marks," she added abruptly. "'Tis passing strange that a Devil-possessed woman treated by Bishop Frederich hasn't the scars to prove it."

Later, Brielle recounted the conversation to Adam. His reply was predictable.

"Candida can never be trusted again. Be kind to her if you will, but be watchful. Promise me you'll not be alone with her. I'd not have you hurt in any way."

She promised readily enough. When Candida came to greet her the next morning, she even found herself looking for evidence of a lingering anger. Instead, after the formal greetings and questions of health, Candida was apologetic.

"I could not believe what Mother Georgina told me I had done," she said, ignoring Honoria's disbelieving stare. "When she said I'd accused my dearest friend of murder, I nearly fainted from the shock. I became deathly ill, I assure you. Then I realized that you would know—everyone would know—I'd gone mad from my terrible grief for Royce."

Brielle was silent for a moment. It seemed that
Candida felt she'd undergone the most distress of anyone involved. Deathly ill, indeed. Had the dagger
found its mark, she thought, 'twould have been real
death for me. But—that was Candida's way. What happened to her was always worse than what happened to
anyone else. It was as if she were blind to all feelings
and fears that were not her own. She gave a mental
shrug, smiled, and leaned forward, kissing the tall
woman on the cheek.

"It's wonderful to see you well again," she said
gently. "We'll think no more about the past."

"Agreed," Candida said, and smiled widely. "'Tis
over, after all. Sit down with me and tell me the newest of London fashions! I did so envy you, staying there
in Westminster Palace. How lucky you are that our
queen deigns to recognize you as a member of her
family."

She chattered on as the party—the two noblewomen
and a determined Honoria, joined by Arabella as they
left the great hall—went up to the gallery and into the
solar. A maid was sent for mead and small cakes, to be
consumed as the conversation went on. It was midday
and past when Adam's arrival broke the talk and
Candida rose to leave.

"We will see each other often now," Candida said
brightly. "I look forward to company on my visits to
Turnbull. The shops in the village are better every day,
Brielle. You will think you're in London."

After she left and Honoria took Arabella from the
solar to give Adam and Brielle their privacy, Adam
gave his wife a doubtful look. "So friendly so soon?"

Privately, Brielle herself felt Candida had ignored
the gravity of her actions. She had spoken of her attack
on Brielle as if it were a little contretemps, an awkward and stupid misunderstanding. But then, if truly
she remembered none of it, 'twould be as some weird

tale to her. She answered Adam with an excuse for
Candida.

"She cannot remember what she did and scarcely
believes what she's been told of her actions. No doubt
it lessens her feelings of shame or regret. It's just as
well, don't you think? We can be friends again."

Adam frowned. "See that you remember her attack,
wife. 'Tis only by the grace of a stumble that you live."

Brielle did not argue. For once she felt the safe-
guards Adam wished her to take were sensible. If
'twere her life alone, she thought, she might take a
chance. But there was another life to consider now.

Within a week the two women seemed the best of
friends again. Candida remarked on it gaily, saying
friends may have a falling out, but true friends came
together again. Brielle smiled and agreed, for what
she'd said was right. But there was a slight reservation
in Brielle's mind as to the term *true friends*. She fought
her suspicion, but it stayed. And so did her escort. Honoria or Arabella, at times both, accompanied the two
noblewomen on the trips to Turnbull or on their pleasure rides, and so did two men-at-arms appointed by
Adam. The men stayed at a discreet distance, not listening to the ladies talk but watching them constantly.
Candida finally grew annoyed.

"They are so grim-looking, those men! And I am so
tired of the company of your maid and your companion. We can never gallop our horses when we ride."

"You can," Brielle pointed out gently. "At this time,
I shouldn't." It was the first time either of them had
mentioned her pregnancy, even obliquely. Candida's
mouth quivered.

"It so happens," she said, "that I too am carrying a
child. If 'tis a son, he will inherit Castle on Tyne. But
you're too interested in your own condition to notice
mine."

Automatically, Brielle glanced at Candida's waist-
line and her breasts and was shocked into silence. It
was true. She had noticed that thin Candida was putting on weight, and she had laid it to the fresh air,
exercise, and the good foods of autumn. Now she recognized the signs of burgeoning breasts and thicken-
ing waist, though the rest of the tall figure was much
the same as before. So Hugh had relented. There
would be a baby, after all.

"You are quite right," Brielle said, half ashamed. "I
hadn't noticed. But I am happy for you and Hugh.
'Twill be the most beautiful gift you could give him."

Candida rode on in silence for a time. Then, as they
drew a little distance from the others, she spoke again.
"You are the only one I've told," she said. "Not even
Hugh knows, for I want to keep it a secret for a while."

"From Hugh? Why? I should think he'd be delighted."

Candida adjusted her cloak nervously. "But—if anything went wrong, he'd be sick with disappointment. I
don't want that to happen."

Brielle smiled. For once Candida had thought of
someone else. "I understand," she said softly. "I will
say nothing."

The harvesting of oats and barley had started, the
scythers took to the fields east of Castle on Tyne, and
all day long the scythes swung, their wide blades flashing in the hazy light. The binders followed, gathering
the grain into heaps, tying it in sheaves for the carriers
to take it inside the castle walls. There the threshers
flailed the grain from the stalks and poured it into
great wooden vats for the winter. Lids were hammered
tight to foil the rats and squirrels; the vats were stored
in the upper floors of the old donjon to keep them dry.
It was a time when every villager was busy and the
streets were free of lounging men and beggars. A good

time, Candida said, to do their fall shopping for spices,
for warm clothes and other winter supplies. She had
already gone twice alone.

"We will be able to go where we will, without pushing through crowds," she said to Brielle. "We can ride
out to the goat farm for milk. Our midwife tells me
goat milk is best for strengthening an unborn babe and
the woman who bears him. We should buy some for
ourselves."

Brielle agreed. The weather was wonderful for riding, and her spirits were high. They set out in midmorning and by noon had done most of their
shopping. The men-at-arms that guarded Brielle were
encumbered by bags and boxes, but their load was not
heavy and they kept up as the women headed for the
goat farm on the northern edge of the village.

Candida raced ahead, more excited, Brielle thought,
than the day's activities deserved. But Candida often
had odd moods. Brielle urged Angelique after
Candida's mare, and then, approaching the small barn
and smaller house where the goat farmer lived, she
slowed a little, hesitating as a band of five mounted
men, some of them in mail, came around from behind
the barn and galloped toward them.

Staring at the leader, Brielle suddenly whirled and
shrieked at Honoria, who, with Arabella, was far behind.

"'Tis Marc de Rohan! Run for help!"

After an instant of shocked fright, Honoria and Arabella swung their horses back toward the village, kicking them into a gallop. Brielle sent Angelique on a
dead run after them. The two burdened men-at-arms
shouted a challenge, unslung their battle-axes, and
charged the attackers. But de Rohan slipped to the
side and overtook Angelique with ease. He laughed as
Brielle raised her whip to slash at his face, ducked
away, and a moment later swept her small body from

her saddle to his, whirling back toward the melee behind him. He grabbed her whip and tore it from her grasp, tossing it aside. Then, drawing his sword, he galloped toward the men-at-arms, engaged in fearsome battle with de Rohan's knights. Two of the knights lay motionless on the ground; the other two still fighting.

"Leave off," Marc yelled, "or I kill your lady!" He laid the blade along Brielle's soft neck menacingly. One man-at-arms was already down, and even as de Rohan spoke, the other fell, struck while distracted by the threat to Lady Brielle. Marc laughed again, a high, excited screech cut short by another urgent voice.

"You'll not forget our bargain, Sir Marc?" Candida stood on the ground beside them, her hair loose, her dress ripped from one shoulder. As Brielle stared, amazed, Candida carefully tore the dress a bit more. Looking up, Candida's violet eyes slipped past Brielle without interest and met de Rohan's black gaze.

"Remember," she added, "you promised to wound me slightly, so I may claim I fought to save the woman and failed. I must not be suspected of leading her to you."

Marc's upper lip lifted in a wolfish grin, exposing his strong teeth. "No one will doubt your innocence," he said, "when you are found." His sword flashed down in the afternoon sun like one of the scythes in the fields, and Candida dropped to the ground, her neck nearly severed, her throat spurting her life out in a red fountain, dyeing her bared breast.

Brielle shut her eyes and gave a thin, despairing cry. *"Mon Dieu!* You have *killed* her!"

"Fool!" he spat at her, and sheathed his bloody blade, slamming it into the scabbard. "Are you stupid enough to grieve for your betrayer?"

"You murderer! She was carrying Hugh's child!"

Marc laughed loudly, turning his horse north.

"Hugh's child? Was that her pretense? 'Twas an imp, impregnated in her by that incubus in priest's robes, our Bishop Frederich. Why do you think he treated her so tenderly?"

Brielle thought of Hugh and his efforts to keep peace. How stupid she had been; how wise Lady Martha. She looked back at the body lying there and closed her eyes again, half fainting, feeling the horse beneath her begin to gallop.

De Rohan paused as they reached his two remaining men. One of them was bleeding badly; the other, a young knight no more than sixteen, trying to stop the flow. De Rohan shook his head. "Come! We've no time for that." He headed across the fields toward the forest, and with a clatter of hooves, the men followed. Catching up, the young one shouted a question.

"What of the two women who rode away?"

"I know neither of them," Marc said. "Nor were they close enough to recognize me if they've seen me before. They can't say who it was who killed the men and took Adam Dunbarton's wife. Still, Adam will suspect me. We can't go home until I finish with her."

"Henry must go home, sire. He is bleeding badly."

De Rohan slowed and turned, cursing. It was true. The other man was swaying in the saddle, his face a greenish white, blood running from a cut in his side.

"Then go," de Rohan growled at him. "I hope you make it. I've lost too many men today." He kicked up his horse to a gallop as the injured man turned slowly to the east.

Clinging hard to the pommel of the saddle, Brielle came to full consciousness of the danger that faced her. When de Rohan had satisfied his anger and lust, he would kill her, too. From what he said, he thought himself safe. But Honoria knew his name. If he killed her, he would die. That much she knew, for she knew Adam.

Then there was another, numbing truth—Candida
had led her into Marc's trap and died for her pains.
Brielle thought of the child who had died also and
prayed: *Mary, Mother of God, hold out your arms for an
innocent soul.* Her own babe moved within her, and
despair gripped her heart. Would it be the same for her
and the babe she carried?

Marc set a straight course for the forest and the hills
and valleys it covered to the north, and rode hard,
looking behind them often until they were within the
first line of trees. Then he seemed to feel safer, though
he kept traveling through the forest at a good rate of
speed until the ground sloped upward again, toward
the top of the first hill. Then he slowed and looked
around.

"There's good cover here," he told the man who
rode behind him, "but we'll take no chances. They may
bring dogs with them. We'll find the nearest stream
and ride in it up the valley. They'll not find us until
we're done with the woman, and perhaps never. In
any case, there will be no proof we took her, even if
they find her."

Brielle took in a long breath and straightened. "You
will die, de Rohan, if you kill me. Adam will know
'twas you—I called your name to my companion."

De Rohan grabbed her long hair in his mailed fist
and held her while he dropped his reins and slapped
her hard, the rusted links of steel across his palm cutting her cheek. He looked at the bleeding scratches
and snarled, curling his lip.

"Damn you, bitch! Today you learn to keep your
mouth shut!" He slapped her harder, knocking her
nearly off the saddle, grabbed the front of her velvet
gown, and pulled her up again. She felt blood running
down her cheek and reached to wipe it off.

"Leave it alone, whore. I like to see your blood run."

Her eyes moved to his face and saw first a blur, then

as her eyes cleared, an expression of satisfaction, almost a smile. And even as she watched, he was pulling a knife from his belt. So he liked blood, she thought, and remembered the spurting fountain from Candida's white neck. Was that how she would die? She put out her hands, palms toward him, in an unconscious gesture of denial. He laughed out loud and grabbed the heavy velvet gown again.

"So you would say me nay, my lady? 'Twould avail you nothing! When I am through with your body, my young friend John will pleasure himself on what is left. Let me bring him to the ready now, with the sight of what lies beneath that gown." With a thrust of the sharp knife and a quick swing upward, he cut her gown and shift from waist to neckline, baring her full breasts. She cried out, grabbing at the gown to pull it together, and he slapped her again, laughing as she gasped for breath. The knight came near, staring at them both.

"Are you going to take her down, sire?"

"Not yet. She's sent my name to Castle on Tyne, and we've traveling to do. There will be a search party after us by now." He stopped, wrestling with Brielle as she tried to slip from the saddle. "Leave off, you bitch!"

"Sire"—the knight spoke absently, his attention caught by Brielle's rounded belly as she gritted her teeth and leaned away, struggling against Marc's grasp—"the woman is carrying a child." He looked away from Brielle's half-naked body as if shamed himself. "Perhaps we should let her go."

"Never!" Shaking his head, Marc kicked up his horse again. "What better revenge against my prime enemy? Dunbarton will lose both his wife and his child. Come, let us find the stream. We've an hour or so of traveling if we care to be safe."

Turning to follow, John looked past de Rohan, who

was still attempting to hold Brielle still. "Sire! Look ahead!"

Caught by desperate hope, Brielle looked forward, praying to see someone less cruel, less vengeful, someone who might take pity on a helpless woman. Staring, she felt nausea and terror tighten her throat.

A band of filthy Scots were coming through the woods, dressed in their furs and rags, carrying their axes. They came as to a feast, half running on their short, bowed legs, grinning like wolves.

De Rohan jerked her around and held her in front of him, displaying her half-naked body to the Scots.

"Now," he said in her ear, "you'd better stop fighting. If they get you, you will think of me as a gentle lover."

James Spencer, steward of Castle on Tyne, often walked in early afternoon on the top of the curtain wall that faced the village. Now that Mistress Woolford rode out nearly every morning with Lady Brielle and returned at midday, he'd made a habit of watching for her from the top of the wall. She kept her horse always at a gentle trot, and her graceful figure swaying in the saddle was a pleasurable sight. But today, when he saw her and that gangly Arabella both clinging to horses traveling at a wild gallop, he turned at once and ran down the stone steps inside the next tower like a boy in his teens. He burst from the door onto the cobblestones shouting for Adam.

Adam, inside the armorer's forge, heard him and ran out. Out of breath, Spencer grabbed him by one arm and got a few words out.

"Something happened to the Lady Brielle! Honoria is galloping hard for the gates."

Adam frowned. "Perhaps her horse ran away with her."

Spencer shook his silvery head. "She is beating him

to make him run faster! Get your horse, you young
fool!"

Adam turned and ran for the stable. Behind him,
Spencer put a shaking hand to his head and looked
after him, wondering if he'd just lost his position in the
castle. *Young fool?*

When Honoria and Arabella came pelting across the
drawbridge and into the bailey, Adam, Kiernan, and
Marsh Nelson were mounting their horses. The two
women rode straight into the midst of the huge warhorses, and Honoria gasped out a message.

"Marc de Rohan has Brielle! For God's sake, ride
fast!"

Adam's worried expression turned into a mask of
fury. "Where was he heading?"

"North," Arabella broke in. "Straight toward the
forest. I looked back often to see if they changed
course."

Adam was gone, galloping across the drawbridge.
Kiernan spoke rapidly.

"How many men?"

"He brought four, but he left with two. Our men-at-
arms fought hard before they died."

"Where is Lady Candida?"

Arabella was silent, looking at Honoria. Honoria
took a deep breath. "She was standing on the ground
at the goat farm when we saw her last, talking to de
Rohan. When we looked back afterward, I couldn't see
her—but I could see she wasn't on one of the horses.
Please, Sir Kiernan, go *now!* Our sire will need you."

Kiernan whirled his horse toward the gates. "On to
the forest! Marsh, get the pack of alaunts and follow
me. Druid would track Brielle through fire."

28

Adam, slowing his horse as he came to the goat farm, saw the goat keeper, his wife, and his two half-grown sons standing in a circle on the beaten ground in front of their house and staring down. He turned toward them, and they scattered like chickens when a hawk flies low. He chased the man, leaning from his horse to grab the man's shock of hair.

"Hold on, you fool! Were you here when the Dunbarton ladies were attacked?"

"'Twas none of my doing, sire! See for yourself! Two of the de Rohan knights lie near the pens, and two of your men-at-arms from the castle are in those weeds. They fought like warriors. We couldn't help the ladies!"

Nor could they, Adam thought. They would have been killed for interfering. He released the man and rode back to the spot where the family had gathered and looked down at the stilled body there. Candida had lost her ethereal beauty. Her face was frozen in the rictus of death; ants had found the gaping, empurpled wound in her neck. The long blond hair was stiff with blood. Adam whirled his horse and spurred for the forest in the distance, sick at heart. *Brielle!*

He was halfway to the trees when he heard the howling of the hounds and knew Kiernan and Marsh were coming. He was grateful that someone had thought of the dogs. The tracks here in the fields were easy to follow; the forest's root-filled trails were not. Yet he kept going, pushed hard by an awful fear.

* * *

De Rohan had now been traveling up the hill for some little time, staying in the thickest part of the forest growth, finding streams and following them until they disappeared. He'd threatened the Scots by charging them with his warhorse and his broadsword; John had run one of them down and cut him badly, and the Scots had retreated. But the sight of one or two slipping along in the forest showed they were staying close, watching for a chance to attack.

Somehow Brielle had found a space inside her mind and retreated to it. There was a strange peace there, a feeling of being far removed from the scene around her and the threat of rape and death. She had watched the stocky, grinning Scots who ran the woods around them and noted that they argued amongst themselves and often fought each other senselessly. Also, when de Rohan's horse stumbled over sharp rocks in the stream, the Scots stole closer, their axes raised.

The young knight—de Rohan called him John—had stopped talking. He rode along, sometimes ahead and sometimes behind, did whatever de Rohan required, and was otherwise quiet. He did not look at her. It gradually came to her that John was no longer pleased or excited. De Rohan, she thought, was beginning to notice that himself.

"We will soon be in the place I remember," de Rohan said. "Another few moments should see us safe." He reached over and slapped John on the shoulder. "One of us must stay on his horse and watch the Scots. But if you swear to be quick, you can have the first taste of the woman."

John shook his head. "She carries a child, sire."

"And what of that? Afraid she won't have room for that big stick you carry between your legs? She will, I promise you."

The knight shot a sheepish look at Brielle and shook

his head again. "I have no desire for her. A woman with child should be honored and protected."

De Rohan blew out his breath in disgust. "A woman with child is no better than a sow full of piglets. And this one fights like a spitting cat. You wait! Once you see me take her down, you'll want to try it." He reached around Brielle and took a nipple between his fingers and twisted it, hard, grinning and keeping on until silent tears ran from her eyes and dropped on his dark hand. Suddenly, as they came to a clearing, John reached over and grabbed de Rohan's wrist.

"Let her alone."

"Take your hand off me!" Enraged, de Rohan shook off John's grip and turned his horse up the nearest bank, taking his reins in the hand that held Brielle and drawing his sword with the other. "Come at me, then! We'll see who gives the orders here."

John jerked his own sword from the scabbard, his face stiff with angry fear. "What? You want a fight while you hide behind a woman? Where should I aim my blows?"

Brielle reached out and grabbed the reins where they lay against the stallion's thick neck and pulled back, hard. The stallion reared up on his strong legs, whinnying and fighting the bit. Cursing, de Rohan dropped his sword and grabbed past Brielle, clutching the saddle to keep from falling. There was a rustle in the thick undergrowth behind them, and John shouted and charged, slashing at the Scot who was reaching for the sword. The Scot was gone as quickly as he'd appeared.

With some dignity, John dismounted, picked up the sword, and handed it to Marc silently. Mounting again, he turned back.

"I will accept your challenge when this misadventure is over," he said. "For now, get on with your plan. But don't injure the woman."

"My plan," de Rohan said between his teeth, "is to leave the woman raped and dead. Nothing less will revenge me on Dunbarton. If you've not got the stomach for it, go home."

John reddened and whirled, facing him. "Perhaps 'tis you who has the weak stomach, to take out your grudge against a man by hurting his helpless wife. Are you afeared to take on Dunbarton himself?"

With a roar of rage de Rohan drew his sword again, kicked his horse around, and charged toward John. John sidestepped, turned, and was in the trees, weaving amongst them, yelling back.

"Set the woman down, and I'll meet your challenge!"

Crazed by anger, De Rohan swept Brielle off the saddle and dropped her to the ground. Charging across the clearing, his evil face contorted, he yelled at John again.

"Come at me, you dog! Your death is on your own head!"

Brielle climbed to her feet, clutching her gown together and turning swiftly to the downward path. A small chance, but she had to take it. She ran, while behind her the clashing of sword on shield, the whinnying challenge of warhorses, and the shouts of fighting men drowned out all other sound. She was past the first turn when two Scots stepped out and grabbed her arms. Grinning and chattering in their strange tongue, they dragged her with them into the deep woods. Their odor, their filthy, sore-ridden skin, and their rotting teeth made her stomach clench. She thought of praying to God for help, but all that came to her mind was something Honoria had said: *Stay out of the forest unless you're with men, for 'tis full of wolves.*

If these be men, she thought, give me the wolves. 'Twould be a cleaner death. And for a moment when the Scots stopped jabbering, she heard a faint howling in the distance. Perhaps she would get her wish.

Adam, reining in his stallion where a hoofprint showed plain in the mud near a creek, struck onward as fast as the knotted roots and thick underbrush would let him. The sound of Druid's belling howl was getting closer. The hound would pass him soon and then lead him aright. His muscles, already tight enough to burst, tensed harder. This time he'd kill! In his heart he knew de Rohan was living his last few minutes on earth. The Devil, he thought, must be laughing, readying a hot place in Hell for that dark soul. Spurring his horse, he plunged forward again, remembering that over the top of the next rise was a small clearing, one that all the hunters knew. He'd look there; 'twas a place de Rohan might choose.

Halfway up the rise, he heard a hoarse shout, a squeal from an enraged stallion, and a shriek of rage. His own horse flung up his head and challenged, leaping up the widening trail with fresh strength. They burst into the clearing, and Adam saw de Rohan sliding from his horse, sword in hand, running toward a recumbent body.

A red mist of fury bloomed before Adam's eyes. His broadsword leaped into his hand, his heels sent his stallion flying, shaking the earth beneath his hooves. De Rohan whirled, his jaw dropping, his eyes staring as Adam's sword came down and split a widening trail from shoulder to groin. His parted body fell forward, his face in the dirt, and a widening pool of blood spread slowly but evenly around him.

Adam turned, his eyes clearing, and looked at the body he'd thought was Brielle's.

Pushing himself to a sitting position, John stared back, dazed. A giant of a man sat on a pure black stallion, and de Rohan lay split open and dead at his feet.

He pushed himself up then, and hobbled forward, looking at de Rohan in disbelief.

"He meant to kill Adam Dunbarton's wife," he said. "I had to stop him. Then he was ready to finish me off." He fell to his knees and bowed his head. "May God bless you, my lord, whoever you are."

Adam laid the edge of his sword across the knight's neck.

"I am Adam Dunbarton. If you are lying, I'll kill you. Where is my wife?"

"She left us when I fought de Rohan," John said, "but we've been followed all afternoon by a band of Scots. They may have her."

"God help her! Which way did she go?"

"The way you came, my lord." John hesitated, listening. "Wolves! We must find her!"

"Hounds," Adam said. "They'll find her for us. Come, if you're able."

"I'm able." John hobbled rapidly toward de Rohan's horse, crawled on, and swung around, following the black stallion.

At the first sound of the deep-throated rising-and-falling howls, the Scots quarreling over Brielle stopped, listened, and began running away. Wolves or hounds, the Scots feared them. Too many Scots had died when a pack found them. Swinging an ax got one or two, but the others went for the throat while the first died. The Scots had learned to run.

Brielle had begun to hope. She couldn't tell at first whether the sound was wolves or hounds, but as the faint sound grew, she recognized Druid's voice leading the pack. She jerked away from the men holding her and ran back toward the trail.

A one-eyed Scot ran after her, caught her, and jabbered wildly, pointing at her loins, sweeping back his rags and showing her his rigid shaft. It was plain what

he wanted before he let her go. She kicked him and
screamed.

"Druid!"

The Scot grabbed her and flung her across his shoulder. She hung there, the breath knocked out of her, as
he ran up the hillside and into the woods again. She
breathed in as deeply as she could and called again,
weakly.

"Druid!"

A hundred feet below, Druid turned from the pack
and went leaping up the rocky hillside. Seeing from
above that the huge hound was quartering off from the
trail, Adam turned and did the same. He'd heard nothing, but he trusted the hound to find Brielle, alive or
dead.

The Scot ran as fast as he could; faster as the baying
drew near. Then when the noise of one deep howl echoed from the rocks ahead of him, the Scot knew he
was followed. He left the hillside and plunged down
into a glade he knew, where a fallen tree and its dead
branches had formed a cave beneath it. He leaped over
it, falling in a huddle with the woman. Quickly he
drew his long knife and showed it to her, his one eye
glittering. He pointed at her mouth and at his empty
eye socket, then held the knife point over her eye. That
too was plain enough. If she made another sound, she
lost the eye.

She clamped her lips shut and prayed. But when she
heard Druid's bell-like tone coming near, she did make
a sound. A small sound, a mere breath of a moan, a
noise no human ear could hear. And then she lapsed
into something near sleep, near death, a fear so deep it
drowned her. Down, down, and down, until her pulse
slowed, her breathing grew faint.

Watching her, the Scot was suddenly terrified. It was
like a spell, like a witchwoman from the Highlands,
going into a trance. He drew back, his knife wavering

in his hand, and at that moment a huge dark shadow plunged over the top of the windfall roaring for vengeance. Druid never hesitated. He tore the throat out of the Scot, shook him once, and dropped him. Then he crouched down beside Brielle and whined, touching her still body with his long nose. His soft mourning sounds led Adam to them.

Shocked and afraid, Adam went to his knees and slipped his arms beneath Brielle, holding her close. She was limp, her bruised face cold against his cheek, her breathing shallow and halting. He had seen Candida's nearly headless body, he had killed de Rohan in a fury he'd never felt before, he saw now the dead Scot and the bloody ax he wore, and he was overcome by horror. He grew cold with the fear of losing Brielle to this rampage of senseless violence. Tears came to his eyes and spilled hot on her cheeks. She stirred and sighed, wondering if she dreamed of Adam.

"Don't leave me," Adam whispered. "Don't break my heart. I love you more than life itself."

She opened her eyes and looked straight into his, and blinked when another tear dropped and struck the bridge of her nose. She reached up and touched his wet cheek. She felt her heart melting, her fear and hurt dissolving away. He was here.

"I would come back from Paradise," she said softly, "just to hear you say that."

They rode toward home after sundown, with lanterns brought out from the castle by men-at-arms. The pack of wolfhounds coursed ahead in the dark, and Adam led the rest with his wife cradled in one arm. His knights, along with the young knight who'd earned the honor of joining them, followed at a short distance to give them privacy.

"I see the stars," Brielle said, gazing upward. "They are beautiful tonight." She sounded impossibly happy.

Adam sighed. Now that she knew the hold she had on him, proud Brielle would be harder than ever to manage.

"I trust you will be less foolhardy in the future," he said, glancing down at her sternly, "now that your judgment once again has been proved wrong."

"Yes, my love."

The arm that held her tightened: *my love.* It had a nice ring to it. Better by far than the common "my lord." He hoped she'd continue it. But in the meantime he would set her straight.

"You will stay in our manse until we are sure there are no ill effects. And later, when you leave the castle walls, you will be attended constantly by at least two of our knights."

"Yes, my love." She shifted a little, curling against him. "But—why?"

Adam drew a long, resigned breath. "Do you need to ask? After this, surely you know there are dangers in careless behavior. We have enemies."

"Who?"

"Why, I—well, everyone has enemies, my lady. I cannot name one at this moment, but—" He glanced down at her and frowned.

"I don't mind the knights," Brielle assured him hastily. "It's good to have strong friends. I'll do whatever you say."

"Fine." He rode on, lost in thought. Nearing the castle walls, he spoke again. "I'm still trying to think of a name—a face, even—that would count as an enemy of ours. Surely we have one. Everyone has a few."

"Well," Brielle said, and it was hard to tell in the lantern light whether the amber eyes were laughing or serious, "I can't think of one, either. But if an enemy is a necessary part of life, perhaps we can make our own. Or mayhap a traveler will come along looking for someone to hate. If not, we shall have to put up with nothing more nor less than friends, family, children, and each other.''

Adam smiled and rode on. That had a nice ring to it, too.

Let best-selling, award-winning author Virginia Henley capture your heart...

Experience the Passion and the Ecstasy

Meagan McKinney

☐ 16412-5 No Choice But Surrender $4.99

☐ 20301-5 My Wicked Enchantress $4.99

☐ 20521-2 When Angels Fall $4.99

☐ 20870-X Till Dawn Tames the Night $4.99

☐ 21230-8 Lions and Lace $4.99